AWOKE

AWOKE

THE UNSEEN WAR SERIES

BY K. T. CONTE

SugarCane Publishing

Published by Sugarcane Publishing
6 Liberty Square, Boston MA 02109
www.sugarcanebooks.com

First Edition: February 2024

ISBN-13: 978-0-9992259-3-6
ISBN-10: 0-9992259-3-6

Cover design by Kristina Liburd, Ana Grigoriu-Voicu
Interior design by Kristina Liburd
Printed in the United States of America

Contents

To my beloved Honey Bee, before you were a twinkle in mommy's eye, this book was written for you.

I

Katya's Affliction

Damn it, it was supposed to be a no-vision-having night. The kind of night filled with dancing, sore feet, smeared makeup, and memories that will stick with you and make you chuckle when you think back on them.

I really wanted that kind of night.

Before I left my house, I looked at myself dead straight in the eye, daring my reflection to fight me. "Katya, don't mess this up tonight. You are normal. Normal. Not one weird thing about you. There are no strange, faraway looks in your eyes. You don't see weird fleshy things, flickering lights, or hear screeching noises that no one else hears. You're gonna enjoy the bottom of a beer mug that you convinced some hot college guy to get for you. You'll dance, laugh, and have a good time. Because that's what normal eighteen-year-olds do."

I should have seen it then – my reflection smirked at me, knowing damn well it wouldn't happen.

But I genuinely tried. And everything seemed okay at first. Arriving at Jillian's Bowling and Bar for Amie's birthday party, I greeted my best friend Cynthia and escaped to the restroom.

I had just sat down in the stall when I started to feel the unfortunate but now familiar creepy-crawly feeling dancing on my skin.

My stomach did that "rollercoaster, about to go down the hill" drop, and my arms' hairs raised. My skin warmed up to alarming heat levels as I was about to go supernova. Someone unfamiliar with my condition would probably think I was erupting from the inside out. When my vision started to get small and dark, I remembered all those complaints my mother made over the years about menopause.

Damn, I really don't listen.

I felt myself sigh as I began to see things and people I had never seen before. Places I had never been to.

A huddled group of sweaty, burly men, laughing together and pointing at me.

Lukewarm water lapped over my feet as I stood on a large rock in the middle of a lake.

A dimly glowing orb in a room covered in silks overlooking a castle courtyard.

Blue eyes, shining brighter and brighter, that had me frightened and mesmerized—

The scenes constantly flashed so quickly that I never understood whether I was experiencing someone else's memories or, God forbid, my memories. It sounds wild even to think that I could forget something so entirely that I'd not know whether I had been there in the first place. My life, unfortunately, has always been complicated. Not remembering something that then returned violently into my psyche without provocation would be just one more complication on a very long list.

"Katya! Where the hell are you?"

I'd never wanted to strangle and hug someone at the same time. Cynthia's shrill voice interrupting me brought me *very* close to that impulse. The visions were quickly disappearing. As the tingling started to lessen, the last image of the bright blue eyes lingered. I tried desperately to hold on. But the longer I grasped for it, the faster it seemed to erase from my head. Then it was gone.

Nothing. Nothing to analyze or call back. All gone. The only thing that remained was the nauseous feeling in my stomach, the impossible heat coming from me, and the sense that I had lost something.

Every single time. It was the same every time.

I heard, "Kat? Katya Stevens, what the hell is taking you so long?"

A green pair of heels clicked against the bathroom tiles toward my stall, and the sound helped to center me. I needed a minute to keep my dinner from coming up and to cool off. The abrupt knocking at the stall door startled me, and I could feel my stomach churn again from the adrenaline. Sighing, I made myself presentable and slammed the door open.

"Damn it, Cynthia, could you be any louder?" I sucked in my teeth loudly. "I was in the middle of something!"

With the sweat pouring down my forehead and the groggy look I had on my face, Cynthia recognized my symptoms and immediately became concerned. "Are you okay? Did you have another episode?" She reached out to me, but I dodged her touch; I hated her touching me when I was sweaty like this.

"Yeah, I just finished. I thought I was about to hold on to something when your high-pitched voice scared the crap out of me."

Rolling her eyes, Cynthia smirked. "Literally or figuratively? Doesn't smell too bad in here." I gave her the finger. She had at least the decency to grab a few paper towels and pat down my face. "I'm only trying to make you smile, Kat. Sorry about the yelling, but you were taking too long. I don't want to miss a second of this party. Of all the times to have visions on the toilet!"

"Girl, you crazy?" I hissed." What if someone heard you?" I quickly checked the two other bathroom stalls to ensure we were alone. I headed to the sink to freshen up and wash my hands. "Cyn, you're acting like I enjoy these visions, flashes, or whatever you want to call them. They come out of nowhere." My shoulders sagged in annoyance and confusion. "I'm just so done with this. This last month has been a nightmare, and I wish they would stop."

My best friend studied me. "Do you remember anything this time?"

"If I did, you know you'd be the first to hear about it."

"Maybe you should talk to your mom about—"

"Cyn, are you really going to finish that sentence? Do you enjoy me having my freedom? To come and go as I please? If Mom gets wind of this, she will think I'm having another psychotic episode and have me back in therapy sessions like when we were kids. I'm not going back to that time, Cyn." Cynthia looked at me, concerned, hearing the hitch in my voice. "I'm not going back to pills and sessions and people looking at me like I'm nuts or possessed. She has enough to worry about with work, not to mention leaving me alone at home with the shakes."

She looked at me sympathetically, aware of the anxiety in my eyes. If anyone else looked at me like that, I would hide away from them in a heartbeat. "I'm sorry I brought it up. We'll leave it alone. Everything is normal, right?"

I strengthened my trembling smile for her as she kissed me on the forehead. "Right." I turned to the mirror and wiped the sweat off my arms and neck. Fortunately, my halter dress allowed me to air out the heat I was still feeling.

"Man, I wish I had some deodorant."

Cyn giggled and began to fish inside her clutch. "Don't ask me why I brought this with me. It was a random thought, but something told me to bring this." And she pulled out a travel-sized deodorant.

And I burst out laughing. "Are you serious?"

"Kat, I swear. I have no idea why I brought it."

I applied it, looking at her through the mirror. "Your twin senses were probably tingling. See? It's times like this that make me think people need to be best friends with someone who shares their birthday."

Rolling her eyes, Cynthia handed me a towel to dry my hands and leaned over my shoulder to gaze into my mirror. "Just say I'm the best," she whispered.

I gave her a happy look and blew her a kiss. "You are the best, Cyn."

"Your other half?"

"The best half."

Cynthia winked at me and began to ruffle her curly red locks, adjusting her green halter dress and makeup. My best friend had looks that were out of this world. Pert nose, flawless complexion, not one blemish. She came out of the womb with looks that any model would pay for. She knew it, and so did everyone else.

People thought she was stuck up, but that wasn't the truth. Cyn had moments of pride but also a heart of gold. She always protected me at every chance, ever since we were kids. She always had this sense of just being there when I needed her. I did the same for her. We called it our "twin sense."

As we preened and fixed our makeup, she threw me a sideways look from the mirror. "I can see it's still bothering you. But at least there weren't any tremors this time. Maybe you calculated wrong about your visions and the shakes happening at the same time. I just want you to relax, okay? Don't drive yourself crazy over this. Just let it go, Kitty Kat."

I nudged her out of my mirror. "Do not call me that. I can't stand that nickname."

Cynthia giggled. "Whatever, K.K. Look, tonight is about having fun. We only have six weeks left of our last high school summer. The birthday girl is waiting for us by the pool tables and is having a mini freakout. You both can't be freaking out at the same time. I can only handle so much. Pity me, please?"

Sighing but smirking, I nodded. "I guess I have to be the stronger one here, seeing as I'm the oldest."

"A technicality. You're only like a few hours older."

I grabbed her by the shoulders and pushed her towards the door. "Yes, yes. Now, give me a second. I'll meet you outside." Cynthia gave me one last look before her heels clicked out the door.

Chuckling to myself, I shook off the distracting thoughts. Cynthia was right. I couldn't let anything ruin Amie's night. When Cynthia and I celebrated our eighteenth birthday last month, only a few genuine friends, including Amie, made an effort to spend time with us. Amie never expected anything in return, unlike most people in our class.

We both had parents with jobs that were considered liquid gold for vultures. My mom worked in sports management, which meant VIP access to top-tier events. Cynthia's folks were involved in the film industry, their names attached to every significant movie shot in Boston. We enjoyed the perks, but it was like a dam burst when our classmates caught wind. Opportunists, haters, and gossipers suddenly turned their sights on us.

At first, the downpour of gossip and backhanded comments had kept me up at night. These days, not so much. The negativity was just background noise compared to the weird drama and visions rattling my head, which is why Amie stood out. She wasn't after anything. She just enjoyed our company, plain and simple. Truly thankful for her friendship, Cynthia and I promised to make her eighteenth birthday party a hit.

And it almost hadn't gotten off the ground due to the tremors.

Six months ago, small tremors started shaking up the eastern region of the United States, and they'd become more frequent since then. What is insane and also a seismic phenomenon is that the tremors have occurred more here, in Boston, than anywhere else. While a few of Boston's iconic buildings have suffered some damage and a few individuals have been injured, people were mostly freaking out about having this many earthquakes here in the Northeast in the first place.

The scariest thing? For the last month, my visions were happening in tandem within minutes with the shakes. But nothing has happened so far, so Cynthia may be right about my calculations. I didn't want to entertain the thought that I could be responsible for putting everyone at risk. It just wasn't possible.

Amie's mom, Mrs. Espinosa, was a bundle of nerves, wanting to cancel the party because she feared "the big one" might strike while we were downtown. Cynthia and I strategized, convincing Cyn's mom, Alexa, to reason with her. Our argument? The emergency alarms would alert us, and besides, couldn't "the big one" hit anytime, anywhere? That's what we told Alexa to say, anyway. Did she? Who knows. What matters is the party's still on, and we breathed a sigh of relief.

I adjusted my dress, slid my clutch under my arm, and sighed. I stepped out of the bathroom, making a beeline for Amie and Cynthia.

Seeing their smiling faces reminded me, no insisted, that I had only one goal tonight.

I was going to have fun, dammit.

2

A Humiliating Encounter

"Katya!" The evident relief in Amie's voice alarmed me as she frantically motioned for me to come over.

We'd convinced Amie to remove her larger-than-life glasses and replace them with contacts for her birthday. Her usually curly nest of hair had been transformed into a sleek style that framed her thin face. Her ordinarily pale cheeks looked alive with blush and color. She'd even swapped her dull plaid clothes and high-knee socks for a fashionable dress out of my closet.

Amie Espinosa turned into an even prettier hot chick when the effort was put in. But instead of being on cloud nine, the birthday girl held her stomach with a panicked look that screamed she was going to be sick.

"Amie, are you okay? Why do you look like that?"

Amie took a deep breath, hoping to stop her dinner from rising up in her esophagus. "Cynthia is trying to convince me to find a guy and get his number. It's crazy, right?"

The growing smirk on Cynthia's face and avoiding my eyes confirmed her mischievousness. Somehow I'm pegged as the troublemaker when, in reality, it's usually the redheaded beauty beside me. But I couldn't help but return the smirk to both of them. "You know what, that's a fantastic idea. We are finally around men instead of those immature asses at school. Besides, what better way to ring in your birthday Ames but with maybe that first kiss?" I looked around carefully. "And it doesn't hurt to look for ourselves either," I muttered.

Amie looked at me questioningly. "Katya, what do you mean? Is something going on with Roger?"

Ah, yes, Mr. Basketball Hotshot, Roger Simmons. The high school star and I started dating before the news broke about my mom. We were sweet at first - thoughtful moments, late-night calls. But as his basketball fame rose, Roger changed. We became the "Oreo Couple" of Benson High. No matter how often I protested those racist names, Roger brushed it off, telling me to "calm down" and "stop making a big deal out of it."

His nonchalance irritated me. Why couldn't he understand how much it hurt? I wanted a boyfriend who would cherish and protect me, not dismiss my feelings. Sometimes a dark flush would creep up Roger's neck when I pressed the issue, and he'd abruptly shut down further discussion. The times I almost smacked him...

Over time, Roger acted noticeably controlling about who I spent time with or what I wore, claiming he just wanted "what was best" for me. But his idea of what was best for me increasingly aligned with what drew attention to him.

I keep hoping the sweet boy I first knew will return. But too often, I've caught flashes of anger in Roger's eyes when he assumes no one is looking. They disappear quickly, his charming facade sliding back into place. Hope can sometimes be a terrible chokehold, especially when your reasoning tells you to move on. But parting ways with Roger has proven emotionally messier than I've been willing to handle. So I've done business as usual, ignoring the warning signs.

Amie was my focus for the night.

"Don't listen to me, girl. Tonight, we are all about you! Let's look around, see who is here, and relax. But if you don't feel comfortable and want to stay where you are," I gave her a meaningful look, "you can stick around the table with your mom and family."

Amie glanced left to see her mother, a sweet woman but terribly misguided in fashion, wearing a loud, colorful dress that screamed disco era. Mrs. Espinosa had also been glugging cocktails, talking loudly, and cackling into her cell phone. Amie's family was a mix of much older cousins, aunts, and uncles who looked uninterested in staying at the table, were utterly bored, or had just decided to nurse a cocktail or two themselves.

With a determined look, Amie said, "Oh hell no. Which direction do you want to go? Left or right?"

I beamed. "That's my girl!"

We guided Amie from the set party area into a larger room with several pool tables and a large bar. Save a few bulbs scattered around and a few strobe lights flashing colors in the room, there was barely enough lighting for customers to get around, mingle, and watch the countless sporting events on the TV screens mounted on the room's walls. The pool room's red and blue strobe lights made everyone's shape askew and misshapen, trying to stay corporal in this world. Like they were nocturnal creatures skulking around to find a new activity since the moon had made an appearance.

It struck me odd that we thought it was normal to creep around a room with minimal lights, loud music you can barely talk over and call it socializing. Then again, how much could I really judge, seeing as I wanted to do it — to be seen as an adult mixing in a dark room looking to get alcohol in my system and throw my inhibitions to the wind.

I watched a group of college students yell and argue, foaming at the mouth, over a game of pool in a room adjoining the main bar. Competition always succeeded in getting people aggressive and unresponsive to reason. If I didn't know better, their inconsequential rage had their eyes flashing red, which was stupid, obviously. It must have been the strange lighting reflecting off their eyes.

As the fight unfolded, a man watched the argument behind the group. His dark, greasy hair fell over his eyes, but his wide maniacal grin showcased his enjoyment of the spectacle. From the nervous energy that had him clenching his seat to the bouncing of his knee, you could tell he wanted to participate, but something held him back.

To the left of the fight revealed three guys, not much older than us, whose attention had strayed away from their pool game. Our lovely frames naturally caught their eyes, and they began to nudge each other, overtly pointing in our direction and attempting to make eye contact.

I involuntarily kissed my teeth. *Meh, it's a place to start.* Flipping my dark, coiled hair over my shoulder, I asked, "Girls, there are some cute guys over there. Why don't we step a little closer?" Neither one said a word. Looking in the opposite direction, Cynthia and Amie had odd, glazed looks. Their jaws were slightly open, their eyes wholly unfocused or, should I say, focused on one spot alone and frozen in place. Gobsmacked. Looking for the distraction, I said, "Hey! What are we looking at?"

Once I followed the trail they left behind and found it, I completely understood.

A small dining table area by the room's entrance sat opposite the pool tables. A man stood tall next to the table in the corner, staring intently in our direction. His short-cropped dark curled hair crowned a chiseled caramel face with a pert nose. His frown only called attention to his full, masculine lips. Despite the dim lighting, you could distinguish the lines and planes that defined his built chest, muscular arms and legs, and well-developed back. His chin donned a slight shadow that only added to the allure of his physique.

At first glance, you could have pegged him for a model, but for some reason, I immediately thought he was an MMA fighter instead. The way his hand gripped his glass of beer and how his knees were slightly bent—he was a signal short of moving at a moment's notice. His eyes never left our direction - like he knew something could happen at any second. I was flooded by my sudden need to get a better look and to get closer, but I also felt that his being there was just *wrong*.

An odd pulse and shiver rattled through me as I watched him, and the desire to stare at him disappeared. A slight earthly tremor shook the room as soon as the shiver ended. With bated breaths, everyone stopped moving and waited for the shaking to cease or increase.

"Oh God, do you think this is it?" I overheard a waitress say to a coworker. "My sister said she was watching a talk show, and they were teaching everybody what to do if the 'big one' comes."

The coworker shook his head. "No, it's not gonna be the shakes. The big one is about the water. All our water will dry up, and this whole country will turn into a desert. See California's drought? Just the beginning, sweetheart."

I rolled my eyes. These doomsday people just fed into the paranoia and fear. There was a lot of talk of the "big one," but no one could say what the "big one" was supposed to be or how it was supposed to feel. Was it supposed to be a massive earth-splitting earthquake? Was it gonna be a gigantic tsunami? No one really understood what was going on. As much as they had their brave theories, the concerned and nervous expressions on everyone's faces betrayed their thoughts; they were looking for any clue from anyone else that they should bolt from the room. The hot guy, however, continued to stare intently at the opposite corner, unfazed by the tremors.

The tremors lasted only a minute, and everyone returned to their activities, less at ease. It also effectively broke the hypnosis on the girls as well. "Hunny. He. Is. Gorgeous. What do you think?" Cynthia said breathlessly. "If I already didn't have Steve, I'd talk to him."

"Y-y-yeah," I stuttered, unsure if it was due to attraction or an underlying fascination with his wrongness.

"Amie! Go talk to him!" Cynthia exclaimed.

Amie immediately paled and started to back out of the room. "Chica, are you crazy?" she screeched. "I'm not talking to him! I can't. I'm not like you, the Redheaded Bombshell, or Katya, the Nubian Princess. Or the neighborly hot sisters from other misters or whatever stupid names everyone else calls you! Why did I think I could do this again? You know what? I'm not a grown woman—I'm a punk. I'm just going to go back to our table and—"

Cyn grabbed the scared silly girl before she could dash from the room. "Amie, love, take a minute. Just breathe." Amie still looked ready to bolt as her eyes glossed with tears.

"Hey, hey," I said, rubbing her shoulder. "Come on now. Talk to us."

She took several calming breaths and said, "I don't want to make a fool of myself. I've told you I've never done this before, and maybe this isn't meant for me."

I drew her in my arms and gave her a tight hug, "Babes, we want you to be happy. Remember all those talks that we've had about you wanting to live freely and not be shackled by everyone's expectations of you? We promised ourselves to not be held by what happened in the past. Ames, you just need to live a little! And have you even seen yourself tonight? You are gorgeous and stunning; any guy would love to have you. You are smart, sweet, and witty when you give yourself a chance to be. Just believe in yourself."

Cynthia nodded. "Look, babes, if we think you can do this, then you can do this. He doesn't look like he's with anyone. What's the worst he can say? 'No, I'm good?'"

Amie looked at the both of us before sighing deeply. "All right. I'll try."

Cynthia's smirk grew to a grin. "Remember what we talked about. Just introduce yourself, make eye contact to exude confidence, and listen. He seems friendly enough. Remember, we live for today!" Amie took another calming breath before ambling to the table. With every step she took, our friend fought desperately to hold in the desire to hide away.

"Cyn, is this a good idea? Maybe she isn't ready for this yet," I said, gnawing at my bottom lip, suddenly feeling like we had sent Amie to the slaughter. We kept a few paces behind our trembling friend to hear the exchange.

"Of course she is. Wasn't the entire point of this adventure to convince her mom to have the party here so that Amie could experience something more than her house, our houses, and school? She cannot go to college next month living like a hermit with her only enjoyment binge-watching sitcoms." Cynthia tossed her fire-red hair over her shoulder and looked me in the eye. "Why?" she asked, her eyebrows arched. "You don't want him, do you?"

"What? Girl, please!" I scoffed but felt the heat rise in my cheeks. I would rather suck on creepy hair guy's left big toe than admit that I found Corner Guy ridiculously attractive and that I was a bit jealous that Amie was getting a chance to speak to him.

Cynthia wasn't fooled and smirked at me. *Damn her.* "Okay. If you say so." Unfortunately, we had taken too long to pay attention because Amie had already approached the man. She wasn't saying much, but he was saying quite a bit. Not able to hear what he was saying over the din of the bar, I quickly stepped closer to listen.

With a Scottish brogue, he said, "Why can a man be left alone without having some chit, a poorly dressed one, come up to him and ask him such stupid questions? Me in high school, lass? Really? Can a man just stand around and enjoy themselves without having some bird act ridiculously dull and idiotic?" His voice rose in volume at this point, and several people and staff members were now staring at them. Corner Guy looked around and seemed angrier because people were staring.

"Why don't you do me a favor?" he lowered his voice, giving Amie the dirtiest look he could muster. "Take your timid, haggard, lumpy body out of my sight and allow me some peace and quiet!" He slammed his glass on the table, splashing Amie and ruining her dress. Without another look, the man stalked out of the room.

Unable to hide her embarrassment, Amie turned around and ran for the bathroom, with Cynthia and I running after her. We found her hiding in a stall, sobbing loudly.

Wow. I did not see that happening. What a jerk! Furious, I knocked on the stall door, begging Amie to come out.

She slammed the door open, her eyes bloodshot and her nose a running faucet. "That was fucking horrible. What the hell was his problem? What did I do that was so bad?"

I could not stop the incoming train of guilt coming for me because I got her to approach a stranger. I took Amie into my arms and held her tightly against me. "Don't you dare cry, sweetie. You do not listen to him. You are beautiful, and no one can say anything to change that. I'm going to make him pay for that. I got this." Taking in my friend's sorrowful expression, rage swelled within me. I turned to Cynthia, shifting my clutch underneath my arm. "Take care of Amie. Tell her mom that she dirtied her dress and needs to go home. Grab a cab and make sure no one else sees her. I'll catch up with you later."

I turned for the exit only to have Cynthia grab my arm, "Wait, where the hell do you think you are going? You don't know who that guy is! He could be a complete psycho."

"Cyn, I know you are usually the one who flies off the handle, but I cannot sit here and not get that asswipe. You don't talk to people like that! It took Amie everything she had to go up to him, and he treats her like this? I'm going to tell that bastard off, and he's gonna apologize!" Not giving Cynthia a chance to talk me down, I quickly walked out the door, down the stairs, and out of Jillian's.

3

Secrets in the Alley

What a jerk! I was furious with myself for convincing my poor friend to go out on a limb, but equally, I was pissed off at that guy. As I exited Jillian's main lobby, I found his tall form stalking down a side street opposite the entrance. He was moving further into downtown Boston's cement maze of side streets, private alleyways, and the like.

"Hey, asshole! Stop right there!" I shouted over the honks and beeps of the taxis passing by, searching for fares. No response and no reaction to my yelling. The jerk either didn't hear me, or he ignored me. Either way, it only ticked me off more. I ran after him, darting between cars and taxis, narrowly avoiding trapping my heels in the large cracks of the broken cement sidewalks. "Hey, stop!" Pushing through the crowds aimlessly finding their next venue, I focused on cornering that rude Scottish guy, knowing I would chew his ear off.

My heels tapping against the pavement filled the air as I blindly ran after him, not realizing he'd ducked into another alley several feet ahead. I turned the corner, getting ready to yell again when he stopped in the middle of the path with a man kneeling. The same creepy-haired man from the corner who stared at the arguing group back at Jillian's. I then realized I'd been blindly following a guy who might be a psycho. *Not a smart move, Kat.* I was about to run in another direction when I heard the kneeling man cry out.

"Please," the kneeling man pleaded. "Please, Kyrios. I'm not ready to go yet. There's too much I want to do still!"

Another quake started shaking the ground again, much more potent than earlier. I could hear the surprised shrieks of people running away from older buildings, fearing the shakes might topple them or send rubble careening to the ground. Then I heard an unearthly sound, like grating nails running against a chalkboard, that only amplified the moment's chaos tenfold. It brought a painful ache to my core that I never knew I could feel like those same nails dragged me down into a dark abyss with no way out. I covered my ears, hoping to lessen the noise and the ache.

"Do you hear that?" the Scot said over the screeching. "It's already searching for you, tearing up the ground and people in its quest. All because it wants to devour you. At least you had the decency to leave that crowded bar. How thoughtful of you," he sneered.

"Thoughtful? Those assholes couldn't care less that I'm gone. And I couldn't care less if every Wanter devoured them," he yelled. "I only left because I was trying to escape from you," the man sniffled.

"You know the rules, spirit," the Scot said harshly. "You've had your time. You need to leave now before you become more of a liability. The Stuffer or the Craver is around the corner." The ground shook with intensity as if the tremors were approaching us. In the corner of my eye, several feet away from the alley entrance, I saw an opaque shadow. The shadow had the shape of a nine-foot-tall, incredibly obese person but with spikes as long as a forearm covering it head to toe. The shadow took another earth-shattering step toward the alley and gave another soul-shaking scream.

"No, please! I'm not ready. I haven't gotten back at those deserters. Those who made me what I am now!" His pleas fell on deaf ears as the Scot raised his open palm over the man's face. A bright blue light appeared from his hand, engulfing the man. The man continued to scream in protest before he vanished.

The Scot whirled around to face the shadow. His eyes glowed dangerously bright blue, intensified by his anger and determination. Only then did he notice me, staring at him and then at the shadow.

The shadow must have sensed that the man was gone because it repeatedly stomped, like a tantrum-throwing child. The shadow's form swelled, making each spike grow to a size as large as a jackhammer. The more it inflated, the more its form clarified and solidified, and the more afraid I became. The nine-foot giant was now twelve feet tall, excluding its mammoth spikes. With blood-red eyes and a noticeable hole in its left shoulder, the dark figure's intentions were clear: destroy the Scot for taking away its prize. And I was in the middle of the battle with no way out of the alley. With each stomp, the foundations of the buildings surrounding us began to crack. The brick building could easily collapse on me.

Before I could register his movement, the Scot was in front of me, shielding me from the shadow. "Run to the other side of the alley now," he yelled. "You don't want to be here when it starts attacking. Go!"

But I couldn't move. I was petrified. *I'm going to die. I don't want to die. Save me, please!*

Then, my vision symptoms returned with the speed of a jet. My stomach dropped, and goosebumps rose on every part of my body. Every hair stood on end. I fought to avoid the nausea and focus on the danger before me.

Suddenly, a gust of unnatural wind swirled in the middle of the alley, spinning into a massive cyclone of dirt, trash, and debris. The dirty storm turned faster, growing as tall as the giant. The whirlwind's body transformed from a muddy brown gust of wind to a glistening silver swirl, like the shiny chrome on a brand-new car.

Before I could study it any further, the cyclone rocketed towards the shadow, like a bullet exiting the chamber of a gun. The dark shadow never had a chance to react as the chrome wind ran straight through it, effectively cleaving it into two equal pieces. It gave one last scream as its right and left limbs went in opposite directions. I stood in disbelief and watched the dark figure's body pieces crash to the ground and disintegrate into red, glowing particles that sunk into the concrete.

Where the hell did that come from?

Then the same odd pulse that gave me the shivers earlier came back stronger and rammed my core painfully more than the chalkboard scream. It suddenly became hard to breathe. My heart pounded painfully fast. I broke into a sweat and then felt freezing cold a moment later. Every inch of my body vibrated like it was ripping itself apart and coming back together. I stumbled back into the alley's wall, desperately gripping my chest and head.

Someone help me.

I shut my eyes, trying to control the pain, but it was too much. I heard a woman's blood-curdling scream, only to realize that the scream was my own. My lungs felt constricted, and I was left gasping for air. I felt a tear open between my heart and lungs in my pain and panic. It was an intense, hot sensation—as if a new organ was coming into existence. The organ felt fresh but also felt like it had always been there. Something I didn't remember, but I did at the same time. It was a feeling that scared me, but I understood it completely. I looked down at my hands and noticed my palms glowed blue. My whole body began to glow, shining brighter with every passing second.

Then, as quickly as it began, it was over, draining all my energy. My body returned to normal, my knees buckled underneath me, and I went straight to the ground. As my head hit the pavement and my vision began to blur, I remembered seeing the Scot approach me. Out of the whole experience, the look he had then freaked me out the most. His eyebrows met in the middle of his forehead, and his lips formed a pout. His eyes no longer glowed, but he looked at me as if I were the strangest thing he had ever seen.

4

The Reaper's Visit

I woke to the comforting smell of lavender, bringing up memories of my home. A pair of down pillows cradled my throbbing head. Shifting my head to look, these pillows looked exactly like those I had at home. A familiar set of ivory cotton sheets pooled around my body.

Wait. I am home—my actual room. How did I get here?

The pictures of my mother and father smiling at the cameraman were on my tall oak dresser, just as I remembered. My closet door was slightly ajar from the amount of clothes stuffed inside. My wall mirror atop my vanity stared back at me, reflecting my confusion and wonder. I studied my face, checking for injuries—my long, black, coiled hair looked like a rats' nest, but nothing marred my dark skin. My dress had some stains, but everything was intact. In awe, I couldn't believe I was really in my room. *Was that all a dream? What really happened with Corner Guy?* Unfortunately, on my first scan, I'd missed a pair of blue eyes watching me from the corner. I soon noticed them.

Jumping out of bed and clutching the wall, I said in a panic, "What are you doing here? How did I get back here?"

The Scot remained silent, observing me. Now, in good lighting, I could do the same. Warm caramel skin and a few freckles dotted his face along the bridge of his nose. His frown deepened as he crossed his arms, and a stray curl of his dark hair dipped on his forehead. He never lost his focus on me as he quickly ran his hand through his hair. He still displayed that nervous energy—ready to pounce on me if necessary.

The better lighting confirmed what I'd observed at Jillian's. His long black jacket did nothing to hide the strong arms encased in its sleeves or his muscular chest. Even his long legs in his black jeans looked sculpted. His square jaw was clenched; a muscle pulsed by his ear. His eyes were the most arresting part of him: they were the most beautiful shade of blue I had ever seen. It was not purely blue but an array of blues and grays that were utterly fascinating. This man could have been conjured from my dreams. But this wasn't a dream; it was reality. He was a stranger, sitting on my vanity chair, watching me and waiting expectantly. His attractiveness meant absolutely nothing.

When he still didn't answer me, I said in a clipped tone, "I know you have a clear command of the English language as you verbally chewed out my friend. So, answer me. What are you doing here, and how did I get here?"

For a moment, I thought he would ignore me again. He suddenly leaned back into the chair, his gaze never leaving me. "I brought you here."

My eyes widened. "How did you know where I live? Did you break into my house?" I looked around for my purse and couldn't find it anywhere. "Where's my purse? Did you steal it? I'm barely eighteen. Hope you didn't think this was going to be a good steal. I don't have anything valuable."

The Scot rolled his eyes in amusement. "Peace, lass. I hardly need keys to enter anywhere, thank you. As for your purse, it's probably back at the alley."

Crap. Well, there goes my money. I pulled the sheets closer to my body. "You still haven't answered my question. How did you know where I live?"

The Scot smiled a smile I found gorgeous and annoying all at the same time. "I looked around. It wasn't too hard to find. Now, if you are done asking your questions, I have some questions for you."

My eyebrows disappeared into my hair. I crossed my arms over my chest. "I don't think you are in any position to give me any orders, seeing as you are trespassing and were a complete jackass to my friend. That was completely uncalled for, asshole. Okay, so you weren't interested in her, but the name-calling? The yelling? Not to mention, your tantrum ruined what would've been her eighteenth birthday party!" I could feel myself getting riled up again, remembering Amie's tears. "I mean, do you know how much it took her to go up and talk to you? What kind of person—"

"You know, lass," he interrupted, annoyed, "the least you could do is be grateful that I protected you and even brought you here. A true jackass would have left you lying there, fainted."

My bravado quickly faded. "I fainted?" A slight tremor shook the house, and I closed my eyes, trying not to panic. I hated being home during the shaking. I felt them more at home than anywhere else. Being home alone with semi-constant earthquakes made a horrible combination. Again, the Scot didn't seem to be bothered by it. His attention was on me. But any easiness the Scot displayed before had disappeared, and he resumed his leaning stance.

"Don't you remember what happened?"

My eyebrows furrowed, trying to remember. *What exactly did happen?* Images flashed through my mind: me running after the Scot into the alley, the kneeling man, the shadow, the Scot's burning eyes. I bolted even further away, putting a clear distance between us. "Whoa! What the hell happened? What was that dark big thing?" I clutched my chest, remembering the tightening. "My chest and my head! What did you do to me? What did you do to that man? Where is he?"

The Scot's eyes showed the same intensity as before in the alley. "You don't remember what you did?"

"What did I? I didn't do anything. Look, my guy, all I saw was that massive shadow thing, you telling me to run away—thanks for that, by the way—and then that tornado taking it out. I mean, how the hell does a tornado form in the middle of downtown Boston and then take a shadow monster out? How did the shadow monster get there in the first place?"

The Scot shook his head incredulously. "She doesn't know. How is this possible?" he whispered to himself. He looked at me. "You did something. Remember."

I looked at him, not sure what to think. I just stood there behind him. *What the hell did I do?*

Remember.

Chills fell over my body as I felt something building up in the middle of my body, right behind my heart. My heart clenched, causing me to grab my chest. I started to panic and clamped my eyes shut, trying to figure out how to make it stop. As I concentrated more, the feeling sent a pulse through my body, and the goosebumps rose again. It felt like a caress—a greeting.

Hello, the voice from inside me said. My eyes snapped open to find the Scot, no longer sitting on the chair but on my bed, much closer to me than before.

"W-w-what are you doing? Did you do that?"

The Scot shook his head, inspecting me like some fascinating science experiment. "No, that's all you. And I want to know how. What power is that inside of you? I mean, you are definitely a human. But I've never seen a living human exhibit that type of power. You're not one of those spiritual clairvoyants, are you? With the TV commercials, who can talk to the dead? I always thought those stories were rubbish."

I slunk closer to my bedroom wall, shaking my head. "Why wouldn't I be human? And what the heck are you talking about?" I inched closer to my closet, hoping I still had that baseball bat from pee wee in there —just in case. "Look, this is all new for me, and I'm not a fan of strange things happening to me without an explanation. I just want to know what happened in the alley. Who are you? What was that dark figure? And what happened to that man?"

The Scot studied me slowly, assessing me from head to toe. Feeling uncomfortable, I crossed my arms to cover my heaving chest. "All right, lass," he said after a few moments. "I will tell you what happened. But are you sure you want to hear this? There are things that once you hear them, you can't run away from them." I felt that his warning went a bit deeper than just the incident in the alley.

In the back of my mind, something said, *He's right. If we step out into this, we could be stepping back into a world we swore we wouldn't talk about anymore. We have to think about Mom. We can't put her through that chaos again. We promised to be a normal teenager.* I wanted to tell the Scot that I'd changed my mind and would decline the information because I didn't want to leave the realm of normal I had built for myself over the last twelve years. Because everything about him screamed that he would pull me away from my carefully crafted world.

But I couldn't say it. I even tried to, but my mouth and tongue remained shut.

Instead, that small voice inside me said, **It's time.** Time for what? I wasn't sure. But before I knew it, the words I wasn't sure I wanted to say spilled out of my mouth.

"Yes, I want to know."

The Scot sighed and motioned for me to sit. I chose the forgotten vanity chair, pulling it back towards my bedroom door. Easy exit, just in case. He sighed, rolling his eyes and crossing his arms. "I have a working theory about what happened tonight," he started.

"So, you don't know what you did tonight?" I asked, already frustrated.

"No, I know what I did. I'm talking about you."

"I want to know what you did before we get into what I did. The way I see it, you did it first. You explain yourself first."

The Scot clenched his teeth, his facial muscles again pulsing. "Fine. We'll go in order. But before I say what I did, I need your solemn oath that whatever is said in this room shall go no further. Not that anyone would believe you, but I want to know whether you can keep a secret."

I looked at him skeptically. But with his eyes bearing down on me, I finally said, "All right, you have my word."

The Scot stared me down, and I looked back at him unflinchingly. "Shake on it?" he finally asked. I nodded and reached for his hand. Our handshake went on only for a few seconds before mine instantly went warm. No, scratch that. My hand was on fire!

I wrenched it out of his grasp, yelling, "What the hell are you doing to my hand?" Now impossibly hot, my hand had an odd mark branded into the middle of my palm. "Did you just brand me?" I asked incredulously.

The Scot smirked. "Just a little insurance."

I could feel myself losing whatever patience I had with the stranger. "What the hell does insurance—"

"Don't worry, lass. Your hand already is better, right?"

I frowned and looked down again. My hand looked and felt normal —like the branding was an illusion. But was it? I distinctly felt the burning. I opened my mouth to say something but couldn't find the words to express what happened. Satisfied, he returned to his explanation as if the incident never happened. "I had been tracking someone at the pub when your friend interrupted me."

"The man from the pool table?"

"Yes. I was curt with your friend because her awful attempts at flirting allowed the man to run. I cornered him in the alley. What you saw in the alley wasn't murder. The man was already dead."

I snorted and sucked in my teeth. "Right, because dead people hang out at bowling bars and beg to be spared from murder all the time."

He smirked, studying my derision. "You'd be surprised at what the dead will do to get what they want."

"Hey, I thought we would be honest with each other here."

"I am. It's up to you whether you believe it or not."

I sighed and crossed my legs. "Okay, fine. I'll play. Let's assume the man in the alley was already dead. Where did he go?"

"A human spirit that doesn't cross over after death causes an imbalance here in this plane, which we call the Live Realm. To correct this imbalance, I sent him to another plane, the Room of Apofasi, for judgment. He would have become a liability if he had stayed in the Live Realm longer. When spirits don't cross over, their energy acts like a beacon for some pretty ugly beasts."

"Wait a minute. You sent a dead spirit to this place, the Room of Apofasi, to be judged?"

The Scot nodded, studying me again. "Yes. Spirits like him, and unfortunately, many more like him, are the reason behind these tremors and the unearthly screams you heard. That massive shadow beast was from another different plane—a much more dangerous plane. That beast was screaming. Its steps caused tremors around the Live Realm, and it was looking to devour that male spirit and absorb any remaining power he may have had. Simply put, the beast was hungry."

His face remained grave, though there was a slight glimmer of amusement in his eyes as he watched me process his words.

"Huh." I took a moment to digest and say my following sentence without losing my temper. "You are saying you sent a dead man, who happened to be looking for a good time at a bar even though he's dead, to some other world to be judged to keep a giant shadow from finding and eating him. Did I get that right?" He nodded solemnly. "Right. And you have this ability because...?"

"I am a Kyrios." The name returned a memory of the man in the alley: *"Please, Kyrios. I'm not ready to go yet. There's too much I want to do still."*

I eyed the Scot suspiciously. "The man did call you Kyrios. What exactly is a Kyrios? Sounds like a cereal."

He smiled eerily and leaned slightly forward. "I've been called many things over the years. The Ankou in Celtic. Hades. The Shinigami in Japanese. Angel of the Dark, though the angel is a misconception. Far from it, actually."

My eyebrows rose, and I felt my jaw unconsciously drop. "Dude, what are you saying? You're..."

"The Grim Reaper? Death? Yes, all of the above."

5

Unburdened

"You're kidding, right?" I couldn't contain my laughter any longer. The giggles pealed out of me with a vengeance. "You're Death? Come on, seriously? Stop pulling my leg."

The Scot shrugged, leaning back, getting comfortable on my bed. "Eh, I'm not much of a fan of the name Death. It's a misnomer, but when you deal with dead spirits and monsters, people jump to familiar names. Most of us call ourselves Kyrios."

Right. Of course. Whatever else would you call yourselves?

This was starting to get too real for me. The Scot couldn't tell from my laughs, but I was inwardly freaking out. Because, on some level, I could understand him. And I did not want to understand, not one bit. "You know what, I think I've heard enough for today. Wow, look at the time. You must be busy with...you know, Death stuff. So why don't I show you the door and—" Another slight tremor shook the house, but this time, I could hear another chalkboard scream not too far away that made my hair stand on end. "What was that?"

A cell phone started to buzz. The Scot pulled it out of his pocket, took a quick look at the screen, and made a phone call. "Samuel, send two men down to the Quincy-Weymouth quadrant. We've got two

Shatterers running rampant. Repeat: Level one Wreckers. I'm dealing with the anomaly still."

With a click of a button, his attention was back to me. "Got two more of those shadow beasts you saw earlier appearing nearby. They probably sense that jittery energy you give off and think you're a human spirit. You may want to calm down there. You're attracting the wrong attention. I had to redirect my men to deal with the incoming problem. Like we don't have enough to do already."

My eye began to twitch. "What did you mean by 'your men'?"

The Scot grinned, clearly enjoying himself. "You can't think one person is sending all the deceased to judgment? Many of us Kyrios are stationed all over the Live Realm. I am in charge of the Boston/New York spirit area. It's been keeping me busy lately, a bit out of the norm. But then, the entire world is going through this right now—increased tremors, odd energies affecting the weather, the increase in unexplainable phenomena. People not acting like 'people.' I haven't been this overworked in a very long time."

I held up my hands for him to stop—I was starting to feel like Alice falling down the rabbit hole. "Nope. No more. Unable to can. This can't be real. You can't be real. This is probably a vision! Yes, this is a vision that has lasted a bit too long. Please, Katya, please snap out of it."

The Scot smirked, studying his hand. "Visions, huh? Is that what we are calling this? I thought we were going to be honest here." He mimicked me from earlier. "Put everything out there for everyone to see."

"What the hell are you talking about?"

The Scot resumed his intense stance from earlier. "What I am talking about, lass, is that secret you are hiding in your pretty little head."

"What do you mean?" I asked, lifting my head with more bravado than I felt. "I don't have any secrets. Besides, how the hell would you know?"

"How do you think I got you back here? How did I know where you lived?" He pointed at my head. "Call it another of my gifts, but I know an interesting little world exists there. Your father passed away when you were six years old. Your mom's a busy sports lawyer who goes on many trips and is away most of the time. You stay at home alone or with your best friend, Cynthia Maroney, who you call your 'twin.' You just graduated from high school at the top of your class. You're considered a popular girl, though you don't like it. You want to be a dancer but have avoided applying to dance academies because you don't think you're good enough. All since you are rather clumsy. I saw a couple of spills you had in the past week that would've broken a burly man in half."

I was stunned. "Are you telling me you invaded my privacy and went through my mind? I have every right to call the police for this! Would you please just get out of my house?"

My shouts didn't move the Scot. He waved his hand nonchalantly and got even more comfortable. "It was a quick read, simply to get your information. I promise you I didn't delve any further. And we both know you are not calling anyone. I am not going anywhere. I am your only chance of figuring out what in the world you are." He paused, looking for some disagreement from me.

"What do you mean, what am I? I am human!"

"A human with an extra pinch of weird, am I correct?"

Weird.

Oh, that word brought out so many feelings and memories. None of them were warm and fuzzy. Just feelings of loneliness, shame, anxiety, and fear. Of days being stuck inside a room and having people question me repeatedly, demanding to know why I knew obscure facts about people I didn't realize. Telling me that I was making things up about horrible accidents that occurred years before I was born. "Stop lying, Ms. Stevens. You didn't see that." Of my classmates whispering things they heard from their parents. "Oh, that's the weird black girl from down the street." Of seeking refuge in our family room and sitting on the window bench where I could stare out at the street and watch people and cars go by. Where I could pretend I knew where they were going and what they were thinking instead of going off of what I could see hidden from them in plain sight.

Because it was always safer to pretend than to find the absolute and ugly truths about the world.

My face must have gone ashen because the Scot had the decency to look abashed. "Oh, sorry, you don't like that word, right? Apologies, but we need to get to talking about tonight. You saw things tonight that most humans would not, lass. You can't deny that."

"Get out!" I walked briskly out of the room and bounded down the stairs with the Scot hot on my heels. Usually, I loved my house; it was the safest place in the world. On the first floor, the grand foyer welcomed visitors into my beloved family room, with warm colors painted on the walls, luxurious cushions, and comfortable couches to sink into and forget your troubles. The Scot behind me demolished any sense of safety I usually felt. He kept close to me as I made for the next room: the kitchen.

"For the love of God, you are infuriating!" the Scot growled. "You want further proof?" He turned on the television on the kitchen counter. Instead of the usual late-night talk show, a breaking news report interrupted with the headline "ERUPTION AT MOUNT SAINT HELENS." Several pictures and videos of Mount Saint Helens, near Portland, Oregon, showed a fearsome volcano erupting steam, rock, and ash into the Washington air.

"Mount Saint Helens released a ferocious roar about two hours ago without much warning," the male newscaster explained. "Scientists are baffled at how the quiet volcano suddenly erupted without its usual buildup before the eruption. Dangerous seismic activity builds up slowly, and potential eruptions are closely monitored. Since 2008, Mount Saint Helens has been relatively quiet, according to geologists. But that all changed just an hour ago when the volcano went from an unprecedented one to four point five on the Richter scale, blowing its top and burying about forty people within its ash cloud who couldn't get off the mountain in time. We have not been able to determine the property damage quite yet."

What surprised me were the creatures surrounding the volcano. Forty-foot-tall white beasts with grotesque humanoid figures—either spikes, holes, or boils covering their bodies. They were clear as day, helping the volcano, throwing more ash into the air, and destroying homes. But no one reacted, screamed, or pointed at them. They were invisible. Except the Scot could see them. And he could see that I could as well. I didn't dare say a word.

"These creatures are the same monsters you saw in the alley tonight. They are called the Want or the Wanters. Do you think this volcano is bad? This is just the tip of the iceberg. And that feeling in you that's scaring you? Your visions? It's all playing a part. Something is brewing underneath the surface. Because the Want don't do such things on a grand scale. Accidents, yes. Loss of life, definitely. Any disaster creates more human spirits to eat. But this? This is more. You are reacting to this. Or at least something inside of you is reacting."

The Scot approached me slowly, probably fearing that I would bolt. "Now, as I was browsing through your mind index, I did see something locked away, like a vault within a vault." I looked at him as he continued his explanation. "The mind is quite similar to a house with many doors. Some doors, like your name, home, or family, are readily available. Others are locked away, like precious memories or hurtful things. You have a dusty door that looks like it's been neglected for years. A prison door. But something's behind that door, lass. Something is bursting at the seams with that same power you displayed earlier. And it's only getting stronger by the hour. So I'll ask ye again. What secret are you hiding in that head of yours?"

The room suddenly felt too small. Memories of Mom crying... A coffin being lowered at a gravesite... Broken bricks all over the sidewalk and the street.

"I can't be mistaken, lass. I know what I saw."

I said nothing as I rummaged through the food in the fridge, finally finding the chocolate syrup. I dipped my head back, squirting the cool, sweet liquid into my mouth and savoring its deliciousness. I felt the Scot watch me inhale the syrup, and suddenly I felt rude. "Would you like something to drink?" I suddenly asked.

The Scot startled. "What?"

"Sorry, I needed a hit of chocolate. Would you like something?" I looked at the fridge door. "Or do Kyrios not need food or water?"

Eyebrows arched, the Scot shook his head in amusement. "I can drink and eat just fine. I don't need it, but that doesn't mean I can't enjoy it."

"Well, you can't have the chocolate. House rule. Even my mom knows not to touch it. What would you like?"

"Water is fine." I grabbed a glass from the cupboard, filled it with tap water, and handed it to the Scot. He looked down at his glass and said, "Back where I come from, we salute each other first before taking a drink."

I shrugged and sucked on more chocolate. "I didn't realize Kyrios had drinking traditions."

"They don't. Cheers, lass."

"Cheers." We both took a swig of our liquid. I felt better but I was unsure of where to go from here. *Could I let someone else know?* It didn't feel safe. When I'd told people in the past, they always had this look that flashed the same message: *liar.* For years, I told myself I wouldn't have to go through this again, but it seemed like I had lied again, only to myself this time.

The Scot must have sensed the turmoil within me because he said, looking uncomfortable, "Look, I know you have no reason to trust me, lass—"

"Katya. My name is Katya."

He gave me a soft smile. "Pardon, Katya. We can only make sense of what happened earlier if you talk. That tornado didn't come from me. But it was powerful enough to cleave through a creature like cheese."

"But it wasn't *me*," I said, exasperated. "I didn't even know what that thing was called until now."

"But you've seen it before, right?" The Scot sighed. "The only way we can figure it out is if you tell me about that door."

I studied my nail beds. "Why should I tell you anything? If it's locked away, maybe it should stay that way."

He said softly, "Because it's my job to know. I haven't given you much reason to trust me. Other than that alley, we might not have ever gotten here. But we did, and I believe there's a reason for it. I was supposed to meet you. And that news report proves that you see much more than you let on. In the past couple of years, you've probably noticed that there have been more unexplainable things happening—extreme weather worldwide. The typhoons, tsunamis in the East, and the super storms destroying lives here in the Northeast. The droughts and extreme heat peppered everywhere. Not to mention people themselves are becoming colder, more pessimistic, and more hateful each day."

The Scot was right about that. I thought it was me being too sensitive to people's emotions. Still, even Cynthia had commented just the other day about how people were acting odd. More and more people were shutting themselves away, becoming superficial and greedier in every sense of the word. At first, I noticed the behavior online, but now it was manifesting in person.

"I'm telling you, these are not isolated incidents. I feel you sense more than you want to admit because you don't want to call attention to yourself. You are afraid. But no one can help you if you don't speak up. You've got to tell me your story, lass. Please."

I suddenly felt the weight of years of secrecy bearing down on me. The burden of my mother's warnings since I was five. The stress of Cynthia being the only other person I could run crying to about all the looks of concern, fear, and worry. The quiet phone conversations coming to an end as I entered into a room. Kids laughing and pointing at me; parents keeping their children away. Most of all, being filled with feelings of shame.

All of it had been buried behind a door in my head. I looked at the Scot, who was looking at me earnestly. "If I tell you," I said quietly. "Can you tell me what's wrong with me?"

The Scot's eyebrows wrinkled together. "I don't think there's anything wrong with you. You have something more than other people. I may not understand it, but if I don't know it, I am sure I know someone who will."

"I don't think there's anything wrong with you." The pit in my stomach started to unfurl, and some anxiety started to melt. The final push came when that small inside voice gave me a nudge. **It's okay, Katya. Tell him**.

6

The Promise of Answers

I worried my bottom lip, praying for strength, and sat at the kitchen table, rubbing my arms for warmth. The Scot made himself comfortable leaning against the kitchen counter. "Start from the beginning, lass," he prompted gently.

"The earliest memory dates back to when I was five. Mom took me out to the playground, and there was this girl named Sara. She had cascading blond hair, wide green eyes, and always had on a purple romper paired with white tennis shoes. Sara was always there whenever I visited the playground."

The Scot frowned, "Always the same outfit?"

"Always," I nodded. "The first time I met Sara, she cried for her mother. My mom always told me to be kind to people when they cried. So, I went up to her, asked what was wrong, and told her not to cry. She told me she felt lonely. I made a promise then, to be with her every day, to play and talk. And sometimes, we'd sit and sing songs together."

The Scot nodded to me to continue. "What made Sara special was that she could see things I could. Like the young man in a white shirt and black jeans who'd walk by daily, listening to his Walkman."

The Scot's eyes sharpened, "What was unique about him?"

"We'd whisper about the red stain splattered across his shirt, innocently wondering if he'd had an accident with ketchup," I said, shuddering at the memory. "Or the pregnant lady who always sat on a park bench near the entrance, massaging her bruised neck, her gaze lost like she awaited someone."

He crossed his arms, "You could see them, and so could Sara. But your mother couldn't?"

"Yes," I hesitated. "Whenever I tried pointing them out, my mom would dismiss it, saying I had an overactive imagination."

"But Sara was different."

"She was. She understood. We spent several weeks together. Then, one day, I couldn't go to the playground. I had a meltdown because I'd promised Sara. My father tried to calm me. When I described Sara, he paled."

The Scot leaned forward, "What did he say?"

"He recognized her description. A girl named Sara had been strangled by her stepfather near the playground. I never forgot my parents' horrified expressions, trying to piece together how I'd known a dead child."

He exhaled slowly, processing the information. "You were seeing spirits."

"Seems so," I continued, "After that, they never let me go back to that playground. I could hear Sara's voice, screaming in pain for help, calling for me. It was the last I heard from her. But she wasn't the only spirit I encountered. And those monsters? I've seen them before. Like that... Wanter from tonight."

His brows furrowed, "You've encountered them?"

I nodded, "In varying sizes. Some as small as a dog, others larger. Whenever I saw them, bad things happened. Accidents, fires, crashes. They were always nearby, causing chaos. It got so bad I had to stay inside. The only friend I was allowed was Cynthia."

"And then?"

"Then one day, after my dad died, it just stopped," I sighed, trying to contain my emotions. "For years, I thought I'd imagined it all. But recently, after my last birthday, it all came back. Those visions... the memories. They're real, ready to ruin my life again. Ready to ruin whatever peace I was able to get. So much for being normal, right!" I laughed mockingly, fighting back the tears.

I cleared my throat, staring at my hands. "I haven't said this out loud in years; somehow, you squeezed it out of me." I sucked another gulp of chocolate, watching the Kyrios process my words. "That's it. That's my secret. So, tell me, am I crazy? A nut job? Am I 'weird'?"

The Scot closed the gap between us and bent down to look me in the eyes, his voice gentle. "No, Katya. I know exactly what you are talking about. I know what you were seeing. I don't understand why."

"But you believe me? You believe that what I saw was real?"

He nodded.

Someone believes me. The dam broke, and I couldn't hold back the tears and relief I felt. Years of denying myself because no one would believe me. Even Cynthia hadn't ever fully admitted that she believed me —she just said she loved me no matter what. All those times of being told I was a liar, I'd almost believed it. And now, someone believed me, believed in me. The Scot remained silent as I regained control.

"But wait, how do I know that you are real? That you aren't a spirit talking to me? That you aren't going to disappear when I try to prove that you are real?"

The Scot softly laughed. "Your friends saw me, didn't they?"

Oh yeah. "But are you dead?"

He hesitated. "It's complicated." He leaned closer, taking my hand into his. It wasn't as warm as I expected, but flesh was in my hand. "I may bring the dead over to the other side, but I am as real as anything in this room. Just as real as the spirits you saw as a wee child."

Unable to hold on, I drowned in his eyes, feeling immense gratitude. "Kyrios..."

"Gregor."

"What?"

"Kyrios is what I am. My name is Gregor."

With his name, an unspoken shift happened between us. Sharing a deep, dark secret about yourself can create a bond that is unfathomable but fitting. We silently stood there until Gregor cleared his throat and stepped away from me. I sat tensely at the kitchen table. Gregor leaned against the counter, his presence seemingly larger than the space around him. "Katya, you have a rare gift. More potent than anything I've ever seen. Not just seeing Wanters and spirits but..." He paused, choosing his words. "You took down the Hungry in the alley."

I blinked. "The what?"

"The Hungry is a second-level Craver, a type of Wanter. There are many Wanters: Wreckers, Cravers, Posers, the Thirsty, Wishers, and Stuffers. Generals are the most powerful among them. A level three is deadly. Anything stronger, and you run."

I tried to digest this. "And the Stuffers? They're the hungry ones?"

He nodded. "They lurk between the Live Realm, waiting to feed on energy. It probably targeted the man, and you. But the extraordinary thing is how you defeated it. Most humans occasionally feel their presence, but you? You created that cyclone. Your energy is... formidable, almost rivaling an experienced Kyrios."

Still grappling with this new reality, I hesitated before saying, "When I first saw you, I felt something ignite inside."

His eyes, intense and curious, locked onto mine. "You felt it?"

Blushing, I admitted, "At first, I just thought it was because my friends found you attractive. But your presence felt... wrong. My friends, they seemed... enchanted by you."

A wry grin tugged at his lips. "Ah, the 'Walk into the Light' syndrome. It's a pull some humans feel toward us. Can get messy, so we keep our distance."

I raised an eyebrow. "Then maybe next time, be kinder to my friends. It took her a lot to approach you."

His face softened. "If given a chance, I'll apologize. That's a promise from a Scot."

I smirked. "So Scots are aware of their attitude issues? Good to know. Thank you."

Gregor met my eyes momentarily, his eyes warm. As he turned to leave, a rush of panic filled me. "Wait! You're leaving just like that? What about everything you just told me?"

He sighed, stretching as if feeling a weight on his shoulders. "I must report back. The Generals and I need to discuss your powers. For now, carry on with your life."

I looked at him and said flatly, "Continue to live my life? I pour out my secret, and you head out?"

He gave a small smile. "Why? Do you want to end your life now?"

I rolled my eyes. "If that is Death humor, it sucks."

His laugh, genuine and warm, echoed in the room. "Katya, just keep low. I'll be back soon." He turned and raised his right hand. A bright light erupted from the middle of his palm. The bright bead of light flew into the air, growing larger until it split the room like a bright blue tear in time and space. He turned back to me as he stepped into the rip. "Oh, one more thing."

The brightness and the power coming from his eyes arrested me. "What is it?"

"Don't get too agitated. Control your emotions. You don't want to attract any unwanted attention."

Before stepping into the tear, he met my gaze one last time, and then, he vanished.

7

Stirrings and Tremors

I woke up with a start, completely disoriented. Cursing the sun for its blinding light, I curled into my sheets, praying the splitting headache away. Unfortunately, my cell phone ringing kept me from falling blissfully back asleep.

"Hello?"

"Katya Elizabeth Stevens!" I fell out of my bed at the sharp tone.

"Cynthia?" I asked as I fumbled with the sheets and propped myself against my bed.

"I've been calling you since last night! If you didn't answer this morning, I would've gone straight to the police because that guy kidnapped you! What the hell happened to you?"

"Cyn, wait—"

"You scared the crap out of me! You never called or texted! Do twin sisters do that? Abandon each other? What's worse is you left me with Amie sobbing! And not just tears, but the sobbing that leaves you hiccupping and snot running down your nose. It was bad enough with just her, but as we were leaving, her mom wouldn't buy that Amie was fine and started to feel guilty for being on the phone the entire time. Then she starts crying drunken tears. You try dealing with a grown woman crying about her daughter crying!"

"Cynthia!" I yelled. "Give me a second. I just woke up, okay?" Silence answered me on the other line. I tried to remember by taking a deep breath and centering myself on the floor. I couldn't remember taking a cab home last night. How did I get home? A look around my room didn't prove anything out of place. If anything, it looked normal. But my clutch was on my nightstand. That didn't feel right, either.

"Excuse me? Can I speak now?"

I shook my head, not realizing she couldn't see me. "Yeah, sorry about that. You woke me up, and I couldn't think straight for a minute there. God, I have a massive headache. Where are the painkillers?" I slowly got up and strolled to my vanity, looking for the medicine bottle.

Cynthia sighed. "It's fine, Katya. Please tell me you are okay."

"Yes, sis. I'm fine. I'm just a bit hazy right now."

"Don't disappear like that again! I was going to come over, but Amie did not want to be left alone. And you not picking up your phone just freaked me out. If you were wondering, which I'm sure you were, I brought Amie to my house for a sleepover. I told her we would hang out today."

I wiped my face, still trying to shake the sleep away. "Sure, whatever. How is Ames doing?"

Cyn sighed. "Not gonna lie, Kat. I know she was trying to play it off in the bathroom, but her confidence took a beating. What happened with that guy?"

Finding the bottle I wanted, I put my phone down on the vanity and placed Cynthia on speaker to free my hands. "What guy?"

She paused. "What do you mean, 'what guy'? The guy you left us to chase after! The guy you wanted to yell at! That guy! Did you lose him?"

Blue eyes. The alley. The shadow. Gregor. It came back with such force that it hurt, increasing my headache tenfold. "Ow!"

"Kat! Are you okay?"

I rubbed my temples, attempting to massage the throbbing away. "Ugh, yeah. It's the headache. Listen, the visions, Cyn—"

"Leave those alone for now. Talking about them always puts you in a bad mood, remember? We'll talk later. Amie's waking up, and I don't want her to hear us talking about this. I will take her to her house to change, and then we'll meet you at Downtown Crossing around 11:30. Okay? Gotta go. Love you!"

I closed the phone, temples throbbing. The weight of last night pressed on me, making it harder to breathe. The memories, fragmented and confusing, threatened to overwhelm me. *There was no way I would have told a stranger my secret. And all that blue eyes, blue light crap. I must have had a dream vision.* Although it would be the first one I could remember.

While searching my closet for an outfit, my cell buzzed again. A quick look at my desk clock showed 9:30 a.m. Not bothering to look at the caller ID, I answered it, saying, "Hi, Mom. Right on time."

"Of course. When would I have missed a phone call with my pumpkin?" I rolled my eyes, smiling. Some nicknames never get old. "Is everything okay? What are you doing today?"

I continued to rifle through my closet. "The tremors haven't been too bad since you left. Though last night was odd, there were more shakes than the previous couple of nights. But Ms. Espinosa didn't cancel the party, thank God! Cyn and I are heading downtown with Amie. After that, I'm not sure."

"You're worried about a party when the world's shaking apart?" Mom's voice dripped with exasperation. I could sense my mother shaking her head. "Promise me you guys will stay safe. How are you doing for money?"

"We'll be fine, Mom. I haven't spent much since you left."

"Are you eating?"

I snorted. "Do you think Cynthia would let me go without eating? She's as bad as you are."

"Just checking. I'm your mother. I need to ask these things."

"Yes, Mom."

On the other side, I could hear my mother clear her throat three times. *Uh oh.* She only did that if she felt uncomfortable telling me something. "Katya, I won't be home like I initially planned. Dallas is experiencing bizarre hail, and we had to push back the negotiations. I will be home closer to the end of the month instead, probably right before school starts. But don't worry. I will be there to buy all of your college textbooks and gear. I promise this won't ruin your experience."

Mom's late return from a business trip wasn't anything new. Being a law partner at Boston's premier sports and entertainment law firm, Mom felt a greater responsibility to prove herself because she was a Black woman. Earlier in her career, she volunteered to take trips to meet with potential sports clients, which meant she traveled all over the country to meet all kinds of sports athletes. But Mom never complained, even when she was away from home for weeks. It was also why she made partner—she took her role as the silent, diligent worker seriously and made the firm tons of money. She didn't realize that I understood that by being a partner, she didn't have to travel as much as she did.

"It's okay, Mom. I know you'd be here if you could."

My mother sighed. "Are you sure? I know I promised to take you to Miami for your birthday, but that fell apart, and the way this deal is going, it is not going right. With video conferences, you would think we wouldn't have to do this. But some of these teams are old school. It's driving me crazy. Not to mention how emotional they are getting! Men always complain about women being emotional. Give me a break. Professional football players are the worst."

I said brightly, "It's totally fine, Mom. And yes, you've said that before. The way I see it, you will have to take me during the school year, right? I'm thinking of Christmas break, but it will be three instead of two weeks. And that means I can get more bathing suits, right?"

It was several seconds before my mother chuckled. "Okay, I'll consider your proposal. Remember, no Roger alone, no parties—"

"Mom! Give me a break!"

Mom chuckled. "Okay, Kitty-Kat. I have to run. Have a good day, and be good."

I got off the phone quickly so my mother could not hear the disappointment in my goodbye to her. My eyes traveled to a family photo taken on a trip to Myrtle Beach. I was six, clutching my father's leg and grinning. Both my parents were smiling down at me, entirely at peace. What I remembered the most about Dad was how much he smiled. And it wasn't an obnoxious smile, but he genuinely just liked to smile and joke around. He loved seeing people happy. It's why I purposely jumped into his arms whenever he'd get home, knowing that tickling was in store for me.

During that particular Myrtle Beach trip, I remember he clung to Mom and me, telling us how much he loved us. That we were his best gift. Shortly after we returned home, the monster sightings became more frequent, and everything changed. Less than two weeks later, Dad died a hero, saving me and a coworker from a drunk driver incident.

The memory of how it all happened was fuzzy; I felt helpless and guilty. I rubbed the only scar I'd received from the incident—a long, crooked scar on my left arm. It constantly itched whenever I thought of that day. Since Dad died, Mom entangled herself with work, becoming a partner, and volunteering to travel without me. She said she does the long hours to give me the life she thinks I deserve. I know the truth. She does it so she doesn't have to remember Dad. I do not blame my mother for running. I don't want to remember either.

My phone buzzed with a text from Roger.

"Hey, party at Devin's tonight. I said we'd go."

I bristled. Roger had made plans without asking - again. He knew I hated that.

"I'm not going. Made plans with Cynthia," I replied and then blocked his number, anticipating his barrage of texts and phone calls. I could imagine Roger's neck flushing with irritation at being denied.

Increasingly, Roger didn't take no for an answer, growing cold or angry when I went against his wishes. Things had changed since sophomore year when he asked me out, tripping over his words.

Back then, his smile made my heart race. We talked for hours nightly. But as Roger's basketball fame grew, so did his ego. His priorities shifted - friends first, me second, my needs last. Once, he raged when I chose an art show over his game, accusing me of embarrassment. Another time, he grabbed my wrist, urging me to stay when I reached for my purse, not liking my dress. His temper would flare, then vanish as quickly, replaced by excuses and apologies.

Even Gregor had the decency to consider my feelings even though he was pressed for time. The universe was telling me something significant here: If I could confide in a dream stranger about a deep secret I've held for years but hesitated with someone who should be my confidante, it was time to move on. It was time to release myself from nostalgia and to stop clinging to what I believed was a "normal" relationship. I wanted to start the next phase of my life and my first year of college free and without baggage.

With a heavy sigh, I erased Roger's latest messages from my mind, resolving to keep him at bay while I figured out my strange night with the Kyrios.

I thought about it as I took a bus downtown. As I scanned for a seat, a sudden and sharp jostle from behind slammed my knees to the floor. It came from a man in a black bowler hat as he breezed past me, exiting the bus's rear entrance.

"Hey, do you mind, buddy?" I yelled at the man's back. As I dusted my knees, straightened my clothes, and found a seat, the man halted by the bus, fixing an unwavering gaze on me. His piercing eyes continued to trail me even as the bus pulled away. I couldn't shake off the eerie feeling. There was something about his staring – it wasn't just passing or casual. It felt... targeted. *Why was he watching me like that?* The hair on the back of my neck stood up, an instinctual warning. Something about him felt invasive, like he was peeling back layers I didn't even know existed.

I felt a tingling behind my heart, like something was stirring. It was the feeling from my vision. I shook my head, starting to panic. *It's a dream, Kat. Your vision, remember?*

An all-too-familiar, yet always unsettling, tremor rocked the streets, effectively stopping all traffic waiting for the tremors to pass. The internal tingling resonated, mirroring the quakes that stilled the world outside. With sweat beading down my neck, I took a deep breath to calm down. After a couple of cleansing sighs, the tingling stopped, and the shakes shortly after. Unfazed, the bus resumed its journey forward into Boston's bustling Downtown Crossing.

8

Hunted

I've always believed downtown Boston was underrated, overshadowed by behemoths like New York City. While towering skyscrapers housed bankers and investors, the city's esteemed colleges and universities studded its terrain. Despite being more compact than many other major American cities, Boston still held its ground.

I cherished my bus rides to the edge of Boston Commons, a sprawling sanctuary teeming with trees and flowers. Here, couples, children, and those on everyday escapades thrived. Lost in my observations, I'd imagine their stories, destinations, and conversations.

The principal pathway in the Commons led directly to Downtown Crossing. The entwined walkways and cobbles whispered tales of Boston's storied past. These brick pathways, a testament to the city's Pilgrim heritage, stretched a mile amidst buildings. These buildings, as old as the nation itself, housed stores brimming with the newest electronics and fashion. Street vendors of various ethnicities hawked their goods, enticing passersby with tantalizing aromas.

Downtown Crossing was a melting pot. Businesspeople, always in a hurry, would cross paths with workers grabbing a quick meal before their shifts. For centuries, it remained a bustling nexus for casual visitors and dedicated shoppers alike. Being there reinforced the idea that, despite our differences, there was a shared human need for connection and community.

As I approached the bus stop, a text from Cynthia arrived, letting me know that she and Amie were at the Underground Food Court. My brows furrowed in mild annoyance. The Underground was a favorite haunt for the popular crowd from our high school. They never quite understood why Cynthia and I befriended Amie. Especially Andrea Pana, who never shied away from her disdain.

We always maintained a frosty truce with Pana. However, I believed she resented how genuine we were and how effortlessly liked we became. The Andrea we met during our freshman year bore little resemblance to the Pana of today.

Roger had once mentioned Pana's failed attempt to woo him early in our relationship. While she never confronted me directly, her animosity became evident when Amie began spending time with us.

I vividly remembered the day Pana first spotted us together. "Did we slip into the Twilight Zone?" she had sneered, "Or did someone lose their way? Shouldn't the nerds be somewhere else? Perhaps Ugly Betty forgot?" Holding back my anger, Cynthia gave Pana a verbal lashing that ensured she left in haste.

But Pana's childish taunts didn't end there. She continued ridiculing Amie about everything imaginable. Despite her initial discomfort, Amie, bolstered by our unwavering support, grew in confidence. Seeing her jabs lose their sting, Pana's focus on us waned. Today, I hoped Amie felt stronger and that Andrea was preoccupied elsewhere.

As I entered the Underground, I quietly prayed, "Please don't let her be there." Unfortunately, God must have been busy because her group surrounded Cynthia and Amie at a table in the middle of the food court. I could tell my friends were stressed from the sounds of the jeers and laughs. Drawing closer, I immediately noticed tears running down Amie's cheeks and smoke coming out of Cynthia's ears. I swore under my breath and quickly made my way to the table. I certainly wasn't paying attention to the slowly rising wave of energy behind my heart.

"Well, if it isn't the chick of the hour!" Pana called out, calling attention to my arrival. I tried to make eye contact with Cynthia to figure out what was happening, but her eyes remained fixed on Pana.

"Shouldn't you be buying some silicon or extensions or something?" I said tersely. "Go bother someone else who gives a damn. I'm done with this high school bullshit."

Unfazed, Pana smirked back at me. "I am surprised you are even out of bed, Stevens. Shouldn't you be a little sore from your escapades last night?"

"Excuse me?"

The posse began to giggle, a bunch of twats. Pana leaned forward and placed her head in between Cynthia and Amie. "I was just telling these two how I saw you last night. In the arms of a guy that wasn't your boyfriend."

I could feel all the blood leave my face. "Wh-what?" The slow-rising energy wave was churning like a hurricane.

Pana cackled. "Oh, come on, Stevens! Stop acting so innocent. I saw you with him. You didn't do half bad, either. He was hot, carrying you around Boston like he couldn't wait for you two to be alone!" She pulled out her cell phone, and on her screen was a dark but relatively clear picture of Gregor carrying me out of the alleyway and turning a corner.

My heart leaped into my throat. *Oh, dear God, they know. They know about me. They saw me glow blue.*

"I just happened to be parking my car near that alley after that shake, and here comes hottie with your black ass in his arms. I wanted to get your attention, but he just seemed to be in such a hurry," she purred. Pana then touched Amie's shoulder, giving her a light massage. "I was just trying to figure out who he was when Sugarplum here tells me you were supposed to defend her last night—from the hottie!" She crossed her arms, looking very smug. "All this time, I was right. It looks like friendship with a freak only goes skin-deep. Especially if there's a guy involved, huh?"

Before I could respond, Cynthia intervened, nose to nose with the offending bully. "Pana, say one more word," she whispered, gritting her teeth, "and I swear I will tear the plastic off your body that you call your nose and boobs!" She grabbed a quiet Amie and me by the arm and dragged us outside.

Heaving, Cynthia stopped a few feet outside the Court with her back toward me. Finally finding my tongue, I cleared my throat, "Guys, it's not what it sounds like. She's making it seem like something it's not. Amie, I never would do something like that to you. I was furious when I left, and I went after him to make him pay for what he said to you."

Amie's disappointment was palpable. With her glasses hiding her red eyes, she glared at me like I'd grown two more heads. "Katya, there's a picture. You're in his arms. Unless that's a new way to fight someone, it looks like you're enjoying his company a bit too much. Maldito, what a birthday this turned out to be."

Cynthia softly grabbed my arm and pulled me aside from Amie. "Listen, I'm not saying you had some sexy rendezvous with the guy, but the picture doesn't look good. You were also commenting about getting a new boyfriend, and I saw how you looked at him." She raised her hand to stop me from interrupting. "I know you wouldn't do it on purpose. But you disappeared. What happened to you last night?"

I shook my head, refusing to get into my whole run-in with Death and spirits in public. That rising wave was giving me a headache. "I will not talk about it right now."

"Why? Kat, will you talk to me?"

I shrugged her off, turning back to Amie, who had taken to hugging herself. "Ames, I swear I didn't do anything. I passed out—"

Amie pulled a moist tissue from her pocket and blew her nose loudly. "Katya, I know you, or I thought I did. Part of me knows that you wouldn't lie to me about this. That you would've tried to defend me. But the other part...I know what you said last night. That picture is real because you haven't denied it."

She put her hand up, blocking my impending denial. "So maybe you saw him, he liked you better, I don't know. I don't want to think like that, but... You don't think I've noticed, but you're not as open as you think. You put walls up, Katya. I thought maybe I was getting through those walls. But I honestly don't know. Maybe this, this guy, is another secret, another part of you you're keeping away."

I felt the morning's frustration begin to build up behind my eyes. "No, Amie. Listen to me. That's not what happened. I would never—"

Amie shook her head and wrapped her arms around herself tighter. "Kat, just give me time. I need time to think. If you excuse me, I'm going home." My jaw brushed the ground as she raised her head and walked away.

At least our time together taught her some pride and not to take crap from anyone, including her friends. I ran after Amie, skirting around the midday shoppers. "Amie, wait!" I called after her retreating figure. More people from the underground trolley swelled into the street, obstructing my view of her. "You don't understand. Please let me explain. I swear that nothing—"

"Katya, the Nubian Princess, strikes again," Pana yelled behind me.

I stopped and slowly turned around to find Pana alone, stalking up to me with a massive smirk on her face. "Newsflash! Katya isn't the all-holy saint she pretends to be! I always knew you got down and dirty. And for some reason, you've been holding out on your boyfriend, too? Two years and no sex? Be careful, Stevens." She licked her lips like a lion licking their chops. "You might find yourself without a boyfriend if you stay a tease. Those college boys are not going to stand for this."

"Would you shut up, Pana? I didn't do anything last night!" I was now very aware of the energy wave beating inside of me. It took everything I had not to react when I only wanted to sit on a yoga mat and do deep breathing.

The smirk on Pana's face only grew. "Then he did all the night's work? You sure you didn't twerk for him a little bit?"

I felt the heat flare in my cheeks, and I snapped. I could not and would not hold back anymore. I have never reacted to the foul things this girl said for years. I was tired of it. I stalked up to Pana and yelled in her face at the top of my lungs. "NOTHING HAPPENED!"

Instantly, the floodgates opened, and all the tingling returned and pulsed throughout my body. Like an echo, it reverberated through the ground and shook the block; however, the Downtown Crossing shoppers looked unaffected, moving on with their business. While I was happy I finally got to act out, my body protested at the wave's release. My lungs contracted, and a wave of fatigue left me clutching my chest. I felt like I had run a marathon and was gasping for air.

Cynthia immediately moved in and pushed me away from Pana, fearing a fight. Pana calmly wiped her cheek off any spittle, still smirking. "I have to say, Stevens, I like you this way. Maybe if you were always like this, Roger would've never approached you in the first place and wasted high school with you. No matter - I look forward to your next breakdown."

With that, she walked away.

Realizing I'd missed Amie, who was now long gone, I stumbled to the nearest bus stop a few feet away and sat on the bench to regain my breath with Cynthia in tow. Less than twenty-four hours from dishing my secret, my life was already spiraling out of control.

"No," I whispered. "No, I am not ready for this. This can't be happening again."

"Katya." I whirled around to find Cynthia looking at me worriedly. "Are you okay?" She took a seat beside me. She gave me a small smile. "I haven't seen you do that since we were kids when you tried to convince your parents about what you saw."

I wiped my face, regaining some composure. "I didn't do anything, Cyn. I swear."

"I know, Kat. I was just concerned about you. We'll talk about it later," Cynthia said softly, rubbing my back for comfort. She bit her lip, looking guilty. "Roger came around looking for you. He heard about last night from Pana."

I groaned, not looking forward to more drama. "Tell me you didn't say anything."

Cynthia sighed, staring up at the towering buildings around us. "Of course, I didn't. But he just thought that I was covering for you. Amie started to tell him about what happened, about the "sexy British guy—"

"He's Scottish," I corrected her absentmindedly.

Her eyebrows cocked. "Sorry, sexy *Scottish* guy, so he went off the deep end, yelling about cheating on him and telling Pana about your sex life. Or your non-existent sex life."

That ass! The moment I see him, I am dumping him! Just as I was about to let Cynthia suffer through the rest of my morning rant, something different distracted me. A peculiar birdlike creature soared through the sky, then vanished upon landing on a building's side. With Cynthia momentarily forgotten, I rose from my seat, trying to spot it once more.

"Kat?"

"Hold on, Cyn."

High above the bus stop, several such creatures circled the Boston skyscrapers. An internal voice prompted me to act, though I wasn't sure what to do. These creatures were unlike any birds I'd ever seen, massive in size and grotesque in appearance with diamond-shaped heads. As I studied them, I realized they all had their gazes fixed on me.

Run, the voice whispered. I began to retreat slowly, the urge to flee growing more potent with each step. "I need to go," I mumbled.

Cynthia gave me a puzzled look. "Kat, what are you talking about? You just got here."

Ignoring her, I could feel the creatures' eyes tracking me. "Cyn, I have to leave. I'll call you later!" I hastened through the crowd, Cynthia's voice fading behind me.

Boston's afternoon shopping frenzy thickened the crowd, forcing me onto the cobbled street. A surge of energy welled up inside me, washing over in rhythmic waves, almost like a sentient radar scanning for danger. Lost in the sensation, I walked right into a man.

From his tattered clothes, battered face, and the unmistakable stab wound, I could tell he was dead. He locked eyes with me, panic evident. "You're like the Kyrios!" he exclaimed.

Confused and unnerved, I stepped back, "No, I'm not." I tried to reason with myself, wondering if I had lost my mind. To onlookers, it must've appeared as though I was conversing with thin air.

Desperation clouded the man's face as he grabbed my hand. My energy responded, reaching out to him. "Please," he begged, "Help me escape. They're coming! I don't want to become one of them!"

Distraught, I changed directions, weaving through the crowd, hoping he wouldn't follow.

But he couldn't.

Suddenly, a chilling sound made me freeze. Glancing upwards, the bird creatures were now perilously close, hanging just thirty feet above. To my horror, these weren't birds. They resembled grotesque pterodactyls with white bony bodies and jagged diamond heads. Their eyes were a piercing red, and their beaks revealed rows of sharp teeth.

Before I could fully process the scene, they swooped down on the ghost. Their massive wings and sharp claws made quick work of him. The internal energy pulsated angrily, suggesting I could have intervened. After a gruesome display, they left only his head and torso, which soon fell to the ground.

The surrounding shoppers seemed blissfully unaware of the horror overhead. But I knew that I was in some serious trouble.

Abandoning all attempts to look normal, I sprinted through the crowd. The creatures' cries grew louder, their wing gusts toppling people and signs.

My only route was a dead-end alley with the high-wired fence mocking my escape. The creatures, seemingly relishing the hunt, floated ominously above. The largest readied to strike. My energy stirred restlessly within, desperate to protect. Overwhelmed, I closed my eyes.

Help is here, my pulse whispered.

As I cautiously opened my eyes, a shadow shielded me. A tall man, his back to me, grappled with the creature. "I thought I warned you," he said in a familiar Scottish accent, "to stay calm."

The man's strength was palpable as he tossed the creature aside, readying himself for the others. They ascended into a fierce aerial battle, their sounds echoing throughout.

After what felt like hours, silence descended. Fragments of the creatures rained down, turning to dust before reaching the ground.

Gregor's steps echoed as he approached. An aura of quiet power emanated from him, my energy recognizing and resonating with his, almost reaching out for him to respond. Half his face appeared human, while the other resembled the creatures, but as he neared, the monstrous visage faded, revealing the creamy tan skin, dark stubble, and blue eyes associated with the Kyrios I knew.

Brushing off the residue, he asked in a voice that sounded both familiar and alien, "Are you all right, lass?" His eyes flitted around my body, carefully checking over any injuries.

My knees buckled, sending me to the ground. As my adrenaline receded and my energy settled, I managed a faint smile, replying, "Never better."

9

Breaking Point

Gregor extended his hand, helping me rise and lean against him for support. He effortlessly ripped into the fabric of space-time, creating a portal that led directly to my bedroom. What would usually take half an hour was done in mere seconds. *Wicked convenient.* He gently set me down amidst my pillows while he settled onto my desk chair. I was grateful for the brief silence, sensing that the Kyrios knew I needed time to process. His patience won out – I finally found my tongue.

"So, the Want, huh?" My words came out muffled as I spoke into my bedding.

"Aye, the Want."

"Ugly buggers, huh?"

"They only get worse, lass. Bigger and uglier."

I lifted my head to look at him. His teasing smirk contrasted with the seriousness of his eyes. "Is that why you changed back there? What was all that about?"

Gregor got up and ran a hand through his hair, now avoiding my eyes. "That was just my body armor when I fight. You have nothing to fear from it," he said, turning his back on me.

Hysterical laughing bubbled out of me, the tension from earlier transforming into a mix of fear and amusement. "No need to freak out?

You're bugging! This whole thing is insane! How do you think I'd act when you've come into my life, turning it upside down and then having the audacity to tell me not to freak out?"

He rolled his eyes, drew his chair closer, and waited for my laughter to subside. "Look," he said quietly. "I understand that this is all jarring. Remember, I didn't seek you out. I'm here to help you. I helped you last night when you could've been alone in an alley. I came to your aid again today when you should've been calm, as I warned."

His jaw tensed, "I do not want to see the world fall apart because some Cravers devour you and unleash chaos using your energy. Everything I've done, including sharing information no living person should ever know, has been to help you. We are both in some uncharted territory, lass. We need to work together, understand?"

My eyes warred with his, searching for some reason to find him untrustworthy. But he was right. I was an anomaly, and he was doing his best. We both were. It didn't make it any easier to accept everything. I moved to the kitchen, seeking the comfort of chocolate syrup, and sensed Gregor's approach. It occurred to me that he allowed me to hear him so I wouldn't be frightened. *Lord knows he doesn't need to make a sound at all. He's flipping Death, for fuck's sake.*

His gaze weighed on me, a mix of curiosity and something more inscrutable. I hugged myself, trying to find a shield in the gesture. "Gregor," I began, voice shaky, "What happened today?"

Gregor shrugged, his eyes never leaving mine. "My guess - you probably had a tantrum."

My eyes narrowed at his accusation. "What?"

"Last night, I warned you about getting agitated. You didn't listen. Your agitation acted like a beacon to those with soul energy. Those Cravers were the quickest to respond."

"Cravers? Those bird-like creatures? They seemed different from what we encountered earlier." I hesitated, recalling the spirit. "Before they got to him, a spirit mentioned I was like a Kyrios. What did he mean? Am I some sort of Reaper? And that spirit... he seemed to die all over again when the Cravers took him."

Gregor exhaled slowly. "You're not a Kyrios. You're human. That spirit was likely referring to your Vis, essentially your 'life essence'. It's connected to your memories, or what most term as the soul. At death, the Vis and soul disconnect from the body. These Cravers, or Want as they're broadly known, need Vis to thrive."

"You possess a uniquely high concentration of Vis. For these Want creatures, your Vis is like a delicacy. Consuming it not only sustains them but empowers them, letting them evolve. The strongest of their kind hunt other high-Vis beings, sometimes even their own kind, to ascend further. It's a ruthless cycle."

He rubbed his temples. "About the spirit you saw today, lingering in the Live Realm post-death typically indicates unfinished business. This could be related to love, revenge, desires, anything really. However, remaining here is dangerous. They risk being consumed and pose a risk to the living. A Kyrios' role is to ensure spirits pass on and to eliminate any rogue Want."

His voice softened. "When the Cravers took him, they essentially erased him. His Vis, his essence, everything. It's as if he died all over again, and now, he's lost forever."

I could only wonder what would've happened to me, and I could feel Gregor's piercing eyes bearing down on me. He was thinking the same thing.

I brushed past him and plopped down on the couch, burying my head in the pillows. "Let's get something straight. I didn't go out today to become food, Gregor. I just wanted to vent for once. Worse, there are these rumors I slept with you last night." I looked away from him but still saw his boyish smirk and blue eyes glittering with mischief.

He said, "Would that have been such a bad thing? I think that you might've enjoyed it."

I threw him a dirty look. "First, you are an ass, and I don't like you. Second, I'm a virgin. And third, a friend from school approached you first, remember? I was supposed to be defending her honor."

"And I am sure if you had given me a piece of your mind, you would have done it soundly."

I rolled my eyes, "I don't need your sarcasm."

Gregor left the doorway and fully entered the room. "I'm not being sarcastic. I've heard enough from you to know your tongue is not one to be trifled with."

Ignoring the sudden fantasy of him warring with my tongue, I murmured, "I think you are just trying to make me feel better."

He gave me a small smile in return. "Is it working?"

"Maybe." I sighed. "I can't go on like this. I want my life to be normal again before the world got all crazy with me at the center of it. What am I going to do?"

Before Gregor could answer, the doorbell rang, and a quick glance confirmed it was Roger. *Of course.*

"Here's another reason for my energy spiking."

"Who the daft is that?" Gregor asked, puzzled.

"Soon-to-be-ex," I sighed. "Please just hide for now."

Gregor ignored my request by crossing his arms and assuming his position against the doorpost.

I closed my eyes, praying for strength. Roger didn't wait for me to invite him in. He barged past me, a storm brewing in his eyes.

"Kat, what's this about you and some guy downtown? Andrea saw him carry you off!"

I rubbed my temples, exhausted. "It's not what she thinks. I got overwhelmed and passed out. Gregor helped me, that's all. He just came by to check on me."

Roger scanned the room, noticing Gregor's presence for the first time. Gregor grinned and offered his hand to Roger. "Pleasure."

Roger ignored it and turned back to me, "So you've been alone here with him? What else happened?" He grabbed my wrist.

I wrenched it away. "Nothing! If anything, you should be thanking Gregor. I passed out in an alley, and he was helping me out last night. Gregor is a foreign medical exchange student from Scotland," I lied smoothly. "He's been a perfect gentleman! I would never cheat on you. But right now, I want to be left alone."

Hurt and irritation warred on Roger's face. "You're my girlfriend,

Katya," he said through gritted teeth. "I'm not leaving you here with some stranger. Let's go."

Gregor quickly stepped forward. "Sorry, Rodney—"

"It's Roger."

Gregor flashed him a phony, apologetic smile. "I'm sorry. Roger. Katya should rest at home tonight. She should not be going anywhere."

"Like I give a fuck what you have to say. She's not staying with you."

He reached for me again, but I recoiled. "No, Roger! I've had enough of your jealousy routine whenever I talk to another guy. I'm tired of your selfishness and I am tired of you using me for clout. I can't do this anymore." I was so close to slapping him that I could feel my energy churning underneath my skin.

Roger flushed crimson, hands clenching. "Can't do this, or can't do me?

"Honestly, pick one. I don't care anymore, and I don't give a fuck. I'm not going to the next phase of my life with you and this idiot thing we call a relationship. It ends here."

"Planning to replace me already?" He glared venomously at Gregor. "I see how it is."

"Not that it's your business anymore, but I just want space to be by myself."

"Space to be with him, right?" Roger growled, taking a step towards me.

Gregor stepped in between us, power crackling around him. "I believe the lady asked you to leave her be."

A cruel smile stretched Roger's mouth. "For now. But once she gets this phase out of her system, she'll remember how good it was with me, and she'll come back." He held my gaze, new darkness swirling behind his eyes. "I am her home."

With that chilling promise parting shot, Roger stormed out, slamming the door behind him. The sound reverberated through the house like the closing of a chapter in my life.

"Well done, Katya," murmured Gregor in front of me. "Your lover seemed rather volatile."

I sighed, the weight of Roger's thinly veiled threat lingering in the air. "You have no idea." I avoided eye contact with Gregor as I swept past him and entered the family room again. "It's done. I'm tired of avoiding everything that makes me uncomfortable. And don't say lover. It's creepy."

Gregor looked puzzled. "Did you not love him?"

That I genuinely didn't know. But I didn't want to look indecisive in front of Gregor, so I said, "I wouldn't have been with him for two years if I didn't."

Gregor arched an eyebrow, smirking. "Being with someone doesn't mean you love them. It just means that you have a habit you can't break."

I scowled at him. "Now it's broken. So, this conversation is now officially over. Moving on, doctor, what are our plans for tonight?" I asked.

"We're dealing with your Vis and your erratic emotions. During your argument with the boy, I had to quickly put up a shield in case you started to get out of control."

I gnawed my bottom lip. "I did start to feel it bubble up."

He nodded. "The stronger the feeling, the greater the power will flare. The more powerful the flare, the more dangerous it becomes for you."

"So, when I got pissed off downtown—"

"It sent off a signal to every Vis creature up and down the North-eastern corridor. The small Cravers got there first. Who knows what else could have answered that call?"

A chill ran up my spine as I thought about what I had seen, both in the past and present. "Gregor, this Vis... why do I have so much? How do I even begin to control it? Every answer seems to open up ten more questions."

Gregor smiled crookedly. "I assumed they would. That's why we are leaving."

"Leaving? Where are we going?"

Gregor raised his right hand and concentrated on its center. A bright blue portal opened, like the one we'd entered earlier. I couldn't help but feel the awe and fear of seeing Death before me, cutting through the fabric of time and space so easily.

"We are leaving the Live Realm and going to the other side."

10

Welcome to Ager

Gregor's crossing-over announcement sent me reeling. "The other side? Wait, does that mean I have to die?" I shoved my hands into my pockets and angled my body further away from him. "Look, Gregor, you are cool and all. I'm feeling the whole quiet brooding you got going on. But I'm not trying to die."

Gregor rolled his eyes and offered his hand. "Don't be stupid, lass. No one is going to die. They know you are coming and are allowing you passage without death."

"Who are they?"

"The Generals – leaders of the Kyrios. They will explain everything to you. But you need to come with me. We need a place where we can talk without the chaos of your world," Gregor hinted. I raised an eyebrow, prompting him further. "A place beyond the veil, Katya." The thought was daunting. But with everything spiraling, perhaps a step into the unknown was what I needed.

I nervously studied the blue effervescent portal in my living room. "I don't know about this," I said, licking my lips, feeling uncertain. Crossing over dimensions to the realm of the dead didn't seem like a wise or safe idea. *What would happen if I couldn't leave? What would then happen to Mom?*

"Katya."

The soft timbers of the Gregor's voice broke through my anxious thoughts, causing a spike in my heart rate. I was transfixed, unable to turn away from his face, his glowing eyes. "You have trusted me with your story. You have trusted me to fight for you. I need you to trust me again. No harm will come to you. I promise."

Standing next to Gregor, with the ethereal portal shimmering before us, I realized how little I truly knew about him. Was I willing to entrust my fate, my very life essence, to this enigmatic being? As I glanced sideways, catching the determined set of his jaw, I felt an inexplicable pull. He seemed more than just a harbinger of death – there was something innately protective about him. But could I really trust him in a realm unknown?

After a few moments, I closed the gap and grabbed his hand, enjoying his warmth. I allowed Gregor to pull me into the portal. I thought we would have to travel within the portal to our destination, but we stepped to the other side.

Initially, we met white mist, fog, and clouds with the sun fighting to peep through, already disconcerting, seeing as we were just in the evening back in Boston. The thick fog made it difficult to see, but Gregor knew where to go. We'd walked for several minutes when the mist began to clear, and a large shadow in the distance became clearer. The closer we got, the larger the shadow appeared. Finally, as if we flipped a switch, all the fog and mist cleared to show the Great Wall of China. Or something that looked amazingly like the Great Wall of China. This white brightened brick wall stretched as far as the eye could see, disappearing into the horizon like an endless serpent, embodying the other-worldliness and mystery of the realm.

However magnificent the wall appeared, it was nothing compared to the towers beyond the wall. Five blazing white towers created a castle beyond the wall's entrance, which looked large enough to fit thousands of people. The pointed caps of the towers reminded me of a trident piercing the cloudy sky, boldly displaying its strength and intimidating onlookers.

"Is this the Room of Apofasi?" I asked breathlessly.

"No. The Room of Apofasi is solely for the judgment of dead souls. This place is Ager, the Kyrios' headquarters." Ager unveiled itself to be a realm entering into twilight. The horizon gleamed with a soft, silvery light, casting long, whispery shadows on the cobblestone paths below. Unlike any I'd seen in the Living realm, an endless canopy of stars painted the sky. Ager's air had a peculiar quality – cool and crisp, tinged with a fragrance of ancient parchment and burning cedarwood. The quiet hum of energy was palpable, like a gentle heartbeat echoing through time.

We headed for the immense wall's entrance, guarded by two tall men. The men wore black jackets, pants, and boots similar to Gregor. And they were both incredibly and devastatingly handsome. They could be featured on the cover of a fashion magazine that would just be called "Handsome." I wondered if being gorgeous was a requirement to be a Kyrios.

One of the men stepped forward—a blond man with brown eyes— and said, "State your name and business."

Gregor didn't miss a beat. "Kyrios Gregor escorting the living Katya Stevens to the Generals."

The two men's eyes fell on me, and I tried very hard not to squirm underneath their inspection. "You may enter," the blond guard answered, and the large gate shot up high in the sky. Gregor nodded curtly, took my arm, and marched forward.

What was beyond the wall was as imposing as the wall itself. The massive towers, centered in the middle of the main compound, were pristinely clean and new, though they looked impossibly old. Surrounding the center towers were much smaller, less imposing, and scary buildings. The entire "town" looked like it came out of a history book on sixteenth-century England. I half expected peasants to stream out of the smaller buildings wearing dirt-stained rags or the rich to stroll down the streets with powdered wigs and white stockings.

Instead of peasants, there were Kyrios everywhere. Men and women from different races and ethnicities worldwide, all similarly dressed to

Gregor. Some Kyrios were running in packs, doing drills. Some were transporting large loads that resembled industrial-sized potato sacks. Others were lounging around, laughing and talking to each other, but still on alert for any alarm. It felt like I'd entered a military base, and I told Gregor so. He slightly smirked but kept his eyes forward. "In some ways, you might liken us to a military," he said quietly.

"But I thought you guys were Death. Why would you need to be militant?"

"The generals will answer your questions later. Let's keep it moving." Some of the Kyrios stared at us as if sensing that my presence in Ager was unusual. I ducked a bit closer to Gregor and followed him quickly. We headed towards the tallest tower, stationed in the middle of the four other large buildings surrounding it. But when we entered through the main door, there was no way to get anywhere. No stairs, no elevator. And the only platform I could see was at the tower's top.

"How are we supposed to get up there?" Gregor hoisted me up into his arms, bridal style. I was immediately struck by how easily he pulled me into his arms and the strength I felt emanating from him. I felt like I could sink further into him and be surrounded by safety. Realizing that I was on the verge of possibly doing something embarrassing, I half-heartedly attempted to leap out of his arms but gripped his neck. I shrieked, "What are you doing?"

"Just hold on tight," he answered and jumped up. The rush of jumping several hundred feet high got the best of me, and I screamed the entire way up. When we hit the platform, I released my kung fu grip on his face, leaped down from his arms, and adjusted my clothes. "That wasn't so bad," I said, refusing to make eye contact with him.

Gregor gave me a sideways glance, his finger trying to dislodge the screech I left in his ear. "Really? I think my ears disagree with you."

Still refusing to look at him, I brushed the imaginary dirt off me. "Well, who are we meeting here?"

"We are right here," a voice said from behind.

My head shot up, and I subconsciously inched closer to Gregor. Four men and one woman stood before me, all wearing the familiar all-black

Kyrios uniform, with one exception: a long medallion necklace hung around each person's neck. A different presence about them indicated they were in charge. Without effort, power radiated from them. My tingling within felt lighter with them, enjoying their energy.

Gregor dropped down to one knee and placed his hand on his chest. "Generals."

A relatively young-looking, tall man came forward. He had dark hair cropped low to his brow, olive skin, and piercing light brown eyes. The best artisans out of Rome must have sculpted his body. There was no way that a physique like that could've come naturally. He seemed to be the strongest from the energy I felt from him alone. The man smiled down at Gregor and, with a Middle Eastern accent, said. "Relax, Gregor. No need for protocol around us."

Gregor straightened and smiled, "I'll always stand on ceremony when it concerns you, mentor."

The man's laugh boomed against the walls. "You always did, my boy. A Scot isn't a Scot without his traditions." He then turned to me and bowed slightly. "You needn't be afraid, child. You are amongst friends here. My name is Nabil." He motioned to the other Generals behind him.

"Ms. Katya, I present the heads of security, research and advancement, operations & barrack life, and training. Together, we are the leaders of the Kyrios. We oversee all operations regarding the Kyrios and spirit transfers from the Living Realm to the Room of Apofasi."

There was something off about Nabil. While his skin was smooth, almost youthful, his eyes bore the weight of countless memories, stories, and eras gone by. I'd seen such depth in elderly people, those who'd lived long and storied lives. But on someone as young-looking as Nabil, it was unsettling.

Sensing my discomfort, Nabil smiled at me serenely. "I'm sure you have many questions, yes?"

Not trusting myself to speak, I nodded.

"Very well, let's adjourn to the next room while we explain it to you. Gregor, you may continue with your duties. You're dismissed."

I cleared my throat loudly and edged back to stand directly before Gregor. "Um, Nabil, I don't want to be a pain, but I would consider it a personal favor if you kept the only man I know here around. I am very aware that I am amid powerful harbingers of death. I'd feel better about this situation if he was here to help me process everything."

Gregor didn't speak a word. He lowered his head, waiting for his leader's decision. Nabil looked at the other Generals, who shrugged and turned around to enter another room. Nabil smiled, though not as widely as before. "Fine. Gregor, you may stay. Follow me." Without waiting for my thanks, Nabil and the other Generals entered the next room.

Gregor relaxed from his stance and began to stroll forward with me in tow. "You know nothing would have happened to you," he said quietly. "I don't need to be here."

I shook my head. "Cut me some slack. I don't know anyone else here. I trust you more than the entire Kyrios force combined. I won't talk to them unless you are with me."

Gregor looked over his shoulder at me with exasperation and amusement. I arched one of my eyebrows and crossed my arms. "Don't look at me like that. You think I'm being childish. Think of it as me self-preserving myself, hmm? Plus, I bet you also want to know what they know."

He turned back around with his smirk shining on his face. "Enough with the cheek, lass. You're getting your wish."

11

Devine Design

We entered the next room. The hum of advanced technology was almost palpable. On the walls, screens showcased scenes from around the world. I took a moment to absorb it all, feeling a slight shiver run down my spine.

The Generals were already seated at the large oval table. Nabil, at the head, turned to me, his gaze probing. "Ms. Katya, what do you know about the Kyrios?"

I took a deep breath, the scent of the room – a mix of dust, old wood, and something metallic – filling my nostrils. I remembered what Gregor had told me about Vis and the role of Kyrios. "Aren't you like Soul Police? You bring souls to judgment, right?"

Nabil sighed deeply, a sound that held a weight of centuries. "Something like that. You see, the Live Realm is made of positive Vis. When you die, your soul and your personal Vis leave your body. The Vis is supposed to return to the Live Realm, and the soul needs to enter the Room of Apofasi to cross over. However, there are times when a soul is so tied to the Live Realm that their anger about dying or having to crossover changes them. They hold on to their Vis, which changes them physically until they are the beasts chasing after you today. In the last 100 years, there's been an increase of souls changing into Want creatures."

"What! Those disgusting bird Cravers that tore apart a human soul were once humans?" I said, horrified. *What could hold someone so much that they changed into those things?* I couldn't stop the rise of emotion, knowing I unfortunately had a hand in that soul's demise.

Nabil nodded, his jaw tensed. "That's just the beginning." He leaned in closer across the table. "The Want creatures' main desire is to be in the Live Realm. It's unnatural for the dead to stay in the Live Realm, so they need Vis. They take it from other dead beings, effectively destroying the soul." His voice was a sad melody, filled with sorrow.

"It's continuous destruction. Outside of the Live Realm, there are two places for deceased souls. Paradiso is for those who have passed judgment, and The Abyss is for those who failed or have turned themselves into the Want. The Abyss isn't a secure prison, though. They always find ways out."

I frowned. "How do they manage that?"

He offered a rueful smile, raking his hand through lush dark curls. "The Abyss is another plane—the poorest mirror image of the Live Realm with no Vis. A Want creature has three choices. First, they can wither away and die a second death."

I looked around the room, eyebrow furrowed. "Does that happen often?"

Nabil's harsh laugh cut through the tension. "No. This is a rare choice for a creature who is hell-bent on returning to the life they once had or getting the revenge they want."

"Second, they can survive and absorb. It means they feast on other creatures and take their Vis for strength. That's why there are different levels of power within the creatures. The highest rank is called a General, just like Kyrios do here.

"Third, they can use whatever Vis they have to pierce the veil separating the Abyss and the Live Realm and enter the Live Realm in search of more Vis to sustain themselves. Every time they enter the Live Realm, they are causing themselves harm. But it furthers their main desire—more Vis and the ultimate destruction of the realm they can't enjoy anymore."

"I'm assuming the creatures probably choose two or three, right?" I interjected, shaking my head.

"Correct," Nabil affirmed. "They desire nothing more than to destroy the world they cannot live in anymore and destroy their Kyrios wardens."

"Don't they just make you all warm and fuzzy inside," I muttered. "Also, I have to say, this seems like a terrible system. Who created this?"

Gregor cleared his throat. "God, Katya."

"Wait," I interrupted, trying to keep my thoughts from spiraling. "When you say 'God' created this system, are we talking about the same God from the Bible, from church?"

Gregor nodded.

A memory flashed before me. I remember sitting in church pews, listening to sermons about God's love, judgment, and the afterlife.

I would never be an atheist, but throughout my life, with all the craziness and heartache I'd experienced, I thought now and then that I must have pissed God off. My relationship with God was mainly what Mom had told me and what her parents had taught her. She always ensured that we went to church when she was home. Mom didn't want our white neighbors to think she was too good to attend the local black church. She tried to maintain whatever ties she had with them like my grandparents did until the day they died.

Unfortunately, I never felt a connection. The congregation's passive-aggressive comments and thinly veiled gossip always made me feel like an outsider.

But it wasn't that I despised God because of those people. I never understood why he let them use his name for their agendas.

Hearing that God made this system brought more questions. "God created this system as punishment for the Want? Did he create you guys, too?"

Nabil leaned back in his chair, satisfied with my rapt attention. "All souls, whole or damaged, have a place. The Abyss, Paradiso, and the

Live Realm all serve a function to preserve a balance in this universe. The Abyss was never meant to be punishment—the Want creatures turned it into one by harboring their hatred. As for us, we Kyrios chose this calling."

"Calling?" I looked around, noting how some of the Generals looked down at Nabil's wording. Nabil cleared his throat loudly, causing them to sit alert again.

"Yes," he continued. "We chose to function in this hybrid world of living and dead as wardens but also to serve a function for maintaining this balance. When the Want creatures break out, it often leads to battles. Many of these bleed into the Live Realm, causing disruptions like dangerous weather due to the shift in Vis."

"Wait a second! So events like earthquakes and tsunamis result from unbalanced Vis?" I remembered my encounter with Gregor and the silver tornado.

"Not always. But the worst ones often are, especially when the Want creatures try to absorb Vis in the Live Realm, causing disruptions and chaos," Nabil explained.

I took a deep breath, my mind reeling. *This is heavy.* Those creatures I saw on Mount Helena and many other instances of chaos in my life – that chaos finally has a name.

"If that is the case, isn't it best to destroy them all? Isn't your priority to protect humans?"

Nabil's eyebrows rose. "Our role is containment, not destruction. We act when they intrude into the Live Realm. There's been an uptick in their intrusions recently, and it's not solely because of you. Something's amiss in the Abyss." I touched my chest subconsciously, trying to feel that essence within me.

"Shifting the conversation to your current situation," the female General called, "I have a few questions for you."

My eyes darted to the woman. "Yes. I'm sorry, General...?"

She smiled softly. Beautiful, with almond-shaped eyes, high cheekbones, long midnight hair, and heart-shaped lips. "General Michiko. I am the head of Scouting and Intelligence. I had Gregor bring you here to discuss your extraordinary well of Vis."

I looked eagerly at the soft-spoken woman. "General Michiko, do you know what is wrong with me?"

Michiko shared a look with the other Generals, shifting in their seats, "'Wrong' is not the word I would use, dear. And we don't have an explanation yet. As far as we know, we have never encountered a living human with such immense Vis reserves – the well of energy within you. We've been charting you since you entered Ager, and your reserve has grown exponentially in the past hour we have been together."

Alarmed, I checked over my body to see if I was glowing. However, everything looked normal. I asked, "Is that a bad thing? Will something happen to me?"

She sighed, massing her temples. "I cannot answer this question until we have more time to study you. Tell me, has anything been different for you? Gregor told us that you could see spirits when you were a child but that it stopped twelve years ago, only to return now. Has anything happened?"

I didn't know whether I wanted to be annoyed that Gregor shared my personal story or grateful that I could speak about my troubles to others who could help decipher my issue. "After my eighteenth birth-day, I started to experience some flashes or visions. I could never really remember them. The last vision I had was the night I met Gregor."

I almost added, *"And there's an odd voice in my head that talks to me when it's quiet, or when I feel incredibly confused about what to do,"* but I decided against it. I understood that I was talking to spirit wardens in another dimension, but I was very sure hearing voices in your head was not a good sign in any dimension.

Michiko opened a small portal, reached in, and took out a pad of paper to begin writing furiously. "The visions seem to coincide with the abnormal activity in the Abyss. Gregor did say that he felt a small abnormality when he met you. Perhaps the Want creatures might have noticed it too and been looking for you, mistaking you for a recently passed soul. But your Vis reserve has almost awakened from a deep slumber since meeting Gregor and that incident in the alley. It's why the creatures have been actively looking for you these last thirty-six hours."

"If they could consume you, then they could move up the food chain quite readily," Nabil piped in. "I reckon any creature that devoured you would instantly become a General."

I furiously thrust a hand through my hair, fighting back the fear and anger that was starting to build. "So now what? What do we do?" I asked tersely. "I know you are trying to help, but so far, all you have done is thoroughly scare me, blow my mind about God, tell me that I'm strange, that I'm Wanter food, and could effectively bring more destruction if I get eaten." I sighed and said a bit louder, frustrated, "What is the point of this conversation if you can't tell me what I am or how I fix myself?" Warmth expanded and engulfed me from all sides. After several seconds, the feeling stopped, and it got cold again.

The room was silent for several moments before one of the Generals spoke up. With a Russian accent, he said, "The main point of our meeting is for you to learn to control yourself." I looked at the General who'd just spoken. A silver-haired, still relatively young-looking man raked his eyes over me with slight annoyance. "We have enough to worry about with Wanters constantly causing trouble. We have another situation in the Abyss that is causing more Wanters to break into the Live Realm, and we can't figure it out yet—"

"Why don't you just pop into the Abyss and take a look?" I interrupted fiercely. "For God's sake, it can't be that difficult—"

"Because it is forbidden!" he said sharply. "We cannot go in as we please, like the Archs and Phims."

"Raf!" Nabil said sharply, and the silver-haired General paused to take a deep breath.

In a softer tone, Raf gritted out, "We must play by the rules. However, we can hardly get control over the Abyss situation because your tantrums are a risk to the Live Realm. Your job is to learn to calm down and not act like a toddler!" He hissed out the last bit from his tight lips.

Shaking my head, I crossed my arms, looking anywhere but at the Russian. "I want nothing more than to not to be a problem, General. My entire life since I have been born, trouble has followed me. So, I apologize if my fear and anxiety are too much. But dammit, I am trying here." Gregor reached underneath the table to squeeze my knee as a warning.

Nabil threw the silver-haired General his own warning look. "General Raf is trying to say that we brought you here because we wanted you to be informed. We also wanted to discuss your role in this conflict and hope we can help each other. While we are trying to maintain the balance, you might find receiving some Kyrios training for protection helpful. Your Vis reserve is very similar to ours. If you can control your Vis, you'll be less likely to be a threat to others around you. And perhaps you'd be an asset to the Live Realm."

Not trusting myself to speak, I nodded.

Nabil nodded as well. "Raf is in charge of training here and will supervise your progress." The Russian man nodded. He then pointed to a dark-skinned, impressive General that reminded me of someone. "General Lamar oversees security here at Ager. He will ensure you remain safe here and in the Live Realm." Lamar gave a soft smile that I returned.

Nabil then gestured to the burly red-haired General, who was grinning in my direction. "And Victor oversees hospitality and energy consumption. He ensures everyone is taken care of and that things are running smoothly. You will not have too much time with him. Michiko will continue her research, and I will check your progress periodically."

"And your position, sir? What do you do?" I asked quietly.

Nabil smirked. "I, my dear, am the head General and oversee everything. I communicate with other departments and sometimes God himself." He looked at Gregor. "I believe that your work here is done here, Gregor. Ms. Katya, you will begin your training immediately."

I did a double-take. "Wait, you mean right now? How long is this going to take?"

Raf shrugged. "As long as it takes for you to grasp basic principles. Could be a few days."

I frowned. "Oh, that's not too bad –"

Gregor interrupted softly, "For full disclosure, one full day here is three days in the Live Realm. Four days here could be two weeks back at home."

My eyebrow rose. "General, I can't disappear like that! My friends and mother will freak out if I'm not there. They are going to think something happened to me."

Michiko quietly reached over and touched my hand, "Ms. Katya, do you understand that we don't completely understand how bad it will get? You could be a threat to yourself and to the people you care about."

I knew Michiko had a valid point. I felt like an accident waiting to happen. That poor man's soul back at Downtown Crossing was a perfect example. And what if Cynthia or Amie were around and got hurt?

But then, I could only remember my mother's anguish after Dad died. My mother desperately tried to stay strong after the casket was lowered into the ground. I did as well, but I couldn't help but grasp her hand as we took several steps away and said to her softly, "We'll be okay, Mommy." Overwhelmed, I nearly crumpled under my mother's weight. She fell to her knees, sobbing into my hair. "My baby. I'm so sorry."

I put my most conciliatory look on my face and lowered my eyes in deference. "Generals, please. Give me a Live Realm week to get my things in order. I only have my mother, and I don't want to put her through stress if we can avoid it. I promise to keep my temper in order until I can come back here for training. Or can we do something to curb my power in the meantime?"

To say Nabil was annoyed was an understatement. The Head General furiously raked his hand through his hair while trying to keep a pleasant smile. It looked more like a grimace. He motioned to Lamar, who looked me at pensively. "What do you think?"

Shaking his head, Raf interjected, "She should stay. We don't need her to attract any more attention. That energy can become volatile at a moment's notice." I bit my tongue, trying to hold back my retort.

Victor stroked his thick beard. "However, there is only so much we can do. Technically, she's not part of our domain. And we don't need the higher-ups to claim we are interfering with human life."

General Lamar shrugged. "I agree. I think we can trust her to be good. From Ager, we could monitor her. If her Vis levels surge out of control, we can bring her in immediately." He looked at me sternly with a hint of a smile. "As long as the young lady remembers to stay calm, I don't think it should be a problem."

I nodded earnestly. "Yes, sir. I promise I will do my best."

Deep in thought, Nabil drummed his fingers on the table, then sighed. "It is only because you are still of the Living that I am even considering this. But we will allow you time to get your affairs in order. We will have a Kyrios stationed by your home for additional protection. That is all. Everyone, return to your posts."

"Nabil, sir," I called out, halting the Generals in their departure. "I'm sorry, but I have one more request."

Nabil looked at me unflinchingly. "What is it?"

I swallowed, got up from my chair slowly, and slightly gulped. "Could Gregor be the one who watches me until my training begins?" I asked quickly.

"Katya!" Gregor hissed. "What are you doing?"

I refused to look at him, still babbling. "Again, I'm very grateful you have been educating me about this whole mess. And it's not that I don't believe that any other Kyrios couldn't protect me. From what I've seen, they all look competent, as do all of you. I mean, my Vis immediately responded to your strength. It's just that I have a level of trust with Gregor. He has already helped me understand quite a bit about Ager and all of you. I could be much more useful to you if I am at ease and not agitated about having another stranger look at me, expecting me to explode." I bit my lip, trying to get control of my nervous energy. "Please allow him to stay with me."

Gregor finally moved in front of me and knelt before the Generals. "Generals, my first duty is to oversee the Northeast quadrant. Yes, I understand I have set up a repertoire with Ms. Katya. I do believe anyone could oversee her protection. While I am flattered, I believe she feels gratitude towards me and is a bit uneasy about the ordeal. I request that I remain at my post." He never looked up from the floor.

The Generals looked at each other, silently communicating. Nabil sighed and said, "Gregor, we have complete confidence in your ability to oversee the Northeast. However, this will take precedence until we better understand the child. Nor do we want to start this relationship on a bad foot, yes?"

He smiled at me widely, but I could see it was forced. "Gregor, you are now ordered to remain as Ms. Katya's guard until further notice. Your second in command will take over. You shall guard her with your life and not allow anything to absorb her Vis. The last thing we need is the Want getting their claws into her."

"Thank you, Generals," I said softly, watching Gregor remain unmoving on the floor.

With a dramatic sweep of his coat, Nabil exited the room.

12

Under Watchful Eyes

Michiko and Victor slowly followed Nabil, muttering goodbyes. Raf and Lamar remained behind. With a stare fixated on me, Raf said, "You must return here in a week. You will get your affairs in order and return here with Gregor. Then you are mine."

Fantastic. "Will this only take a few Ager days, General Raf?"

"It will take as long as you need to get control of your energy."

"But that could take months, years."

Raf shrugged. "What is time when you are dead?"

"But I'm not dead."

"You will be if you don't control your Vis." He left the room, not waiting for a response. "I will see you in a week, Ms. Katya," he called over his shoulder.

I massaged my face, feeling annoyed. "It's going to be just fantastic training with him, huh?" I muttered to myself.

I looked to General Lamar, who still showed the kind smile from earlier. "This is a lot to take in, isn't it?" he asked softly. His voice's soft, soothing timbre seeped into me and threatened to unleash the tears I was surprised I was even holding. I nodded. "Things will come easier with time. I'm sure you will surpass our expectations," he said softly. I gave my new favorite General a shaky smile.

General Lamar snapped his fingers, opening a tiny blue sliver in the middle of the room. He reached in and pulled out a silver bracelet. "In the meantime, I want you to wear this bracelet. It will allow us to track you and your energy level. I'm sure Gregor will keep you safe; however, I prioritize your safety." With a snap, the metal bracelet, inscribed with odd hieroglyphic-like markings, infused together and was officially stuck on my wrist.

"What language are these markings?" I asked, observing the bracelet closely.

Lamar grinned. "Older than time. Think of them as a direct line to yours truly. You'll understand more later."

"And this really will keep me safe?"

"You are a precious commodity, dear. All of us will be watching you," he said, leaving with a wink.

I turned around to find Gregor looking at me, very displeased. "What's the matter?" I asked innocently.

He closed the gap between us and whispered, "Not here. Let's go." He took my arm and led me hastily out of the Center Tower. He barely said a word as we walked back through Ager, out the main gate, and back into my family room. A quick look at the clock told me that it was midnight. It had only felt like an hour in Ager, but we were gone for three!

The moment the portal closed, Gregor finally took a deep breath. Not letting go, he led me to the couch. Knowing that I had made it back safely into my domain, with my inviting window bench calling me, I wanted to laugh out loud and twirl like a child. I had adventured into the world of the dead and lived to tell the tale. But Gregor's stormy eyes curbed that desire. "We need to talk," he said briefly.

I bit my lip, nervous about requesting him to stay with me. "What do you mean? Is this about you being my protection? Look, I –"

"I almost don't know where to begin." Gregor interrupted, and I noticed he looked ashen. "First, you can't be disrespectful to Nabil, the head of the Kyrios. Second, you lost your cool until quiet Raf, who never speaks unless spoken to, was sharp with you. And after all that, you ask one of their Majors to abandon his post to babysit?

I gnaw on my bottom lip, "Hey, I resent the babysitting! I didn't want to start over with someone else!"

He ignored the interruption. "It's just not done this way. The Kyrios, Ager - they are ancient and set in their ways. There are protocols and manners to follow—spoken and unspoken. I understand that this is your first time with them, and I probably should have explained this to you before we left. And perhaps the Generals understood and took pity on you. But in the future, you must watch your tongue. It is a miracle that the Generals were in a good mood, or they could have turned you down flat and locked you up!"

I was about to interrupt him again about the babysitting when his last sentence hit me. "Wait, what?"

Gregor ran a hand through his tousled hair, looking less frazzled than he had just a few minutes before. "You are an unknown. An enigma. Something that could upset the balance within the realm, like the Want. They could have taken you into protective custody if they had willed it."

"But Victor said they didn't have the authority over me because I'm human."

He gave me a side glance. "Aye, and they could have found it if they needed justification."

I closed my eyes, letting my head fall back on my shoulders. "I've heard that phrase way too many times. Police taking you in 'for your protection.' That's absolute crap. Just say what you mean. You mean prison."

"Something like that." Gregor kneeled before me, bracing his arms on either side of me. "Katya, take this from someone who knows. Don't be the reason for your loss of freedom. If you can't control your Vis, they will not hesitate to contain you."

I searched his eyes, looking for an answer. *Does that mean he was imprisoned?* "Would they kill me?"

He hesitated but shook his head. "The Kyrios do not kill the living.

We bring souls over. However, the Generals could have gotten the okay from the higher-ups to place you somewhere within Ager for safe-keeping."

"The Generals kept saying that. Who are the higher-ups? What does that even mean?"

Gregor sat on the couch beside me, hunched over and draping his elbows over his knees. "You know, Katya, there's a hierarchy in our realm. We Kyrios aren't at the top." He conjured a sphere of light, three silhouettes dancing inside. "See the winged figure there? Those are the Archs."

"You mean, like Archangels? Like real-life angels? Big fluffy wings? Chubby-looking things?"

"Correct on the wings, though not as fluffy. And an absolute no on the chubby. Think deadly warriors with wings and powerful weapons."

I instantly pictured Gregor with only wings on his back, bare-chested with a cloth covering his bottom half. I shook my head to clear the arousing thought. I studied the silhouette a bit more. "What's their role in all of this?"

Gregor looked uncomfortable. "If we are the 'Soul Police,' they are weapons of the judge. They follow orders. Whatever comes down from on high, they will execute efficiently."

"You don't sound like you like them," I observed, his lips thinning.

"More so, they don't like us." He cleared his throat. "Then it's the Phims that could overrule us all." He pointed to the top figure that looked like an ordinary man, and I said so to Gregor.

The Kyrios chuckled darkly. "One hundred percent far from it. They may take this form, but it's not their true form. They are called the 'fiery serpents' for a reason. Consider them to be the right hand of God himself. God gives them the order, and the Phims send it down the chain." He rubbed his chin. "Now that I think about it, we haven't got a Phim directive in a hundred years."

"Is that a good thing or a bad thing?" I asked softly, afraid of the answer, of what it could mean for me.

He cocked his head to the side. "Not sure. They only appear if they're convinced something is upsetting the balance. As Nabil explained, they will do whatever is necessary to keep that balance in check."

I understood Gregor's unspoken warning. *I could disrupt that balance.* "Wait, the Phims could order my death? Just like that? They can't do that," I said slowly. "I have the right to live my life too. Where is the justice in that?"

He chuckled darkly again and stared at the ceiling. "Justice. If only true justice ever existed. It's a fine idea, but nothing is ever that clear cut, even in death." He turned to meet my eyes, almost pleading with me. "They can detain you, and they will if you don't learn to control your emotions and your Vis."

I stared into Gregor's eyes, searching for a hint of deception but found none. A myriad of emotions swirled within me—fear, disbelief, anger. *Was this truly my fate?* I took a deep, steadying breath, rubbing my arms for warmth. Never in my wildest dreams did I think that because just because I existed, I was a threat to many. That I could be 'dealt" with, without my feelings being considered – for the greater good and all that shit. "All right. I get it. But I'm not doing it because of the threat of angels. But because I want to go back to my normal life. Whatever the hell that means now."

Gregor also visibly relaxed as he saw my acceptance of the situation. "Good." For a moment, I felt an urge to tell him about the swirling doubts in my mind, but I held back.

I looked down at my lap, fiddling my hands. "I thought for a moment you were upset that I asked the Generals about you staying with me."

Gregor's eyebrows shot up in genuine surprise. "Why would you think that?"

I shrugged, studying my hands. "I don't know. You didn't say a word on the way back, and the way you looked at me when I finally turned around, I thought I overstepped my boundaries with you."

Gregor smirked. "I don't mind staying with you, lass. I had to say all that because I don't want there to be any implication that we had a closer relationship than appropriate." He paused momentarily, studying my face for a long moment before clearing his throat and looking away.

"We Kyrios are not allowed to maintain ties to the Live Realm. If the Generals thought there was any possibility, I would have been ordered to release you to someone else."

"So Kyrios can't have any...friends in the Live Realm."

He shook his head though his eyes searched for me. "If by friends, you mean relationships, then no. If we get too attached to this ever-passing world, we could create anchors for ourselves, which could tear us apart if we had to choose between being with humans or completing our purpose." He looked down at his own hands. "There are tales, you know. Of a Kyrios from eons past, ensnared by human charm."

I raised an eyebrow. "Ensnared? Makes it sound like a trap."

Gregor chuckled, the sound echoing softly in the room. "Well, humans have been known to be...captivating."

I giggled, "Why am I getting the feeling that you don't take this too seriously?"

"I do! Now, hush, lass. Let me finish the story." He relaxed back into the coach, mischief glittering in his eyes. "Let's see, the story says he was forced to choose. A choice so profound it echoed through our kind for a millennium. The higher-ups somehow learned about the disturbance he and the human he fell in love with and had him banished from Ager. His fate remains an unsolved riddle amongst us."

His words both delighted and disappointed me. I was happy that he was thinking ahead and trying to protect me, but I couldn't get involved with him either. Gregor sounded like he didn't put much stock into this story, but it didn't mean he would potentially put himself at risk. Considering the Archs and the Phims, it was best to do what I needed to do and exit as soon as possible. Because in the end, Gregor wasn't likely to get attached – it was me at the risk of doing something stupid. I was starting to expect too much from him because he saved me. Or maybe because he was the first person to believe me.

I inwardly rolled my eyes at myself, hugging a nearby pillow. *I'd barely known this man for forty-eight hours and was already thinking romance?* I just told Roger I wanted to be by myself, and now I'm considering having a relationship with literal Death. I always made fun of girls getting too attached to guys so quickly after getting a little attention. *I refuse to become a hypocrite and a "pick me," no matter how strong this connection and pull to Gregor grows.*

I cleared my throat and asked, "What will you do now?"

He arched an eyebrow. "What do you mean?"

I looked around. "I don't know. Do Kyrios sleep, eat?"

"We don't need hours of sleep or food, but we can sleep and eat should we choose. We must stop by Ager occasionally to get our fill of Vis to sustain ourselves. That's what General Victor is in charge of."

My nose wrinkled in confusion. "Is there any Vis in Ager? Where does the Vis come from?"

Something in his manner shifted, and he quickly said, "Everywhere and nowhere."

Sensing there was more but having no energy to pursue it, I shrugged. "Okay then. Where are you staying?"

Gregor stood up and looked around. "This room will do just nicely." He began fluffing a nearby pillow.

I shot up from my seat. "Excuse me? You are staying here?"

He placed his hands on his hips and smirked. His lazy and careless stance infuriated me even more. "How do you expect me to protect you, lass? I need to be close by so you don't go off the deep end and have an episode."

Rolling my eyes, I plopped down on my couch, bringing my knees into my chest. "It's almost like you Kyrios forgot how the Live Realm works. I live with my mother and next door to my best friend, who might as well be my second mother. How am I supposed to explain you to either one about you living with me?"

The dim glow of the lamplight washed over the room, casting soft shadows. Gregor joined me on the vintage couch, its old floral patterns peeking through the dim light, throwing his arms behind his head and stretching his long legs. "I'm sure you'll think of something other than the truth. You certainly did last time." He winked, chuckling softly.

"Yeah, a lot of help you were." I freed my hair from its haphazard bun, easing the ache behind my head. "I can't just hide all of this from my mom. If I explained, she might understand."

He shook his head, though his eyes never left my long curls or neck as I massaged the stress away. I wish I could say that I didn't notice him watching me and didn't massage my neck longer than necessary, but that would be a lie.

"Since Ager, the Abyss, and Paradiso came to be, it's been decided: the living shouldn't know the secrets beyond death. Even the Generals telling you what they did would be considered a big infraction. Hence, we must keep this quiet and not call attention to ourselves. That's why I had to mark your hand the night we met—to keep the secrets. Fewer people know, the better."

"Decreed by who?"

He gave me a look. "Who else?"

God again. "You try explaining why you're going to be gone for an unknown amount of time to your mother," I muttered. The rumblings of my stomach reminded me that I hadn't eaten at all. Being at the mall with Cynthia seemed like days ago. I stood again and crossed over Gregor's legs. "I'll make some dinner. Is there anything you are allergic to..." I trailed off and looked at him. "Never mind. You are not human. It's not like I can kill you."

I made for the door when Gregor called, "Katya."

I turned around. Gregor hadn't lost his relaxed position on the couch, but his eyes betrayed his easy stance with a certain amount of heat and intensity. "While this may be my duty, in the six hundred years that I have been a Kyrios, being here is much better than dealing with the dead. The dead, they're predictable. The living? Full of surprises. And you, Katya? You're the most intriguing of them all." His lips curled in a restrained smile, but his eyes remained intense and unreadable.

His words left a mix of emotions in me. Flattery, fear, surprise. I tried to brush off the swelling of emotions, reminding myself of the perils that lay ahead, but his words, like a tune, played repeatedly in my mind.

I returned his smile and exited the living room quickly. As I cooked dinner for myself and Death in my living room, my smile refused to be extinguished.

13

Mornings with Death

The following day, I awoke to my alarm blasting several feet away. The sunlight pouring through my open drapes kept me from falling back asleep. Groaning, I reached my arm over to hit the snooze button but could not reach it. I slowly raised my head from my pillow to see an opaque wall giving off a slight energy. I looked around and found that the wall surrounded my entire bed like a dome. And I had no way out. Instantly, I felt my palms sweat, and a pounding started in the back of my head. I tried to get up but felt another wall only several inches above me. Blood raced through my veins as I pounded on the invisible walls, searching for an opening or weak spot.

The panic finally rose from deep within my belly, and I began to scream.

"Gregor! Gregor! Help me!"

I furiously pounded on the wall, tears streaming down my face. My throat began to hitch, and I started to lose my ability to breathe properly. Just as I was about to let out another scream, the walls suddenly came down, and a pair of arms encased and brought me close to a warm chest.

"It's all right. I've got you. Nothing to fear." All the fear, anxiety, and apprehension I had harbored for the past few days hit me, and the floodgates opened. I'm unsure how long I cried, but the warm arms never left me. Calloused hands caressed my hair and head, easing the tension away. A soft breeze blew through my window, sending lavender and vanilla scents to relieve my panic. Gentle words of comfort finally brought my sobs to a low hum.

As my tears dried, I became aware of the shirtless Kyrios cradling me. Underneath my cheek, I could feel the patches of dark hair sprinkled about the broad chest. With every movement, the muscles rippled, displaying his great strength and fitness. His sandalwood and moss scent filled my senses and stirred the small yearning I put away the night before. Without having to look, I knew Gregor was a sight to behold.

I slowly raised my head from his chest, my eyes cast downward. "I... I'm sorry about that. I, um, don't do well in closed places."

Gregor had slightly released his tight hold on me but kept me close. "No, it's my fault. I put up the barrier around you while you slept to keep your Vis contained in a smaller area in case you released anything while you dreamt. I should have made it bigger." His posture was relaxed, but his eyes betrayed his distress.

I shook my head, wiping my face, "You couldn't have known about my claustrophobia. It's okay."

He looked me over, checking for any injuries. "Are you sure you are all right?"

I nodded, trying to clean the snot running down my nose discreetly. "Not particularly attractive right now, but I'm okay."

Gregor chuckled, tucking a stray hair that escaped my silk bonnet behind my ear. "I don't know about that. You are still quite the sight even with bogeys in your nose."

The unfortunate but familiar lurch in my stomach returned, painfully reminding me that the gorgeous Kyrios was in my bedroom, holding me. Everything I feared was coming true because I did not want to leave his arms. I wanted his lips to descend to mine and relieve me of my breath. I wanted him to explore the warmth expanding through my body. *Come on, girl. Look beyond the pretty face. Don't be that girl!* It didn't help that I also wasn't dressed for company. After dinner the night before, I'd only thrown on an extra-long tank top, which didn't leave too much to the imagination.

Knowing that I needed to move before I did anything foolish, I pulled back from Gregor. "I should probably get out of bed."

However, during my panic attack, my feet had gotten impossibly tangled in the sheet, starting my descent to the floor headfirst. Gregor caught me before any physical damage could be done. But his actions only placed my head in his lap and my hands against his chest. The quiet strength I had felt against my cheek doubled against my hands. His strength enveloped my entire body, tightening me like a string on a bow. I felt nothing but safety and arousal, which murdered my self-restraint.

Gregor's grip tightened slightly around my shoulders, searching my eyes. "Are you all right, Katya?"

I nodded, not speaking for fear that my mouth would betray me. The Kyrios and I were frozen, waiting for the other to do something. For several long moments, neither of us moved, maintaining close contact. Until my stomach growled in protest, freeing us both from our electrified captivity. Smirking, Gregor said, "I believe your body is protesting its further maltreatment."

I felt my cheeks flare and cleared my throat. "Looks like it's time for breakfast." I allowed Gregor to scoop underneath my bottom to set me on my feet. I quickly adjusted the tank, knowing and feeling his eyes rake over me again. Gregor finally had the foresight to avert his eyes as I reached for my robe, cinching it tight around my waist. "It's been an eventful morning, huh?"

Gregor gave me a crooked smile over his shoulder. "A Scotsman never leaves a damsel in distress, especially not one under his protection."

I unwillingly let out a snort. "Whatever, Kyrios." I smiled bashfully as I snatched the bonnet from my hair, undoing my twists and shaking out my curls. "Care to join me for some bacon and eggs?" He followed me out of my room and downstairs into the kitchen.

Gregor sat at the small kitchen table. "Whatever you are offering,

I'll take it, lass. I miss the taste of food. Your cooking last night has me craving meat and hash."

As I moved about the kitchen, I could feel Gregor's eyes watching me, surveying my every move. Flustered, I thought of any question I could ask him. "Tell me about Scotland."

A small smile appeared on his face. "Aye, Scotland. There's no other place like it in the world. The Scottish Highlands are the lushest green you'll ever see. It is the one place in the Live Realm that could honestly take your breath away."

I smiled wistfully, whisking eggs in a bowl. "I've always wanted to go abroad. My mom has been to Europe, but she's never had the chance to bring me. School always got in the way. Or work. Or it just wasn't the right time." I bit my lip as I remembered how my mom would be fearful of leaving anyone who might be helpful to her if I had an "episode." Unfortunately, she never wholly believed me when I said I was all the better after the ability disappeared.

Gregor made himself comfortable and poured himself a glass of orange juice, relishing its taste. I would have laughed at him if I wasn't trying to actively not look at his naked torso. "If you ever have the chance, you should! The isles of Scotland truly are one of a kind. It's like the Princess of the Earth made it her palace. The most beautiful hills and mountains, the freshest air in the world. It is truly the gem of the entire planet."

I smiled as I continued to cook our breakfast. The bacon sizzled adequately in the pan, browning the right amount. "I always knew I wanted to go. When was the last time you were up there?"

Gregor got quiet, sitting at the table again. His knuckles turned white, gripping his armrests. "Been too long. Too many memories." I couldn't help but notice the faraway and sad look in his eyes. It was the same look as the night before. It was the same look I've sometimes seen reflected on my face. Understanding him completely, I didn't press him. I distracted him with food.

Plating our scrambled eggs and bacon, I brought our breakfast to the kitchen table. Gregor dug into his with the gusto of a man on a fast for months. With a groan that tore through my defense, the Kyrios looked at me with gratitude. "Lass, this food! What magic did you use on it?"

I giggled, taking a bite of mine. "It's called spices. Not necessarily groundbreaking, Gregor."

He nodded. "Aye, it reminds me of the years I was stationed in the Caribbean for many years before taking over the U.S. Northeast quadrant."

"You've been everywhere, huh?"

He grinned. "There hasn't been a corner of the Live Realm that I haven't seen— just the humans and landscape change. Also, the language and food," he shrugged. "It keeps it interesting, to say the least."

Ruefully, I added, "It's a perk of being dead, right? What's time to you?" Calling back General Raf's words brought me back to the plan I had started to formulate to explain my soon-to-be disappearance. "So, what are you doing for the rest of the day?"

"What do you mean? I'll be with you."

I paused and eyed him. "I guess it's fine for today, but I need to visit Amie before leaving with you. I don't want this incident with you and her to be a thing before I leave."

He looked up from his plate and smiled tightly. "Everywhere you go, I go, remember?"

It was just not my morning. "Gregor, you can't come with me to talk to Amie. How am I going to explain you and apologize? I'm pretty sure she will not react well if the man who insulted her on her birthday comes with me as my escort."

"What would you have me do, Katya?" he asked, annoyed and dropping his fork. "You're essentially the loose cannon here. I need to be around to ensure you don't send off any signals. Someone needs to keep the people around you safe."

Eyes narrowing, I said, "I can keep my cool, Kyrios, okay?"

Gregor leaned in and smirked, "Haven't seen much of that control yet."

I forgot about the food, huffed, and threw down my napkin. "I'm starting to get sick of everyone dictating my life. I used to do it by myself, you know. Since I was a kid, I've been by myself because I can handle it all myself. But now all of that is gone. Now, I can't do anything without a shadow following me."

"Aye, a shadow that's here only because you wanted it! Because you needed me to keep everyone safe!"

"Because I'm a liability, right? That I couldn't possibly keep everyone safe myself?"

"Katya, since we've met, things have only gotten worse. I shudder to think what will happen when your reserves stop growing. Which, by the way, they haven't!"

Ignoring the growing heat in my hand, I let Gregor have it all. "I'm trying to keep cool, but it seems like the universe, and you want to remind me constantly that I'm a ticking time bomb. Who wouldn't react to that, especially when their life has been turned upside down? And for your information, my temper could be excellent if you would give me a friggin' chance!" I turned on my heel and was out the door. Gregor was hot on my heels.

"Oh, and I suppose this is an example of you keeping your temper? I can't wait to see you perfectly calm!"

"You know what, I've had it up to here with you men! Why must you—" Gregor's hand suddenly clamped down on my mouth, stopping my tirade. I wrestled against his grip only to realize that his attention wasn't on me but something moving outside. He brought me closer against his chest, clamping down on my waist.

"Don't say another word," he whispered. "Something is nearby."

My eyes widened, and I strained to listen. A screech and beating wings could be heard not far from the house. *Cravers were nearby.* I closed my eyes and focused on the Vis bouncing inside me. It took several breaths to calm myself down, the inner energy quieting with each exhale. After several minutes, the internal power had stilled, and the Cravers' screams faded into the distance.

Gregor released me shortly after it went quiet. "That was unusually fast. They are certainly coming out to play more than usual. What are they up to?" He scrutinized me from head to toe. "Have you finally realized your temper is precariously balanced on a cliff?"

I bit my lip, feeling ashamed. "Look, I'm trying, okay? I don't want to fight, but you need to give me room to breathe. I'm having a hard time with this, and I'm used to being alone. Let's start over, okay?"

I took a deep breath. "Hi, I'm Katya. I'm a human with some weird abilities. I have only-child syndrome, and I don't like not getting my way. I'm a work in progress and asking for some patience."

The Scot smiled ruefully. "Katya, I'm Gregor, a Grim Reaper here to protect you from deformed evil souls looking to devour your soul. I will do my best to give you some space, but I want you to know that this is all for your well-being." He tugged on a curl softly. "And you're not alone anymore. You can lean on someone else for a change."

"It'll take some practice. But it's still gonna be weird with you being there when I meet up with Amie, Gregor. Unless..." I trailed, and Gregor's apprehension spiked when he saw my smirk grow. "Do you remember when we first met, and you said you would apologize to her? I can invite the girls over, and we can have you do it then. It will also help me apologize to Amie."

Gregor put his hands on his narrow hips and sighed as well. "Fine. It still gives me the chance to be close by."

I beamed. "Thank you. I'll contact Amie. Perhaps we can meet later this afternoon?"

He smirked, giving me an all-knowing look. "Whenever you wish, lass. Wouldn't want to deny you."

Choosing to ignore him, I stretched, feeling a sudden coolness against my skin. "I guess I should probably get in the shower." Gregor's gaze was fixed on me, more intense than before. Confused, I followed his line of sight and felt a rush of warmth coloring my cheeks. My robe and tank had shifted, revealing more than I intended. I pulled it close, trying to shake off the thrill his stare elicited.

I gave a nervous chuckle, hastily drawing the robe around me. "You better get back to your breakfast, Scotsman. You don't want it to get cold."

Gregor shook his head and cleared his throat. "Of course. I'll be waiting for you while you get ready." And with that, he returned to the kitchen.

I swallowed, watching the play of muscles on his back as he walked away, increasing the distance between us. I rolled my eyes as I made for the bathroom. *I need a cold shower.*

14

Pizza, Apologies and Hidden Desires

After several begging texts to Amie and a call to Cynthia for help, Amie finally relented and agreed to meet at my house that night. Considering the threat of Wanters flying around all day, my home was the best place to be for me. I ordered a couple of pizzas and waited for Amie to come. Cynthia promised to stop by later to ensure we were "back to lovey-dovey friends again."

A few minutes before Amie arrived, I called Gregor into the family room. "Gregor, stay in the other room until I call you in. I need to talk to Amie first, and then we can bring you in for your apology. And make it a good one, will you? Make it look like you are sincere but that you're also afraid of my wrath."

His eyebrows arched. "I'm supposed to fear you, now? You're such a wee thing." He chuckled as I pinched his arm. "Who'd ever fear you?"

I put my hands on my hips, trying to look menacing. "Plenty of people, Scotsman. Don't you know the most fearful thing in the world is a woman's wrath? Add a black woman to the mix, and you'll be ducking for cover!" Gregor guffawed, like I'd said the greatest joke. I was slightly amused as well. "Anyway, go into the kitchen, and I'll call for you."

The doorbell rang. I pushed as hard as I could against his retreating back, not that it would've made a difference. "And keep quiet." He wordlessly entered the kitchen. I looked over my reflection in the mirror by the door, ensuring my high bun was messy enough to look careless but chic simultaneously. I opened the door to find Amie looking much better than she had the day before. More color had returned to her cheeks, and the light had returned to her eyes, still covered by her glasses. Her curly hair neatly framed her face. She had again given up her plaid clothes for a t-shirt and shorts this time. She tentatively stepped into the house.

"Listen, Kat, I—" Amie began, but I pulled her into a tight hug, cutting her off. The faint scent of her perfume, a mix of cherry blossoms and amber, wafted to me. "You don't need to say anything," I whispered, feeling the tension between us begin to dissipate. She clung to me as we held each other, realizing we both needed that human contact for a bit. I released her and was relieved that no tears had fallen – genuine affection looked back at me. I took her by her elbow and led her to the family room. "How's the last forty-eight hours been?" I asked, sitting on the couch.

Amie let out a sigh and sunk into the couch beside me. "Meh, not too bad. When I got home, my mom was screeching about my eyes and let out a string of Spanish curses that I won't share. I told her I was fine and my friends looked out for me. The rest of the day was just her feeding me because that's what Dominican mothers do when they feel emotional. My dad just asked me if I was okay at the end of the day and was satisfied that I said yes." She gave a crooked smile. "What about you? Are you okay? I know Pana was saying some ugly things about you."

I rolled my eyes but returned her smile. "Yeah, she was. I got upset, came home, fought with Roger, and then we broke up."

Amie sucked in her breath but then cocked her head to the side. "You know? I'm not that surprised. I wondered when you would be real about your relationship."

I rolled my eyes, chuckling and tucking a pillow into my side. "I'm so embarrassed, sis. How did I let it get this bad?"

"You liked him because he was pretty to look at," Amie said matter-of-factly. "There were some good moments, right? And you are loyal to your own detriment, babes. But you woke up, and that's the more important thing." She relaxed back on the couch. "This news now makes sense now."

"What do you mean?" I leaned in closer, intrigued, as a playful smile tugged at the corner of Amie's mouth. She cocked an eyebrow, her tone dripping with mischief. "Pana. This morning, she was bragging on Instagram. I'm assuming it's because of Roger."

"Whatever. Pana can have him. I'm better off." I immediately thought of the man hiding in the room, waiting for his cue to enter. I cleared my throat and put on my most peaceful look to not give away my next course of action to Amie. "But I didn't ask you to come over for all that. Ames. I wanted to give you a proper explanation of what happened that night."

Amie looked away, studying her nails. "The guy was a mamagüevo. End of story."

Knowing that being called a "cocksucker" wouldn't make Gregor pleasant, I winced. "He was definitely a jerk and should have never spoken to you like that." I paused, biting my bottom lip. "But I wasn't lying when I said I passed out. You were right that I sometimes keep a lot of myself. And it's coming from a place of hurt and smashed expectations."

"Because of your dad?" Amie asked softly.

I gave her a crooked smile. "That, among other things." I reached for her hand and stared into her eyes. "I know that seems really selfish of me, but I promise it's not meant to hurt you. Ames, you are genuinely one of my closest friends. Very few people see me like this," I gestured to my home. "I don't bring people here unless I care about them. I care about you and went after that guy because he hurt you. Vengeance was on my mind alone. I swear it."

Amie held my gaze briefly before asking, "Then what happened that night?"

It was on my tongue to tell her everything, but a slight burning ache on my palm stopped me. That damn brand Gregor put on my hand was aching. *It could sense I wanted to tell the truth! Damn that Kyrios.*

"That guy, Gregor, ended up helping me out that night. That's why he was holding me. I passed out in the alley after chasing after him. He took me to get checked out. He ended up being a medical student. When I did come to, I had a chance to yell at that asshat for what he did. And we had a chance to talk."

Amie's eyes rounded. "What did he say to you?"

I stood from the couch and smiled down at my friend. "Why doesn't he tell you himself? Gregor?"

Gregor silently appeared in the doorway, causing Amie's gaze to linger on him, her eyes a mixture of surprise with unmistakable interest. *It must be that walking into the light attraction Gregor had talked about.* The Scot entered the room, giving me a glare for my insults, and sat down on the couch with a healthy distance between them. "Hello, Amie. My name is Gregor. Or maybe you know me as mamagüevo or asshat." He stretched out his hand for hers.

Amie's gaze shifted to Gregor's outstretched hand, her eyes betraying the storm of emotions she was battling. Memories of the insults and embarrassment she'd received replayed in her mind. Amie only hesitated for a few seconds before she reached over and slapped the Kyrios in the face. Her hands vaulted to her own, surprised at her actions. I could only watch, feeling my eyes pop. The room stilled. Gregor looked at Amie for a stunned second before a deep laugh escaped his lips. His laugh was so infectious that it pulled laughter out of us both.

Once Gregor calmed down, he said, "I guess I deserved that, huh?" His face sobered a bit. "I told Katya the day we met that if given the chance, I would apologize to you. On my honor as a Scotsman, I am deeply sorry that I offended you. I was not in the best of moods that night and didn't mean to take it out on you. I hope you can accept my apology."

Amie's eyes filled with that dreamy look again, and she didn't immediately reply.

"Amie?" I asked.

She jumped as if she had just awoken. "Yes, I accept your apology. But don't think you can charm me to get into my good graces for a second. I think still think you're a dick."

Gregor smirked, draping his arms over his knees. "I believe that Katya would agree with you. I don't want any ill will between us. Or Katya will never let me hear the end of it."

I pursed my lips, sitting back down in the middle. "That's right. The wrath of a black woman," I declared, lightly punching his shoulder.

"Yes, yes. Please allow me to save face, you mean horrible woman," he teased.

"Oh, this is nothing, hunny. I've been known to reduce monsters to dust simply because they pissed me off," I joked.

We smiled at each other until I caught Amie watching me with sharp eyes. "Are you sure there's nothing between the two of you?"

I jumped, not realizing I started leaning towards Gregor's embrace. "Nothing! Gregor can't get into any relationships anyway."

Her eyebrows furrowed. "Why?"

"Well..." I fished for something. Desperate to deflect and protect our secrets, I blurted out the first thing that came to mind. "Gregor's not into any hetero relationships. He's gay."

Amie's eyes reflected understanding, while Gregor's eyes flashed with surprise and anger.

"Katya, what—"

I clapped a hand over my mouth, looking horrified. "Oh, I'm so sorry, Gregor. I didn't mean to out you. I didn't want Amie to get the wrong idea about our friendship. I just wanted to be clear that you are essentially off-limits, right?" I gave him a look, daring him to refute my story. And he opened his mouth to do so when the front door opened and closed.

A sudden burst of energy filled the room. "Katya Stevens, why am I just learning that you broke up with that ass Roger—" Cynthia rounded the corner to find us staring back at her, showing the same surprise. Before I could even formulate a response, her gaze shifted to Gregor, her eyes narrowing suspiciously.

"What the fuck?" Cynthia's voice, mixed with surprise and irritation, demanded attention. I winced, her tone reminding me of all the times we'd navigated high school dramas. "Cyn, now just wait a – "

"What's he doing here?" she hissed back. "I heard online that you and Roger broke up, and he's telling everyone you cheated on him with this...person. Thanks for telling me, by the way!"

Since we returned from Ager, I'd been dying to call Cynthia and tell her everything to help me process what had happened. But Gregor's heated warning flared up each time I reached for my phone. He clearly didn't understand how best friends worked. The unspoken promises, the shared secrets. It wasn't just about protection—it was about trust. Even now, the truth was right on my lips again, ready to be spit out. But beyond the heat radiating up my arm, with the threat looming over me, something held me back from saying the truth. There's only so much weirdness one person can take before saying, "This is too much." I didn't want Cynthia to get to that point.

"God, I didn't fucking cheat! Gregor helped me back in the alley. He came over to check on me yesterday, and Roger assumed that we were sleeping with each other. I broke up with him last night. I was going to tell you when you came over, Cyn." I met her eyes, hoping she would drop it. "Gregor is here now because he wanted to apologize to Amie. Which he did, and she accepted."

Cynthia looked at me and then gave Gregor an evil look. "Excuse me, Greyson—"

Gregor's eyebrows arched up. "It's Gregor, lass."

My fiery red-haired friend plastered a smile on her face. "Whatever. I'm just going to grab my friend for a little chat in the kitchen. You don't mind, do you? Amie, be a dear and keep the guest entertained." Cynthia grabbed me before anyone else could speak and entered the next room.

Feeling a sense of deja vu, I braced for the incoming interrogation. "What is it, Cyn?" I said as casually as possible.

"Don't you 'Cyn' me!" she hissed. "You are keeping something major from me. I can feel it. He's now a medical student? You know I can tell when you are lying, and right now, you're lying about him. I want the truth, Kat. I can't protect you unless I know what's going on."

I looked down and studied the sandals on my feet, feeling incredibly helpless and increasingly frustrated with the Kyrios, the Want, and everything in front of me. If I didn't say something that would please Cynthia, it could become a massive fight, and I couldn't allow myself to lose my temper. "Cyn, I love you very much. You are my sister in every sense of the word. I totally understand your confusion, but—"

"Kat, we've been through a lot. I know what you are going through. The visions, that smoldering heat, those dreams! Babes, you know that I'm here for you, right? I can handle it. Just tell me." Her eyes reflected all the concern for me my mother would have. I nearly broke—maybe she could handle it. Maybe she wouldn't run from the room screaming. I took a deep breath, memories of all our shared secrets over the years flashing before me. This was one more. One big one. I opened my mouth to spill, but a searing heat shot up my palm. The pain was so intense that I imagined the smells of smoke and charred skin wafting from my palm.

"Fuck!" I hissed, gripping my hand between my knees.

"Katya! What's the matter?" Cynthia grabbed my hand and studied it for some injury. I shot a dark look at Kyrios sitting in the family room. He merely crossed his arms and waited for me to return. Cynthia followed my gaze and watched me as I winced and massaged my hand. As the searing pain ebbed away, she gently grabbed my chin, forcing me to pay attention. "Katya, look at me. What's going on?"

As much as I couldn't stand the Kyrios's tactics, I had to admit I was a bit relieved. I could not willingly give Cynthia a reason to leave. I could not handle having another person reject me because of my "weirdness."

I stared into my best friend's eyes, hoping that she would gain some understanding, see through my actions, and not hold it against me for the rest of our lives. I wrenched my face away, surprising her. "I burned my hand earlier, and it's just acting up." I took a step back and avoided her perusal. "Look, Cyn, it's no big deal." I walked out of the kitchen and to the nearby bathroom just outside the family room, feeling an additional shadow follow me.

Studying my reflection, I smoothed my hair, ensuring it was secure in its bun. "Gregor and I are friends, and he's hanging out with us. There's nothing suspicious about it. He helped me out the other night, and he's not so bad. Stop being overprotective." Cynthia's face flushed with anger. She stared at me as I pretended to preen.

"You're not going to tell me?"

I gave her a funny look. "There's nothing to tell."

"Is that the way you want it? Fine. I'll play. Gregor's your friend. And that's it."

I nodded.

Cyn turned to stare directly at Gregor. I knew two things were going to happen in the next moment. Either Cynthia would take this denial gracefully and leave it alone. Or she would start screeching, alerting the neighbors of our disagreement. Her eyes cooled, and she made a beeline for the Kyrios, who secretly watched us while chatting with Amie. I rushed after her, hissing, "Cyn, what will you do? Please don't embarrass me!" Cynthia stopped short several feet before Gregor, staring hard at him. He stood up from the couch, wary of another slap from Cynthia. Gregor's stormy grey-blue eyes locked with Cynthia's rainforest green, and I wasn't sure whether I should intervene.

"Gregor," Cynthia said authoritatively.

Gregor slowly lowered his arms, maintaining eye contact with Cynthia, and nodded.

Cynthia paused for another second before saying, "I accept you. You'd better not hurt my friend. Guard her with your life."

Gregor nodded solemnly.

Amie and I shared a look before Amie giggled. "Cynthia, way to be melodramatic! I don't remember you telling me that when I became friends with Kat."

Cynthia smiled, though her eyes didn't leave Gregor's. "You don't have a pecker, sweetie. Our conversations would be categorically different if you had the same parts." Amie and Gregor laughed heartily while I rolled my eyes, unable to hide my smirk.

Breaking her gaze, she looked down at the pizza on the coffee table. "Oh great, you got food. I haven't had lunch yet." And just like that, the tension was gone. My two friends ate with the Kyrios for the next hour and had a decent conversation. They asked him about Scotland, and he told them stories about his home's beauty and the places he had traveled to.

I watched over them, feeling a mixture of happiness and wistfulness. I had so few people where I could feel like myself. As much as I knew that Gregor could not have any permanent ties here, I increasingly appreciated his help and presence.

Watching the three of them laugh and talk over pizza reminded me that I was leaving in less than a week. I still had no idea what I would tell Amie, Cynthia, or Mom about why I had to leave. I knew that there wasn't any reason that would be enough for them. I had the strongest feeling that it would be a long while before I could return to this—the simple luxury of eating pizza at home with friends.

After Amie and Cyn left, with promises to meet up the following night, I felt increasingly alone. *How could I leave home, my sanctuary? How could I leave my family and friends?* I quietly told the Kyrios I would read for a bit in my room.

"Katya," he called.

I stopped at the bottom of the stairs and looked back at him.

He stepped forward, his blue eyes shining with understanding. "The hardest burden to carry is duty. Even the strongest of us have moments of doubt and worry. But the greatest battle is whether you can do what needs to be done. I can feel the swirl of indecision and concern within your spirit." Gregor stepped closer and laid a hand on my shoulder, squeezing it lightly.

"Is my Vis acting up?" I looked around, waiting for a monstrous screech.

"No," he said softly, tugging on a stray curl. "That is just me understanding you a wee better. Take solace in the fact that what you are feeling is completely human. To not feel this would make you...well, a Wanter. Don't feel guilty for feeling this way. Revel in it, embrace your human and move forward."

My nervous lip-biting returned. "Gregor," I said, looking down. "I know what I have to do. I know I have to protect them. It's just, I have this feeling that something bigger is coming and—"

"Katya, one step at a time. We can only concern ourselves with what today's troubles are. Whatever is set for the future, we'll handle it together. Remember, you are not alone anymore."

Feeling my lower lip tremble, I bit down harder to stop any potential tears. "How could I possibly forget, with you towering over everyone here?"

The Scot chuckled. "Aye, how else do I remind you I'm here?" We both laughed at that, clearing any further tension.

"Thank you, Gregor." Before thinking about why I should not do it, I closed the gap between us and softly kissed the Kyrios' cheek. He stayed still, looking down at me unblinkingly. His eyes showed his complete surprise and perhaps a hint of attraction. The familiar warmth I ignored returned with a slam, and the urge to give him a more significant kiss grew. To enter his embrace and get acquainted with his body. To unleash every desire searing through me, knowing he could take it all. I cleared my throat, turned, and ran to my room. "See you in the morning!"

As soon as I closed my bedroom door, I let out a silent wail. *How could I have done that?* He was probably mortified that a living human just kissed him. He was probably already planning how he would let me down gently with a speech he'd probably used before: "I'm dead and a Grim Reaper, and you're alive. This can't work." With my heart beating out of my chest, I prayed to all that was holy that he would not bring it up tomorrow and that he would pretend that nothing happened.

As I snuggled underneath my blankets, I reflected on my duty and resolve to do what was right. We had to leave before my mom got home.

If I see her, any resolve I have now will reduce to nothing. I might say to the world, "To Hell with you all."

15

The Night Before Goodbye

As soon as my eyes closed, I found myself in a dream.

I was at a serene lake, surrounded by a vast forest of the most beautiful fir trees I had ever seen. Even the sweet smell of moss and aromatic pine filled my senses. In the middle of the lake was a large yet smooth rock about the size of a sedan, and I was floating over it. Every time I looked around to figure out a way down, a cool mist covered the entire lake, making it impossible to see anything else. Then, I sensed that someone was watching me through the fog. I called out for several minutes but only heard the softest of whispers.

And just as I made out what the whisper was saying, my alarm clock rang so loud and surprised me that I fell straight out of bed. Thankfully, the Kyrios did not rush upstairs to find me sprawled on the floor eating carpet fibers.

Now effectively awake, I dressed appropriately before heading downstairs and into the family room. I found Gregor sitting on the couch watching the news—a 4.5 earthquake had just hit Los Angeles the night before. Wordlessly, I grabbed a bowl of cereal from the kitchen and joined him on the couch. I was relieved to learn that there were no reported deaths. Several buildings were damaged, but it could have been worse. I avoided watching the wreckage as I didn't want to see Wanters out at play, but their screeches came loud and clear through the reporter's live feed at the scene. Every scream brought a distinct ache to my core that made me want to run and hide. And the reporter at the scene was none the wiser of the danger surrounding her.

Gregor noticed that I was nose-deep in my cereal, "You should get used to seeing them. To deny their existence is to reject reality."

"I'm not denying their existence. I don't enjoy looking at them. They are hideous, and it saddens me that humans are capable of turning into that." I took a bite and wiped the dripping milk from my chin. "What could you hold so much that you turn into...that?"

I missed the flash of pain on Gregor's face as I got up to return to the kitchen. "It could be many things, not just material greed, that could rip a soul apart," he called after me. "Just remember, humans are very complex creatures—now and in death."

I returned to the couch and turned down the TV. "I get that, but looking at and focusing on those things so early in the morning is still terrifying. I'd rather talk about our night tonight."

"Katya, about that—" Gregor began.

"You will accompany us as we discussed, act as the big bodyguard you are, and keep all of the icky Wanters away." I raised my eyebrows, daring him to refuse to go and bring up anything but the plans I was discussing. Especially not the kiss that I gave him the night before.

Gregor said nothing but nodded. I gave him a solid pat on the back. "Good, it's settled. The girls will be over later today. I'll be in my room, packing some of my stuff and figuring out my letter to Cyn and my mother." I stood up, stretching and cracking my fingers. "You can keep yourself occupied, right?

He stood from the couch and pulled out his phone from his pocket. "I'm sure I can, lass. I'm just going to call into my squad to check in."

I edged closer to him and poked him in his rock-hard abs. I couldn't resist the urge to touch him, and I needed to stop. Touching him led to other thoughts, and I couldn't afford to have those thoughts. "Does that mean you're leaving? I thought you had to stay nearby."

"And I will be. Don't fret. I'll be on the roof for a bit." He snapped his fingers, opening a bright blue rip. "Do keep calm while your minder is away," the Scot smirked.

"Ha ha," I said drily. He grinned and disappeared.

The rest of the day was a whirl. I packed most of my personal belongings and started to write an email to Cynthia and my mother, scheduling them to send after I'd left.

As I tried to write my notes, I realized the gag order radiating from my palm didn't allow me to write much, so I had to be a bit creative. Hopefully, when I did return, neither one would take my letter to heart and go too crazy.

As I put the final touches to my mother's email, a notification flashed from the dean of my future college. He welcomed us and applauded our accomplishment of entering college; he looked forward to seeing us all at orientation at the end of the month. And it made me laugh out loud – the world is at risk of imploding from the dead breaking into our plane, and the dean is excited about an ice cream party for first-year students.

As much as I hated going through so many changes at once, I'd rather be aware than oblivious. My understanding gave my family and friends a chance to survive.

Interrupting my gloomy thoughts, Cyn sent me a text.

"Let's go to Nicky's. Arcades and my boyfriend! Be over in about an hour and a half or so."

I sent a quick *"Okay,"* finished the email, quickly showered, and dressed in the sweetest red sundress I could find. A sweetheart neckline with a hem ending mid-thigh. Knowing this would be my last outing in a long while, I wanted to make sure I looked utterly captivating.

The setting sun blazed bright oranges and reds through my skylight, and I suddenly felt compelled to take a selfie video. I sat in the middle of my room, sitting on my desk chair. Turning the recording on, I sat in the chair, twirling as fast as possible until I lost control. The chair toppled over, sending me into giggles at my stupidity. I stared back at my reflection on the phone screen, at my wide grin. "No matter what happens, Kitty-Katya, you are amazing. Don't forget that."

As I started putting my final makeup touches and fluffing my kinks to large curls, I called for Gregor. I didn't hear a sound. Rolling my eyes, I dashed downstairs, calling for him again. I peeked in the living room and didn't see a soul. Then I noticed that water was running in the bathroom. *Is he taking a shower?*

I slowly inched my way to the door. Straining my ears, I heard the soft musings of his voice. *He's singing.* The song wasn't exactly in English, but the tone was so captivating that I didn't realize that the water had stopped running and footsteps were behind the door.

And that's how Gregor found me. Right behind the bathroom door, like a deer caught in headlights. What caught me off guard was the masculine, sculpted beauty that stood before me with only a towel wrapped around his waist. Had it not been for my nails cutting into my palms, I'm sure I would have jumped him, tossing my reservation out the window. If I had not been so distracted, I would have seen how his breath slightly hitched at my appearance, his eyes darting between my hair, neckline, and legs.

The Scot spoke first. "Do you need something in the bathroom, Katya?" he asked gruffly.

"Yes," I said huskily. I cleared my throat. "I just need to get...something." I licked my lips. My eyes dropped to the floor. "I thought Kyrios don't need to shower."

He shrugged, bringing the towel slightly lower with his movement. "Being in the Live Realm has me picking up some old habits. Never hurts to be clean." He brushed past me into the living room. Not wanting to make another fool of myself, I pretended to grab something in the bathroom and ran to my bedroom.

I closed my eyes as I leaned against the door. *It is getting harder to be around him. I don't think it's particularly fair to have Kyrios look so ethereal and perfect! Who wouldn't want to die if a man like that could lead you into the forever sunset?* A knocking sound at my door startled me out of my inner thoughts.

"Katya? Let's get this over with. Are you ready?"

I opened the door to find Gregor in the same drab, black-on-black ensemble. My disappointment must have been evident because he asked, "What's the matter? Is there something wrong with my clothes?"

I smoothed my sundress down, refusing to look him in the eye. "Can you wear anything other than black combat gear? It has to look like you changed, or the girls will be suspicious." I shuffled back into my room and grabbed a magazine. I flipped it open to a male model I had admired a few days before. "Do you have anything like that?" The male model wore a dark navy and brown button-down short sleeve shirt, and washed denim blue jeans—trendy but casual. Gregor took the magazine from me and studied it.

"You want me to look like this?"

"Or something like this." I then felt highly uncomfortable. *Who was I to dictate what this man wore?* It wasn't that serious, and I started to sound like Roger when he would assess my clothes when I was going out to a party with him. "You know what? It's okay, Gregor. I can make something up." I took the magazine and returned it to my desk. "I'm sure the girls were more focused on your..." The words died in my mouth when I returned my attention to Gregor, who had miraculously changed his clothes to mirror the model's outfit within seconds: the shirt, the pants, even the stainless-steel necklace, and tan boat shoes.

If I had to compare the magazine model with Gregor, the Kyrios would win— every time.

The Scot smiled and performed a pirouette. "How is this?" The striped button-down showcased hs chest and forearms, elongating his tall frame. His jeans gripped his body but effortlessly fell against his legs. Even his simple boat shoes made me feel a bit jittery.

"How did you do that?"

The Kyrios gave me an all-knowing grin. "Lass, just because it looks like I changed my clothes doesn't mean I did. I just changed the appearance of it. Why do you think we all wear the same thing? We can change our clothes at will, whatever the situation dictates."

I merely grinned. "You are full of surprises, you know that?"

Gregor tapped my nose and returned the grin. "Took the words right out of my mouth. Come on, I wouldn't want you to be late."

* * *

Cynthia arrived promptly, her eyes bright with anticipation. Expecting to wait, she used her keys to enter and sat on the couch. She was shocked to find me ready, arm-in-arm, with Gregor in the foyer. "Gregor, are you a miracle worker? Who would have thought that Katya could finish on time?"

"Hey, I'm not the only one who's fashionably late!" I retorted.

"I'm here on time, aren't I?" She looked me over with a calculating eye. "Turn around, let's see." I obliged, twirling to showcase my sundress and Roman flat sandals. Cynthia nodded, rubbing her chin thoughtfully. "Looks good. Your turn."

Cynthia followed my exact movements while I looked over her outfit. She had on a green sundress with off-white polka dots and wedge shoes. Cute but sassy. I nodded. "It's giving, girl. You may proceed."

Gregor gave us both a look. "What was that about?"

Cynthia clasped her hands behind her back and circled Gregor and me. "You see, my dear man, when ladies step out for an evening—"

"Cynthia, shut up already! We're just checking each other's outfits. No big deal." I grabbed my purse off the coffee table. "Geez, Cyn. No one is trying to hear a lecture, damn!"

Cynthia looked at me haughtily. "If you'd been more patient, I would've reached that point. Why do you always have to rush me?"

"Why do you have to be such a know-it-all?"

"Why do you have to be such a brat?"

"You must be talking about yourself!" I took a step closer to her.

"I call it like I see, baby. You want a pacifier with that crying and whining?" She took another step closer to me, our noses dangerously close.

Gregor looked between us uneasily. "Ladies, let's not let our emotions get—"

He was interrupted by our burst of laughter and giggles. I leaned on my best friend's shoulder and grinned. "You ate that pacifier line. I'll have to remember that for next time."

Cyn winked and kissed me on my cheek. "You can borrow it anytime." We let out more giggles as we looked at the dumbfounded expression on Gregor's face. "Oh, Gregor," Cynthia said, shaking her head. "You men sometimes just don't get us, do you?"

Another knock at the door announced Amie's arrival, and with a quick, approving look over her lovely romper and hair, we all clambered into Cynthia's car. *"Mom and Dad are away for the next two days, so we can use the car as much as we want."* The ride to Nelly's Pizza and Arcade was quick—a fifteen-minute drive from our homes.

Sitting on the edge of the Fenway neighborhood, between bustling businesses and homes, Nelly's Pizza and Arcade was brimming with people when we arrived. We headed to our usual corner, dragging Gregor behind me. As soon as the door opened, we could smell the rising pizza in the stone brick ovens, the sweet sugar twisting into cotton candy at the concessions, and hear the clangs and bells from a won jackpot prize game. To my surprise, however, we were greeted by a group of people smiling widely at us. Cynthia had prepped our friends before we arrived. Our favorite corner was set up with several tables.

"Better with a cool crowd, right?" Cynthia shouted over the music. I smiled. I couldn't agree more. Cynthia and I often say we can count our genuine high-school friends on both hands. They were our friends because they all had something we prized greatly – no bullshit and straight honesty. That group from school was waiting for us, ready to have fun.

"Guys! Welcome!" Steve shouted gleefully. Cynthia's dark-haired boyfriend came from behind one of the counters and greeted his girlfriend with kisses and a hug. I always did like Steve. He was the type of guy that you could hang out with, tell him some crazy secret stuff, and know he would never tell a soul. Cynthia and I met him a year and a half ago when we learned about Nelly's and its famous pizza. I noticed how starry-eyed Steve had gotten after meeting Cyn and knew my friend would be happy with him.

Samantha, a sweet girl who loved to tease as much as she loved to laugh, said, "Kat is here! And who is this yummy person behind you?"

Before I could say anything, Gregor threw a hand up to say hello. "I'm Gregor."

Samantha stepped up first to shake his hand. "Hello, hello, hello! That is a lovely accent."

I nudged her back to her seat. "Stop being thirsty, girl." I gestured towards the Kyrios. "Gregor, these are my friends from school. You just met Samantha. The guy behind her is Ben—we go way back to middle school. The tall blond is Don. The ginger is Ally, and the guy wrapped around Cythina is her boyfriend, Steve. This crew is what Cyn and I like to call the Fab Five. They're not fabulous, but the name rolls off the tongue, and there are five of them."

The crowd groaned, throwing napkins at me while giving a rousing "Hey!" to the new visitor.

"Kat, hunny." Samantha swiped a slice of pizza delivered by one of the servers. "We were just talking about you. Roger is spreading the word on social media that you two broke up. How are we doing, girl?"

I rolled my eyes and flipped my curls over my shoulder. "Girl, please. I'm the one who ended it. And good riddance; he was an ass." I sat down, noticing Gregor scanning the room as if assessing potential threats. Once his shoulders slightly relaxed, I tugged on his arm to sit beside me. He immediately got comfortable and poured himself a drink of Coke.

"I'm just glad you finally saw it. We," Samantha pointed to the others, "were all hoping you were gonna figure it out."

"Damn, everyone was just waiting for us to break up?" I huffed.

I looked around, and all their nods confirmed Samantha's sentiment. "We didn't want to push, but we were hoping! It just took a bit longer, but hey, you made it! Not to mention with a sexy man to boot."

Amie took a seat next to Samantha. "Sam, I thought the same thing too. But she swears up and down that they are just friends."

She and Samantha shared the same skeptical look.

"What happened, Kat? American boys can't be your friends either?"

With beautiful onyx skin, Ben stepped forward behind Samantha with a twinkle in his eye.

I smiled, rolling my eyes. "Don't be jealous, boo," I crooned. "Gregor is just a good-looking friend with a better shot at me than you."

Ben barked with laughter. "Oh, Kitty, you wound me!"

I hit him lightly on the arm. "You know I hate that name!" I looked back to Gregor, smirking in his cup. "Okay, enough. Gregor is here to hang out with us, so let's show him a good time. No more questions about our relationship."

We gathered around the table as Steve returned with more pitchers of soda to pass around. "Gregor," Don yelled over the arcade noise, passing us drinks, "how old are you?"

"I'm twenty." *Good, just like we rehearsed.*

"Do you work, or are you in college?"

Crap! We never discussed this. I frantically looked at Gregor, hoping he would make eye contact. But he took a deep swig of Coke, smiled, and said, "My job is protecting Katya from unwanted predators."

The crew laughed, mistaking his literal words for humor. Gregor smirked but chose not to clarify.

Ben slapped him on the back. "Makes sense. Kat has a knack for finding trouble."

The Scot gave me a sly look. "I believe it."

I grimaced, "Hey, why don't we just have a good time instead of talking about the stupid stuff I do?"

The night went remarkably well. The guys talked about sports and guy stuff with Gregor, and the girls needled me with constant questions about my new "friend."

"Katya, you lucky bitch! How did you even find him?" Ally asked, her eyes never leaving the Scot.

"She said he's a medical student who happened to save her in an alley, but we met him at a bar on my birthday," Amie said mischievously. She cleared her throat. "Apparently, not only is he hot, but he's also a knight in shining armor."

Ally leaned forward in her seat, tapping my arm. "Spill it, hunny. How is he?"

Samantha and Ally looked pointedly at me, and I suddenly understood what they were asking about. "Oh my God. We are NOT doing that."

Cyn rolled her eyes, giving me a smirk. "Guys, stop it. Kat's innocent! Why bother asking?" She smiled at them all, daring them to challenge her protection. "She's waiting for when the time is right."

Their jaws nearly hit the floor. "Are you kidding? How could the timing be any more perfect?" Samantha exclaimed.

"Keep your voice down!" I hissed. "And no, I'm not blind. We're not like that, okay? What part about friends don't you get?"

"Oh, I get it," Ally said grumpily. "He's gay!"

I rubbed my forehead, slightly frustrated, and shared a look with Amie, who shrugged. "Yes, that's exactly it."

"What!" the girls chorused, clearly disappointed. Except for Cynthia. She had a pensive look on her face and kept studying Gregor.

"That is so unfortunate!" Samantha grumbled. "It's always the good ones! He is so polite, charming, and everything else in between. I mean, that's just...ugh, look at him."

At her insistence, I did. I watched Gregor as he talked with the guys. And the odd thing was that they acted like they had known each other for years. Gregor suddenly turned and looked at me, catching my eye. Completely relaxed, his brilliant gaze softened as he looked me over, checking if I was okay. With a wink, he returned to the boys' conversation. Though the entire exchange took only a few seconds, it sent my heart into an upheaval.

Unfortunately, a slight tremor followed shortly after. Everyone paused, waiting for the weak earthquake to stop while I closed my eyes and tried to calm down and keep the excitement out of my heart. I'd forgotten my impending departure for a short while, and remembering brought my mood crashing down.

Once my heart rate slowed, I knew that the signals I was sending to the Wanters would also cease, ending the tremors. Once I found my control, I looked around to find Cynthia watching me closely and Gregor giving me another look before returning everyone's attention to the festivities.

After some more pizzas, laughter, and dart contests, I stepped outside to get some fresh air. Ever the protector, Gregor was right behind me, checking me over. He walked over to where I was leaning against Cynthia's car. "I'm fine, Mr. Bodyguard. It's just that I'm having such a great time, and it's sad to think I'll miss all this when we leave."

Seeing my sad expression, the Kyrios unexpectedly brought me into his arms for a hug. I could feel his lips against my forehead widen to a smile. "It's not goodbye forever. Who knows, maybe you'll be back before they miss you."

I let out a sigh, secretly enjoying Gregor's tight hold. The waning summer heat had cooled, and the Scot's hug chased away chills. "What were you and the guys talking about?"

"Oh, the usual small talk. Briefed them a bit on you and my world, of course."

"What!"

Gregor laughed heartily. "Are you daft? Of course not."

I pouted and pushed him away, "That was mean, Gregor. They were so into your stories, they would've believed it."

Gregor returned his arm around my waist. "Don't worry, lass. They mainly teased me about you all night. Talked sports, girls, you know."

I rolled my eyes but smiled, accepting his embrace. "Fine, you can keep your manly stuff."

Gregor sighed happily. "You know, I'm glad you convinced me to go. Being back in the Live Realm feels good. I've missed just being a person."

I turned to face him, feeling particularly giddy. "Oh yeah! You were alive?"

"Yes, a long time ago. But that was then, and this is now. I'm just enjoying the now."

Smiling, I teased, "And you were worried something was going to happen."

Gregor nudged me and gave me a smirk. "I wouldn't be so sure. There was that tiny spike in your power when I looked at you."

I froze and then studied my hands closely. "Ah, it was just the girls being, well, girls. They pointed you out, started putting ideas in my head—so it was nothing."

Gregor's eyebrows furrowed. "What did they say to you?"

I bit my lip and looked up to the inky dark sky to avoid his gaze. "Something like you were pretty much perfect. And it's too bad that you're gay."

I expected him to get on me about calling him gay again. But the Scot didn't say a word for several minutes, and then he asked, "What did you say?"

I cleared my throat. "Well, I agreed. I mean, it's unfair how you Kyrios are put together. You are perfect beacons calling souls to cross over. And you! You're sweet, kind, and polite, among other things." I worried my lip further, closing my eyes to hide my mortification. "I just played along with them. I'm human, and you're not. Besides, it's not like you'd be interested in me or anything."

Gregor's thumb brushed against my bruised lip, impeding my gnawing. I suddenly became very aware of the intimacy of our bodies. He had moved just so that he had me pinned to the car using his body. Our knees could not move without touching.

Gregor slowly moved his finger down, slightly caressing my lips. "Why would you think I wouldn't be interested in you?"

Unable to speak, I shrugged my shoulders, my eyes pulled in by his bottomless grey-blues.

His thumb gently traced the contours of my cheek as his hand cradled my face. "Allow me to correct that misunderstanding, then."

16

A Kiss Amidst Chaos

Holding his breath, he leaned in slowly, his lips brushing against mine. When I didn't move away, he touched my lips again with more pressure. Soon, I responded in kind. As I let out a slight groan, the Scot shuddered, releasing his inhibitions. He flicked his tongue against my lips, seeking entry.

The total pleasure I had ever felt was nothing compared to Gregor's kiss. Every single nerve was alive, and every sense was electrified. Even my inner spirit, my source of power, bubbled over with joy, fluttering excitedly inside me. I couldn't help but wrap my arms around his neck and bring him closer. Every lick, every groan, and every caress emboldened Gregor, and I couldn't move an inch.

Shivers ran up and down my spine, and his clean scent of soap, sandalwood, and moss had me almost begging for more. I yearned for more—more friction, more of his body pressing against mine. My temperature was rising, and my hands began their exploration. Into his hair, massaging his scalp. The Scot's hands delved into my hair, traveling downward to my hips, grabbing and molding my ass. He moved us so my back arched against Cynthia's car and into his chest, leaving me gasping for air. More hands, more friction.

More.

Full-on passion collision.

As Gregor nipped my right lobe, sending me spiraling, we didn't notice my heart rate and fluctuating energy. It grew so much that it became a pulse that shook the ground underneath us. The forgotten bracelet from General Lamar began to beep loudly. We froze, with reason and duty intruding abruptly on our moment.

Gregor quickly pulled away, his breath ragged and his eyes wide. "Fuck, what was I thinking?" he hissed, turning his back on me. I understood why he reacted as he did. I understood why he was frustrated at that moment. However, I couldn't stop the wave of rejection hitting me as he grabbed his curls, cursing under his breath. He turned back and closed the gap again, "Katya, breathe deeply and try to calm down."

Blinking back tears, I took a deep breath to bring my power down when the bracelet sent a zap to my wrist, causing me to cry out and spike my energy further.

I desperately tried to relax but couldn't find my equilibrium, like something kept hitting my internal panic button. "I'm sorry. I didn't—" A loud, heart-stopping screech froze us and had us staring at the sky above. My power pulse had not just attracted your run-of-the-mill Craver this time. Something much larger, uglier, and with much sharper teeth had emerged from a new eighteen-foot black hole in the sky, like the blue rips that Gregor created to cross over to the other side.

The towering humanoid creature, five stories tall, was clad in white, bony scales. Its elongated claws could rip the street to shreds. One swift kick from its long, webbed feet could have taken four buildings, and Nelly's down flatter than a pancake. But its head was the most terrifying part—it wasn't located where one would expect shoulders to be. The familiar, diamond-shaped head was lodged in the middle of its chest, with bone armor protecting it from all sides.

Gregor immediately pulled out his phone and began barking orders. "Patrol fifty-eight, I have one Devastator—Wrecker, level two in the southwestern quadrant of zone thirty-two. Requesting backup to arrive in the southeast. With the human anomaly. I repeat, with the human anomaly." Gregor didn't hesitate, gathering me into his arms and jumping high.

"Gregor, wait! Cynthia and the others!"

He landed on the roof of the building next door and headed opposite Nelly's. "I know. If we suddenly leave, he'll have a tantrum and possibly cause more destruction. We must lure him away from everyone to someplace more remote. The patrol will either send him back to the Abyss or destroy him. We'll head to the industrial complex." Over his shoulder, the Wrecker could tell its intended target was moving quickly away, and it roared in anger. It stomped quickly towards us, but not without taking out electric poles and two nearby homes. Screams could be heard from underneath the rubble.

Shortly after, three men ripped through their blue portals and fell in line with Gregor. They ran and jumped from roof to roof with precision and speed. "Sir," a steel-haired man said. "What are your orders?" They stopped on a nearby rooftop, still in sight of the terror chasing after us.

"The human must stay within my care. Take Williams and Carey with you three and take it out. Ensure that no human casualty occurs."

"Sir!" the three men chorused and disappeared into the night. Gregor continued to run until we reached the industrial complex and stopped at the highest rooftop available, with the Wrecker not far behind. The hideous thing seemed to smile, savoring the chase of a new power source. It whacked an empty water tower off a nearby apartment building and launched it in our direction. Gregor dodged to the left to avoid the massive missile but didn't notice the incoming debris that followed the water tower.

"Look out!" My scream came two seconds too late. A large metal girder knocked him back, whipping me out of his arms and into the air.

Free falling doesn't happen as fast as one would think. Not to me, anyway. Everything happened in slow motion. My body rocketed fifty feet higher, twirling like a human cannonball, and then resumed its descent. Somehow, I could flip myself upright but was closing in on the Wrecker. Even with no words, I could tell it was pleased that it could snatch me midair, devour me, and absorb a new source with just two steps.

And I was terrified. I didn't know which terrified me more: hurtling towards the ground or getting captured by the Wrecker. All I could think was, *This can't be the end. I need to do something!*

Within seconds, a blinding white light launched itself at the Wrecker, splitting into four spears and embedding itself into the Wrecker's limbs. The creature let out a terrible screech and came to a halt. The spears disappeared in a white blaze, but the attack had created searing holes in the Wrecker's armor, leaving the creature heaving for breath. *I had attacked it. That blinding white light came from my chest!* I was so mesmerized by the attack that I briefly forgot about the ground approaching me. Gregor flashed underneath me before I could scream for help, murmuring, "I've got you."

Before the Wrecker could take a furious step forward, five other Kyrios had surrounded it in an odd formation. One stepped forward to taunt the beast while two positioned themselves at the Wrecker's feet and the remaining two high on rooftops, at level with its claws. With a shout, four of the Kyrios raised what looked like glowing swords and slashed away at the beast's limbs. Dismembered, the Wrecker fell to the ground with a surprised roar, leaving its armor open around his face. The remaining taunting Kyrios quickly scaled the giant beast and embedded his sword in the middle of the Wrecker's forehead. With one last roar of agony, the creature disintegrated into nothing.

The steel-haired Kyrios returned to Gregor's side with a salute. "The creature has been destroyed, sir."

Gregor nodded. "Return to your post."

The five saluted with a chorus of "Sir!" and disappeared, once again, into the night.

I hadn't spoken to Gregor since we left Nelly's, and I still couldn't talk. Gregor quietly dashed back to the pizza parlour to find that two nearby homes, partially destroyed, had police surrounding them and that the road leading to the residential street was blocked off. Thankfully, no one was seriously hurt, and people blamed it on a gas leak-turned-explosion. Of course, there was no evidence of any gas leak; however, the human mind will make excuses when natural logic fails them, and the supernatural seems to be the next obvious choice. I wondered whether the immediate grasp for a "logical" answer was a by-product of Kyrios involvement. *No one must know the ongoings of the dead.*

Everyone at Nelly's crowded around the police tape to get a closer look at the destruction. Gregor and I surreptitiously entered the crowd from the back and pretended to be just as shocked as everyone else. Our group could not stop talking about how Nelly's shook from the reported gas explosion. Gregor remained quiet as I spoke robotically and added, "Wow" or "I know, right?" when necessary.

Cynthia remained quiet in Steve's arms, looking inexplicably exhausted. She observed us both and asked, "Where were you two when all this happened?"

I shifted uncomfortably. "I needed some air when Gregor came out to check on me. We were outside when the shakes started, so we ducked for cover nearby until it stopped. We figured it wasn't safe to go back inside."

She narrowed her eyes but shrugged it off. "Right, it wouldn't have been safe in Nelly's, but you could've been killed from the explosion." She gave me a quick peck on the cheek and made for the car, which had somehow remained unscathed. "I just want to go home. Let's get Amie," she said with an unfounded, scathing glare at Gregor.

No one uttered a word the entire ride back.

The intensity of the unexpected kiss with Gregor lingered, unlike anything I'd ever experienced. If water were always that electrifying, I would never stop drinking. *Why had he kissed me?* I didn't know what made him go that far, but I liked it. I wanted more despite the danger—what if I became an anchor for Gregor and he was forced to leave?

I stared at the bracelet on my wrist. *What had happened back there?* The bracelet's malfunction had made me lose more control not contain it. I massaged my head, grateful no one got hurt; it could have been much worse.

Cynthia's apparent animosity toward Gregor puzzled me. She had always been protective, but this was different. But she knew nothing that would make her dislike him so much. There's no way she could.

We dropped Amie off first. I stepped out of the car to give her a proper hug. Everything in my spirit told me that this was a night of goodbyes. *This would likely be the last time I'll see her for at least a few weeks.* "Kat, you scared me and Cyn," Amie started softly. "We had no idea where you were and—"

"I know, babes." I gave her a watery smile. "I really am sorry about that. But we're fine, okay? Gregor did take care of me." I smoothed her frayed edges and bangs back to clearly see her eyes. "This is gonna sound weird for me to say, but I'd never purposely make you worry. You and Cyn matter to me."

"Like family?" she asked, her lips raised in a timid smile.

"Like sisters, Ames. Love you, girl." I hugged her tightly and waved goodbye as Cyn returned to our homes a few blocks away. We pulled into Cynthia's driveway, and the silence was palpable.

I glanced at my best friend. "Cyn, I'm sorry I worried you earlier—"

"Love, you have nothing to apologize for." She glanced disdainfully at Gregor in the back seat. "It's not as if you had anything to do with tonight."

The hairs on my neck prickled. *What was she suggesting?* "Cyn, why are you looking at Gregor—"

"She's right, Katya," Gregor interrupted. "You had nothing to do with this, so let's move on. A situation like tonight won't happen again."

I inwardly groaned. Gregor was already heading in the direction I desperately wanted to avoid. With a nod, he exited the car, leaving Cynthia and me. The Kyrios walked away and disappeared, turning to the next block. *He's probably going to circle back into the house.*

I looked at my friend sternly. "Cynthia, I get that you were worried earlier, but what's your problem with Gregor? It's as if you are blaming him for what happened tonight!"

Cynthia stared down at her steering wheel. She didn't seem to have even heard me. "Katya," she said thoughtfully. "Be careful, please."

I gave her a puzzled look. "You think there's going to be another gas leak?"

She shook her head and finally met my eyes. Filled with unshed tears, my best friend took a deep breath and steeled her voice to stress the seriousness of her words. "No, it's not about that. Katya, you need to promise me you'll be careful. Yes, I worry about you. You scared me half to death tonight when you disappeared, and we couldn't find you. You cannot leave this car without promising me you will stay safe."

To say I was alarmed was an understatement. Cynthia was not the crier – I was. She was the one to hold me and comfort me. I wanted to interrogate her to understand where this was coming from, but how could I when I had my own secrets?

I embraced her, her orchid and vanilla perfume easing my anxiety. "Hey, don't cry. It's going to be okay. I still don't understand your mixed feelings about Gregor but don't worry about him. He is a good guy. I will be fine, I promise."

Cynthia sniffled, gently wiping her eyes. "Call me later?"

There wouldn't be a call, babes. I'm sorry. I gave her an extra squeeze. "You got it." I exited the car and walked across the lawn into my home.

Waiting for me in the foyer with a detached look, Gregor said quietly, "Katya, we need to talk."

Uh-oh. I walked away from the stern Kyrios to sit on the couch, mentally preparing myself for either a lecture or a speech of deprecation. "I know. I know we do. We—"

"Major Gregor!" A man in the Kyrios uniform stepped out of the blue-silver portal into the living room.

Gregor looked at him grimly. "Sargent Davies. What brings you here?"

The younger Kyrios cleared his throat. "General Nabil has sent orders that you and Lady Katya return to Ager immediately."

"Did he say why?"

"He simply said they had found something regarding Lady Katya that she might want to know."

Gregor nodded, looking thoughtful. "We shall return shortly." The younger Kyrios returned through the portal without another word. The Scot cleared his throat, not facing me, "Katya, I guess our talk will have to wait?"

"Yes, I think so. I'm just going to change quickly." I dashed past him and made for the stairs.

"Katya," he called after me, his eyes never leaving the floor. "I would bring everything you need for an extended stay. Something tells me we won't be coming back."

I knew it. "No problem." My feet didn't falter as I made for my room, hearing Gregor's deep sigh.

As I changed into a T-shirt and black leggings, I questioned if taking him out was a good idea to begin with. I sent my goodbye emails ahead of schedule, grabbed my packed backpack, and took one last look around my bedroom, etching everything into my memory.

My eyes particularly lingered on a picture of my parents, smiling at me, across the room on top of my desk. I quickly crossed over and gave them each a kiss. "I will be back," I said to my mother's portrait. "I promise." And with a certain finality, I shut the door to my room.

I wondered whether anything that happened that night would lead to any good later.

17

The Prophecy Unveiled

The moment Gregor and I entered Ager, we knew something was off. As we made for the grand gate, the sentry guards, instead of the aloof stares we'd received previously, immediately dropped to one knee. "Welcome, Lady Katya," one guard intoned, his voice filled with an unexpected reverence. "And to Major Gregor," the other added, his tone echoing with respect.

I immediately looked at Gregor and whispered, "Lady, who? What's their issue?"

Gregor's eyebrows furrowed, ushering me forward, "I'm as puzzled as you are."

After instructing a low-ranking Kyrios to guard my belongings, we walked through the courtyard toward Central Tower. I expected to see a spectacle again, to watch these warriors practice their arts. However, most of the Kyrios stopped training to watch us. Some of them fell to their knees or just gaped at us. I could hear the whispers: "Is that her? Can't you feel her Vis? Wow, she's really here."

I tugged on Gregor's arm. "What is going on? Why are they staring at us?" I whispered.

Gregor looked around suspiciously. "I have no idea. But we will find out soon." In a loud, clipped tone, he said, "Everyone, return to your duties immediately."

"Yes, sir!" And they did, but not without lingering stares or side glances. We cut through the crowd quickly, ignoring the bows and staring, and entered the Central Tower. Every step inside the imposing white tower, which radiated with the power of the Generals, felt like a step toward the gallows. Gregor scooped me into his arms, and I automatically put my arms around his neck to prepare for the high jump. But he didn't move. His gaze held a depth I hadn't seen before, a mixture of emotions I couldn't quite decipher.

"What's wrong?" My arms unconsciously tightened around his neck, grazing the nape of his hair.

He continued to look at me wordlessly. Something shifted in his eyes that I could only guess was confusion, suspicion, and perhaps longing. The same longing, I knew my eyes reflected back as well.

He finally shook his head, dispelling his momentary desire and returning to duty. "Nothing. Let's go."

With one leap, we reached the top of the Tower to find the Generals waiting for us again. I expected to see cross looks, to receive a complete dress down – "*How could you kiss one of our Majors? You put everyone at risk again!*" However, their energy was calm, almost serene. They even slightly bowed their heads. Nabil had a grand but fixed smile. If Nabil could still smile at me after the scene I'd caused on my last visit, something was seriously wrong.

"Okay, can someone tell me what's going on? Why's everyone acting like this?"

Nabil chuckled softly. "Please, Lady Katya, there is no need for alarm. We found some answers about you, and we're simply treating you with the respect you deserve."

How big of an answer could it have been for the Generals to act like this towards me? I worried my lip. "I am genuinely afraid of what this revelation might be."

Nabil gestured to the previously used conference room. "Why don't we adjourn to the other room then?"

The General nodded and quietly shuffled inside. Gregor began to turn to leave the tower, but Nabil stopped him. "Gregor, your presence continues to be required. You will remain with Lady Katya."

Gregor nodded curtly. I gave him an annoyed glance. *Didn't he know I didn't want to be alone with these people?* The only being in this tower I trusted was him.

We assumed the same seats, and I patiently waited for someone to begin talking. The Generals looked at each other, wordlessly deciding who should explain. Michiko lost the battle of the wills and cleared her throat. "Well, my lady—"

"I'm sorry, but why is everyone calling me that? I am not a lady or a princess or anything like that. General Michiko, please call me Katya."

Taken aback, Michiko looked to Nabil, who nodded his assent. She cleared her throat again. "Katya, as you know, I began researching when we left this room. After many hours of searching our libraries, I came across an old tablet sent by our Lord as a record of creations."

"Our Lord? God, you mean?" I asked, looking around.

Michiko nodded. "Within the record, his Lordship spoke of the First Battle with the Want at the beginning of time. The fierce battle had taken many souls on both sides, but Our Lord was victorious in sealing Drachen, the leader of the Want, and his creations below the Live Realm in the Abyss."

"And I am assuming Drachen is what we call the devil?"

Michiko nodded again. "However, Our Lord understood there would be a time when the Want would try to regain power and storm the Live Realm. We Kyrios have been on the front line, protecting the Live Realm along with the Archs—"

"Archangels, right?"

Nabil sneered. "Another department, another story. Continue, Michiko." *Hmm, interesting reaction.*

"But within the record, He spoke of an entity he would leave within the Live Realm. A power unlike any other, with portions of His own dominant power. One who would be alive but with the power of the dead, with the ability to call and control Vis from both realms. The one who would be the decider of the Live Realm's existence."

Lamar added, his eyes glittering with a small smile, "The record called this power the Balancer."

Michiko took a deep breath, glaring at Lamar's interruption. "Yes, the Balancer would be the bridge between the dead and the living, with the ability to see beyond the apparent and look within to determine the true purpose of a soul."

"What does that mean? True purpose?" I asked, a sinking feeling in my gut.

The Generals exchanged uncertain glances. "We surmise it might be a form of discernment," Nabil offered, his tone cautious.

Michiko cleared her throat, continuing, "I am also assuming this discernment has to do with the Balancer's main purpose: to protect all the realms – Live, Abyss, and Paradiso."

The Generals fell silent, watching me process this new fable. I didn't want to hear the next part. I already knew what they were going to say. And I wanted no part of it. But their continued silence and waiting elicited my next question. "What does this have to do with me?"

Michiko moistened her lips. "Based on our readings, your innate ability from childhood, and the surge in your power during a time of unusual Abyss activity, we believe you possess the power of the Balancer, Katya."

My entire world completely went off kilter. A continuous loop of "No" echoed in my head. The pregnant silence became more awkward, and I shook my head, refusing to accept this fate. "No, you got it all wrong," I finally croaked, finding my voice. "There's no way that I could be that."

The entity, the power inside of me, nudged me and spoke for the first time in days. **It's true**.

My head continued to shake. "There has to be some mistake. Whatever this fable is, this Balancer, I am not that. I'm just a..." The phrase "normal, average girl" seemed too ridiculous to utter. "This can't be true." I looked to Gregor, my eyes pleading for some help. "This is a joke, right?"

His blue eyes bore into mine; his eyebrows raised and his jaw tense. He didn't say a word.

"I'm afraid Michiko is very correct, Lady Katya." Nabil stood from his seat and walked to the other side of the table, his eyes never leaving mine. "It seems that your meeting Gregor came precisely on time. It was more than likely foretold. Around the same time Gregor discovered you, we discovered several breaches made by Wanters between the Abyss and the Live Realm worldwide."

He gestured to the ceiling, sending Vis above our heads, forming an image as if there were a projector. Mountains and a large forest surrounded a large city, bustling with activity. However, a black tear was in the air, towards the back of the city near the tallest mountain. And it poured out monsters.

"This is just one example out in Denver, Colorado. Tears like this have been occurring all over the Live Realm. New York, Sydney, Tokyo, you name it. These holes are small enough now that most Wanters leaving are level one forms. We are managing the small droves, but the breaches do have the potential to grow."

"But that's not our only concern," Victor added, his voice gruff from lack of use. "The effects of the breaches themselves are being felt everywhere. The negative Vis and the Want seeping out of the Abyss hits humans like a virus, making them colder, darker, and more selfish."

I took a closer look at the tears and the various Wanters leaving, all of them of a smaller size than I had seen before. "Doesn't it look like they are fleeing the Abyss?"

A few of the Generals chuckled, easing the tension in the room. Nabil smirked, "We are still trying to figure out why these holes are occurring. I believe this may be Drachen's attempt to breach the Abyss wall and begin gaining a stronghold in the Live Realm."

"And what's Drachen's goal here, again?"

Nabil shrugged. "In a word—destruction. Just like other Wanters,

Drachen wants what he can't have. He'll destroy it so no one else can have it. But we will not let his desire destroy millions of souls."

He looked pointedly at me. "Before these holes become any larger, you must go to these cities, use your power, and deal with the tears."

"Me?" I squeaked.

"Yes, you. You will start with the largest tear so far, Los Angeles. Our forces are maintaining order for now, but they'll need your help soon." A new image of the West Coast city came to life on the wall. Car accidents, small and large, plagued the streets of downtown LA. Drivers brawled in the streets over the most minor fender benders. Ambulances and caretakers fought to get to those seriously hurt. Those avoiding troubles ran from the carnage, attempting to swallow them up. And perched on almost every human shoulder were small Wanters, whispering in their ears.

It felt like my life had turned into some twisted video game. I closed my eyes, unable to stop shaking my head, "This is too much. You need to do your research and find your actual savior. Because it's not me. I can't even control my Vis." I stood from my chair, ready to leave – all of this be damned. "Find yourself someone else."

Raf stood from his seat as well, looking very annoyed. "You know what? Perhaps she's right. Our Balancer can't be some spineless girl. This one can barely keep her faculties straight, let alone be the one the realms need now."

Michiko stood as well. "Wait a minute, Raf. You know I'm right! I've shown you all the records!"

Lamar rubbed his chin, looking thoughtfully at me. "I told you all she would react this way. Raf, you can't have your way on this one. She's young. You can't possibly think that she would take this calmly. A seasoned soldier would be in shock."

"But at least a soldier would understand that he must act. She says she will not. So what good is she to us?" Raf eyed me with derision. "We have no use for her, and she's already seen too much." Raf looked at Nabil, "I believe my way is the best way, Nabil."

They shared a look before the Head General sighed, rubbing his brow. "You are correct, Raf."

A manic grin grew on Raf's face. "Hold the boy down."

Nabil immediately understood and jumped on the table, kicked Gregor in the face from his chair to the floor, and pinned him down.

The Scot immediately began to struggle. "General, what are you doing?" With a flash, Raf had a large sword in his hand, poised to strike.

"Taking care of this problem." He leaped straight in the air and charged at me with his sword raised over his head. I stared as Raf made his descent. Just as he was about to swing his hand down, one thought came to my mind: *Protect*. My hand unconsciously raised over my head, and an opaque shield formed around me. Just like the one Gregor had erected around me while I slept.

Amazed, I gently touched the covering, feeling a hum as my inner power responded, **I will protect you**.

I looked to my left to find Raf standing beside me with a smug look. "If you won't accept what we say, perhaps you will heed your heart. Denying who you are isn't going to make this go away. The sooner you realize this, the sooner you can accept your purpose." His sword disappeared with another flash, and Raf smiled for the first time. "You can relax the shield, girl. No one will harm you."

Feeling some of the adrenaline dissipate, I nodded. It took me a few tries to relax, but I finally took down the shield and sat back down. Nabil released Gregor, helping him back up, and returned to his chair. "My lady, I am sorry we had to do that. But we knew we had to make you realize your power is real. You cannot stop this as much as you cannot stop breathing."

I thought back on the questions I had asked about myself, constantly asking myself, "Why?" Amid those questions, I never thought I would get an answer I would hate even more than having it unanswered. As much as I wanted to scream that all this fate stuff was bullshit, I felt within me a begrudging acceptance. Maybe it was because I could feel a caress from within, trying to ease my anxiety. Or perhaps I was tired of fighting who I was any longer.

Nabil smiled again. Seeing his smile made me uncomfortable, no matter how attractive he was. Like a kid in a candy store ready to devour a feast he knows he shouldn't have. "Your training should begin immediately, and you will be housed here in Ager until you have gained enough training to close the tears. Once the threat has been dealt with, you can return to your Live Realm life. Can we agree on that?"

All of my premonitions have come true. Nothing is going to be the same. But I nodded. "Guess it can't be helped? Thank God I put things in place before we left." I sighed and tried to rub the tension out of the back of my neck. "Let's get started."

All of the Generals grinned. Nabil clasped his hands with extra vigor. "Wonderful. Raf, begin training tomorrow. Gregor, you will continue as Lady Katya's protector indefinitely until further notice."

Gregor slowly rose from his chair, keeping his eyes on Nabil. "Sir, perhaps another person might be better for the position."

My heart dropped to my stomach. Nabil looked over him with a calculating eye. "Has something happened that impairs your ability to protect Lady Katya?" *They don't know about the kiss!*

His eyes shifted minutely over to me, and my eyes pleaded with him silently to not compromise himself.

"No, sir."

"Then I see no reason to change my mind. You will do as you are commanded. Lady Katya will be housed in the Marble Tower. Take residence there as well."

His body went rigid with anger, but he answered, "Yes, sir."

Nabil turned to the other Generals. "I think we are just about done here, Generals. Shall we adjourn?" The Generals nodded and, one by one, left the conference room. Lamar was the last one to go. He winked and said, "This may not have been in your plans for your life, but I am glad you are joining our group."

I appreciated his sympathetic look and felt like I could be honest. "General Lamar, I am scared outta my mind. I don't think I can do this."

He patted me on the back. "My dear, you don't know how important you are. You are exactly what we have been waiting for. Don't forget that." The kind general left the room with a slight bow, leaving Gregor and me alone.

I slowly stood from my chair and looked at Gregor carefully. "Gregor, look, I know we need to talk—"

Gregor stepped back, placing his hands behind his back. "Lady Katya, shall I escort you to your room?" His voice turned cold, uncompromising.

I bit my bottom lip, swallowing back the emotion building up. Brick by brick, I could feel the wall Gregor was building between us, and did it ever hurt. "Come on, don't do this. You know I don't want to be called that."

Gregor didn't meet my eyes and said quietly, "Unfortunately, I haven't been given leave by the Generals to address you otherwise, so you will have to excuse the formalities, my lady." He bowed in a way that I could only take as condescending. "To your room, *Lady* Katya?"

18

New Allies, Old Hurts

I rolled my eyes dramatically at the Scot and walked past him. He quickly caught up and led me to the main lobby from the conference room. Gregor scooped me up and jumped twenty feet to the entrance floor below. Hastily, he put me down after we landed and walked out the door. The Scot moved briskly, looking over his shoulder occasionally to ensure that I was still following him. We walked through the courtyard and made a slight left at the entrance gate toward several smaller towers.

Gregor cleared his throat. "The barracks, where most of the Kyrios are housed to rest between assignments, are set on the other side of the Ager compounds. These towers," he pointed before us, "are for the higher-ranking Kyrios. The Generals are housed in the largest tower here. You will be housed in the second largest," the Scot explained without looking at me.

"Where are you normally housed?" I asked quietly.

"The barracks. As Major, I could be housed at the Marble Tower. It's considered a perk some Kyrios can't wait to have—a room to yourself. However, I was raised to prefer family and closeness over solitude. My Dah always told me that being alone breeds selfishness that you don't know is there until you're tested. To combat that, you remain close to your kin, so you never forget what and who you are fighting for."

My eyebrows furrowed. "Family is really important to you, huh?"

Gregor's cheeks rippled as he clenched his jaw. He nodded and did not offer any more information.

We walked the rest of the way in silence. The giant tower within the set was a sight to behold. Like the Taj Mahal's ambiance, the General's building was made of unadorned white brick that shone with a gem's brilliance. It had large windows that faced out to the courtyard where we stood, surrounded with gold engravings, the meaning of which I could not make out. I saw a large canopy bed plush with pillows through the lowest window. It reminded me of the fairy tale my mother had told me about Rapunzel and her long locks of hair. If Rapunzel had been trapped in this tower, I doubt she would have minded it too much.

The second tower was similar in grandeur, just not as tall. We entered the second tower through a side door. Thankfully, there was a set of stairs. Again, in silence, we reached the top of the tower to find several rooms. He led me to the last bedroom at the end of the hallway. The room had the same large canopy bed with scattered plush pillows on the mattress and floor. The room also had a view of the courtyard and the main gate. I looked around, pretending to inspect the room but waiting for Gregor to say something.

"Is everything satisfactory, my lady?"

I crossed my arms and gave him my own piercing stare. "Gregor, enough of the theatrics. I get it. We messed up back there."

His expression hardened, eyes narrowing slightly. "It's not 'we,' my lady. I messed up. That should never have happened."

I studied my nail beds, avoiding his gaze. I was simping over this 'earth-shattering' kiss, and he regretted it all. Worse part? I know why our being together is problematic for him. I know I could be a liability; he would have to separate from me if the Generals caught wind. I understood why he was acting this way, but it didn't stop the hurt nor ease the ache at his distance. "I'm not going to say all that because…" I let the words fade as my courage failed me. "Look, I don't want this to affect our friendship. Can we go back to before Nicky's?"

"I think it's best we put some distance between us. You came across a different Gregor. A Gregor that let his human nature get the best of him. A Gregor who temporarily forgot his duties to these realms. A Gregor that could have put everything in jeopardy. He is no more."

My eyes blazed with anger, "Just like that, you're just going to step back and what? We're not friends anymore? I trust you the most here and came here because of our friendship! How are we supposed to—"

"I know my place!" he exploded, his face distorted by anger and his eyes dangerously flashing. "I am a group leader that keeps humans safe daily from dangers. Any distraction from that is a liability I cannot afford. And it's about high time you grow up and understand you can't get everything you want, Lady Katya." He opened his mouth to say more but hesitated. Shaking his head, he stalked to the door. "If you need me, I'll be down the hall." And with that, he slammed the door.

I grabbed the first thing next to me and threw it at the door. Unfortunately, it was simply a pillow that didn't quite reach the exit. But it did make me feel a bit better for a moment. Then, the weight of the entire world settled onto my shoulders. Tears rushed down my cheeks, all my frustration, fear, and anxiety breaking the dam. I didn't even make it to the bed, collapsing beside the discarded pillow, the wooden floor beneath me sodden with tears.

The following day, I awoke bewildered and sore from the hard floor, finding myself in the bed that I had previously ignored. The sleek silk sheets slid off my shoulders, pooling on the floor.

How did I get up here? It must have been Gregor. My heartache surged painfully at the thought of him. *He's right, Kat. This is just going to be one of those things. Ugh, did you have to fall for Death, girl?* I never thought he would have just turned away from me, divorcing himself from our bond. Frustration swelled as I massaged my temples.

Now a bit removed from their announcement, there were holes in some of the explanations the Generals gave me. Why would the Balancer be needed? Couldn't God fix this problem? And why did it feel like the Kyrios had some animosity toward the Archs, at least Nabil? Shouldn't they be working together? And Gregor's statement the night before— he had been alive at one point.

What had happened to him?

I wasn't any closer to these answers, and the only person who could shed some light told me he needed to distance himself. Sighing, I got out of bed and stretched when I heard knocking at my door. I opened it to find the Scot himself, with a fathomless look in his eyes. "I trust you slept well, my lady."

I snorted, knowing very well he already knew the answer. Instead of the easy retort resting on my tongue, I said, "What are we doing today, Gregor?"

He assumed a position that sadly reminded me of a butler: arms behind his back and nose in the air. "You will be training with General Raf this morning, and we will start our meditation exercises in the afternoon. Lieutenant Young Jae will escort you to the courtyard and the training room."

Biting my bottom lip, I said softly, "I thought you were to stay by my side."

My comment only angered him. In a steely voice, he said, "Other matters need my attention. Young Jae will be with you shortly." The last I saw of him was his back, retreating out the door.

Growling, I couldn't help but punch the many pillows on my bed. *Other matters that need his attention? What am I, then?* I stopped shortly and thought, *Wait, he is a big deal here. This is a military base. He probably does have other things to do.*

Oh geez! And he's been babysitting me for the past few days. I could only imagine the workload that was probably waiting for him. The last thing I wanted to do was cause Gregor more trouble. Feeling all the anger drain out of me, I pulled a couple of pillows by the window, kneeled down on them, and gazed out the window. Noticing my backpack by the corner, I unpacked my belongings and arranged my toiletries and hair products on the windowsill. My hands traveled to my hair, began to detangle my curls, and set my hair in flat twists. *At least everything here is in silk. Don't have to worry about my hair too much.* I watched the crowds of Kyrios move in and out of the gate for several minutes before I heard a knock on the door as I finished my last twist.

"Be right there!" I called and started to step away from the window when I heard a female voice call out, loud enough for me to hear, "Gregor! You're here!" Curious, I stretched my head further to find a blond woman running swiftly toward the towers with a giant smile. She made a beeline for a dark-haired man who caught her as she jumped into his arms. Feeling like I was intruding, I began to turn my head when I realized the dark-haired man, who was now traveling through the courtyard, was Gregor. And he was smiling!

Don't get jealous. Don't get jealous. Do NOT get jealous, Katya Elizabeth Stevens! A full-on explosion would've detonated had it not been for another knock at the door. "Sorry!" I shuffled to the door, plastering a smile on my face. I opened the door only to have my jaw drop to the floor.

Before me stood a man who could easily rival any model on the runway. Jet black hair, swept back into a low ponytail, framed almond eyes that held a warmth, making them nearly impossible not to get lost in. The drab uniform couldn't conceal the strength of his physique.

Realizing I was staring, I backed away from the door, "I'm sorry. Are you Lieutenant Young Jae?"

"Yes, Lady Katya. It is a pleasure to meet you."

I sighed inwardly. *Even his deep, husky voice sounds like music.* I held out my hand. "Please call me Katya. I hate formalities."

Young Jae slightly bowed over my hand and kissed it. "Of course, Miss Katya. Rather than calling me 'Lieutenant Young Jae,' you may call me Jae. My friends call me something ruder, so let's stick with Jae."

I couldn't help but smile at that. "You're not serious like the others."

"Someone has to lighten the mood around here, Ms. Katya." He gave me a serene smile that I returned. "So, before we begin your training, I've been asked to give you this." He snapped his finger, forming a rip portal. He stuck his hand in and pulled out a box. "This holds your attire for training. I hope you find it pleasing."

"I'm sure I will." I took the box, trying to shake the mesmerized look from my face.

Still wearing an easy smile, Young Jae nodded. "I'll wait for you outside." He looked around once and closed the door behind him.

I sighed deeply, this time letting the sound fill the room.

I went to the adjoining room in the suite and found a bowl filled with water. I splashed my face and wiped it down with a nearby convenient towel. I returned to the bedroom and approached the box on my bed. Inside the box were a pair of oddly soled shoes and a black bodysuit. I slipped into the outfit without complain and noticed immediately how much lighter I felt. Like I weighed close to nothing. Like I could run for miles—and I hated to run! Looking deeper into the fabric, I could see a blue and gold thread that shimmered slightly under the black top layer. As I experimented moving, I noticed the blue threads shining brighter than the gold. Shrugging, I met Young Jae outside my bedroom. I didn't miss Young Jae's appreciative glance across my body as I stepped out.

Offering his arm, he said, "Please follow me."

19

In Raf's Arena

The cool breeze brushed against our skin as we stepped onto the stone-paved courtyard, where the soft hum of distant conversations and stomps of boots on the ground floated in the air. I surveyed my surroundings –Kyrios were bustling to and fro. The barracks had been initially hidden behind the Central Tower. I saw large homes of various styles, reflecting diverse cultures, spread across acres of land. Some houses had ornate carved wooden facades reminiscent of ancient European towns, while others bore intricate mosaics that sparkled under the sun, echoing Middle Eastern and North African aesthetics. Given the number of buildings, I imagined the number of Kyrios working was in the thousands. Young Jae noticed my study. "Do you have questions that I can answer, Ms. Katya?"

"What is this place? How big is this? How did this come into being?"

He paused for a second before starting. "It is said that when God created the Live Realm, Archs and Phims were already plotting to overrun and rule it as their own kingdom. They were jealous that God had provided a place for humans but wouldn't create anything remotely close for them. So Drachen, a high-ranking Phim at the time, sent his underlings into the Live Realm to wreak havoc."

"So the first Wanters were Archs and Phims?"

He nodded. "They were the first Want Generals, the strongest Wanters in the Abyss."

"Are the original Generals still there? After all this time?"

Young Jae stopped; his eyebrows raised. "You know what, I am not sure. We don't come across too many generals very often. If we do, something serious has happened." Looking back at me, his smile returned. Young Jae's dark hair caught the light as it moved, and he held a glint of mischief. Despite the strict rigor of his uniform, there was a lightness in his step, a carefree tilt to his chin.

"Back to my story, my lady. When the first Wanters entered the Live Realm, early humans couldn't see them. They were only aware of the major disasters they were suffering from and the cruelty of their own people. The more powerful Archs-turned-Wanters kept a humanoid form and sowed dissension and chaos among the humans."

"God must have loved that," I said ruefully.

Young Jae smirked, "Actually, that period in the Realms was called God's Great Silence because the remaining Phims did not receive any orders for a long time. So many lives were taken in the struggle, and souls failed to cross over. It was a win-win situation for Drachen. He destroyed God's loved creatures and added to his army. The remaining Archs, still loyal to God, had their hands full."

"But then, how do the Kyrios play into this?"

Young Jae smiled at my enthusiasm. "A group of souls during that dark time had particular Vis gifts. The ability to see, strengthen, and manipulate it into physical forms. In their own way, they fought back against the Want. When they died, they sought God to give them the power to fight against the chaos wreaking havoc on their fellow man. That drop of humanity and compassion in these souls compelled God to create Ager to house the first responders to chaos in the Live Realm."

I took in the realm and the souls working around the clock. "These people are from all over the world?"

Jae gave me a soft smile. "Answering the call to keep humans safe."

"And everyone just ends up speaking English?" I squeaked incredulously.

The lieutenant doubled over in laughter. "I'm not speaking English. I only know Korean. That's just part of the power of Ager. All tongues shall speak in one accord. To me, you are speaking Korean."

I couldn't help but giggle along with him. "That was a weird question, sorry. This, all of this, is just amazing. It's one thing to hear about God at home but another to see all of this in person."

"Trust me, there is much more to learn. I am sure General Raf is eager to teach you. Ah, which reminds me. The other Generals wanted me to remind you that General Raf is a bit unorthodox in his methods." He gave me an apologetic smile, "I would stay ready."

We talked amicably as we headed toward the training dome. I had wanted to ask Young Jae if he knew why Nabil disliked the Archs but got distracted by the massive training center we'd entered. The dome, made of a semi-translucent material, stood well over one thousand feet high. It loomed proudly against the landscape, reflecting the skies and surroundings like a giant opal. However, the impressive dome had no weapons inside. Our steps echoed against the cement floor as we entered. "Is there anyone else joining us for training?"

"General Raf ordered that the training dome be for your use only this morning."

My annoyance flared. "I don't want special treatment. I'm just like everyone else."

Young Jae smiled kindly at me, giving me a sympathetic look. "Ms. Katya, I respect your humility. But you are very far from the truth. You can't feel what it's like to be in your presence. Your energy, your power, is palatable, almost electric." His eyes warmed as he met mine. "You are very much special." Under his gaze, I had no choice but to melt and smile.

"Ah! I see you made it on time!" We both jumped at the sound of General Raf's appearance. He stood behind us, still looking menacing and scary. "Young Jae, you may return in six Live Realm hours to escort Lady Katya back to her chambers."

"Yes, sir." He bowed slightly, winked at me, and whispered, "Go knock 'em dead!"

As he exited the dome, I turned to Raf and asked, "General, why can't I return by myself? I'm sure the lieutenant has other duties to accomplish rather than babysit me."

"It is not about babysitting. I intend to exhaust you, so you might need an escort to carry you back."

General Raf circled around me, studying my physique. I took the moment to assess him in return. His ice-blue eyes pierced through me, contrasting starkly with his chiseled face. The striking white hair seemed out of place with his relatively young face, but it somehow fit all the same. His attire was similar to mine, but his sleeveless bodysuit allowed me to admire his biceps and shoulders. What took me aback were the scars I hadn't noticed before. Even his face was marred with scars. I imagined each scar telling a silent story—a jagged line running across his forearm, a puncture mark on his collarbone, and a particularly deep gash on his hand.

"Sizing me up, are you?"

My eyes snapped to his face, and a smirk awaited me. I stood a bit straighter. "Maybe I am."

"Good. You should always be aware of what your enemy can do before you act." He stood tall with his arms behind his back; his eyes didn't reveal anything. "The point of our lesson is for you to better understand your Vis and protect yourself." He snapped his fingers, and a rack filled with weapons appeared on the right side of the room.

"If there is one thing you must leave with today to protect yourself effectively, never underestimate anyone, including friends. Be aware of everything around you. The better you evaluate your situations, the better your chance of surviving." He walked over slowly to the rack, speaking over his shoulder. "What do you know about the Want?"

I crinkled my nose, not realizing this would be a quiz. "Basically, they are souls that didn't cross over and are turned into monsters that you guys destroy or whip back into the Abyss."

Raf's hand rested on a long wooden staff, quietly assessing it. "That's it?"

"I mean, what else is there to know?"

Raf threw me a look. "A lot." He snatched a staff from the rack and charged at me like the day before. In the air and ready to kill. Realizing his aim, I rolled away in time for him to slam into the floor with such force that it created a large crater. My eyes widened. He hadn't stopped himself this time.

In a flash, Raf again jumped up with the staff above his head, poised to strike. His eyes were devoid of mirth or jest. He was out to kill. The air grew acrid from dust and debris. It was thick enough already that I lost sight of Raf.

"General Raf! Wait! Why are we doing this?" I cried out, desperately trying to find his location.

His voice came from the dust, nowhere and everywhere. "I'm asking you the same question. Why are you doing this? Why are any of us doing this?"

I looked around wildly, but I couldn't even find a shadow.

"It is imperative for you to determine your answer to those questions. You can't use your Vis to its full potential if you don't know yourself. Your enemy can easily come behind you if you don't know them." A poke at my back and a hand on my shoulder gave me the answer I sought. "Like this—and then extinguish your life." Raf's breath on my nape gave me creepy goosebumps, sending my heart into a tailspin..

He released me, and I turned around to face him. He moved the staff to his shoulder and gave me a hard stare. "Indeed, there is much more for you to know."

Annoyed that I got caught so quickly, I just nodded. Raf relaxed in my quietness, brought the staff down as a cane, and leaned on it. "Lady Katya, understanding the origins of the Want is crucial."

"Yes, I know all this, General. These souls overstayed in the Live Realm. They got angrier and bitter until they died again. They are only motivated by anger, selfishness, jealousy, and envy."

Raf sighed, leaning on his staff. "I'm not supposed to give you my opinion, but you know what my hope is for you?"

I looked at him, signaling him to continue.

"I'm under orders to teach you to protect yourself. Some of us would see you fighting the Want. But perhaps your role is just meant to restore the balance between the two conflicting realms. You potentially could bring peace to the Want they desperately lack, and you could save the humans targeted in the oncoming chaos."

Again, that savior thing. I internally cringed. But I knew better than to say that to Raf, so I said, "I understand."

"Good." He tossed me the long wooden staff. "Now, with an understanding of our adversaries and their motives, we must strategize our approach. As Kyrios, we use hand-to-hand combat and wield our Vis simultaneously. Only Vis energy can cut down another Vis creature."

He materialized a new staff and stretched it over his head, the definition of his abs showing through his body suit. "We don't have much time to teach you theories, so we will do it the old-fashioned way. You need to learn to bring up your Vis purposefully instead of instinctively. Use that staff as a guide for your power." He said this with a glint in his eye.

I swallowed hard. "And what exactly is this 'old-fashioned way'?"

"Through practice. Legends say the most formidable Kyrios can converse with their Vis."

My eyes narrowed, thinking of the voice within me. "What, like a conversation? Vis can talk back?"

He shrugged. "I'm not sure. It was said that the first Kyrios could speak to their Vis as guides. As though their energy was sentient." Raf smirked. "Honestly, who can say? I've never met them nor achieved such a connection myself. But who knows, Balancer, maybe you can." Raf began maneuvering his staff through his fingers, striking at imaginary foes to the left and right. "Let's see if we can bring it out on purpose! I won't be as hard as a few minutes ago, but I'll give you a good whack if you aren't paying attention. Raise your staff," he ordered.

"But I've never fought with a staff before!" I cried, secretly looking for an exit.

"No time like the present to learn. And don't just fight. Protect. Feel out your Vis!" Raf said, smirking.

The General charged from the left, swiping at my head. Instinctively,

I raised my staff to block it. Raf held and threw his weight into this staff, pushing me back with a wide grin. "Good, let yourself feel it out. You may have skills you never knew about."

"Last time I checked, I was a class A klutz," I grunted, trying not to fall over under Raf's weight.

With a grin, Raf jumped back. "You just haven't been in a situation where you had to be serious. Life or death should be motivation enough." His eyes hardened. "Come at me, my lady. Hit me right here." He pointed to his right shoulder. "Touch me here, and we will call it a day."

I frowned. "Okay." I ran towards him, but Raf disappeared, to reappear behind me.

"Too slow."

I swung hard behind me and hit dead air.

"Oh, come now. Where's that feisty spirit? You will never get anywhere with that attitude." He disappeared to the other side of the room, a thousand feet away. "Unless you want to hit me, to take me down literally, there is no way you will get close to me."

I gritted my teeth. "How the hell am I supposed to hit you if you disappear like that?"

He chuckled. "It's called quickstep. I'm sending my Vis to my legs and feet to boost my speed. And you're right. If you wanted this to be a close combat exercise, you just should've asked." I raised the staff up as a samurai-like I had seen Gregor do. Sweat trickled down my forehead. *At least he can't do any real damage with that wooden staff.*

"Don't do that," Raf barked.

I glanced around, puzzled. "Do what? I didn't make a move."

"You just let your guard down. Essentially, you just shouted to me, 'I don't think you can hurt me with that staff,'" he mocked me in a high-pitched voice. "Is that right?"

I gaped. "How did you...?"

Raf shook his head. "Years of combat have taught me to read every nuance, my lady. And I wouldn't be so sure about your theory." He lifted his staff to mirror my stance. "One of the benefits of controlling my Vis is that I can make anything into a weapon." With that annoying smirk, Raf flicked his staff downward. His staff glowed a bright purple, becoming a Vis-covered blade. His razor-sharp Vis blade hit the floor, sending acrid dust and particles in the air. Coughing, I waved my arm to clear the air and saw the cement ground split until the widening crack stopped at my feet. My eyes bulged in fear as Raf slowly walked toward me with a dangerous purpose in his eyes.

Move! Come on, girl, move! You'll be in pieces like the floor if you don't move. Just move, dammit! But I was paralyzed with fear. I wanted to run and protect myself from the slow-coming madman. But all I could sense in the room was the powerful and intimating Vis rolling off Raf in waves. Every bone in my body vibrated painfully, as if an immense and heavy pressure was being pushed down on me, demanding I lay on the ground to ease my suffering. The only thing I could smell was the sweat rolling down my face as my body fought to keep standing straight and not bow from exertion.

Why do you persist on your own? Just ask for help, my entity said.

Raf's words came back to me. *Um, right. So, hey. A little help?*

A soft sensation ebbed into me that made me feel more light-hearted, even as Raf's energy was crushing me. It felt like my Vis was chuckling.

Close your eyes and just focus on me. I did as I was told. **Your own fear hinders you, Katya. It is not his Vis you should bow to. But he should bow to yours.** A deep sense of pride I didn't recognize started to swell inside me. **It's time to remind that soul who you are. Raise your staff with both hands towards the end.**

Like this? I moved my hands closer to my body, gripping the ends of the staff.

That's right. That pride you feel? Feel it build and spread all over you. It's a pride that won't be silenced by Raf's repressive energy. Do not falter. I will help you. Swing your staff now!

Opening my eyes, I found Raf only a few feet away, his energy still pressing down but now only affecting me minutely. I took a step forward and swung my staff vertically. The prideful swell erupted, traveled down my arm, and through the wooden staff. The Vis burst into a wall of energy, splitting the entire room in half, engulfing it in a bright blue light and slamming into the dome wall with a force that shook it.

It was over as soon as it happened.

Well done.

I dropped to my knees, exhausted and unable to see anything before me – more dust erupted in the air again, clouding everything. *Did I hit Raf? OMG, did I kill him?* As the dust settled back to the ground, I made out a shadow about fifty feet ahead of me. It was Raf with his arms crossed over his chest and head tucked in. He was surrounded by a shield, unharmed. He released his stance, and his shield shattered into glass pieces and disappeared. "I didn't expect that from you yet."

"Neither did I," I panted.

The General closed the gap between us and knelt down to my level. "My lady, you're exhausted because you've never used your Vis like that. Think of it like running; it's all about building stamina." He smirked. "But you should feel accomplished. You nicked me." A small cut glared back at me just below his shoulder on his arm.

I smirked at my instructor. "I almost thought I killed you."

He laughed heartily. "You're not quite there yet, my lady. But in due time, you'll be able to conjure a Vis dome encompassing this entire arena."

20

Lost in the Labyrinth of the Soul

Ager's sun cast elongated shadows on the ground as we sparred. Raf's training weighed heavier on my limbs with each hour, and my staff felt like it was made of lead. After several grueling hours of ducking from Raf's staff and sending my Vis through my own staff, I was so grateful to hear a clear call of salvation. The sound of crunching gravel heralded Jae's approach as he stepped into our training circle with an easy smile. "General Raf," Jae called out behind us. "I've come to collect Ms. Katya as you directed."

"Ah, Young Jae. Right on time." Raf turned, hiding a smile. "Be careful, my lady. You almost seem happy to be rid of me. Until next time." The General bowed and exited a shimmering blue portal, zipping tightly behind him. And I immediately collapsed on the ground on my back. Covered in sweat and dust, I must've been a sight with my hair frizzled into an afro, crying out for a shower.

However, Young Jae didn't seem bothered. His smile grew as he turned his attention to me. "Did your session go well?"

I rolled my eyes but couldn't help but laugh. "Yeah, it did. I am starving, though."

Jae extended his arm and hoisted me quickly back on my feet, letting me lean on his shoulder. His warm cedarwood and amber scent crept up and shivered across my spine. "Then let us return to your chambers for a scrumptious lunch, shall we?" I took his arm and paraded back to Towers in high spirits. With each step, some fatigue passed until I felt as if I never had my session with Raf. When we arrived at my chambers, the soft amber light of late afternoon streamed in through the windows, casting dappled patterns on the rich, velvety curtains and silk pillows. Jae followed me inside, sitting on my windowsill, studying my toiletries. Amazed, I bounced on my toes, with enough energy to a marathon to Jae's amusement.

"If you're already feeling better, that's your suit and Ager. Part of the realm's power is to heal us when we feel depleted. It's also deep routed in the fabric of your suit." He stood back and removed his over jacket, revealing a bodysuit molded to his sinewy body. Jae sent a flare of Vis through his body, highlighting the blue and gold thread I noticed earlier. "The glowing thread absorbs Vis and feeds back into our body, giving us strength."

"That's amazing." I touched the sleeve of his jumpsuit, surprised at the tingle of power underneath my fingertips. "Is that why you guys can go non-stop?"

He smirked, throwing back on his jacket, "Oh yes, non-stop and all night." Jae took a few purposeful steps towards me, his height towering over me, sending a sexy smile that had me unconsciously leaning towards him. "Unbelievable perks, wouldn't you say?" the warmth of Jae's breath raised my own temperature.

I scoffed, hiding my laugh and feeling drawn into his charisma. "Oh really? I thought Death was only focused on the job. No time for wicked pleasures."

Jae grinned. "Not all of us, Katya. We did live once. We know how to have fun once in a while."

That brought back something Gregor said about his family. I stepped back and took the seat Jae abandoned, pulling my frizzled hair in a high ponytail. "You guys did all live before, like as actual humans?"

He gave me an amused but puzzled look, stepping closer and closing the gap again. "Of course. Where did you think we came from?"

Before I could answer, the heavy oak door to my room creaked and swung open, revealing Gregor's imposing silhouette framed in the doorway, holding a tray. His eyes took in the close proximity Jae and I inhabited, and his blue eyes immediately cooled. Even the temperature in the room turned icy despite the direct afternoon sunshine. "Lieutenant Young Jae. You're still here. Is everything in order?"

Jae quickly saluted his superior. "Of course, sir. I ensured that Lady Katya had returned safely to her room, sir."

Gregor looked between us with a calculating eye, his jaw tensing rapidly and gripping the tray tighter. I couldn't help but feel a bit guilty – as though I had been unfaithful in some way. "I am sure she is safe once she enters the room. You may return to your duties."

Jae quickly nodded but returned his sight to me with an impish twinkle. "Until tomorrow then, Ms. Katya," he murmured quietly.

I gave him a small smile. "I look forward to it."

With a sly wink, Lieutenant Young Jae was out the door.

I smiled to myself. *At least I have one friendly face here.* Gregor's icy displeasure rolled off him as he placed the tray on the desk with a slight slam; a vein throbbed at his temple. "I hope you made inroads with training," he said quietly.

"I was able to surprise General Raf and nick him on the shoulder. I think that made inroads, don't you?"

He visibly relaxed and smirked out of the corner of my eye as I made my way to the lunch tray. The food smelled terrific— noodle soup steaming gently, ham & cheese sandwiches with fresh green lettuce peeking out, and mixed tropical fruit glistening with water droplets. *Oddly, all my favorites.* Gregor stood off to the side and watched me eat. But not much else was said. The heavy, pressing silence made me twitchy, so I asked, "Where did you get the food from? I thought you said Kyrios don't need food."

Gregor barely removed his sight from the floor. His face took on a tight, controlled look. "Human food; this is different."

"How different?"

"Is the food inedible?"

I started. "No, not at all. It's quite good."

"Then you shouldn't worry yourself about it." I got the hint and ceased any more attempts at idle chatter. When I was done, Gregor finally moved from his corner, rolling his shoulders. "Are you ready to begin our training, my lady?"

Resisting the urge to roll my eyes, I nodded.

The Scot looked me over, not betraying a thought, "Please sit on the floor. Are you familiar with deep breathing exercises? Similar to what's used in yoga?"

Gregor instructed me to begin deep breathing for about three minutes and try to calm every nerve in my body. By the end of the three minutes, the tension within the room had oddly dissipated. I cracked open an eye to see that Gregor, too, was doing some deep breathing. He must have felt my eyes because his own immediately opened.

Silently, we both surveyed each other for several seconds. I didn't want to go through this tension. I wanted to tell him I would ignore whatever I felt if he returned to normal. I just wanted him to return to the man I'd met only a handful of days ago but who was already becoming my closest confidant.

But he'd made himself very clear. I could not become a distraction for him. If only he would talk about it; we might find some middle ground.

His granite eyes pierced into me, and somehow, his gaze reflected everything swirling inside me: hurt, caution, displeasure, yearning. Gregor swallowed hard, fighting back his emotions. "I'm going to continue your Vis training and control. We're going into your soulscape to find your Havadar."

"Soulscape? Hava-what?"

Gregor softly explained, "Your soulscape is where your soul resides, and your inner Vis is stored. And it's also where most of your dreams take place. Not those nonsensical ones where you dream about flying fish or deep-sea giraffes."

"But I like those dreams," I smirked, eliciting a small smile from the Kyrios.

He continued, "It's where your soul connects with your mind and communicates. Most people can't see their soulscape since it's shrouded by the mind's visual stimulation, but the soulscape is the true home of your soul and Vis."

Seeing my baffled expression, a ghost of a smile flitted across his face. "You'll understand in a moment." A magnificent sword appeared with a flash of blue light that seemed to ripple the air, resting elegantly on his lap. From the point to the hilt, the entire sword was a coppery color with the occasional silver diamond decorating it, embedded down the middle of the blade with a dark marble hilt. "This sword is a Havadar."

I studied the blade closely, "It's beautiful." The sword resonated with a power that I could now say was Gregor's signature energy.

"This is Dusk, my Havadar. Every Kyrios can wield a weapon created from their inner Vis. We also call it a heart protector because it's forged from within the wielder's heart. The Havadar only responds to the wielder and cannot be wielded by anyone else." His sword hummed quietly; then it disappeared again.

"Where did it go?"

"Back inside of me, inside of my soulscape. Because you wielded weapons during that Wrecker episode after –" he hesitated, not wanting to say *our kiss.*

"Nelly's?" I offered, grimacing slightly.

Gregor cleared his throat, rolling his shoulder again to ease his distress, "Correct. The Generals think you might be able to call a Havadar. We are going to find out. If you have one, it could help you better control your Vis."

"Does my having a Havadar make me Kyrios?"

Something indiscernible flittered across his face. "No, you're just a complicated human with extraordinary abilities." He raked his hand through his curls and sat on his knees.

"I want you to lie on the floor and continue your deep breathing."

He adjusted my position to ensure I was in the middle of the floor. As I closed my eyes and continued breathing, Gregor murmured in my ear, "I'm going to push you into your soulscape. Fair warning, it's not going to feel pleasant."

Keeping my eyes closed, I began to ask, "What do you—" The words died on my lips as I suddenly felt enormous pressure on my chest. I had heard the expression "an elephant sitting on your chest" before. I never had one sit on mine, but I think what I was experiencing felt eerily similar. As I gasped for air, I heard Gregor whisper, "Do not fight it. Let me in. Sink into yourself. You need to relax."

Sure, pal, easier said than done. But I tried to ignore the immense discomfort, allowed my mind to shut down, and tried to relax. It came much easier than I realized, and soon, the pain was gone.

"That's it, easy now, good girl," Gregor murmured.

My eyes remained closed as I tried to listen for Gregor but heard nothing. I cracked open one eye to find that the floor underneath me had changed from wood to a smooth, dark marble. I raised my head slightly to see myself in an opulent room filled with doors. The walls were covered in sand-colored granite, with several torches lit and mounted on the walls. The doors were of dark mahogany but void of any knobs. I looked to each end of the room to find no end. It was an endless, silent hallway of doors. Not even the flames from the torches made a crackle or a hiss. Above us was awe-inspiring – infinite stars and galaxies shimmering in blue and purple shades down at us. I felt a mix of awe and trepidation. The vastness of this place was both beautiful and intimidating. I wondered if every soul had a place like this or if mine was unique.

Something shifted behind me, and I yelped in surprise. Gregor groaned softly and propped himself up from the ground. "Ouch, that entrance was a bit harder than I thought. Your soulscape was putting up a fight there."

I said nothing as he rose from the ground and stretched his arms. My mouth went bone dry at seeing the Scot in a toga. Hot desire surged in my belly as I devoured his chest, barely covered by a sash of white linen wrapped around his waist and ended at his knees. His thighs were clad in worn leather sandals. The firelight only glistened his light caramel skin, making dips and cuts of his muscles more defined. The soft lighting only gave me a better look at how fit he was.

Realizing I was staring, I cleared my throat and looked down the endless hallway. "Why are you wearing a toga?" I asked.

The Scot looked down at himself and chuckled. "The attire we find ourselves in reflects a significant era of your souls' journey. The toga might represent an ancient connection or a reflection of your soul's most impactful incarnation. Be thankful an older era chosen wasn't one where we could be utterly in the nude!"

I pursed my lips, desperately trying to get the image of a naked Gregor out of my head. "Wait, souls reincarnate? Past lives?"

He smirked. "We've never received confirmation. But it is possible." Gregor shook his legs, "I'm surprised at how comfortable I am here. Usually, soulscapes try to push intruders out. Outside of that initial entry, yours has been pretty inviting."

I didn't want to delve too much deeper into why my soul was so accommodating to him. I began to look deeper down the endless tunnel when I realized that my clothes had changed into a toga, too. The more I thought about it, the more I felt slightly different. I rose from the floor, sighing. "I wish I could see myself."

No sooner had I said it did a mirror materialize out of thin air. I whirled around and sputtered, "H-h-how did that just happen?"

Gregor grinned at my wonder, "You are forgetting this is your soulscape. It does answer your desires."

Ha! Right, soulscape. We are in the world my soul created. Simple enough? I returned to the mirror to find that I had indeed changed. Not only did the one-shoulder floor-length toga fit my body perfectly, but my skin had a slight otherworldly shimmer, and my hair went way past my back. My ephemeral image freaked me out. Sensing my discomfort, the mirror vanished. Running a hand through my hair, I returned my attention to the Scot watching me, sending my hormones into over-drive. My heart hammered in my chest as an unexpected warmth crept up my neck and face. The sight of him, so different yet familiar, stirred feelings I wasn't ready to confront. Nor did Gregor want me to.

"What now?"

Gregor sighed and rolled his shoulders. "We are here so you can find your Havadar. So tell me – where do you feel we should go?"

"Where do I feel like going? What kind of question is that?"

"Be still. The answer will come."

I mirrored Gregor and rolled my shoulders. I began the deep breathing exercises and hoped that something would come up. I remembered my earlier training and the entity's words about asking for help. *Hey...um, it's me again. Not sure where I should be going. Some direction, please?*

I didn't hear an immediate response and thought perhaps I couldn't speak with my power in the soulscape. However, my heart rate slowed considerably after a few seconds, and something within me just clicked. A searing heat surged through me, so intense that it felt as though my veins were aflame, radiating from the core of my being to the tips of my fingers and toes. Then, a slight tickle of Vis energy sent a signal out from my center, and with each tickle, the signal continued to grow like a pulse reverberating outward from within my core. The signal became a sonar searching throughout the entire soulscape. For several moments, I stood erect, waiting for the answering call back. For something to echo back to me. It soon found its mark.

"There." I pointed down to the left corridor. "We need to go this way." I didn't bother to wait for Gregor's response. My feet led me way down the endless hallway. As we passed the doors, soft sounds could be heard behind each one that decorated the hall. Sounds of laughter, tears, anger, and sorrow.

"What are behind these doors?" I asked the Kyrios, my first question in about fifteen minutes.

Gregor eyed me carefully, gauging me. "These are your memories."

I blinked. "My memories? If I open a door, I can see my memories?" Curious, I approached a door where loud laughter could be heard. Before I could reach for the door, Gregor grabbed my hand.

"Once you open a memory door, it's difficult to leave. Our memories tend to trap us from moving forward, particularly if it's strong. I suggest that you stay on your current quest."

I felt an inexplicable pull towards one of the doors, a familiar lullaby faintly echoing behind it. It felt comforting yet melancholic. Gregor's warning echoed in my mind, but the temptation was undeniable.

I dropped my hand, realizing it had been the first time since our argument that we'd had any contact. I didn't know until that moment how much we'd touched before, how these new barriers held us back so much more. Disliking the residual ache his touch left, I focused on the echo. "Fine. Let's go."

We continued to walk down the hallway, the signal rapidly getting stronger the closer we got. Finally, as we approached a door, the signal within me grew insistent. The door was very similar to others we had passed by. Except it was completely silent.

"This is it." I looked at Gregor with apprehension. "What do I do now?"

A small smile graced his features. "Trust your instincts, Katya. They'll guide you in this place more than any advice I can give."

Determined, I thought, *'I want answers.'* As I resumed deep breathing to discern my next move, I heard the entity's voice speak clearer than ever.

Hello, Katya.

21

Mika's Revelations

In a flash of a moment, my surroundings had changed. No longer with Gregor and hovering above a familiar lake from my dreams, I took in the serene surroundings. Gentle ripples flowed across the lake, framed by distant tree-lined shores. An ethereal mist veiled everything, lending a dreamy atmosphere. It felt oppressive yet comforting all at once.

And I wasn't alone.

"Hello?" I called out. "Anyone there?"

You know I am here, the voice echoed everywhere. **Why do you question that?**

I looked around for the source, but no one came into view. "Show yourself."

Would you feel better if you could see something?

I nodded, not particularly trusting my voice.

Suddenly, a gale of wind surrounded the rock I floated over, forcing me to crash down onto the rock itself. The wind was such a force that I ducked down, hoping not to get pushed into the water. When the wind died out, I opened my eyes to find the mist had solidified into a replica of myself. But her eyes—ancient and wise—betrayed her true nature. I was staring at the beginning of time, where wisdom was first born, and all understanding stemmed from.

"Does this satisfy you?" my copy asked.

Finding my voice, I asked, "Who are you?"

She softly smiled. "I am a part of you. You may call me Mika, your reflection and guide."

Speaking with this carbon copy of myself was so unsettling that I couldn't meet her eyes. Seeing all-knowing enlightenment within my body was a bit too much to handle. "Okay, Mika. I've heard you speak to me before, several times now. Are you my Havadar?"

A serene look fell over Mika's face. "Yes and no. I am your guide to your purpose, a gateway to your Vis.

Resisting the urge to roll my eyes, I said, "That doesn't make sense. If you're my Vis personified, shouldn't you also be my Havadar?"

Mika shook her head. "There are many things that will become clear in time. This is not one of them."

"I don't understand. Why did you choose me? I am not anything special!"

"You were chosen to be the Balancer, a power that would awaken when the Living Realm would fall into great peril."

All types of alarms went off in my head. "What do you mean 'would fall'?"

Mika only glanced sympathetically. "Another moment that will become clear in time, Katya." She placed a hand on my shoulder. "This is overwhelming, yes. But I assure you, you can do this. You were created for this purpose. The sooner you accept this, the easier it will be for you."

Mika then grazed her hand down my cheek; the most sensory-calming scents followed – chamomile, lavender, and earth. "You don't have to be brave with me." Her fingertip brushed away a tear; I didn't realize I was crying. "I am here to support you. But I can only go as far as you allow me. All the tools you ever need are right here." She gestured to the domain we stood in. "It is up to you to begin the work and up to you to finish it."

I stared at the calm mirror image of myself, the surrealism of this ordeal catching up with me and robbing me of my breath. A rocking chair, reminiscent of the one I used to have in my bedroom, appeared underneath to catch my collapse. Mika wordlessly rubbed my back as I resumed my breathing exercises to calm down. "Mika, I don't know about this. This is more than I bargained for. All I ever wanted was to be normal. This isn't normal."

Mika looked amused. "Normal is really in the eye of the beholder. Your normal isn't everyone else's. It will all come to you soon." She took a step back and took my hand into hers. "Now, back to your true mission. You Havadar is not here."

"How can that be? Gregor said the Havadar is a part of the soul."

The slightest shadow passed over Mika's face so quickly that I must have imagined it. "Gregor is correct; however, it was made separate from you for your protection. You will need to go back home to find it. Unfortunately, an obstacle is waiting for you."

"What do you mean?"

Mika closed her eyes, her eyes swirling behind her closed lids. "Before you came to Ager, the Wanters had been watching you, trying to decipher your nature. They aren't pleased that the Kyrios now protect you. It is more than likely that they are awaiting your return to the Live Realm. They will use your mother as bait to make you yield to them."

"You mean absorb me," I said, fighting back the panic.

She nodded. "Yielding to them puts the Live Realm in jeopardy. But you could possibly free your mother from harm. You have not completed your training, so perfect Vis usage may not be possible, even with me guiding you. What will you do?"

My face twisted in confusion. "What is there to choose? I'm going back for Mom."

"Even though it could put billions of souls at stake? What of the men, women, and children you are meant to protect and to save?" She looked at me, probing.

"I..." I stopped, realizing she had a point. Could I sacrifice the safety of billions for one person, even my mother? My thoughts raced beyond comprehension at the decision in front of me. I looked up at Mika, searching her wise eyes for some answer, some indication of what I should do. "Can't I save both?"

She returned my gaze, looking sympathetic and embracing me. "Are you asking me? Or do you want me to endorse the decision you will make?" The decision was mine alone. If I saved my mother, the Wanters could destroy everything. But I didn't know if I could live with myself if I abandoned her. There had to be another way...

She suddenly looked up to the sky. The mist began to clear, allowing me to see the landscape slowly disappearing. "Your mate is getting anxious about you. It is time I send you back. And Katya? Remember, everything happens for a reason."

Mate? My brow furrowed in confusion, but before I could press her on what she meant by 'mate,' Mika suddenly sent a palm thrust to my chest, sending me to the ground. I bolted up from the floor, gasping for breath, when I realized I was back in my room in Ager.

Gregor was kneeling over me, gasped in surprise. He immediately brought me into his arms, kissing my forehead. "Oh, thank God!" He smoothed over my edges and hair, gingerly holding my cheeks. "You are okay, Kat. Breathe in for four, hold it for seven, and release it for eight. Follow me."

I coughed, trying to fill up my lungs. "What happened?"

He didn't answer; he just continued to mimic the deep breathing until I started to follow. When my heart rate finally lowered to safe levels. Gregor finally answered, "When we were at the door, you went into deep breathing and suddenly collapsed. I thought the stress of being in the soulscape was too much for you, so I brought you back to your body. Then you stopped breathing," he shakily muttered. His hand traveled to my neck, massaging and easing muscle tension, almost making me groan. He rested his forehead against me, his warm breath sending a delicious thrill through me. "When you still didn't respond, I was about to start some emergency measures when you returned."

I met his warm and concerned gaze, shuddering from his proximity and the sweat crawling down my back. "Man, that was intense."

Gregor lifted my face and searched my eyes. "Where did you go?"

"I spoke to someone... or something. Her name is Mika. I've never encountered her before, but she claims to be my guide and the gateway to my Vis.

"What did she say?"

"She was as cryptic as the rest of you, speaking in riddles and telling me not to fight it."

The Kyrios chuckled and tucked a strand of hair behind my ear. "Sounds like she knows what she is talking about."

"Says the king of confusion and mixed signals," I joked softly. But my barb only reminded him of our new barriers. Begrudgingly, he released my face and sat back on his hunches, stretching our distance as much as possible. His eyes shuttered closed, locking away his emotions again for duty's sake.

"Well," he said, clearing his throat, "I'm glad you made contact. Now we can move forward in your training."

I shook my head, standing up to hide my hurt from his gaze. "Not yet. She said my Havadar isn't inside me for my protection and that I need to go home to retrieve it." I paused, collecting my thoughts. "Mika also mentioned that my mother could be in danger."

Gregor frowned. "What's going on? Why would your mother be in danger?"

"The Wanters are using her as bait. How long have we been in this realm?"

Gregor rubbed his chin, "It's been twenty-four hours here, so three days have passed in the Live Realm."

"Mom's probably be back home now. And she's probably freaking out about my email to her."

He grunted, "What did you tell her?"

"To divert her attention and prevent her from worrying too much, I told her that since she couldn't come home in time, I was going to go on vacation without her to Scotland with the Scottish man I met," I looked at him purposefully.

Gregor chuckled, incredulous. "Of course, you added me. Give her a place to direct her anger. If you were my daughter, I wouldn't take that news very well."

"I know it's terrible!" I said, fighting my giggles. "I need her to be angry with me rather than freaking out about my safety." I took a deep breath, knowing my mom had a whupping with my name at home.

"Gregor," I began, "I'm aware of the stakes, especially with my energy going nuts periodically. But I need to go home to get my Havadar and make sure my mom is safe. Can we do something to make sure that we can keep everyone safe? Without sacrificing anyone?"

The Scot shook his head. "Katya, I understand, but I'm sorry. I can't authorize your leaving."

"Let's speak to the Generals, then," I said evenly. "They want me to get my Havadar, and apparently, it's back in the Live Realm. Leaving it there could also be a problem." I offered a hand to Gregor to help him stand. "I know what's at stake here, Gregor. If we devise a plan together, no one will get hurt."

Our eyes locked, a mix of defiance and something deeper pulsing between us, and a battle of wills ensued. For several minutes, we said nothing, sizing each other up and searching for the other's commitment to the overall mission. Finally, Gregor blinked, grabbed my hand, and stood up. "Okay, Katya. I believe I have a solution that might appease both sides."

Hope flared inside me, making my voice inadvertently upbeat. "What's your idea?"

Gregor's expression darkened. "I think I know a way. But let me think it through." He raked a hand through his curls. "I'll come get you for dinner. The Generals want to see you."

Before I could respond, he strode out, the door shutting firmly behind him. My burst of elation quickly withered. While we'd made progress, an uneasy feeling still gnawed at my core.

22

A Dangerous Proposition

I jolted awake later that afternoon, realizing I'd fallen asleep from exhaustion. Slightly dazed, I trudged out of bed to answer the knock that had awakened me. Gregor stood on the other side, his expression unreadable. "Lady Katya, I am here to take you to Central Tower." His eyes raked over me with a sudden hunger that caught me off guard. When he caught himself, he turned away, averting his eyes, "Do you want a minute to freshen up?"

I looked down to find that my bodysuit had unzipped down the middle, showing quite a bit of revealed skin down to my navel. Cheeks enflamed, I quickly adjusted it and stepped out of the doorway. "I'll be out in a minute." I closed the door, finger-combed my hair, and adjusted my afro into a top bun.

I exited my room to find Gregor already walking down the hallway. "Let's go to dinner, shall we?" I hustled to reach him and finally caught up at the tower's base. We walked in silence to Central Tower, though I did risk a couple of glances Gregor's way. If he saw them, he never acknowledged them.

"Are you going to tell me what the plan is?" I asked softly as we walked through the courtyard.

His jaw clenched. "I will ask them to put you in a soulbind."

I stopped short. "A soulbind? What the heck is that? And why do you look so tense?"

Gregor paused, his gaze still evading mine. The mention of the 'soulbind' weighed heavily on him, making his typically steadfast demeanor falter. "It's the only solution that can work. If they allow you to do this, I'm sure the Generals will come to the same conclusion."

I slowly moved closer to the Scot, lightly touching his arm. "Look at me. What's going on?" Gregor cleared his throat before turning towards me. Even as the sky darkened, his eyes shone brightly with worry and trepidation. "A soulbind is essentially a Kyrios prison. If a Kyrios changes sides or becomes a liability, a soulbind is the soul's version of handcuffs. It's normally meant for those who have lost all control and begun to change into the Want."

I could feel my brows arch high into my hairline. "Kyrios can change into the Want?"

"Any spiritual creature can." Gregor's eyes bore into mine, quietly conveying something to me. "Becoming a Want creature is simply a matter of choice, of where your loyalties lie. To change your loyalties from peaceful interaction to absolute destruction by a Kyrios is not tolerated, especially because we have pledged ourselves to fight. The Vis bind can be a horrible device used to cause immense pain. After several hours, the soul can only take so much."

Horror-struck, I demanded, "And you want to put that on me?"

"No!" Gregor shook his head, rubbing his forehead, exasperated. "I hate that I've even come to this conclusion at all. But I know how the Generals think. Their concern is not your mother but the entire Live Realm. They need to protect all humans from not just the Want but you too." Gregor inched closer to me, grabbing my shoulders desperately. "I know I said it's painful, but there are levels to a Vis bind, and it won't be as nearly destructive as it could be if you were a Wanter. At most, you would feel pressure inside of you. Not crippling pressure, but you will feel it. But anything longer than three Live Realm hours could be damaging."

His jaw clenched, and I could feel the anxiety rolling off him. "Katya,

I am concerned about this. I have a feeling that something could go wrong, and since I have...taken you under my protection, I am advising you not to do this. I can send someone else to collect your mother and put her in a safe place under our protection. You don't have to go personally. We will figure out something, but we must keep you safe."

It was the most emotion I had seen from Gregor since we met. Unconsciously, I caressed his cheek, feeling stubble tickle my fingertips. "Gregor, do you know why I feel relatively calm about this?" I waited until his eyes met mine to continue, "Because I know you will do everything you can to keep me safe. I trust you with my life." His eyes widened and swelled with emotion, his jaw clenching repeatedly.

I wanted nothing more than to close the gap and kiss him senselessly until he found the comfort he needed. At that moment, I understood the desperation he hid about keeping me safe. I had burrowed behind his defenses and taken a spot near his heart just as he did to me.

I also understood why there were measures to remove any distractions from Kyrios. Here was this proud Major, filled with anxiety because of me, because he was worried about me. What would they do to him if they learned about us and our ties to each other? Would they put this soulbind on him? Would they cast him out? I imagined taking all of my garbled feelings for him and throwing them behind one of the many doors within my heart. I steeled myself for what I was about to say and hoped that he wouldn't take it to heart too much.

"As much as I appreciate your concern," I said, dropping my hand and stepping back from him. "we will go through with this. If the soulbind is the recommended step, then that's what we'll do. You do your job and only concern yourself about my security. Anything else is unnecessary." I walked away from him, gazing towards the tower to avoid his reaction.

No further words were exchanged, and he only made contact with me when he dutifully gathered me in his arms and jumped to the top floor where the Generals were waiting for our arrival.

We found the Generals in a room across from the conference room we had visited before. This round room appeared similar, except for the round table and the one table setting where I assumed I would be sitting. *Looks like I am eating by myself.* The Generals stood from their chairs and gave me slight nods.

"Lady Katya, so glad you could join us," Nabil said with an easy smile. The others murmured similar greetings, although Raf's smile was more genuine. I answered with a small smile and took my place at the table. They were waiting for me to say something, so I didn't disappoint. "What is the occasion for this meeting?"

Nabil glanced at Raf and said, "My lady, we wanted to ensure you're well. Raf mentioned your progress in training. However, your session with Gregor today raises concerns. Your training will intensify, and it's paramount you cooperate. We want you to succeed. The fate of the entire Live Realm is resting on your shoulders." His guarded eyes held a hint of insincerity.

I took a moment, gathering my thoughts. "There is something I want to say."

Michiko, two seats away, encouraged. "Speak, child."

I met the eyes of the other Generals and Gregor's impassive gaze. I sat back in the chair, hoping to express confidence in my relaxed pose. "I'm returning to the Live Realm to retrieve my mother and locate my Havadar. My internal guide assured me of finding my Havadar upon my return."

Nabil slowly rose from his seat, his anger palpable. "Haven't we stressed the dangers of returning before you have mastered your power?" he said softly. "The dangers you pose to others?" The room suddenly became stifling. His anger became more than just a feeling, but a physical force that pressed against me. A quick look around the room told me that the other Generals felt it too, but they didn't nearly feel as oppressed as I did.

The control over my temper slipped. I felt my power surge, mingling with my anger and perhaps a bit of Mika. I rose from the table as well, matching his soft tone. "And have I not made it clear that I must return? This is not a debate but a discussion of my decision. I must do what must be done. I do not take this lightly and have considered those lives when deciding. And please refrain from throwing your energy at me. It's uncalled for. This is no way to conduct a meeting amongst equals." My voice became more unearthly, and a bright azure light radiated from my body.

Nabil weighed the situation, then reluctantly sat, his gaze still locked on mine. Once seated, the tension eased slightly. I steadied myself, then turned to Gregor. "You had a suggestion?"

Snapping to attention, Gregor addressed Nabil, "With Lady Katya's consent, a temporary soulbind could protect her and others during her visit."

Raf shot Gregor a sharp look ."Is this necessary? I'm sure Lady Katya should be able to handle the visit. What of the dangers to her?"

Gregor nodded. "I understand, and I share the same concerns. However, if only done for a limited time, it would protect others around Lady Katya and allow her to complete her desired tasks."

Lamar explained, "Her Havadar, an extension of her power, is vulnerable. If it's truly in the Live Realm, we must retrieve it. Imagine if our enemies obtain it."

Disturbed, I said, "I thought a Havadar couldn't be wielded by anyone else."

The Security General clarified. "Normally, yes, but we don't know the effect of having it outside of you will do. Theoretically, the Havadar may have formed its own personality or state of mind without you controlling it. It could be converted into a Wanter."

I worried my bottom lip. "I don't like the idea of someone using a piece of me against me."

Raf grunted, "It's unavoidable. We do need it. If Gregor is with her, there should be no issue. She's capable of protecting herself." He grinned, looking at me.

Victor nodded his consent, and Michiko eyed me closely before saying, "Let her go. We have more to lose if she stays."

Lamar folded his arms over his chest, looking down at his forearm. "As long as Lady Katya understands the dangers she faces, I concur."

I nodded. "This may be the only way to save everyone."

Nabil, barely containing his frustration, conceded. "Very well. Return within three Live Realm hours of departure. Any later, and there will be consequences." Abruptly, he departed. "This meeting is adjourned."

As if sensing my uneasiness at Nabil's departure, Raf grunted, "Don't worry about him. He's used to getting his way since he's been here the longest." He crossed his arms, grinning manically. "If only you could wield your Vis like that all the time, I'd be a happy soul."

I grinned as well. "Well, piss me off enough, and I just might."

The room lightened with shared laughter. Victor then summoned, "Sophia!"

Footsteps echoed from the main foyer as they approached the dining room. A tall blond with pale skin entered, holding several plates in one hand and a pitcher in the other. On closer inspection, I realized that this was the same laughing woman I had seen Gregor with earlier in the courtyard. I quickly looked away, not wanting to catch her eye.

Victor introduced, "Lady Katya, meet Sophia. She aids both Lamar and me. She'll serve you tonight."

"Generals, will you join me? I understand you don't need food, but I'm told you can enjoy it," I asked brightly.

The Generals all shook their heads no. Lamar also stood, "We simply stayed to ensure that you had settled with your dinner. We shall leave you in Gregor's capable hands." Lamar looked at Gregor. "I shall meet you at the gate in the morning, Gregor. I want to ensure that all goes well."

Gregor stood from his chair and gave his salute. "I shall see you in the morning, sir."

With that, the Generals made their way out, murmuring their good-byes and goodnights. I nodded and smiled at each, appreciating their support.

Sophia served me with an unmistakably cold demeanor. Trying to be amiable, I met her gaze, but she looked away with disdain. I focused on my meal, sensing her tension and fighting the urge to cuss her out for her attitude.

Sophia straightened and turned to Gregor with a slight smirk. "Is there anything else I can do for you, sir?"

Gregor, curtly dismissing Sophia, joined me in the awkward silence.

I began eating the food set before me– a lovely golden-crust chicken pot pie. *Another favorite.* I could feel Gregor's gaze on me as I ate.

Unable to stand the silence, I cleared my throat, wiping my mouth, "I hope you understand my point earlier."

The Kyrios nodded. "Of course."

His simple answer pained me as much as our earlier exchange. But I knew I had to stay stronger to protect him, no matter how much I wanted to embrace him and coax the worry lines out of his forehead. Finishing my meal, I said, "Tomorrow is crucial. I should rest." I rose from the table and began walking towards the door, realizing I was alone. Gregor still sat at the table in deep contemplation.

"Gregor? Are you coming?"

He met my gaze, warmth returning to his eyes, "My lady, wherever your journey takes you, know I'm always by your side."

23

The Homecoming

Gregor escorted me quietly back to my room. While his last words filled me with a slight hope that he would be friendlier moving forward, his walls were rebuilt brick by brick with every step toward the tower. *It's for the best.*

Once we reached my door, Gregor murmured, "Your training will have a slight adjustment tomorrow, presumably to accommodate the successful location of your Havadar. You will not train with General Raf in the morning but in the evening. We will resume our training session the next day."

I nodded and reached for my doorknob when I stopped and said, "Gregor, I am sure everything will be fine tomorrow." I made eye contact with him. "We're going to come back here in one piece. I'm sure of it."

For several moments, he only stared at me. He opened his mouth to say something but shut it abruptly. "I'll see you in the morning, my lady." With a curt nod, he was gone.

Still fatigued from our adventure into my soulscape, I quickly changed out of my clothes into a nightshirt, plopped down on the sea of pillows on my bed, and stared at the ceiling above me. My last thought was whether getting the drop on a Kyrios was possible for pissing you off royally. As I closed my eyes, the world shifted around me, and the familiar confines of my room faded.

Suddenly, I find myself in a city. Smack dab in the middle of the street, within what looked like a financial district. Towering buildings with imposing windows stretch as far as the eye can see. But instead of maple trees, the streets are lined with palm trees. Is this Florida or California? I wonder.

My eyes dart side to side, looking for some activity. I run down the street, looking for anyone: a cart vendor, a businessman on his phone, a cabbie searching for fares. Nothing, not a soul. In a blind panic, I suddenly dart around the corner. But I stop short. I finally find someone about one hundred yards before me.

She's a Kyrios—a tall blond with immensely cold eyes. Sophia. She stares me down, considers me carefully, and then smirks. She saunters towards me with a carefree ease. On the other hand, I feel like lead, unable to move an inch. She extends her right hand and materializes a long, thin blade and hilt as black as her bodysuit. Her Havadar. The freezing glint and the murderous intent in her eye tell me everything I need to know. I look frantically around for anyone to stop this mad woman.

Gregor finally appears, walking from another intersection towards us. Sophia must sense his presence because she stops and looks at him expectantly. I try to speak, but my mouth won't move. I pray that my eyes convey my panic and gratitude now that he is here to save me.

Yet the closer he gets, the more I can see the unforgiving line in his jaw, the cold nature of his eyes. Eyes that glitter dangerously red. Eyes of the Want.

Bewildered, I open my mouth to say something but fall mute again. Gregor doesn't break my stare until he is shoulder-to-shoulder with Sophia. He grabs her by the hair and roughly pulls her to his lips for a punishing but passionate kiss.

My heart races to the pit of my stomach and sends me crashing to the ground. As the two Kyrios release each other, Sophia turns gleefully in my direction, her eyes glittering red. Within seconds, she's launched into the air with her Havadar above her head, intending to send my head in the opposite direction from the rest of my body.

I awoke with a scream that would've shaken the dead. Sweat poured from my brow as I tried to steady my racing heart, the remnants of the dream still haunting me. I heard heavy steps approaching, the sound growing louder. I braced myself, and to my relief, Young Jae burst through the door.

"Ms. Katya! Are you all right?" He sat down at the edge of my bed with concern in his eyes. Jae looked me over anxiously as I caught my breath. The shock and anger from the dream robbed me of voice, and all I could do was shake my head.

"Oh, my lady," Jae crooned. "What has upset you so?"

I continue to shake my head, grasping at the blanket covering me. Young Jae inched closer to me, snapped his finger to open a small blue portal, and reached inside. His hand returned with a cup of water, and I desperately gulped it down, dehydrated. Young Jae gently takes my hand and sends the cup away when no water is left to drain.

"Do you wish to talk about it, Ms. Katya?" he asked softly.

"I think I'm just stressed," I reply quietly. "The world's weight is on my shoulder, and I am just trying to be strong." I massaged my face, trying to wipe away the remnants of the dream. "How did I get here? I... Don't you wish you had complete control of your life? That you could live how you want and not how the universe planned?" I whispered brokenly.

Jae inched closer, "May I speak frankly, Miss Katya?" I raised my eyes to find him staring at me intently.

"I would prefer it."

He paused momentarily, watching me, "When I was a child in Korea, my father had high expectations of me taking over his business. Really, he pounded into me that it was my destiny."

I raised an eyebrow, "That sounds tough."

Jae nodded, "Every day was a reminder of the heavy mantle waiting for me. Yet, my heart yearned for simpler things: to lay in the fields, watch clouds, and pen down fantasy tales. Sometimes, I wished for a different life, away from the one my father envisioned for me."

"Did you get the life you wanted?" I asked gently.

Jae gave me a sad smile. "No, I never had a chance to. But sometimes

I think about what it would have been like if I had focused on being the best version of my father's dream? Maybe something in between—completing what was expected of me but still able to do it my way? I believe that you are in the same place, Ms. Katya. Find a middle ground that makes you happy but still fulfills your purpose. Follow your instincts."

His fingers grazed over mine, sending an unexpected jolt up my arm. The sensation slowed my thoughts, anchoring me in the moment. "I won't probe you about your dream. I know that's personal. But sometimes your dreams are clear messages from your instincts."

I raised my eyes to find his eyes glittered mysteriously.

"They will not steer you wrong," he said, his eyes never leaving mine. His hand squeezed mine, instantly filling me with warmth and slight trepidation. *Woah, is this something romantic to him?*

"Thank you, Jae." I returned the squeeze but quickly released it. The young Kyrios continued to look at me earnestly. "Ms. Katya, I think you lack someone looking out for you. A friend."

A friend? I thought Kyrios shouldn't have human friends. I gave Young Jae a crooked smile. "You are right. But I don't think Nabil will be offering friendship anytime soon."

Jae chuckled, giving me a rueful smile. "No, Nabil is not one to make any friends. Enemies, yes. Friends, no." He leaned closer and said softly, "If you need help or have any questions, don't hesitate. Just simply come to me and ask."

"I think I might take you up on your offer."

The Kyrios beamed, and I was again taken by how attractive I found him. He rose from my bed and gave me a sweeping bow. "To think I should serve such a beautiful lady. My afterlife is finally complete."

I rolled my eyes but laughed softly. His words reminded me of an earlier conversation we had. "Jae, I do actually have a question."

"Of course. What is it?"

I suddenly felt odd asking—it felt like a personal question. But my curiosity won. "You've mentioned twice about being human and having a life before. How did you get to Ager? How does one become a Kyrios?"

Jae stiffened and suddenly looked uneasy. "The formation of a Kyrios is not an easy explanation. The beginning is different for everyone, but it's all the same in the end. The epitome of internal warfare."

Before I could ask him to elaborate, the door suddenly burst open, and Gregor charged in with his eyes blazing. "Lieutenant, what are you doing in her chambers?"

Jae instantly saluted Gregor and said promptly, "Sir, while I took over your watch, Lady Katya was experiencing a nightmare and was giving off copious amounts of energy. I came to investigate and to ensure the Lady's safety."

Gregor glanced me over, checking Jae's story out. With the nightmare I'd just had and remembering our necessary distance, I avoided making eye contact and instead busied myself with the blanket covering me. His relentless stare just made me feel more uncomfortable.

Finally, Gregor's attention returned to Jae. "Very well. You are dismissed."

Jae nodded. He then turned to me and gave a curt bow. Right before he returned to his full height, he gave me a slight wink and walked out the door.

Gregor remained at the entrance, his brow furrowed. "Are you all right?" he asked quietly.

I smoothed my hair, adjusted my bonnet, and fluffed my pillow. "Yes, I'm fine," I said curtly.

"Do you want to talk about it?" he asked slowly. The soft husk of his voice made me want to melt into his arms and continue to cry, but Jae's words about the middle ground helped me stand firm.

"Thank you," I turned my back to him, clutching my pillow. "But it's probably best that I go back to sleep. We can talk later, soldier."

He nodded, and as he made to leave, the words came out before I realized it. "I wouldn't mind someone keeping me company while I fell asleep, though." Not facing him, I expected to hear a resounding "No" and a door slam. I listened to his footsteps as he grabbed the stool near the window, the scrapping of the chair as it was set by the door, and his steady breathing as he watched on as I eased back to sleep.

* * *

A soft rapping on the door awoke me from my uneasy sleep the following day.

"My lady, we are scheduled to leave for the Live Realm within an hour." Gregor's soft brogue carried through the closed door. "Are you awake?"

"Yes," I said groggily. "Give me a couple of minutes. I'll be out in a little bit." The ensuing silence was my answer. I dragged myself out of bed, my feet heavy against the cool floor. Approaching the basin, I gazed into the mirror. The reflection staring back was a mess: hair freed from its tied silk, tired eyes, and the undeniable weight of uncertainty. "It's going to be a long day," I muttered. After several water splashes, I felt slightly more awake, though not entirely.

I changed into my original Live Realm clothes and made enough effort with my makeup to look like I had been traveling with my paramour. Satisfied with my outward appearance, I opened the door to find Gregor patiently waiting. The image of him, handsome but dutiful, raised questions.

Is Jae right? Should I pay attention to that dream? Could Gregor betray me? That can't be right. He did kiss me. He must feel something for me.

He was just caught up in being human. You know that, Katya.

But he's been looking out for me too. To his own possible detriment. Why worry about putting me in a soulbind if he would betray me?

As my internal battle ensued, I stared at Gregor with utmost intensity. When it went on longer than necessary, the Kyrios cleared his throat. "Lady Katya? Are we ready to go?"

Snapping back to reality, I cleared my throat, hiding behind my curls. "Yes. Sorry." I quickly made for the stairs, not waiting for him to answer. He caught up with me quickly, and we made our way to the main gate in awkward silence.

"Are you sure you are all right?"

"Of course," I said with false cheerfulness. "Let's hurry. Wouldn't want to keep General Lamar waiting now!" Sure enough, General Lamar was waiting for us at the gate. The General nodded in our direction while Gregor gave him a salute.

"Good. You're here. Let's get down to business." He looked me over carefully and then continued. "The Vis bind, as explained, will be imprisoning your energy. You have three hours before the Vis bind begins to affect you more severely."

He stepped closer to the both of us. "I cannot stress the risk that you are facing. There is no telling how your soul will react to this. Gregor, any sign that the Vis bind is at its limit, you must bring her back immediately to me."

Lamar crouched down to meet me at eye level, eyes boring into me. "My lady, I give you one command. You must stay calm. While your control improves, your Vis is still linked to your emotions and adrenaline. Any bump to your Vis could bring thousands of Wanters searching for that power, devouring and destroying anything in their path."

Fear and trepidation rippled through my face; Lamar gave me a slight smile and pat on the shoulder. "Don't worry. The entire Kyrios force is here to protect you. Besides," he shot a knowing look to Gregor, "I know Gregor would give his life force to protect you. Isn't that right?"

Gregor's facial expression betrayed nothing, but his eyes widened slightly. "Of course, sir."

Lamar's smile grew. "Good. Let us begin then." He closed his eyes and pressed his palms together; a crackling sound grew louder. As he sent more power to his hands, a bright amber light streamed through his fingers, giving his dark face an eerie glow. He then separated his hands, stretching and molding the light until it formed a sphere in his right hand.

Then, without warning, he thrust the sphere into my center, leaving me gasping for air and sending me careening to the ground. The elephant feeling returned, but this time, I felt completely numb. I could still feel physical sensations: the coolness of the floor and the warmth of Gregor's hand as he helped me back up. But I felt numb, as though

I was in shock from the severe loss of someone special. Being unable to feel Mika within me felt like no other loss I had ever experienced.

"The bind holds. You have three hours. Good luck, my lady." Lamar gave a quick nod and left for Central Tower. Still shaken, Gregor bore my weight gingerly as he led me through the gate and to the exit portal point.

Gregor studied me as we walked further away. "How do you feel?"

"Like I lost my best friend," I said quietly. "I don't like this, Gregor."

He grimaced and walked a bit more quickly. "Then let's get this done quickly so your best friend can be returned to you."

With a quick snap of his fingers, his bright blue-grey portal opened. Five seconds later, we stood outside a block from my house in an alley behind a bodega. The air felt different, lacking the familiar essence of Vis. Perhaps it was because I had been in another realm. The air wasn't the only thing different. My once pristine neighborhood now lay in near ruin. The pavement, where kids used to joyfully ride their bikes, was now riddled with cracks and potholes. The homes, which used to stand tall and well-maintained, now appeared lopsided, as if they'd seen too many harsh years in just a matter of days. The vibrant green lawns were replaced with patches of brown. Everything looked so... desolate. In the distance, I could hear many sirens managing people, probably causing mischief due to the uncertainty. *The Wanters have been very busy.* I shook my head free. My mother first.

I asked, "Why didn't we appear inside the house?"

"I checked it before I opened the portal on this side. There were a handful of souls throughout the entire house."

Feeling a sense of dread, I bolted down the street and toward the house. Yellow police tape greeted me, covering the door. A small crowd of the neighbors parked themselves on the lawn, quietly murmuring to themselves. Just by the door, we saw three uniformed policemen walking around the foyer, brushing the walls, looking for prints.

I couldn't see Cynthia, but I could hear her bawling uncontrollably. "She never does this. I know something bad has happened to her. I can feel it." A quick look at the driveway revealed my mother's car parked at an angle. As if she had pulled in quickly and bolted inside of the house.

"Um, Gregor, remind me, how many days have passed?"

"As of now, four and half days."

I looked back at the Kyrios beside me, who looked equally concerned. We walked over the police tape, past the three occupied police officers, and into the house. We found Cynthia sitting beside my mother on the family room couch, softly saying something. My mother was hunched over with her head in her hands. Her dark hair looked frazzled like it hadn't been combed in days. Both looked exhausted and bedraggled. My mother was still wearing her work suit, something she never keeps on once she gets home after a trip. I looked around, not knowing what to do or what to say.

Before I could ask Gregor for advice on what to do, I heard my mother say, "Katya?"

Every single head swiveled to the middle of the foyer. I could only squeak out, "Oh, hey, Mom."

I quietly stepped forward as the police officers, Cynthia, and my mother stared at me. I cleared the ball of anxiety from my throat and tried to chuckle. "What's going on? Did someone die or something?"

"Did someone die?" my mother repeated hoarsely. "Where have you been?" Suddenly, my mother's grip clamped around my shoulders, shaking me. Her eyes were wild with fury, worry, and relief—each emotion fighting for dominance. Her voice trembled, but there was a razor's edge to it. "Do you have any idea what you have put me through these four days? Where the hell have you been?"

"I told you, Mom. Traveling with my friend here," I explained, attempting to sound nonchalant. If I started stuttering like an idiot, the whole story would be blown. I looked back to Gregor, who was as still as a statue.

My mother saw where my attention went. She took a moment to size up Gregor. Her gaze piercing as if trying to unravel his very essence. "Who the heck is this?" The entire room held its collective breath, waiting for my response.

Cynthia suddenly found her voice and screeched, "That's him. That's the guy she was last with!"

"Everyone stay where you are," a stern voice commanded behind us. I turned, facing a tall blond man wearing a crisp black suit and a bowler hat standing at the top of the stairs. His piercing dark gaze fixed on mine, scrutinizing, unblinking. I felt like prey under a hunter's watchful eye. A chill ran down my spine; there was something eerily familiar about him. As he descended the stairs, the room's atmosphere grew tense, everyone anticipating his next move. Even the average residual Vis energy in the house seemed to disappear.

As much as I wanted to question this odd sensation, making sure my mother didn't commit my murder was my priority. The bowler hat man said, "My name is Detective Sloan, and I'm in charge of this investigation. Are you Katya Stevens?"

I gulped. "Yes, sir."

He crossed his arms and arched his eyebrows. "You have been gone for four days with this man?"

"Yes, that's true—"

"And who might you be?" Detective Sloan asked icily, emphasizing every word. He paced deliberately around the room, taking a moment to look over Gregor from head to toe. The weight of the room's attention shifted to Gregor, every eye bearing down on him, expecting an answer or a confession. "What's your relationship with this girl?"

"He kidnapped her!" Cynthia yelled. "He made her write those emails to her mom and me because he kidnapped her."

I rolled my eyes and threw my arms up in frustration. "Cyn, really? Does that make any sense to you? I'm right here. I left on my own. And I came back on my own. Gregor is not my kidnapper."

"Then answer me." My mother was suddenly behind me, with her eyes blazing with anger. "I'm not going to ask again. Who the hell is he?"

I stepped closer to Gregor, looking over everyone in the room. "I would tell you if you would just give me a minute," I said crossly, hoping to buy time, "I would gladly tell you who Gregor is."

What I hoped to be a dramatic pause only ended up ticking off my mother. "Get on with it, young lady!" she barked.

"Gregor is—"

A warm hand firmly took mine, and I found Gregor looking down at me with a loving intensity that took my breath away and sent heat to all the devious parts of my body. "Ma'am," he began, his voice unwavering, facing my mother directly, "What Katya's trying to say is that I am her husband."

24

Eloped Secrets

The silence that fell over the room was deafening. Mom and Cynthia's simultaneous exclamation shattered it: "WHAT?"

I quickly schooled my shock as Gregor slightly squeezed my fingers in a warning. *Wait till we're alone, Scotsman.* The arousing thought of confronting Gregor later sent a twinge through my soulbind. Taking a deep breath, I addressed the room, "Yes, Gregor and I were married in New Hampshire three days ago."

As the room became a cacophony of shouts and shrieks, I bit my tongue, feeling the tightness of my Vis's bind. Gregor, sensing my struggle, tightened our grip. Detective Sloan, looking both bemused and irritated, whistled sharply for silence.

"Enough. Everyone sit down." Cynthia and Mom reluctantly shuffled into armchairs, their eyes never leaving Gregor or me.

Gregor gently raised and kissed our joined hands as we sat on the couch. Behind the sweet gesture, however, was a silent message: *Take my lead.*

Detective Sloan stood with his arms crossed, looking amused. "Ms. Stevens, you were reported missing two days ago. You left behind a puzzling email, which, according to your family, is uncharacteristic of you."

I shifted uncomfortably. "Yes, I sent those emails."

He sat on the coffee table directly before me, his arms draped over his knees. Something about his energy raised the hairs on my neck. "Now, after four days, you return with a husband who isn't even the man you were supposedly dating?" He paused, consulting his notebook. "Roger Simmons?"

"Roger and I broke up before all of this. You can ask him that."

Gregor, voice icy but polite, interjected, "Detective Sloan, instead of berating my wife with questions, I think it is best to begin at the beginning, don't you think?"

Detective Sloan shot Gregor a terse look, then nodded. "All right, start from the top."

"Yes, we met in the alley, and after I helped Katya return home, we both realized that we had ties to each other many years ago. The first time we actually met was ten years ago."

He cuddled closer to me, embracing me and gently smoothing my hair. "This beautiful little girl befriended me when my family and I first moved to Boston. Though it was only a few months, she was everything to me." He chuckled to himself as if actually remembering this fabricated story. "She was such a sweet girl and treated me so well that I never forgot about her when my family moved back to Scotland. I have been in love with her since I was twelve years old," Gregor said earnestly. His recounting of our "history" was so vivid and heartfelt that I almost believed him. Playing my part, I ran my fingers through his curls and leaned against his shoulder, enjoying the proximity I wouldn't have later.

"Over the years, I often thought of her. I berated myself for never having the courage to tell her how I felt." Gregor turned to me, his eyes shining brightly. "Imagine, after all this time, that I would find her again, in complete serendipity. I couldn't let this moment pass without telling her how I felt. I just never thought that she felt the same about me." He squeezed my hand gently to prompt me to say something.

"Yes," I said breathlessly. "I had a soft spot for him since way back, but when he moved back to Scotland, I thought I would never see him again. Gregor coming back into my life was simply a miracle. And I didn't want to let him go again." On cue, he leaned in with a gentle kiss on my cheek; it was as much a comfort to me as a performance for the others. But as I felt the fluctuating emotions pulling at my bind, I struggled to keep a neutral expression.

Cynthia and my mother weren't convinced.

Mom burst out of her chair, raging, "I'm not going even to bring up the fact that you are only eighteen, you are supposed to start college in days, that your whole life is ahead of you and shouldn't have even thought about getting married," my mother said through her gritted teeth.

"But why did you write that email?" She grabbed the nearest vase and threw it against the wall, glass splintering everywhere. "You expect me to believe that you leave home, leave me to travel with a man you met at eight years old? I want the truth now! Where the hell have you been?" she screamed.

Her demand for the truth cut me to the core. All I could see was the turmoil Mom suffered through because of me. Tears pricked the corners of my eyes, and a slight tugging at my core from the bind had me inhaling sharply. I had hoped that no one noticed it, but Cynthia was watching me a bit too closely. "What's the matter, Kat?"

"Mrs. Stevens, I strongly urge you to take a deep breath and sit down," Gregor said quietly but authoritatively, shifting in his seat to shield me. Despite Gregor's protective stance, Mom, eyes like daggers, tried to catch my gaze.

I refused to look up. The floor and my hands were much more captivating. Besides, I knew she'd see right through me when I looked at her.

"Mrs. Stevens, please. While I understand you are upset, screaming does not help the situation," Gregor said carefully. For several minutes, Mom remained silent and standing. I slowly looked up to find she was staring through rather than at me. A sudden chill danced on my back, but no one noticed the involuntary action or the sudden shift in my mother's eyes.

"Mrs. Stevens?" Cynthia asked quietly. "Are you going to sit down?"

"Oh... Um, yes. Yes, I will." My mother quickly sat in her chair as if standing had suddenly burned her. I quickly averted my eyes to Detective Sloan, who had been watching all of us. His eyes lit up, a spark of anticipation dancing within them. He gave an eerie smile and caught me in his stare. *I want him gone. Now.*

"I don't think you're necessary any longer, sir," I said, addressing him directly. "I think my mother's reaction proves why I did what I did. And Cynthia," I rounded to face my best friend, "you would've tried to convince me to stay or tried something to make me forget about Gregor completely. You haven't kept it a secret that you don't like Gregor! Why would I have told you anything?"

Cynthia chewed on her bottom lip, looking somewhat contrite. "Kat, I act the way that I do to protect you. And I was right! Married?" She spits the word out with venom. "This isn't right, nor was this planned for you!"

I smiled sadly, looking down at my hands, hoping I looked contrite. "I understand everyone is upset, but I love him and just wanted to make my own choices." I made a show of clutching Gregor's hand to my chest. "I just want to live my life with my husband."

Gregor's eyes softened, his free hand caressing my face. "I love you, too." His following kiss was purely perfunctory, but even the slight brush of our lips sent an intense stirring within me, tapping into a bed of desire. I wanted to climb into his lap and never let go. It also caused a more significant twinge through my bonded energy. I hid my discomfort behind a smile, but Gregor wasn't fooled.

I turned back to Detective Sloan, whose face twisted in disdain at our open displays of affection. "Like I said, we no longer need your services. I'm of age, and we eloped in New Hampshire. Nothing more to discuss. At least with you, anyway."

Detective Sloan gave me a funny look and then smirked. "Of course, I tried to explain that to your mother." He turned to my mother and said, "The missing person just didn't want to be found. Your daughter

has disregarded her feelings for you and has tied herself to this man."
He paused. "Mr...?"

"MacGregor," Gregor growled.

"Gregor MacGregor?" He asked dubiously.

Gregor's chest puffed up slightly. "Aye. All of Scotland knows about
us. The clan of the MacGregors is one not to be trifled with." His brogue
came in a bit stronger than usual.

Detective Sloan smirked, a hint of arrogance playing at the corners
of his lips, and addressed my mother, who oddly hadn't said a word.
"Kids these days get into all sorts of mischief. But they always return
home. Always. Mrs. Stevens, I leave your daughter's fate in your hands.
Do your motherly duty." My mother nodded. I didn't appreciate how
her eyes looked blank or how Detective Sloan told her to be a mother.

He actually commanded her to be a mother. What the hell was that about?

Gregor and I shared a look. The clock was ticking, and the detective
needed to go. The Kyrios rose from the couch and put out his hand for
a handshake. "I'll walk you to the door, Detective." The two men left the
room, leaving me with my quiet mother and flushed best friend.

I tried my best friend first. "Cyn?" I asked carefully. "Say something."

The redhead pouted. "What can I say, Mrs. MacGregor? Apparently,
I can't be trusted."

I rubbed my temples, trying to keep calm. "Cyn, please. Let's not do
this. I cannot lose my cool right now. I didn't come back for this. I came
back to explain—"

"Explain why you left that sorry-assed email, right!" She screamed at
me, tears streaming down her face. "I thought I lost my best friend! I
have every right to lose my cool!"

"Listen, I promise to explain it to you both, but we can't do it here.
We have to get my mom out and in a safe place. Cyn, just stop acting
crazy for a second and listen!"

"I'm crazy? This whole thing is insanity!" Cynthia exclaimed. She
turned to Mom, who still sat unnervingly quiet in her chair. "Right,
Mrs. Stevens?

My mother snapped out of her stupor—her eyes finally focused.

"Yes, Cynthia, it is insane." She rose from her seat and grabbed my arm. "Katya, can I talk to you in your room? Now?" The pressure at my elbow told me there wasn't much room for discussion. I nodded, and we briskly made for my bedroom. As we left the living room, my heart sank when I realized Gregor hadn't returned.

My mother closed the bedroom door, but she didn't immediately face me. With her back turned, she said, "Okay, where have you been really?"

My heart dropped to my toes. "What do you mean, Mom? We just went over—"

She whirled, her eyes widened in anger. "Stop it!" she hissed. "I raised you, Katya Elizabeth Stevens. I know all your tricks. Do you think I don't know when you are lying?"

"Mom," I pleaded, feeling the discomfort grow. "I need you to let this go. Please. There are more important things to discuss, but we can't do it here." Forget the discomfort. A full-blown headache was coming on.

"Tell me now, Katya," her voice dangerously low. "Where have you been? Who have you been with? What have they taught you?"

Been with? Taught me? Alarm bells going off, I said, "Mom, really. Can you stop? We don't have time for this." Irritated, I turned away. But turning my back on her was one of the worst things I could have done. She grabbed me by my shoulders and turned me around, her fingernails digging into my skin. Her grip tightened enough to make me yelp out in pain. But it was her visibly calm face that freaked me out the most. "So, you refuse to tell your own mother what you are up to?"

I shook my head, not trusting my voice. Her eyes studied my face as if memorizing it. I saw a glint in her eye – a red shimmer that made my blood run cold. "Mom?" My voice quavered. Her only response was an eerie grin. A chilling realization washed over me, knotting my stomach. *This isn't my mother. That's a Want creature inside of her.*

"So be it then."

My mother grabbed me by the neck and slammed me into the hard-wood floor. Wood splinters flew everywhere as the force of her blow created a body-sized hole in the middle of my room and robbed me of my breath for the second time that day.

I felt Mika slamming into the bind barriers, reacting to protect me. But the Vis bind held, causing me just as much pain internally as my mother on the outside. My mother's eyes glittered, taking on a familiar red look I had seen before.

"Mom," I managed to gasp. "S-s-stop it!" But her inhuman strength kept me in the crater, forcing me down and closing my breathing pipes.

"I'm afraid I can't do that, Balancer," she said, her voice transforming from its usual tone to a high-pitched, cold laugh. The type of voice you imagined in your worst nightmare. "You have been tied with a Vis bind and sent into my grasp. I'd be a fool not to take full advantage of this."

My survival instincts kicked in immediately, prompting me to kick and squirm, hoping to shake her off. However, it just ended with me being in more pain and the she-devil sounding highly amused. "You are weak! The General was worried for nothing! I never thought I would have the honor of destroying the Balancer. My master will be so pleased. To be rid of the threat to everything we've worked for!"

"Where's my mother?" I hissed, desperately gulping for air.

The she-devil's grin became even more prominent, cutting into my mother's cheeks and distorting her face completely. "Mommy is right here, sweetie. Don't you see her?" It raised my mother's hand, which was growing impossibly long nails, poised to strike me in the chest.

Tears streamed down my face, pooling on the floor. I tried to kick my way out, but "my mother" managed to evade each of my kicks or ignore them altogether. The headache continued to build, and Mika tried to rattle the bars holding her prisoner. With the edges of consciousness slipping, I clung to the last thought before my eyes completely shut.

"Gregor..." I whispered.

You know that pivotal moment where the damsel in distress loses hope that she'll get rescued, but then the dashing hero comes in at the nick of time? It actually happened. The claws on my mother's hand drew dangerously close to my heart. Yet a deafening crash resonated throughout the room just as that deadly point seemed inevitable.

The door shattered, and in its place stood Gregor, his silhouette bathed in an ethereal sapphire glow, his eyes ablaze with unyielding fury. The air around him crackled with palpable energy, causing the room's atmosphere to shift from stifling dread to electrifying tension. At any other time, I would have been panting with unfiltered desire.

When our eyes met, his anger flared even more. "Release her, Poser," he commanded. His voice was deep and resonated with a promise of retribution, each word dripping with authority.

The Poser sneered but didn't move her hand from my neck or drop her raised claws. "I will do no such thing. I will have the glory of terminating the destroyer of our plans."

The air grew heavy, almost stifling, as an invisible storm raged within the room. A sudden force smacked the Poser so fast that it unconsciously released me.

Coughing spasms took over, revitalizing my breath. Mika pressed against the bind, rattling her cage, making me feel even sicker. The screeching wouldn't stop, but Gregor didn't move. He stood unmoving with his hand raised, his eyes now blinding azure stars, staring at the source of the screeching. My mother was pinned to the wall, slithering around, unable to move anything but her head.

"Gregor," I gasped. "Please don't hurt...my mom..."

The Scot glanced at me for a second, still unmoving. "Come out of the body, Poser."

"But of course, Kyrios," the Poser said. But then something changed. The wide grin faded, replaced by an expression of genuine fear and confusion.

"Katya?" My mother's voice trembled, free from the coldness and malice of the Poser. Tears welled in her eyes. "Babygirl, it hurts. Please... help me."

"Mom!" I gasped, my heart hammering in my chest.

Gregor hesitated, his fierce gaze softening. Clearly, he was struggling to discern whether this was indeed my mother speaking or another ruse by the Poser.

The Scot's guard lowered momentarily, his concentration faltering.

Seizing the opportunity, the Poser sneered. "Foolish Kyrios, do you think it would be that easy?"

Gregor growled, his eyes once again taking on their fierce intensity. "Come out of the body, Poser. This is your last warning."

However, the Poser chuckled. "But I just have. Didn't you hear? The mother calls out to her daughter. Perhaps you'd care for another conversation?"

My mother's voice broke through, desperate and filled with pain. "Katya, please, make it stop! It's so dark in here."

Gregor glanced at me, torn between the urgency to act and the desire to protect my mother. "Poser, if you harm her in any way, I promise you'll regret it."

The Poser cackled. "Why would I do that? You wouldn't dare harm this body. To remain here means to remain safe." Whatever force pinning the Poser down must have increased because the screeching became louder.

"Gregor, stop!" I screamed.

"Shut up, Katya! Leave the body, Poser! If I need to destroy the body to be rid of you, I will do it. And you know what happens if you don't leave a dead body. I hope you are prepared to remain there forever."

The Poser gave a loud growl, thinking over its options. No one moved. I fearfully looked between Gregor and my mother's pinned body. *Would he kill my mother?* The Poser suddenly grinned widely, stretching my mother's face beyond what a human could do.

"You win, Kyrios. I'm only the Messager." The Poser closed its eyes, and Mom's body started to convulse. I looked on in horror as I watched my remaining parent go through a series of violent seizures. And I had no idea what to do.

A small creature slowly emerged from her chest. It looked similar to the Cravers that chased me downtown but had a tail three times longer than its body. It had wings just as long as its tail. Its beady eyes stared at me as it rose, its red pupils peering into my Vis bind. Its mouth opened, and a small green sphere shot through the window.

Gregor cursed loudly and raised his free hand. Within seconds, a bright blue light emanated from the center of his palm. Gregor's Havadar emerged from the light, slashing the Poser in half. The Poser's cackling laugh, and its body disintegrated into nothing.

25

Protector and Deceiver

I released a breath I hadn't realized I'd been holding. My mom was still pinned to the wall by the invisible force, but her features returned to normal, her head lolling to the side.

My voice breaking, I asked, "Is my mom okay?"

Gregor released the hold on Mom's body and carried her to my bed. "She's unconscious, but other than that, she's fine. She won't remember the attack."

"Katya! Are you all right?" Cynthia crashed into the rubble of my bedroom. She immediately cradled my face, asking, "Are you hurt?"

I nodded. "I'm okay." A complete lie. *This is not how I planned to explain my otherworldly role in life.* I looked at Gregor, searching for answers, but his eyes never left Cynthia.

Satisfied, Cynthia's eyes narrowed on Gregor. With three steps, she stood before the Kyrios, gave him a once-over, and punched him straight in the face. Gregor's face snapped to the side, and I could only stare.

Wait a second. How did Cynthia do that? Aren't the Kyrios known for their superhuman strength?

Cynthia crossed her arms, her tone icy. "I trusted you to protect my charge, Kyrios. How did you miss a Poser entering here?"

Gregor seemed taken aback. "You've got to be kidding me." He massaged his chin and chuckled darkly. "Your energy is... I can't believe I missed it before." He ruefully smiled, his eyes narrowing. "Are you honestly blaming me? You've been here the entire time. Shouldn't you have been on guard?"

Cynthia's red hair crackled with energy as she swelled with anger. "I had no idea where the two of you had gone! Not one word, not a thing! And when her mother got that email, she called me right away. What was I to do?"

"Oh, maybe reassure her?" Gregor retorted.

She began pacing, a signature Cynthia move. She raked a hand through her hair, gnawing on her bottom lip. "In her hysteria, Mrs. Stevens was taken over by a Wanter, probably lurking around before she came home. You would have known that if you had been looking out for the ones you two left behind!"

Gregor massaged his temples, sending his Havadar back to its secret place. "Who else is aware of your nature? This conversation is incredible."

Cynthia's bravado deflated a bit. "I'm not completely sure. It's only been a few months since I've known, and I'm still piecing things together."

Gregor guffawed, raking through his curls haphazardly. "You've been on my case since I arrived, and she doesn't even know what you are!"

"Charges aren't supposed to know until they are ready! You know that!" Cynthia hissed.

Interrupting, I whispered, "Excuse me." Both fighters turned toward me. "I know that this might be a little much to ask for," I said, with my voice rising, "but could someone kindly tell me what the HELL is going on?" I grimaced, massaging my throat.

I turned to my best friend and hissed, "How the hell do you know what Gregor is? How are you talking about the Want and Posers?" I turned to the Scot. "And Gregor, why are you so surprised by Cynthia? Why should others know about her?"

Mika rattled her cage, causing me to wince and gasp in pain.

Both Gregor and Cynthia turned to me in concern. "Katya," Gregor started, his voice gentle, "you need to calm down."

I shot him a dirty look. "Maybe I'd calm down if I knew what secrets were being kept from me."

Cynthia bit her lip again. "I wish it didn't have to be like this, but we don't have time to chat over chocolate. What I'm gonna say next will sound crazy, but you have to believe me." She sighed and took a hold of my shoulders. "Babes, I'm really your twin in a spiritual sense. I'm your Havadar."

I felt my world tilt. "You're my Havadar? Like the weapon that is supposed to be inside me that I wield on command?"

She nodded.

"You realize how crazy that sounds, right? You are essentially telling me that you are a part of my soul. My own energy."

"It's as wild as you befriending the Grim Reaper and not telling me," she smirked. "Why do you think we've been together all of our lives? Why we have been able to read each other so well?"

I thought back to when our bond began, dating back to when we were five. I tried explaining the Wanters I saw on TV to my parents. They'd gotten agitated and had sent me outside to play.

I was crying on my front steps when this redheaded girl from next door approached me and asked, "Why are you crying?"

"No one believes me."

She sat beside me and smiled such a sweet smile. "I'll believe in you."

That day, I felt I'd be okay if at least one person believed in me. That person, whom I've always considered my sister, was essentially a part of me, living in another body.

I said quietly, "I'm sorry I didn't tell you about Gregor. I was afraid you'd freak out and leave me behind. But why can I talk now?" I glanced at Gregor.

"The moment I was able to sense her energy, which is identical to yours, I removed the restriction," he replied. "No point in hiding anything now."

"Cynthia," I said softly, averting my eyes, "how long have you known about the Want? Why did you keep it from me? Why lie?"

"No, Kat, you don't understand—"

I stood up, deliberately accepting Gregor's hand and ignoring Cynthia's. "After all that I suffered with, the images and the creatures, I pretended, NO, tricked myself into believing people were right and I was wrong. Have you been able to see them the entire time? You could've backed me up!" My eyes watered – I could have brought my parents some peace if Cynthia had just spoken up.

Cynthia already had tears streaming down her face. "Please, Kat, you need to listen to me. I wanted to see what you could see, but I couldn't. I was being honest. I only started to see and feel things on our eighteenth birthday. I began having these odd dreams, and then—"

I never caught the rest of what she said. I couldn't hear or feel anything for a moment except utter dread. Something within me snapped, and it sent Mika into a spiral. All I could sense was unbearable pain, and Mika's screams shook through and out of my mouth. I wanted to die right there. My knees buckled, and I clung to Gregor's clothing for support.

"Katya!" Gregor commanded. "What's wrong? Calm down!"

I screamed hoarsely, clutching my throbbing neck, "The Vis bind!"

Gregor passed his hand over the center of my chest, eyes widening in shock. "The Vis bind is at its limit. I don't understand. It hasn't been three hours yet!"

"You bound her Vis energy?" Cynthia shrieked. "Are you crazy? You are crushing her soul!"

"It was the only way to keep her and everyone here safe," Gregor shouted over my sobs. "Her powers could've brought the—"

A sudden shift was in the air. A wave of different spiritual signatures shook the atmosphere, approaching us. It was nothing but pure bloodlust.

"The Want are coming," Gregor whispered. I wanted to know how they knew we were there, but the Vis bind tightened again, causing me to writhe in pain and scream at the top of my lungs. Pain seared every nerve, every cell. The cold floor beneath me felt inviting, beckoning me to surrender to its numb embrace.

The eerie wail of a Craver echoed in the distance, drawing nearer with every second.

Gregor picked me up and shifted me so I could piggyback. "I've got to get her back to Ager. I can't remove the Vis bind myself."

Cynthia blocked the doorway. "No! You are not retaking my charge. I have to be with her."

"Mom," I whispered. "What about my mom?"

"I'll call for backup," Gregor said quickly. "We need to leave the house now." Two quick taps on his phone and two female Kyrios appeared inside the house.

"Major Gregor, a massive fleet of Wanters are moving here. We must evacuate the Live Realm immediately before we are overrun. They have already destroyed two neighborhoods on the way here."

Gregor shifted me on his back. "Collins, grab the Balancer's mother and take her to the safe house in South America. Put as much distance between here as possible before those Wanters arrive. I'm taking the Balancer and her companion back to Ager." Another cringe-inducing scream filled the air. "Go!" The taller female Kyrios gently but quickly put Mom on her back. She was still out cold but breathing.

My voice was a raspy whisper, the weight of my fear making it barely audible. "Please take care of her."

Collins gave me a small smile. "We will do our best, Balancer." They were gone.

Gregor turned to Cynthia. "Outside now." We bolted out the front door to find people running as fast as they could away from the neighborhood. They continually looked behind them, screaming in fright and running even harder. I saw Amie and her mother shoving their way to escape the terror behind them. People were running everywhere. Homes and belongings left behind.

I wanted to call attention to Gregor, to tell him to save Amie and her mom and get them out of the way. But my vocal chords failed me, and I couldn't utter anything.

The three of us turned around and found the oncoming storm behind everyone's terror. What looked like a tornado blowing through the neighborhoods of Boston was large numbers of Wanters. There were Cravers, Wreckers, and others I didn't recognize. And they literally destroyed everything within sight. It was at the very moment that I saw them when the bracelet given to me by General Lamar gave another zap, causing Mika to explode inside of me. The blast within me was so strong that Gregor and Cyn were thrown ten feet away.

The ground trembled slightly as the entire fleet halted. Their gazes, cold and calculating, turned uniformly towards the source of the explosion. The Cravers were going to be the first to feast.

Every ounce of me yearned to stand, to fight. But each effort was like trying to swim against a relentless current, dragging me deeper into darkness. Astonishingly, with the speed of a Kyrios, Cynthia ran in front of me, facing the Wanters coming head-on.

"Finally," she cried, tears mingling with the sweat on her face, "I get to show you everything we are, our power together." She looked over her shoulder and smiled. "I love you, Kat. Don't be afraid. I'll be there with you."

There was a finality in her voice, a weight in those words that clung to my heart. A goodbye I wasn't ready for. Moments of Cynthia protecting me over the years flash through my mind – always there to wipe my tears and stand before taking on bullies. I could only moan in the heap that I'd become, wordlessly begging her not to leave, not to do anything foolish, to come back. On some level, she understood my anguish; she nodded and returned her attention to the fleet. The first Cravers exploded through my house, destroying the second floor. The flying wood splinters, rubble, and debris should have impaled us, but a bright yellow dome shielded us, sending the shrapnel careening in different directions.

"Get her out of here!" Cynthia cried.

How she did protect us, I wasn't sure. But I could only remember that my best friend glowed with the same azure power I wielded, and the most tremendous yearning to join her swelled within me. I vaguely remember Gregor grabbing me and hoisting me over his shoulder. I remember chalkboard screams and more rubble crashing about as we vaulted into an open portal. Gregor ran through the gates over Ager, shouting commands and calling for General Lamar.

I had only reached the courtyard when laid on the cool Ager ground. Running steps pounded the ground. As someone yelled for supplies, I took hold of Gregor's hand and pointed to my convulsing wrist to show him the cause of my new pain. With one look at the bracelet, he wrenched it off with ease. Lamar's concerned face loomed over me, telling me to hold on. Nabil stood beside him, his eyes narrowing and his jaw twitching, revealing his suppressed frustration.

With the bit of energy I had left, with exhaustion singing a siren song to sink into nothing, I gave them both what I hoped was a smile and said softly, "Told you I'd be fine. Piece of cake."

26

Truths Unveiled in Marble Halls

The gentle echo of a voice roused me from the depths of sleep. "Kat, Katya, time to get up." I slowly opened my eyes to a familiar marble stone floor, soft silk wrapped around my body, and a sense of weightlessness. Somehow, I returned to my soulscape.

"How did I get here?" I whispered.

"I brought you here," Cynthia said from behind me. I turned to find Cynthia standing gracefully behind me, her once-short hair cascading past her waist, and she wore a toga identical to mine. The soulscape's atmosphere added a shimmer around her body that enhanced her ephemeral beauty. A deep, intrinsic sense told me it was right for her to be here like a puzzle piece, finally finding its place.

I swallowed hard, my voice barely above a whisper, "So, it's not just a dream? You really are my Havadar?"

She smirked at me. "Well, yeah! There is no way I could have made up something like that. Besides, who else could deal with you but yourself?"

I let out a breathy chuckle, trying to find humor in the surreal situation. "So, in a strange twist, I've been best friends with... myself?

Talk about narcissism." The fire on the nearby torches danced in an enthralling rhythm as though they were amused by its owner's self-centeredness.

Cynthia giggled. "There are worse things in the world to be. You could be Andrea Pana. That's a nightmare you never want to have." We laughed but sobered up quickly at the thought of what everyone back in the Live Realm was going through. Thoughts of Amie, her mother, and even Roger filled my mind with worry.

Closing the distance between us, Cynthia squatted to meet my gaze. "Kat, know this – I love you. I started getting inklings of who I was just a few months ago. Dreams, where Mika spoke in riddles, began to guide me."

"You've met Mika?"

"Ah yes," she smiled gently. "Mika essentially spoke in riddles but asked me one question: did I either want to begin a new life away from everything, away from danger, or help you and fight? Without a second thought, I picked you."

As Cynthia combed and began braiding my hair, memories of us doing this very thing in our childhood flooded back. "Then I started to have flashes of you even when we were apart. I knew when you were stressed or upset. Or feeling particularly excited about a certain Kyrios," she smirked, causing me to blush. "I couldn't say anything because I knew you would've never believed me. I know you wanted to keep the past in the past. I didn't want to drive you away."

My voice wavered, "We're so much alike. I hid the truth about Gregor, fearing I'd push you away. When did you first sense him?"

"The day we all hung out at your house," She admitted, finishing the plait. "Kyrios have a distinct energy about them. I'd never had a chance to be close to him until that day. I knew something was happening, but you said there was nothing to discuss." Her eyes saddened, remembering. "You didn't realize it then, but your leaving without me weakened our bond as wielder and Havadar. I felt lost without you."

I hesitated, biting the inside of my cheek before venturing, "And what about your parents?" The weight of my unspoken questions hung in the air.

Cynthia released a heavy sigh, which seemed to carry the weight of a thousand unsaid words. She settled next to me, drawing her knees close, seeking comfort. "On the day you were born, my parents had a child in the same hospital—a baby girl who went through a hard delivery. Her lungs weren't completely formed, and for five minutes, her heart stopped."

At my horrified look, Cynthia shook her head. "It was her time. Her life was only a few moments long, but she felt her parents' love. That's all a soul needs to feel complete—love. But, to spare my parents, the family that was to move next door to you, from heartbreak, they were given a child, me. My parents were blessed, and I was blessed to have them."

I frowned, struggling with the whirlwind of emotions. "How is it even possible? To have you, another me, in a separate body?"

"Our soul and Vis are immensely large—three times more than normal human standards. Your young body could never hold everything. To protect you, your soul and Vis were split. Half of it was placed into this body. I formed my own consciousness, but I am still a part of you and your Havadar, and I will come to protect you at your call."

"That night at Nelly's," I began, trying to piece things together. "when Gregor and I disappeared, I could fight in a moment of panic. Was that you?"

Cynthia snickered. "Yes, Nelly's! You called for me without realizing it and responding took its toll. The same thing happened that night you met Gregor. You didn't nearly pull as much energy from me, but I could feel something."

"Then you could see the Want this entire time?

"No. Only you had that ability, especially when we were much younger. Mika said you were starting to attract attention, and a Vis bind was put on you at six years old."

"Who did that? Why? And how did it come off?"

Cynthia shrugged, squeezing my hand. "Mika never said who, just that it was time for the bind to weaken." She paused to consider her own words. "Time for what? I'm not sure. But you gotta think...with everything that has happened..."

I shook my head, not fully believing I was chatting with the other half of my soul. I paused, a pressing question nagging at me, "Please understand, I just need to know... Was our friendship preordained? Did you befriend me because of some cosmic duty?"

Cynthia's eyes darted away momentarily, and she began gnawing on her bottom lip, a telltale sign that she was wrestling with something deep within. "Not exactly. I still have a mind of my own. We've fought before and disagreed on things. I'm my own person." She smiled crookedly. "Just because we share a soul doesn't change that I chose you as my best friend. That I wanted to share experiences. That I am happy that we grew up together. We are truly no different than twins."

A warmth spread behind my eyes, and I fiercely blinked it back. *Now wasn't the time for tears.* Overwhelmed, I whispered, "You've always protected me, haven't you?"

With her eyes shining with unshed tears, Cynthia let out a breath she seemed to have been holding forever, and then she pulled me into an embrace so tight, it was as if she was trying to merge our souls again. "Always. Do you remember that accident in your front yard?"

Cynthia and I had been playing in my front yard one afternoon when Cynthia suddenly wanted to go inside for pudding. At first, I didn't want to go inside, but she refused to go inside without me. I had just run in after her when a truck swerved off the road, slammed on the concrete, and skidded right into the front steps. The truck took out the front yard, the front steps, and a quarter of the front of the house – exactly where we had been playing moments before. Cynthia latched on to me for hours after.

Cynthia faced me directly. "A chill ran down my spine, an instinct I didn't understand back then. Mika explained that I could sense The Want caused that accident ...amongst others.

"What other accidents?"

Cynthia's eyes became impossibly sad. She took both of my hands into hers and expelled a deep breath, dreading the truth she had to share. "Kat, it's about your dad—"

I looked at her, confusion gave way to rising anger. "What about him? Cyn, he's been dead for twelve years. What does he have to do with this?"

"Kat, please just listen for a second." The soulscape shimmered uneasily, sensing my unease and growing agitation. The torches' flames flared, and the potent Vis energy rippled in anticipation of a confrontation.

I shook my head, wrenching my hands for her grasp. "Seriously, stop looking at me like that. My dad has nothing to do with this!" I attempted to walk away, but my Havadar firmly pulled me back and pinned my arms to my sides.

"The Want killed your father, Katya." Years of grief, like a dormant volcano, suddenly erupted within me; it took all my self-control not to react violently.

I shook my head, denial surging. "Cynthia Carr, stop it. This isn't funny. My dad died saving me and his coworker in an accident. That's it."

Cynthia's response was only tears streaming down her cheek.

My balled fist fought off the tears streaming down my own cheek. "Cyn, it was a freak accident. Everyone said so. Mom, the police. It was an ACCIDENT!" I screamed.

Cynthia shook her head again, sobbing, sharing the pain that echoed within the soulscape. Even the bright starred ceiling dimmed with my anguish. "I'm sorry, Kat."

My senses, reacting to my turmoil, grew with energy, and I stepped back, repeating my denial. Tearing myself away, I ran down the hall, driven by the need for answers. The turbulent power spread throughout my body and into my head. Tears streamed freely, accompanied by uncontrollable sobs.

I need to find it. If what Cynthia says is true, I must see it myself.

My senses extended out, seeking the correct memory hiding behind a door. Cynthia's desperate shouts echoed against the marble wall, screaming for me to stop, but I couldn't care less. I was going to prove her wrong. She had no idea what she was talking about. Abruptly, I halted before an unassuming door. From behind it, sounds were stifled as if submerged underwater. They weren't silent, just distant.

The echo of Cynthia's sandals on the marble floor grew closer. "Katya, don't! You can get lost in your memories," she gasped out. Her typically athletic build seemed to sag under the exertion of chasing me.

"Be my Havadar and protect me," I said snidely. "Pull me out,"

Her reproachful eyes caused an annoying pang of guilt. Taking a deep breath, I softened. "Please, Cyn. I need to see this."

Exasperated, she threw up her hands. "Never a dull moment with you! Fine, but only your head. Stick it through the door. I'll hold your waist and pull you back out. Remember, you can only watch. You can't change the past."

I nodded, placing my hands on the doorframe. Cynthia's grip was so firm I could almost feel it physically. She braced herself, preparing.

"Ready?" she asked. I nodded again. "Go ahead."

Inhaling deeply, I thrust my head into the wood, half expecting a collision. But the wood yielded, drawing me in.

My consciousness floated above a scene where a younger me, maybe six years old, joyfully skipped alongside my father. His tall frame, crowned by warm brown eyes full of kindness, made my heart ache. They headed for his car parked outside the after-school daycare I often attended.

During the drive, he remembered forgetting an important file at work. Peeking at the young me through the rearview mirror, he suggested, "How about a trip downtown with Daddy, Kitty-Kat?"

Mini-Me bounced in her seat excitedly. "Yeah! Let's go, Daddy!"

Time with Dad was precious. Our secret trips for candy or ice cream and his playful antics were our moments. My mom always got mad about the secret candy or the ice cream when she found out, but I loved it anyway.

The trip downtown was quick. A red-hued sunset bathed the old structure in warm light as they parked before the historic Franklin building. It stood unique amidst modern skyscrapers, a testament to Boston's rich past. It was also Dad's pride and joy as he had restored it.

With the sunset bleeding red over the old building, everything seemed normal. Inside, Dad swiftly retrieved his file. Lifting Mini-Me onto his shoulders, making her giggle, he proposed, "Kitty Kat, since we are already out, let's say we get some dessert for dinner tonight? What would you like?"

Feigning thoughtfulness, I answered, "Ice cream! Chocolate ice cream!"

Laughing, Dad carried me down the hall. As we exited, he bumped into Matt, his coworker. Setting me down, they conversed briefly.

Above, an unsettling sensation caught my attention. Something was flying over our heads. I looked up and held in the scream I wanted to release. Three Wanters, resembling small skeletal-winged Wreckers, swooped into the building. One remained perched on the top of the building, staring at the three of us, releasing a chilling screech.

Mini-Me sensed everything I did. She looked up at my father, hoping that he would feel that there was trouble. But he was none the wiser.

Unwittingly, Mini-Me's fear amplified her energy output, drawing the remaining Wanter's attention. The energy flare was not particularly strong but more intense than any other human could emit. Knowing that absorbing my energy would give it more power, it gave a deafening screech and released a bright orb from its mouth, just like the Poser had in my bedroom. It was calling for backup. Held in place by Dad's grip, panic consumed Mini-Me.

I knew the impending doom this orb signaled. I wanted to shout a warning but was powerless, trapped in the observer's role. I no longer need to be in this memory, but I stayed, reliving the most profound horror life can offer.

Less than half a mile away at the intersection, a car suddenly turned sharply, cutting off traffic, and drove onto the sidewalk. Screams of panic rose as pedestrians ran for cover between cars, sprinting into buildings or angling between the skyscrapers around them. Less lucky people were clipped, hit, or dusted aside by the accelerating vehicle.

Dad spotted the danger first. With adrenaline-fueled strength, he pushed Mini-Me and Matt towards the building entrance's alcove, yelling, "Get out of the way!" But he wasn't as fortunate. The speeding car slammed his left side, breaking his hip. The momentum sent him reeling onto the car's windshield, shattering it into pieces and launching his body over its hood. He crashed into the concrete below on the top of his head.

The car would continue for at least half a mile before crashing into a newspaper stand. Later, we would find out that the driver had claimed that he heard voices demanding that he drive on the sidewalk. He was also a horrible drunk.

It all happened within three minutes.

Stunned at the sudden push, my six-year-old self cringed at the scratches on her elbow and knee. When she noticed that only Matt sat beside her, she yelled, "Dad? Daddy? Where are you?" Sirens could be heard in the distance, and other hurt pedestrians crying for help. But nothing from Dad. Mini-Me eventually found him several feet away, but Matt's protective hold thwarted her attempts to reach him.

A flurry of small Want creatures flew down from the top of the building, thoroughly distracted now by the carnage. It would be the last time Mini-Me would see a Wanter for many years.

I understood why the door was muted. If painful memories remained as loud as the joyful ones, there was no way we could possibly move on. As I watched Mini-Me release sorrowful screams, I was tempted to stay and cry with her. To not leave my father alone. To acknowledge the pain that I had been burying for so long. But Cynthia's insistent tugs pulled me back, and I reluctantly exited.

She looked relieved but had gone unusually pale. "Thank goodness you're all right."

I said nothing as I slid down the wall, bringing my knees in. Tears clouded my vision as realization hit. "Because of me...Dad...". The wave of grief I had hidden for years surged over the dam I had created, and I was drowning. I sobbed and wailed at the injustice, the loss, and the rage I felt. Those creatures stole from my father from me. I grew up without my father because of their inability to move on. Cynthia remained by my side and held me, her body shuddering now and then from what I assumed was shared grief.

When my tears finally dried up, Cynthia's hand smoothed my hair. "Your dad was a hero. His love for you gave him the strength to go against his sense of self-preservation to save you." She pulled me to my feet into a tight hug. "Your dad's sacrifice allowed you to be here and now, to claim your destiny. We have work to do to save the others out there. Amie, our friends from school...even those assholes Roger and Pana."

I chuckled under my tears.

Cynthia offered a weary smile. "But you have a choice. No matter what they say to you. Whatever you decide, I am with you." Cynthia's knees suddenly gave out, sending her to the ground.

"Cyn, what's wrong?" Her skin had gone from pale to transparent, like losing her form in the soulscape.

She grimaced. "I've weakened myself quite a bit here. I don't have much time."

"Time?"

"We need to make this quick. Kat, are you sure about the Kyrios?"

"What?"

Cynthia's body suddenly flickered like a dimming light bulb. She gasped in pain, "Are you sure about them? Do you trust them?"

I hesitated but said, "I believe I can trust Gregor. I do care for him and think he also cares for me. You saw him out there today. I trust him, with my life if I have to.

Despite her condition, her gaze searched mine, finding resolve. "Let's hope your faith in them is not in vain. I need you to say aloud, 'I need you by my side, my protector, my Havadar Diantha.' Say it quickly!"

I grasped her opaque hand tightly. "I need you by my side, my protector, my Havadar Diantha."

A giant white glowing orb left her chest and soared into mine. Every bit of me felt electrified, which I thought was impossible in my soulscape. She shuddered, her body becoming more and more insubstantial. "I gave you some of your soul and Vis back so you can fight," she smiled feebly. "It's not everything—it's not time yet." Cynthia gave another weak whimper. "Tell no one I am your Havadar – Gregor's orders. I'm sending you back. Just remember—be strong, sis."

"Cyn, wait—" Her palm caught me in the middle of my chest, emptying my lungs of air and sending me out of the soulscape.

27

The Balance of Desires

When I opened my eyes, I was surrounded by silk sheets and pillows, an abundance of Vis energy in the air, and a warm hand enveloping my own. Beside me, Gregor had dozed off. *The attack had taken its toll on him as well.* His serene face, framed by unruly dark curls, starkly contrasted with the intense warrior I'd come to know. It tugged at my heart to see the Kyrios, so often the epitome of strength, vulnerable and unreserved in sleep.

I closed my eyes, sinking into myself, ensuring all was well.

I'm here.

My mind swirled with the information I'd learned about my father and the dire state of my home. I sighed internally. What *happens now?*

Mika's gentle presence brushed against my mind. **That is entirely up to you. You know that.**

Well, a little bit of guidance wouldn't hurt, you know! I mentally retorted, rolling my eyes. Sighing outwardly, I opened my eyes to Gregor, staring intently back at me. Not a word was said. But his stormy blue eyes were a symphony of regret, misery, concern, and longing.

My voice trembled as I tried to find words. "What—" Before I could form a coherent thought, he surged forward, clamoring onto the bed and pulling me into a desperate, all-consuming kiss. His hand cradled

225

the back of my head, urging me closer. My pulse roared as our tongues tangled urgently. The sweep of his tongue and the firm pressure of his lips warmed me to the tips of my toes and placed the same symphony within my heart. When breathing became an issue, he released me, keeping little distance between us.

"I almost lost you," he said against my lips.

"Just a typical Tuesday afternoon," I said with a smile.

His soft and genuine laughter was my only reply before his lips met mine again, cajoling and coaxing out of me whimpers and sighs. My hands trailed down his chest, marveling at the firm muscle beneath his shirt. I arched into him instinctively, heat pooling low in my belly. Gregor's deep groan reverberated through me. My skin flushed, and my nipples tightened almost painfully. Sensing my desire, his eyes flashed wickedly as he withdrew.

"Ms. Stevens," he smirked, "Shouldn't you be taking this slow? You just woke up."

Take it slow. His words brought back our self-imposed boundaries. "Oh God, I'm sorry. I lost my head there, and I couldn't help-"

Gregor's hand caressed my cheek, his thumb stroking my lips. "No, Katya. It's not just you. I've wanted this too, and I'm tired of fighting it." He massaged my hands, his solemn gaze melting my reservations. "I've been trying to abide by the rules, the threats about having close ties to humans. But seeing you suffer, seeing you near Vis depletion, destroyed me more than any threat of harm ever could." He settled my hands against his chest, notably against the very low thrum of his heartbeat. "I cannot continue to fight what I feel and be next to you, knowing our time together could be very short."

He closed the distance between our lips, grazing softly and whispering, "*Mo chridhe, mo chorp, agus m'anam tha iad uile agad fhèin.*"

Something within me leaped in pleasure hearing his foreign tongue. "What does that mean?" I whispered back.

"My heart, body, and soul are all yours."

At that moment, even though I still had my reservations and wanted to keep him safe from the Generals or any power from hurting him,

I threw it aside to climb into his lap and pour all my unsaid feelings into him. *Every fiber of my being, every leap of my soul, wants you.* Gregor tightly embraced me, his hand sinking deep in my hair, massaging my neck, gripping my hips to rock against his own. For several glorious moments, everything melted away except for our desire for each other. My body throbbed as his hands roamed possessively. With a pained groan, Gregor gently broke our connection. Gasping for air, I emerged, not allowing him to pull back away from me.

"We have to be careful, right?" I murmured. "I don't want to lose you to them."

Gregor concurred, smoothing my disheveled hair behind my ear. "These moments will need to be behind closed doors."

His brilliant smile took my breath away. "Be sure to keep your hands to yourself in public."

I smacked his chest, chuckling, and melted into his embrace, feeling the warmth and protection only the Kyrios could offer. As I nestled into him, I saw a glinting silver on the nightstand – the remnants of my security bracelet. Memories flooded back, the moment's joy replaced by the grim reality. I pulled back slightly, the weight of unanswered questions pressing down on me. "Gregor," I began, my voice hesitant, "What happened back there?"

The shift in his demeanor was palpable. He reluctantly pulled back, sat me on the bed, and returned to his abandoned chair. "Your soul was in grave danger when we reached the gate. General Lamar almost didn't make it in time to take it off. You've been out of it for about two days here in Ager, about a week or so in the Live Realm."

"That long?" Concern gripped me, and I started to get out of bed, to only have Gregor hold me back by my shoulders. "What about my mom or Cynthia? Cynthia said she was weakened?"

His eyebrows furrowed. "How did you know that?"

I explained everything, including my trip down memory lane. I could feel him changing from the concerned kisser to the dutiful Major of the Kyrios.

"So the Want killed your father." He shook his head. "It's not your fault. The Want have caused destruction even before you were born," he said fiercely. Gregor then shifted in his seat and glanced down at the floor. "Their destruction has touched everyone."

I returned to my original question. "What happened to my mother?"

He looked at me carefully and propped himself on his knees. "Your mother is safe. Collins took her down to Buenos Aires. There hasn't been the same intensity of destruction there yet, so we thought it would be best to keep her there for the time being. General Nabil was concerned that she would become another target."

"How is mom taking it?"

"She's been told that she's in protective custody in response to the terrorist attack in your neighborhood and throughout Boston. She demanded to see you, but we assured her you were safe and at another location."

"And my home?" I winced, already knowing the answer.

He grimaced, "Your home has been essentially destroyed."

I gnawed my bottom lip to keep from crying. My safe haven, the one place in the Live Realm that I could escape to, went within an instant. Gritting my teeth, I hissed, "Just another thing the Want have stolen from me."

I pulled the sheets off and attempted to get out of bed. Gregor intercepted me a second time. "Where do you think you are going?"

I tried to shrug him off. "I want to find Cynthia. She said she was nearby. By the way, she told me of your plan to not tell anyone about her being my Havadar."

Gregor's eyebrow furrowed, and his shoulders went rigid, "Katya, about—"

"Look, whatever debriefing you are about to do can wait." I tried to push past him, but the Kyrios grabbed me by my waist in an unforgiving grip. I tried to push him away, but he wouldn't budge.

"What's wrong with you," I huffed, smacking his chest. "I need to find Cynthia!"

His large body had initially blocked my view of the rest of my room. But in our struggle, my gaze shifted past his shoulder to another bed by my window. A still figure with auburn hair, lay there. Panic gripped me. Going entirely still, I asked, "Gregor, who's that?"

His shoulders sagged in defeat. His blue eyes sought mine, begging me to stay calm. "Katya—"

"Who is that?" I shouted. He allowed me to push past him to see a battered Cynthia looking close to dead. Cuts and bruises covered her once-lovely face, making it almost unidentifiable. Her once-long red hair was singed and uneven. Her skin was deathly pale and looked impossibly cold. I tried to reach for her but was stopped by a shield that covered her entirely. Every shared laugh and secret between us flashed in my mind, making the present sight of her even more heart-breaking. The beautiful soul Cynthia was, and here she lay because of me. Reduced to something unrecognizable because of me.

"Please, Gregor," I begged, unable to see through my tears. "Don't let this be real." Ever since our escape, our bond had deepened and grown more intense. The world was collapsing around me; somehow, he had become my anchor.

Before my legs could give out underneath me, Gregor tucked his arm underneath my knees and held me close to his chest. He carried me back to my bed, the dim light casting shadows on the walls, emphasizing our solitude and the moment's weight. I felt the weight of his concern as his hand rubbed at my back. "Why does it always have to be those I care about?" I whispered. Gregor's tenderness was different, his touch familiar but also unsettling. Our growing bond felt inappropriate, but it was undeniable, given Cynthia's state.

"Katya," he whispered, the urgency evident, "Cynthia's still with us. She's alive, but..."

I looked up, desperate hope flickering in my eyes. "How?"

He frowned. "Her spirit's nearly depleted. During our escape, she must've confronted something... enormous. That fleet—it did unimaginable damage. It took out your house, neighborhood, and three others nearby. She'll recover, but it's hard to tell how long it will take."

"What does Cynthia need?"

"Her Vis is dangerously low as if it almost vanished." I thought of the orb that had left her and went into my chest. *You stupid girl.* "We're force-feeding her energy through that field to keep her consciousness here, but there's something...off."

"What do you mean?"

"Despite the energy we've given her during your recovery, she's stuck in a state like a coma. There's no improvement."

I asked quietly, "Is it because she came into my soulscape?"

"It wouldn't have been easy for her," Gregor said, still stroking my back, "but I think there's something more at play."

"Foul play?" I whispered. I almost hesitated in saying my following words, but I meant what I said to Cynthia—I did trust Gregor with my life, and nothing so far from his actions proved me wrong.

"Gregor, that security bracelet...that was the second time it made me lose control."

Gregor's face darkened, his gaze momentarily shifting to the bracelet. He seemed to battle with his thoughts, choosing his words carefully before he replied. "I know. I asked General Lamar about that. He was puzzled about the malfunction as well. He said that their security team had checked over the bracelet before they gave it to him. He said he would investigate whether anything was happening with their team and others."

"What do you think is going on?"

He turned me to look at me directly, wiping my tears away. "I hate to think that one of our own Kyrios is working against us, but that fleet knew where you and Cynthia were. Something is siphoning her energy away, and we can't determine who is doing it or how they are doing it."

His jaw clenched, and he turned away from me. "Cynthia should have never had to deal with that fleet. It's my fault,"

My heart softened at the grief-stricken look on the Scot's face. I gently touched his shoulder. "What do you mean it's your fault? You had nothing to do with this. Those underworld bastards did this."

"I should've destroyed that message sphere the Poser sent out." He palmed his face. "But I was more concerned about keeping your mother safe."

I remembered Cynthia's intense question about the Kyrios and wondered if she knew something. I looked back at her comatose body. I eased my head into the crook of Gregor's neck, letting the dust of the past few days settle. I knew I had to stop being timid about my role here. The longer I faltered, the more that people around me were hurt.

"Gregor?" I said quietly. His hand stilled, acknowledging he'd heard me. "Do you think I can do this? Be this savior of the Live Realm?"

He wordlessly caressed my tear-stained face, bringing me to a calm peace. "Katya, your best friend risked her soul for her belief in you. You've witnessed the depths of humanity's beauty and cruelty. We need your vision now. And I have no doubt about your capabilities." He smiled softly. "You can end it all. But it's up to you." He released my face for my shoulders. "What do you choose?"

The question of the hour. I closed my eyes, reviewing everything that had happened so far.

"What if..." I started. "What if I just wanted out? What if I can't handle all this?" I locked in on my favorite set of blue-grey eyes. "

His eyes reflected a bit of shock and pain for a moment, but he quickly concealed it by releasing me, setting me on my feet, and standing back. "If that were your honest wish, I'd request that you be released. The Generals, while upset, wouldn't want to keep a soldier here who didn't want to fight. But you couldn't return to the Live Realm as you are now. We'd have to find a measure to make your Vis less threatening and attractive to the Want...but perhaps you could return to normal."

Normal. Something I've always wanted. I stared at the floor, already knowing my answer, but I had to ask one more question. "Do you want me to stay? To take my place as the Balancer?"

"My answer shouldn't influence you."

I crossed my arms over my chest. "I already have my answer. Whatever you have to say won't change it."

Refusing to look at me, he said, "In my opinion, as Major—"

I shook my head, closing the space between us, grabbing his chin to force his eyes to meet mine. "No, you don't get to do that. I don't want the Major. I want Gregor to answer my question."

Gregor studied my face, spending a few moments at my lips, sending tingles down my spine.

"I don't want you to fight," he said quietly.

I swallowed down my disappointment.

I nodded and made to move past him when he grabbed my wrist. "You didn't let me finish."

Sighing deeply, I turned back to him, giving my full attention. He let go, running a hand through his already-tousled hair. I felt he had done that same movement countless times since we'd returned to Ager. "I don't want you anywhere near the fight, the violence, or the ugliness of this war. Every fiber of my being screams to shield you from it all. War is vicious, Katya, and I don't want it to change you. I want you to stay just the way you are."

He picked back up my hand and intertwined our fingers. "Sweet, innocent, caring, feisty, and clumsy." He chuckled when I hit him on the arm. "I don't want you to fight. But I want you to stay here with me, against my better judgment, against all the Kyrios protocols, even against my deepest wish to keep you out of harm's way."

Tears threatened, and I only wanted to forget for a moment. To find solace. And without thinking, my arms curled around his neck, and on the tips of my toes, my lips greeted his. With equal fervor, his hands clutched the small of my back, pressing me closer. But even in the safety of his embrace, the weight of responsibility lay heavy on my heart. *I think enjoying the here and now is the best solution for us. But I need to do my part to eliminate the bastards in the Live Realm.* With one last perfunctory kiss, I sighed happily, "Bye, Gregor," and started for the door.

"Katya?" he said, confused.

I stopped at the door and said, "Or do you want to come with me? No, actually, I need you to come with me."

"What do you mean?"

Determined, I gave him a fiery smile. "I can't get up Central Tower by myself! Someone has to tell the Generals that the Balancer is ready to do some intensive training."

28

Revenge's Seduction

Gregor's smile revealed his relief at my decision. However, he insisted I stay in bed and promised to bring the Generals to me.

As I lay in bed, watching Cynthia flicker occasionally, I thought about our time together in the soulscape. A slow-burning rage smoldered within me, fed by every memory, every wound the Want had inflicted. My parents, both victims of the Want, and my best friend in a coma — all because of a power I hadn't yet harnessed. That had to change, and soon.

A knock at the door anchored me back to reality. "Come in!"

Jae hesitated for a split second before pushing the door open. His eyes lit up like Christmas morning when he spotted me among the pillows. "Ms. Katya! You're all right! You gave us such a scare."

"I'm sorry for causing you worry."

He shook his head earnestly, striding forward. "Please don't be. You couldn't have helped it even if you wanted to." He took Gregor's seat. "Major Gregor asked me to watch over you. How are you feeling now?"

"I've made up my mind, Jae." I looked at him closely. "Can I ask you a question?"

"Of course," he said with an easy smile.

I took a moment to adjust myself in my bed and sat directly in front of him, debating how much I wanted to tell him. "How does one train with their Havadar?"

His eyebrows quirked up. "You found your Havadar?"

I nodded, resisting the impulse to say anything else.

Jae grinned, "That's fantastic news. I assume that's why the Generals are coming."

"What kind of training should I expect when working with my Havadar? I want to understand what I'm in for before I tell the Generals anything. I would've asked Gregor, but he's not excited about me fighting."

"No, I suppose he wouldn't be," Jae said quietly, gauging my reaction.

I blinked. "Why do you say that?"

Jae sat back in his chair and shrugged. "Major Gregor has a reputation of being particularly hard on female Kyrios because he doesn't want to fight them. That is, everyone but Sophia."

I could feel my gut tighten with a familiar hot feeling. "Sophia?" *That blond Kyrios that gave me a dirty look?*

"She's a Lieutenant from the Southern European squad, exceptional with the sword. Gregor enjoys spending time with her. There were rumors that they were together, but that could be baseless gossip." At the sick look on my face, Jae asked, concerned, "Are you getting tired?"

I smiled weakly. "No, just a slight dizzy spell. It will pass." *Maybe my dream about them was a vision?* Clearing my throat, I asked, "How are your skills, Jae?"

He propped himself on his knees. "I'd like to think of myself as exceptional with my sword." With his palm up, a sword appeared in his grip. The very thin blade was pure silver from tip to grip.

"It's beautiful."

He grinned. "Thank you. This is Slumber. His name coincides with my ability to put humans to sleep. We sometimes take passing souls through their dreams while they sleep."

I massaged my chin, thinking. "Can you send messages in a normal human's dream?" It's funny how I didn't fit in that category anymore—I was becoming increasingly comfortable with that fact.

He shrugged. "Yes, but why would you need to do that? The only other time we go into a human's dreams is to wipe out the memory of a Poser invasion."

The thought of the Poser's assault on my mother made my heart ache for her. I took hold of Jae's hands and looked at him earnestly. "I want to talk to my mother and let her know I'm okay. I didn't know that visiting her in her dreams was an option, but I'd like to use it if it is. Going to the Live Realm now is out of the question."

Jae chuckled. "More than you realize. But I think we might be able to do something. Let me ask for General Lamar's permission. As security, he'll have to give clearance."

I nodded. *It's better to have Lamar decide than Nabil.* Loud steps could be heard from downstairs, marking the Generals' arrival.

Jae quickly stood up. "I must go. I do my best to convince General Lamar of your wish."

"Thank you, Jae."

His eyes became unreadable, but he said, "Just remember, help sometimes comes from the most unexpected places." And with that, he was behind the door.

I didn't have a chance to think about what Jae said before I heard voices approaching. Gregor stepped in with General Lamar and Nabil in tow. Lamar looked pleased to see my progress. Nabil just looked guarded and a bit sour. He said with a sweeping and mocking bow, "Lady Katya, it's good to see you up and about. You had us quite worried."

I rolled my eyes—something about him just annoyed me. "So I've heard." I rose from my bed, not wishing to look sick in front of them, let alone Nabil. "Generals, after receiving some new information, I've decided to make a slight change."

Lamar's eyebrow arched, "Which is?"

Nabil stepped forward, silencing my answer. "Before you answer, Lady Katya, you might want to know about the new developments in the Live Realm." He nodded to Gregor, who, with some reluctance, conjured a small green glowing sphere with his Vis. The sphere pulsed with light.

Curious, I stepped forward. "What is it?"

Gregor cleared his throat, shifting his weight. "This is our version of a message sphere, like the Poser's sphere you saw before. It can record messages from anything and be sent to whomever we wish. Well, those who have Vis energy." Dread seeped out from him. "The Generals had several news stations recorded from your area."

"Why do I need to see Boston news?"

"It's not just Boston news. It's news from around the United States."

He waved his hand over the sphere that projected a small image of an anchorman on a news telecast. "Small tremors for the second week in a row. These quakes are not yet life-threatening, but scientists are baffled as to why New York City would have any tremors. As far as scientists can tell, there is no reason for these small quakes whatsoever, but research is ongoing—"

A new image of an anchorman with a Southern accent appeared, her smile brittle. "We're five days into a record-breaking heat wave, and there's no sign of reprieve for the people below the Mason-Dixie line. Remember to stay cool and keep out of the midday sun. Four people have died this week, and authorities expect several more among the most vulnerable population due to heat stroke and other heat-related illness."

The screen shifted, and a new pair of anchors appeared, their expressions grave. "John," the woman stated. "It seems that Southern California might experience its first tsunami. Tell us more about this impending threat."

The man nodded. "That's right, Heather. Due to the earthquake that struck Japan last night, high waves are approaching the West Coast. Scientists believe that the waves will diminish before reaching the coast, but officials have evacuation plans ready just in case—"

The sphere went dark. For a brief moment, silence ruled the room. The weight of what we had seen settled over us, giving me time to reflect on the challenges ahead.

"Similar reports are coming from all corners of the world," Gregor said quietly.

A knot grew in the pit of my stomach. "What's going on? What's happening?"

Gregor reduced the sphere back into invisible Vis. "We were right when we thought the Want were up to something. All of the tremors and heat are clear indications that their efforts are intensifying. We think it could be because you've been named the Balancer."

His jaw was clenched tight, accentuating the muscles along his neck. "Our intelligence is still trying to determine their plans and the reason behind these gate openings. Our original plan for Los Angeles is now more important—that portal has grown a few inches bigger."

I crossed my arms, feeling overwhelmed. "Does that mean we need to go now?"

Gregor shook his head. "Not yet. It's still not big enough for a level-three Wrecker, but it causes some harm. If they are planning a major attack on the Live Realm, they will try to get their heaviest hitters out that gate." His brows were furrowed, forehead lined with worry. "We must find a way to close that gate and frustrate their efforts."

Before I could respond, Nabil interjected, his voice dripping with challenge. "This is what you're up against, Lady Katya. The stakes are high. If you have doubts, voice them now."

He's trying to get rid of me, isn't he? A newfound resolve surged within me. The scale of the problem was immense, but backing down wasn't an option. If God supposedly gave me this gift, no one in existence would stop me.

I narrowed my eyes at the Head General and said clearly, "I've decided to stay and continue my training here to take my place as the Balancer." Their reactions were predictable. Lamar with a smile. Nabil with a curt nod, though there was a slight jerk of his head. As if his attention wasn't wholly on me.

"I'll alert the other Generals of the good news," Nabil said quietly. He turned for the door when I called him back.

"General, I do have a request."

"There always is one, isn't there, my lady?" Nabil asked, rolling his eyes.

"I want to begin training with my Havadar immediately. I'm prepared to fight." Both Generals looked at each other, silently communicating.

Nabil's eyebrows arched. "The point of the mission was to collect your Havadar—your sacred weapon—and keep it from the Want. We never believed you'd wish to wield it in battle. You spoke only of closing the gates. What's brought about this sudden shift?"

"Why does it matter? I'm now capable of fighting at full strength."

"It matters entirely. Why?"

I clenched my fists so tightly that my nails dug into my palms. "The Want are more than nuisances; they're vermin. They've taken everything from me." I answered, my voice shaky. "And now? I'm ready to take everything from them. I intend to eradicate anything remotely Want from every realm."

I stepped forward, close enough for Nabil to feel my breath, my eyes burning with determination and hatred. "If the Want are itching for a fight, fine! The sooner, the better, so I can return to my life. That explanation good enough for you?"

The three men stared at me with mixed reactions. Lamar looked genuinely pleased and broadly smiled, but Nabil and Gregor looked troubled. Lamar stepped forward and palmed my shoulders. "I think training with your Havadar is a fantastic idea. I'll see to your training at once, Balancer. I must say, your Vis is deliciously surging."

I smirked and looked at the enthusiastic General. "I'm ready to start. Thank you, General." He lingered at my shoulders before releasing me.

Nabil cleared his throat and stepped between Lamar and me. "I will allow you to commence your Havadar training. However, I'll provide you with a full protection guard."

Lamar narrowed his eyes. "Is that necessary?"

Nabil's eyebrows arched smugly. "Of course. Havadar training can be quite difficult. Uncontrolled discharges of energy can become a liability. I shall pick some men to be part of Lady Katya's entourage."

Lamar and Nabil locked eyes silently. A war of wills was occurring, and I wasn't sure why. Lamar relented and returned to me with an easy smile. "I will depart now, my lady." With a quick bow, he was gone.

Nabil remained, his arms now locked behind his back. "My lady, this was not the road I intended for you," he murmured. "The Kyrios force is supposed to fight and protect you as you did your part in closing the gates. I will ask you again: are you sure you want this?"

I gritted my teeth, holding back the curses I wanted to throw at him. "General, "I want to defend myself and help rid the world of these monsters. This last trip outside into the Live Realm has just shown me how much I need to learn so I can do my part. That includes fighting and using my power to its fullest."

Nabil smirked. "Oh yes. However, I don't believe this was God's original intention in creating you." He inched closer. "I will do as you ask, Balancer. However, let me state this. You must listen to every command given to you while in Ager—no questions asked. No arguments, is that understood?" He looked me down, assessing me. "We all need to be careful, or you might find yourself in grave danger, splitting yourself from your Vis forever," he said softly.

A chill swept up and down my back. Nabil studied me once more before nodding. He turned to Gregor, who was observing our exchange. "Gregor," he barked, "come to Central Command shortly to discuss the new detail." Gregor saluted, and the Head General exited. Gregor closed the door and gave me a suspicious look.

"What was that about?"

"That's what I want to know."

"Katya, why are you talking like this? When we talked about you fighting, I thought you meant closing the gates, not blazing into battle with your Havadar in hand."

I huffed, sitting back on the bed. I was starting to feel dizzy. "Gregor, it's not really up to you."

Gregor followed me towards the bed and sat back in his chair. "Your welfare is my concern. My job is to keep you safe. Havadar training is one thing; I get you want to protect yourself. But to fight against the Want is completely different. Your role here is just to close the open gates."

Angrily, I stalked over to my window, staring at Cynthia's prone body. "Don't you get it? The Want have been the destructive force for my entire life. People have called me crazy since I was a child."

I turned to look at him, my tears be damned, "You know why I have a weird relationship with God? My overzealous religious grandparents thought I was possessed. They used to keep me locked up in their prayer room—which was a closet—for hours, trying to pray the demons out of me. I would cry and beg to be let out, and they would just thump me with their bibles." I wrapped my arms tightly around me.

Gregor leaned forward, his eyebrows knit in confusion, urging me to continue. I took a deep breath, trying to steady myself, but the weight of the past pressed on me.

"I couldn't sleep whenever my grandparents visited because I was petrified that they would take me from my room and lock me into the prayer room again. All because of the Want. I've changed schools because other parents didn't want their children to play with me."

Gregor looked taken aback, his eyes filled with pity and anger. "I... I had no idea, Katya."

I gripped my elbows, trying to keep the memories from overwhelming me. "All of this happened because those pathetic dead souls simply can't let go of what they can never have. How many more have to suffer?" I looked back at the Scot, who looked stonily back at me. "The world will be better off if I can figure out how to eliminate all Wanters. Every type, every size, whatever."

His jaw tightened. "Seeking revenge is a treacherous path, Katya. You can't fathom the toll it takes on one's soul."

I rolled my eyes. "Before you start your 'good' angel mambo—"

"I am NOT an angel," he snapped. My eyes widened at his outburst. Catching himself, Gregor stepped back, his back straight and shoulders tensed. "You know what, fine. You'll get your wish." He stalked toward the door and reached for the knob but turned back to me. "Just remember, your title is the Balancer, not the Destroyer. We already have one—his name is Drachen."

29

Power's Edge

Gregor didn't return for the rest of the day. As the sun set, hiding behind the brilliant white towers of Ager, a random Kyrios came in wordlessly and brought my dinner. I refused to ask where Gregor was. Fuming, I decided to take the night luxuriating in the tub, conditioning my hair, braiding it down, and preparing for my training.

This war between the Want and humans had started many lifetimes ago, and it felt like my family was suffering casualties for no reason. A war just because God liked us better and the Want is jealous of the life they can't have anymore? My nails dug a bit too deep into my scalp. *I'll destroy anything that even remotely resembles the Want. No mercy, right, Mika?*

My answer was dead silence. *Mika?*

If you haven't noticed, these are the moments where I let you decide for yourself.

What are you talking about? I have already decided.

Again, silence. *Great, first Gregor, now you. Whatever, you two will come around. I'm finally embracing the true potential of my role now.*

Still silence.

Before you give me the complete silent treatment, tell me what's going on with Cynthia? Is she okay?

Your Kyrios was right. She was under attack and could not sustain

her body's full functionality. **Something was trying to siphon her remaining energy. But before the attack could take all of your shared Vis energy, she gave back some of it to you. Diantha has been returned to her wielder.**

I swallowed. *You mean Cynthia is inside of me?*

For now, she has returned home. She cannot speak to you now, but you can wield her once you have mastered your heart.

What does that mean?

Again, silence. For an inner Vis guide, Mika had a lot of attitude.

* * *

The following day, a soft knock awoke me. "My lady?"

Jae's voice filtered through the mahogany door. "Your presence is requested in the training sphere. I'm here to escort you." Within minutes, I was ready, the brisk morning routine of washing up and changing done, and we made our way to the training dome. As I smoothed down my edges, I noticed the vast silence around us. The massive courtyard was usually brimming with souls conducting training or exiting Ager from its many gates to enter the Live Realm. Not a Kyrios in sight.

"Hey, what happened to everyone?"

Jae's shoulders tightened. "Squads are running drills in their respective barracks. It makes traveling around here all the better, right? Nobody to run into."

I frowned. "Running into anyone was never an issue before. Was the courtyard cleared because of me?"

He chuckled awkwardly but took a firm hold of my elbow, ignoring my question. "We'll be late. Come on." We entered the training dome, still devoid of weapons within its semi-translucent sphere, to find several people awaiting our arrival. I recognized Nabil and the pouting Gregor but hadn't had the pleasure of meeting the other four people. Each one radiated a breathtaking allure, their statuesque figures and mesmerizing features quintessential of the Kyrios.

"Lady Katya," Nabil nodded. "Nice to see you up and about. Let's hope there aren't any more accidents."

I bit back the snide retort on my tongue and declared, "Reporting for training, General."

"General Raf is currently dealing with the open gate situation in the Live Realm, so I have asked Gregor to take over your lessons. As for these people, they are now part of your own team – The Quad. An elite crew handpicked by me to fight beside you and protect you."

All four, two men and two women, took a knee and said in one voice, "At your service, Lady Katya."

Feeling slightly intimidated, I managed a quiet "Good morning."

Nabil adjusted his long black coat and closed it around his broad chest. "I shall leave you to the training. Gregor, as we discussed." As he turned, he beckoned to the tallest of the Quad. "Demetrius, a moment." I wanted to try to read their lips, but Jae's sudden whisper pulled my focus.

"Miss Katya," he began, lowering his voice. "I've spoken to General Lamar about your dream request." He glanced around before continuing, "He thinks he can work something out. I'll fetch you later." He paused, his gaze searching mine, "But don't mention it to anyone. It's a bit... unauthorized."

I peeked at Gregor standing to the side, speaking to the other three in the Quad. "I'll pretend I know nothing."

Jae gave me a wink before exiting. The Quad stood by Gregor, looking expectantly at me.

The shortest of them stepped forward with a cheeky smile and olive skin. Her dark, curly hair bounced with each confident step. "I am Zenobia, my lady," she said with a wink. "I am overjoyed that we have the privilege of protecting you."

The tallest guard, who had spoken with Nabil, ran a hand through his jet-black hair, fixing me with an intense, calculating gaze before bowing slightly. "I'm Demetrius, my lady."

The next male guard, with hair so blonde it was almost ethereal, paused and met my gaze before kneeling with a flourish, grinning widely, "I am Sebastian, my lady."

The last was a dark-skinned woman whose eyes were such a soft shade of brown they almost glowed. She took a graceful knee, offering a comforting smile, "I'm Adedoja, my lady. But you may call me Addy."

Feeling very uncomfortable, I said, "Guys, please stand. I'm not one for formalities. Just call me Katya." As they looked at each other, I added, "If you want to serve me, please call me Katya." They seemed to accept that and rose to their feet.

Gregor clasped Sebastian and Addy on their shoulders. "They will be with you everywhere you go, especially during our raids into the Live Realm." *Babysitters, great.* "But they are here now to erect a barrier around the dome. We wouldn't want stray energy to leave our confines and cause damage to Ager." With a nod, the four disappeared. Or it seemed that they did. They were in their respective corners, sitting down with their eyes closed.

"Quickstep?"

Gregor smirked. "I guess General Raf showed you a bit of the technique? Perhaps you'll get there too. But that's for later." He checked each corner before shouting, "Begin!"

The four guards slapped their hands, emitting fierce yells reminiscent of martial artists. Yet, unlike any martial art I'd seen, they glowed, sending beams skyward. These beams converged overhead, weaving a radiant net. I looked on in amazement, feeling the electric buzz of energy in the air and watching as each of the four quietly sat down, meditating. "How are they doing that?"

"Vis manipulation. When you have full control of your Vis, you can be just like that," Gregor said behind me. I turned to say something clever, but seeing Gregor's naked torso left me dull and dumb. It felt like an eternity since we were just at my house, and he was walking around without a shirt, eating breakfast. Gregor must have guessed my train of thought, for he smiled predatorily. "Are you ready?"

Before I could answer, he disappeared. "As you know, this is the speed," he said to my left, "average Wanters can move." I swirled around to see him leisurely standing around. "At most, this is what the General showed you. But the higher-ranked Wanters—" He vanished, then reappeared further away. "They can go three times faster. Tell me, Katya—" He began to appear and disappear in several places at once, blurring around me until it seemed that several Gregors surrounded me.

"Can you even try to follow me?"

The illusion of Gregors continued to swirl around, and a slight panic set in. *How the heck am I supposed to do that?* The cold touch of steel at my neck froze me. A quick look down confirmed that Gregor was pressed behind me with his sword hovering over my aorta.

"In the time you took to figure out what was going on, I could've killed you twice," he whispered. As angry as I was for falling for his ploy, I couldn't help the butterflies in my stomach and the liquid pool running through my veins at Gregor's closeness. Gregor didn't step back but instead pressed himself closer, his sword closer to my neck and his breath sending delicious shivers down my spine.

"Well?"

Suppressing my attraction, I clung to my resolve. "I guess we have our work cut out for us then." I glared at him, giving him a clear message: *I'm not backing down.*

His eyes narrowed, but he chuckled darkly, stepping back and releasing me. "Indeed, there is much work to do." His sword vanished as swiftly as it had appeared. He pulled a cloth from his pocket and threw it at me. "Might want to wipe your neck."

Surprised, I swiped and saw a small drop of blood. *Just wait, Kyrios. You'll get yours.* Taking several steps back, Gregor widened his stance. "The first thing you need to learn is how to control the strength of your ability. Your Vis reserves are vast, but only react when you get emotional. You need to draw on them with a clear head and communicate with your Vis. Have you done this before?"

I hesitated but nodded. "I've done it only once. I created a blast of Vis, but it was hardly controlled."

Gregor crossed his arms, his eyebrows arched. "Then you can do it again. Show me by bringing energy to your hands."

Crap. I raised my hand and breathed deeply. I could sense Mika moving, but she was not moving toward my hand. *Help me out here, Mika. Don't make me look stupid.* If Mika was an actual person, she would've stood before me, waited for several minutes, and then eventually smirked and given me what I asked. I opened my eyes to find my open palm glowing blue. I fought the grin that wanted to burst out.

"Good," Gregor barked. "Now, I want you to create a sphere of energy in your palm like this." He set out his hand and effortlessly got his hand glowing. "Imagine there is a dot in the middle of your hand. This dot can be filled with your energy. Focus your energy on filling that dot until you get a sphere as big as this." I watched as a sphere quickly grew out of his hand to the size of a basketball.

I did as he said and imagined the dot. Inwardly, I sought out Mika. *Can you let me have full reign, please?* Mika shrugged and let go of the control. I was immediately taken aback by how much she'd held back from me. My every extremity swelled with power, an exhilarating yet terrifying sensation. It felt like I held a wild storm threatening to consume me. I could've unleashed its fury a thousand times, and still, with all that, I could feel Mika holding back. My teeth ground together as I tried to concentrate. It was like being thrown into a raging river with waves slapping you as you came up for air. I could feel my body humming with power, shaking with energy.

Gregor's voice pierced through the chaos, a mix of stern command and underlying concern. "Control it, Katya!"

I closed my eyes as I tried to tamp everything down. Sweat was building in my temple from exertion. With every ounce of willpower, I imagined a cage around the tempest within me, trying to contain its wild energy. After several excruciating minutes, the storm calmed, bending to my will, and I regained control.

Expressing a breath, I focused the trapped energy on that stupid dot. A small sphere started to grow, filling me with immense satisfaction. I glanced at the Scot, who crossed his arms, looking unimpressed and even angered. Which only released my own ire. *Why is he looking at me like that? Doing this takes time, and I'm doing my best!*

"Katya?"

Why does everyone get to judge me for wanting to fight? I have every right to avenge my father's death!

"Katya, stop!" I returned my attention to my hand to find the sphere had grown into a giant beach ball. *Oops.* Not knowing what to do, I dropped my hand, cutting off its supply. When the floating sphere began to lose shape and vibrate, I quickly learned that letting go wasn't the smartest thing to do.

"Back up, Katya!" Gregor yelled, his hands doing a series of complex gestures. I took three steps back before the sphere shattered like glass, causing a massive explosion. The world was a blur as the blast sent me flying. My thoughts scrambled, fear setting in. I braced for impact, screaming, knowing I was about to hit the wall at fifty miles an hour.

But it never came. Instead, a familiar, mocking voice whispered close to my ear, "Thought you could use a hand." *Demetrius.* His firm grip yanked me sideways, and his broad chest came between me and the concrete. The force of the explosion still crashed us into the wall. My catcher grunted, but he held tight onto me. We descended gracefully from the crater in the wall, about sixty feet off the scorched ground.

I felt a mix of gratitude and annoyance, especially since Demetrius's smirking face loomed over mine as we touched the training floor. "It's amazing that all that power is in that small body," he said softly, but his eyes were slightly mocking.

"Don't judge what you don't know. I'm capable of a lot more, sir," I shot back.

Gregor quickstepped next to us, looking frazzled. "Are you two all right? Katya?"

Demetrius nodded. "We're fine. My back took the hit. The lady is whole." He crossed his arms, sending a sideways glance, looking amused. "Perhaps we should take this much slower. I don't believe she's ready for something as advanced as this."

I scowled at him. *It's official. I don't like this guy.*

Gregor frowned. "Maybe you're right."

I rolled my eyes. "Look, it's my first day and my first mistake. I'll do better. Come on, let's do it again."

He shook his head, resigned. "Fine. Let's go."

As I followed Gregor back to the center of the floor, Demetrius's taunting voice called out. "I'll be ready to catch you again, my lady." I waved in acknowledgment but was more determined to wipe that smirk off.

Come on, Kat. Get your head in the game.

The rest of the training session went a whole lot more smoothly. With my focus solely on the task, I could form the basketball-sized sphere, first with one hand and then with both hands. After doing it several times and completing several drills to help me practice focusing and controlling my Vis, I was pretty wiped out. It felt like hours had passed.

When my knees started to shake, Gregor finally took pity on me. "I think that's enough for today."

"Fantastic," I muttered. I retracted the last Vis sphere, and my ankle gave out, sending me crashing to the floor. Thoroughly embarrassed, I tried to summon the energy to get up. But my body was on strike. I looked up through my eyelashes. "Just a... give me a second here. I need a moment," I huffed.

The moment lasted for another minute. Gregor's eyes searched mine, a hint of concern breaking through his usual stern demeanor. With a heavy sigh, Gregor stooped down and picked me up, bridal style. The Quad rose from their respective corner and met us in the middle.

Demetrius leaned in, his voice a soft murmur. "For what it's worth, my lady, that's the most power I've seen from a novice. Just... maybe try not to bring the building down next time."

I shot him a glare, but surprisingly devoid of mockery, his words lingered in my mind.

Zenobia gave me a sympathetic smile. "What are your orders, sir?" she asked Gregor.

"Take the night. I'll escort the lady to her chambers and keep watch. Be here by sunrise." With curt nods and a departing smirk from Demetrius, the Quad departed.

"Well," Gregor hoisted me closer to his chest, "Shall we head back?"

As Gregor led me away from the scorched training floor, I couldn't help but steal glances at him. A day hadn't gone by where I hadn't marveled at his good looks. But it wasn't just the looks, but the ease I felt around him. I had never let anyone get so close to me so quickly, and he'd accomplished such a level of intimacy with me in just a matter of days. Maybe it was the way he acted that intrigued me. The way his brow furrowed when he concentrated, the way he held himself—everything about him was a paradox. He could be gentle and ferocious in the same breath. It made me wonder.

"What's on your mind?" He asked, catching my gaze.

I hesitated for a moment, then blurted out, "Do you like doing this? Being Death?" He gave me a look that clearly said, *That's a random question.* I shrugged. "I don't know how to peg you. At one point, you are Mister Military. Other times, you're 'sweet, hold your hand, kiss the pain away' man. Which one is the real you?"

Gregor stopped, studying me, debating internally what to say. "I want to take you somewhere. Are you up for it?"

I sat up straighter. "Of course. Let's go."

30

A Stolen Moment

Gregor held me tightly and then leaped high into the air. We jumped from tower to tower until we reached the highest in Ager. Below us sprawled the expanse of the fortress realm. It was shrouded in clouds. A horizon emerged, dividing the bright clouds in the sky from the dark ones below, painting the pristine white towers gold, orange, and purple. It was a fantastic sight to behold.

Gregor sat down, keeping me in his arms, gazing at the light-changing horizon. "It seems odd in this realm that we would have sunsets. I want to think that Ager was created like this to remind us that time is still running and very fluid. While time runs differently here, everything still feels it—human or not." He sighed. "Or maybe it's just a cruel reminder that life moves on with or without you."

"Does it bother you, life moving on?"

He gave me a small smile. "Sometimes, it does. Sometimes it doesn't. And to answer your question about who I am, why can't I be serious and charismatic? Dutiful and debonair?

Smiling, I said, "I don't remember adding all that."

He chuckled and gave me a soft smile. "I understand the gravity of my role. We shepherd souls to their final resting place and safeguard the living. Nabil emphasizes this duty, ensuring we never lose sight of our mission. Saving souls from destruction is our purpose. Nabil says the Archs don't think much of us because we are not angels. But we are the only ones in all realms that maintain order in the everyday lives of humans."

"If the Archs are so superior, then why don't they come and do your job?"

He frowned. "No, it's not their role. Nor do I think they have the capacity. Archs don't have a shred of humanity. Our human pasts help us understand what it takes to keep destructive evil at bay. That part of the job, protecting people, is important to me."

"Yes, the spirit police."

Gregor's laugh warmed my insides. "Aye, something like that." We sat in comfortable silence when he said, "You know I worry about you fighting."

"Really? I hadn't noticed. You seemed so carefree about it."

He ignored me. "I hoped you'd reconsider. Engaging in combat isn't straightforward, especially when wielding your Havadar—it's both challenging and exhausting."

"Do you want to cripple me?" I challenged. "Why shouldn't I be able to fight effectively? Lethally?"

Gregor looked out to the horizon, his brows furrowed, forehead lined with worry. "We should protect you. Your role should be more peaceful. And I am not saying you shouldn't be able to protect yourself. You have been gifted with the ability, and I'd be a fool not to see it. But your reasons for fighting are coming from the wrong place."

Wishing I had more energy to argue, I said quietly, "I need this, Gregor. I need to feel like I'm standing up for my family, friends, and myself. I need to fight back on their behalf."

"Are you willing to die for it?"

I met his eyes. "I have no intention of dying."

The tension in his shoulders eased a bit, but he held me closer. Silence hung between us for a beat. Gregor took a deep breath, as if steeling himself, and gently cupped my face, bringing our foreheads together. "Whatever comes our way, Katya, I want us to face it together," he whispered, his eyes searching mine. "I'm just worried about the dangers. Worried about what you'll find out there."

I snorted. "I'll be fine. That's what I have you for, right?"

"Oh, now I'm just a convenience," Gregor smirked.

I wrapped my arms around his neck and brought his face closer. "You're my favorite convenience."

"Indeed." Gregor's lips met mine tentatively at first, but soon, our kisses grew urgent, seeking comfort and escape from the chaos around us. My fingers tangled in his hair, drawing him closer as his hand caressed my cheek. The world faded away until all I felt was the thrill of his touch and the vibration of his low groan against my mouth. My enthusiasm seemed to ignite something in him. Gregor clutched me tighter, kissing me with an urgency bordering on desperation as if I were his lifeline in a swirling storm.

I shifted to straddle his lap, desperate to eliminate our distance. We moved together effortlessly, lost in the heady rush of desire. I nipped at his bottom lip, reveling in his sharp intake of breath. Gregor groaned into my mouth, his usual restraint slipping. His hands roamed my body possessively, guiding me against his hardness as I rocked my pelvis. Heat flooded my core.

Trailing kisses along his stubbled jaw, I took his earlobe between my teeth. Gregor's fingernails dug into my back, "Katya," he choked out, his gravelly voice making me shiver. Gregor crushed me against him. I reveled in his loss of control. The power I held over him in this moment was intoxicating. His urgent moans escaped him as he quickened our rhythm. Pressure building, my cries echoed across the empty rooftop. I clung to his shoulders, giving myself over to the delicious torment.

The gusting wind raised goosebumps on our feverish skin, a jarring reminder of our exposed position. Gregor slowed, chest heaving. I pressed my forehead to him, waiting for my pulse to steady.

"Damn," he muttered, a rueful smile touching his kiss-reddened lips. We stayed tangled together a moment longer, foreheads touching, breaths mingling, hearts hammering in tandem.

"Let's get you back. I know you're exhausted." Gregor grinned wickedly. "Wouldn't be fair to keep my student out past her curfew."

I couldn't help but roll my eyes and snuggle closer into his shoulder. "Jerk face," I muttered, yawning. As he sailed through the air to our tower, I could have sworn that I had seen a moving shadow in the corner of my eye.

"Gregor, did you—" The shadow was already gone before I could finish.

"Did you say something, Katya?" Gregor asked, still moving swiftly through the air.

Chalking it to exhaustion, I shook my head no and passed into dreamland.

* * *

A persistent knocking brought me out of a delightful dream the following day. What it was exactly, I couldn't remember. The last fleeting remnant was Young Jae, with wide open arms and a huge smile. I couldn't help the wave of good feelings the dream evoked, and I woke with a goofy smile. After several moments of ignoring the raps on the door and shouts of "Wake Up, Miss Katya," the door creaked open, and an annoyed Jae entered.

"You've overslept, my lady. The major won't be pleased by your tardiness. "

Groaning, I sat up, stretching to shake the sleep from my eyes. Jae's eyes widened as he took one look at me. I ran a hand through my tangled bedhead. "Sorry, I must look a mess without my bonnet."

The flustered Lieutenant quickly turned around, facing the wall. "Um, no, my lady," he stammered. "That is not to say that your hair isn't a mess. But I do like it. It's nice. Not to say that it's not normally nice—"

"Jae, what's the matter with you?" I demanded, still not fully alert.

"You are n-naked!" he blurted out.

As the fog of my restful sleep lifted, I became aware of the cool air against my skin. One look down confirmed I was, in fact, naked. And I had just given Jae a free peep show. I started screaming and clutched the blanket to my chest.

"My lady, please do not scream! You'll alert the entire guard. I'm sorry! I shouldn't have come in. I'll wait for you outside." He made for the door, still looking at me sideways as he exited. Mortified, I remembered that I had quickly stripped down after returning with Gregor, enjoying the feel of silk against my skin and easing myself into a deep sleep. I promptly found my training clothes on the floor next to the bed and dressed quickly, hastily tying my curls in a low bun.

When I did leave my room, poor Jae refused to look at me. "We better get a move on, my lady," he spoke to the floor.

The awkward silence continued to the courtyard until I stopped him and said, "Jae, let's just forget what happened. It's not that big of a deal. It's anatomy, you know?"

He looked at me incredulously. "You don't have a problem with me looking at...you?"

"I wouldn't exactly put it like that." I shrugged, hiding my blush. "The way it happened was embarrassing. But we're both adults. We can be cool about this."

A small smile crept up his face, which I returned. He turned away, lips pressed into a tight, thin smile. "My lady, you forgot about our meeting with General Lamar. I was supposed to meet you after your training was complete."

I smacked my forehead. "Oh crap, I'm sorry. I was completely knocked out yesterday from training. Can we meet today?"

His jaw tightened, but he spoke kindly. "Yes, the General assumed something like that had happened. I've been permitted to collect you from your training session early."

I gave a quick tip of my chin. A quick look around the courtyard showed it empty again. "Are the squads doing drills still?"

"Yes," Jae said briskly, clearing his throat. "Under General Nabil's orders."

Since I'd been here, the Kyrios had always been milling around the courtyard, even when they had things to do. Something felt off, and I couldn't stop my next question.

"Jae, is there anything that's being kept from me?"

He froze. His brown eyes widened in surprise and consternation. "Why would you think that?"

"Call it a hunch. It just seems off to me that everyone just disappeared. Is there something I should know about in the Live Realm?"

Jae relaxed a bit, taking hold of my arm and bringing me closer to him. "Yes, something is going on," he whispered. "But as far as I know, there's no new information that you don't already have," he said, pulling away slightly, his eyes scanning the surroundings. "General Nabil simply feels the Kyrios should be more organized, more disciplined."

"Example of what?"

"Of duty and responsibility, perhaps? I'm not entirely sure. Regardless, the Kyrios have their tasks."

That still didn't feel right to me, and I was about to ask more questions when Jae brought me closer and whispered, "Hold your questions—I know you have many. General Lamar might be the only one willing to address them. We'll meet him tonight."

"All right, I'll speak to Lamar. I just feel like something is off."

He gave me a small smile. "You wouldn't be the Balancer if you couldn't rely on your instincts. I want to help you as much as possible, Katya."

I gnawed at my bottom lip, smiling slightly. "You know, I had a dream about you," I teased.

His eyebrows shot up in genuine surprise. "Did you? What about?"

"I don't remember it all," I shrugged. "I just remember feeling content."

Jae seemed to search for words for a moment. "Dreams can be curious things. But if it brought you some happiness, then I'm glad."

An unexpected thought bubbled up. "Lieutenant, do you think dreams here can be influenced? By the realm or... by anything else?"

Jae looked thoughtful for a moment. "Kyrios don't dream – it's mostly for humans in the Live Realm. There are tales of how the first Kyrios could touch dreams. But they are just legends. Why do you ask?"

I shook my head. "Just a random thought. There's always something new to learn here."

He nodded, "Indeed, but regardless of what you learn, just remember to hold onto what feels right and true to you, Katya."

31

❧

Security's Assistance

Upon reaching the training dome, the Quad members occupied their respective corners while Gregor stood in the center with an unmistakable look of displeasure.

"You're late."

"Sorry," I mumbled, then raised my voice. "Good morning, everyone!" The Quad left their corners and converged in the center.

"Good morning, my lady," Sebastian greeted, bowing dramatically. The others followed suit. My gaze shifted to Gregor, engrossed in an intense conversation with Jae. I addressed the Quad to avoid looking nosy, "Shall we start without Gregor?"

Addy hesitated. "Perhaps we should wait."

Impatiently, I responded, "They'll only be a moment. Let's get going." The guards exchanged glances, bowed, and conceded, "As you wish, my lady."

"Listen closely," I insisted, groaning. "Stop. Calling. Me. Lady. My name is Katya. Let's be casual with one another. And if you're truly my guards, then treat me as an equal."

They smiled knowingly. Addy began, "So, you want to be treated the way we treat each other?"

"Yes! That's exactly what I want. I'd rather be with everyone else in the barracks. I want to be around everyone else. As Raf would say, how else are we supposed to be 'comrades-in-arms'?"

The mischievous glint in their eyes grew more pronounced. Zenobia inquired, her hazel eyes twinkling, "Join us at the barracks tonight?"

I smirked, "If you can sneak me in, I'm in. Is that even allowed?"

Sebastian revealed, "We're assigned to watch someone tonight. Gregor has duties in the Live Realm."

I looked back at Gregor and Jae, still in a heated exchange. "General Lamar has asked to see me this afternoon. Can we do it after?"

Demetrius's casual demeanor vanished. "You're seeing Lamar?"

"Is there an issue?" I inquired, sensing the tension. Before I could dig deeper, Gregor, having ended his discussion with Jae, positioned himself before me, glaring past my shoulder at Jae.

"Given your meeting with General Lamar, our session will be shortened today. I'll have to intensify the training to compensate. Hope you're up for it." His proximity would've been intimate without the uneasy guards and Jae's cold stare from behind. "Lieutenant, I believe you're dismissed."

Jae left without a word. I gently extricated myself from Gregor's grip, whispering, "Why the public display? What about being discreet?"

Disregarding my question, Gregor addressed the guards with a curt tone, "What are you waiting for? Let's get to work."

For the rest of the session, Gregor had me alternate forming spheres in either hand as fast as I could. When I could interchange them at faster speeds, he had me do laps, barking out orders to form spheres while running. He was not joking— he was relentless and a bit mean about it, too.

I was immensely relieved when Jae returned. "Time to see General Lamar, Lady Katya," he announced briskly.

"One minute," Gregor said, equally brisk. He again positioned himself before me, glaring past my shoulder at Jae. He lowered his eyes to mine and smirked, "Is it just me, or are you happy to be rid of me?"

I smirked back at him, "I'd be lying if I said no."

He chuckled softly. "I have to run down to the Live Realm tonight.

I'll be gone for a couple of hours. Sebastian will escort you back to your room after meeting General Lamar."

I nodded and began to turn away when the Scot grabbed my wrist. "Katya," he said suddenly, his eyes searching mine.

When he didn't finish, I prompted him. "Yes?"

After a moment, he released me, his face unreadable. "Stay with the Quad. They'll protect you."

I shot Gregor a puzzled look. "You make it sound like I'm leaving Ager. I'll be here when you return." I turned to find Jae unchanged in his spot across the sphere. For an instant, his face contorted with fury. Then, just as quickly, an indifferent mask slid into place. He flashed an easy smile as I approached. "Miss Katya, shall we?"

I tilted my head thoughtfully. "Ready when you are."

With a courteous nod to the guards, Jae led the way. We ventured past a series of imposing towers, each showcasing unique designs, indicating the distinct roles of their respective Generals. Nabil's tower, the most grandiose, was unmistakably Central Command. Michiko's tower, with its subtle and sophisticated design, was home to the archives, and one could almost smell the nostalgia of ancient books and parchment. As for Lamar's tower, it uniquely featured an array of satellite dishes crowning its apex. We reached Lamar's entrance, where a daunting staircase spiraled upwards.

I sighed, eyeing the climb. "He's at the top, isn't he?"

Jae's lips curled into a playful grin. "Wouldn't you like to know?"

Rolling my eyes, I slouched. "I'm not in the mood for a marathon right now."

With a bashful smile, Jae hesitated and said, "I could... carry you up if you'd allow it." He seemed to blush, an endearing trait.

Surprised and amused, I stepped closer, teasingly raising an eyebrow. "Offering a lift, are we?"

Jae's response was to gently wrap an arm around me, adjusting our position. His eyes, warm and kind, met mine. "Always at your service, Katya."

Laughing softly, I quipped, "With looks like yours, I bet you were quite the heartbreaker back in the day."

He exhaled a faux dramatic sigh. "Ah, the troubles of being irresistibly handsome in Korea. It was a heavy burden."

Chuckling, I playfully nudged him. "All right, Casanova. Let's not let your ego fill this entire tower."

He laughed, and with an impressive leap, we ascended multiple levels. Soon enough, we stood before the top floor entrance. As I moved to knock, a voice from within beckoned, "Enter."

I glanced at Jae, puzzled. He just winked. "Lamar has his ways. After all, he is security."

We stepped into a dimly lit room, the only source of light emanating from countless television screens that covered the walls from floor to ceiling. The soft hum of electronics filled the air, punctuated by the occasional static hiss.

From the ceiling to the floor, screens covering the walls displayed Kyrios' activity across the globe. Some of Gregor's squad in New York stood watch atop the Brooklyn Bridge. In Cairo, Kyrios battled a massive Wanter just a few feet from the Pyramids as terrified tourists fled the tremors.

But the Los Angeles scene seized my attention. A group of Wanters chased two young souls through an alley. The kids' shrill screams pierced the air as clawed shadows nipped at their heels. Just as a Wanter's gnarled hand grasped the shoulder of one child, the screens powered off.

I turned with a gasp to see General Lamar, who had been watching the screens when we walked in, lowering his hand from the controls. His easy smile belied the haunting images. He stood up slowly, his eyes searching mine with an intensity I wasn't used to. "Lady Katya," he began with a tone softer than I'd expected, "I understand you seek answers. And there's the matter of your mother?"

I sat in an empty chair opposite Lamar, still needing a moment to recover from training fully, Jae beside me. "General, will you be completely honest if I ask you something?"

Lamar nodded. "What is on your mind?" As Lamar spoke, I felt Jae's hand gently touch my shoulder; his silent support comforted me. A silent nod passed between us, encouraging me.

"Why do I feel that you guys are hiding something from me? And why do I feel I am constantly pissing off General Nabil? I'm not trying to on purpose, but it's the biggest inconvenience anytime I want to do something or understand something more fully."

Lamar shared a look with Jae before saying carefully, "I won't deceive you, my dear. I've advised Nabil to be forthright, but he prefers secrecy after so many centuries as Head General." He raised his hand, showing a familiar branding. "I am bound to secrecy on some matters, so I cannot divulge too much, but whatever I can give you, I will tell you."

He settled back in his chair, steepling his fingers. "How much do you know of the Archs?"

"That they are archangels, never human, do not like the Kyrios. Though not sure why."

He massaged his chin. "They've looked down on us for over a millennia. While we handle most skirmishes, the Archs deal with the major battles. They don't give us much respect. If anything, they revile us."

"Why is that?"

Lamar shrugged, giving a sardonic smile. "It's been that way for as long as I can remember. And I have been here for a very long time. Just as long as General Nabil. Nabil has craved their respect since they intervened in a demon uprising we failed to contain.

Interesting, they do work together. "Can I ask what happened?" I settle back into my chair, mirroring the General.

Lamar looked distant for a moment, lost in a past memory. "The first time Nabil and I encountered the Archs was a day that changed him profoundly. We were in an assembly hall draped in ornate banners of silver and gold. It was to be the first convention between Kyrios and Archs in over five hundred years."

I closed my eyes, picturing it.

"The room buzzed with murmurs, but everything fell silent when the Archs entered. Their wings shimmered with colors we had never seen.

The aura they exuded was intoxicating. Nabil stood beside me, posture upright, his face alight with hope. He had always revered the winged angels and saw this as a chance for the Kyrios to gain respect finally."

Lamar paused, his face contorting in pain. "But it was far from what he expected. The Archs looked down on us, noses upturned. To them, we were lower beings, mere tools. I remember the exact moment Nabil's spirit shattered. An argument broke out between the Kyrios and Archs, which turned physical. Nabil attempted to intervene but was immediately backhanded by an Arch who pointed at him and uttered with disdain, 'You, Kyrios vermin, should know your place. Serve without question.'"

The room grew chillingly cold. "Those words changed Nabil profoundly. His dreams were destroyed in an instant. From that day on, reverence turned into resentment. He became obsessed with proving our worth, with showing the Archs our power."

Opening my eyes, I saw Lamar quickly wipe away a stray tear. "That moment birthed the Nabil you know now, driven by a need to reclaim our lost honor."

Realization sank like a stone in my gut. "So, he means to use me to gain power over them."

General Lamar leaned forward, his elbows on his knees. "That is my suspicion. You beside us will be a show of force to them. The Balancer—God's own drop of power—partnering with the very things they hate. But now..." Lamar trailed off.

I gripped the chair arms, suddenly incensed. "I'm getting strong, and he wants to control me. Keep me weak and compliant."

Lamar's expression was grim. "How else would you endear yourself to us if we do not protect you entirely? You would be less likely to side with the Archs if it came down to a choice. The other Generals and I had to unite against him to get your combat training approved."

My mind raced, thoughts spinning. "So Nabil wants to keep me strong enough to close gates but weak enough to need the Kyrios against any real threat. But why has he cleared out all the Kyrios from the courtyard?"

Lamar placed a gentle hand over mine. "You noticed? My guess is he wants to keep you close to those he has chosen for you, who won't speak ill of him. So that you will see his good side and work well with him. But we will ensure he doesn't misuse you, my dear." His eyes searched my face tenderly.

"Thank you, General." *I'm going to test the Quad tonight.* "How about my mom?"

Lamar nodded toward Jae. "Lieutenant here tells me you want to visit your mother in a dream."

"Yes. I'm worried about her. Gregor said you have put her in a safe house in South America, but I need to know she is safe." Memories of my mother washed over me—her laughter, the warmth of her hugs, the stories she'd tell me before bed. Her absence pressed down on me, and tears threatened to fall. "I need her to know that I'm fighting to come back. That I'll be home soon."

Lamar cocked his head to the side. "Dreamwalking requires authorization from high up, so going through proper channels would likely get denied."

He smirked. "But rules can be bent."

I grinned and took his hand. "Thank you, General!" He held on tight and seemed reluctant to let go of me.

He paused, a distant look in his eyes. "Your spirit, your tenacity—it reminds me of someone I knew long ago."

I tilted my head, curiosity piqued. "Who?"

Lamar hesitated for a moment, a hint of sorrow shadowing his features. "Sherene, my Major. She is gone now. She was fierce, never backed down, always the first to face danger head-on. Even when things seemed insurmountable, she'd find a way. Just like you." As he spoke, his voice carried a softness, a fond remembrance. He seemed momentarily lost in the past, making me wonder what stories and adventures he and Sherene must have shared.

For several moments, Lamar's mind seemed to replay memories unseen to me or Jae. Uncomfortable, I softly pulled away from his grasp, bringing Lamar back to the present.

"Yes, well, we should get started!" he said happily.

"And you are sure you won't get into trouble for this?"

He let out a hearty laugh. "My dear, I'm head of security. Who is going to tell on me?"

32

A Mother's Plea

General Lamar rose deliberately from his seat, his expression focused and serious. "We're on borrowed time. Let's begin." He and Jae moved the chairs and cleared a space on the floor. "I've kept a close watch on your mother, and she's presently in the throes of a dream." He paused, looking into my eyes, allowing the weight of his words to sink in. "This is our moment." Lamar took a deliberate breath. "Lie down next to Jae. The journey through dreams can be treacherous and intricate for the inexperienced."

Lamar's warning made me uneasy. "The realm twists perceptions, makes spatial awareness unreliable. Strange logic prevails. Lose focus for a moment, and wayward thoughts manifest physically."

I laid down on the floor, shoulder to shoulder with Jae. "Take his hand. This is very important—you must never release his hand. You could even find yourself in the Abyss if you're not careful where you step."

I nodded, a pit of nervousness forming in my stomach. *Why did everything have to be so dangerous? Why couldn't an explanation start with 'This should be a walk in the park for you?'* Gripping Jae's hand tightly, he returned the gesture with a reassuring squeeze. I gave him a weak smile and closed my eyes. I heard Lamar move about the room, flipping on switches before his footsteps were close to my head.

"Since I don't have time to teach you the mechanics of dreamwalking, I'm going to force you in, like you might have experienced while visiting your soulscape. Jae's already there waiting for you."

Before I could mutter, "Oh goody," an immense but familiar pressure pressed down on my chest and my head. When I felt a hand on my forehead, I shot up suddenly, feeling completely confused and disoriented.

Jae knelt before me, gripping my hand. "Shh, it's all right. We're here."

"Where's here?" It looked like we were in the middle of downtown Boston. The empty streets around us seemed fuzzy, details bleeding into each other. This version was distorted—buildings wavered like mirages, and the roads shifted subtly underfoot, as if we stood on the water's edge, with details blurring and melding. Whispers of unheard conversations echoed eerily in the distance, and though the air felt thick, it lacked substance, like we were submerged in a dense fog that our fingers could pass through. It was just like my dream of Los Angeles.

Jae helped me up, not once releasing my hand. "We're in your mother's dream. She's about to show up in a few seconds." I searched up and down the street for some sign of life. But there was nothing. Even the Commons seemed desolate without its typical infestation of pigeons.

"Are you sure this—" I began but stopped when I heard my name.

"Katya? Katya, where are you?"

"Mom," I cried. "Mom! I'm here!" Jae held tight to me. "Don't move from this spot. Let her come."

Sure enough, coming from a nearby street, my mother came around the corner and stopped dead in her tracks. "Katya?" Her voice cracked with emotion. "You're really here?"

"Mom," I choked.

She rushed over, crying, "My beautiful baby girl!" I couldn't hold back the stream, either. I could finally see my mother, even if it was only a dream. Sobbing, she ran into my arms and said, "Oh my Lord, I thought I'd never find you again."

"I'm sorry I disappeared, Mom." I croaked, wiping my eyes. "There's so much going on right now."

"Shh, you'll have all the time in the world to tell me when we get home." She held my hand and turned to leave when I pulled back.

"No, Mom. You don't understand. This isn't real. This is a dream." When my mom's face fell, I said quickly, "I had to let you know I'm okay, but this is the only way I can come to you."

"So..." She looked around, taking in the empty metropolis, finally taking in its desolate manner and lack of flowing air. "This isn't real."

I shook my head. "But us talking is real. I convinced them to let me do this so you wouldn't worry as much."

Mom took a quick glance at Jae. "Who is this, and why are his hands all over you?"

I rolled my eyes. "Wow, Mom, be for real right now. We are talking in a dream, and you want to focus on the man next to me?"

Mom crossed her arms but shrugged. "Okay. Please fill me in because I've heard nothing but stories for several days. First, I'm told our house got blown up due to some sinister plot they can't tell me about. Then, I'm in witness protection and stuck in a house in the jungle with three men I don't know, while my only daughter is supposed to be in a different location. But I can't know what that location is either. It's a miracle I have cracked under the stress of worrying about you. So, talk! Why are you talking to me in my dream, and what does the world going to shit have to do with you?"

I gnawed at my lip, suddenly feeling very uncertain. *This is going to take a lot of work.* "Jae, can I tell her everything?"

Jae gave my hand another reassuring squeeze. "The speech bind that Major Gregor put on you doesn't affect you in your sleep. You can tell her."

I exhaled loudly, "Mom, don't say a word until I'm finished, okay?"

I told her the abridged version of everything with Jae's help. Except for the parts about Cynthia being my Havadar, Gregor and me kissing, and Jae seeing me naked. Her eyes narrowed to skeptical slits, and her lips pressed together, each outlandish detail of my story pushing her further towards disbelief.

When I was finished, her disbelief was palpable. "You expect me to believe that you are God's drop of power that's supposed to save everyone. You work with a bunch of angels—"

"Grim Reapers," I interjected.

"Your father was killed by invisible, dead humans-turned-monsters, and you're going to fight these same monsters? And you tell me all this in my dream?"

I winced. "Look, I know it seems a bit crazy—"

She gave a short laugh. "Girl, you got me...You think? Those sleeping pills are doing a number on me."

I grabbed her shoulders, my fingers pleadingly gripping her as my eyes searched for understanding in hers. "Mom, this is real. Every word."

Jae cleared his throat, "Mrs. Stevens, if I may?" Mom eyed him cautiously but nodded. Jae held out his free hand and focused his Vis on it. Fast wisps of blue energy swirled furiously into a sphere until it crystallized in the middle of his palm. At a closer glance, it was a flower pulsing with a dim light. *I definitely want to learn how to do that.*

"This is a lotus made from my Vis energy. Take it. There is enough energy in it that it will transfer over to real life. It will last for twenty-four hours. When you wake up and find this with you, you will know this is all true." Mom gently took the flower and gingerly put it in her pocket. She quietly said, "It's beautiful. Thank you."

A beeping noise suddenly emerged from inside Jae's uniform. He cursed. "We have five minutes before the General will pull us back."

"W-wait, please, Kat. Baby, don't go," Mom said tearfully. "You're the only one I have left. I couldn't survive losing you, too."

I put on the bravest face I had. "Mom, I'm just going to take care of some business. I'll be home soon."

She bit her lip and smoothed down my hair. "You promise?" she whispered. I had never seen my mother look so lost, unlike when my dad died. I felt a tear slip down as I nodded.

"Promise. I love you, Mom."

Mom sobbed, and she pulled me into an awkward hug. "I love you too, pumpkin. So much." I leaned into her shoulder, hugging her as best as I could with one arm. A sudden swell of emotion gagged me, and I was suddenly grief-stricken; this could be the last time I would ever see her. As she began to pull away, I let go of Jae's hand and closed the distance, giving my mother a bear hug and inhaling her familiar scent.

"Katya," Jae cried. "Don't move!" The two of us froze. "Why in the world did you let go of my hand?"

"I wanted to give my mother a proper hug," I said into my mother's shoulder.

I could hear him huff indignantly. "Well, any sudden movement could open another door to who knows where."

Crap. "What do I do?" I said frantically.

"Don't move. I will carefully move over to you and grab your hand, okay?"

"Okay," I whimpered.

Mom whispered, "Don't move, sweetie." However, her whispering moved her hair just enough that it rested underneath my nose.

I wiggled my nose, but it just made it worse. "Jae, hurry. Mom's hair is tickling my nose."

I heard a shuffling behind me. "I can't move too quickly either. Hold on." I tried to shift away from the hair, but it seemed to go further up my nose. I began to whimper louder, feeling the sneeze coming on.

"Hold on, Katya,' Mom urged.

"I'm almost there, Katya. Don't—"

The sneeze wouldn't listen and came out forcefully. The floor beneath me suddenly liquefied, tearing open a void beneath me. Terror clutched my soul as I teetered over an abyss—a swirling mass of inky clouds that oozed a sinister cold that sunk into my bones. The clouds churned and clashed together with flashes of lightning that would have destroyed me. My mother's grasp on my wrist was my only saving grace.

"Hang on, Katya!" she cried. There was some shouting between her and Jae, but I was too concerned with the dark cloud that had engulfed the entire space underneath my feet. A powerful energy emerged that reminded me of Mika. But it wasn't pure at all. It was...gunk. Just plain nasty. Every possible dark and depressing thought I'd ever had came to the surface and left a cold bite in my heart.

The hairs on my neck prickled - I wasn't alone in the hole. Whatever was there could sense my fear. It was laughing.

A second hand grabbed my arm, and I was pulled back onto stable dream concrete. I collapsed into Jae's arms, shaking uncontrollably. He smoothed my hair, concern etched on his face.

"Are you all right?" Mom questioned me, next to our heap of bodies.

"Yeah," I said shakily. "Just caught off guard."

Jae caught a hold of my face and studied my eyes. He flitted across my face for a moment, then nodded, seemingly satisfied. "We have a minute left. Mrs. Stevens, remember the flower. It will confirm everything."

Mom grabbed Jae's arm and said unflinchingly, "I'm entrusting you with my only child. You promise me that no harm comes to her."

The Lieutenant swallowed but nodded. We stood up carefully, and I gave my mother a final kiss. "I'll be seeing you, Momma."

With tears streaming down her face, she whispered, "I'll see you later, Kitty." Our hands were still gripping each other when she disappeared. The entire Boston dreamscape faded to black.

And once again, I sat back up with a gasp, disoriented. Jae and General Lamar kneeled beside me.

"Was it successful?" the General asked.

Tears streamed down uncontrollably. "Yes," I said brokenly. "Yes, thank you."

Lamar smiled, his gaze intense yet kind. He held his hand, palm up-wards, in a gesture of allegiance. "What wouldn't I do for the Balancer?" Jae tensed, shifting almost imperceptibly between Lamar and me. His jaw tightened, though his face remained impassive. He rose to his full height. "Young Jae, in the ten minutes you were gone, Lady Katya's bodyguards have come for her. See that she is returned to them safely."

"Of course, General."

Lamar bowed slightly. "Until next time, my lady."

"Thank you again, General."

As we exited the room. Jae scooped me up but didn't immediately leap down. He studied my face momentarily and asked, "Are you all right?"

I put on a brave smile. "I'm just happy to have seen her. Thank you for today." I tightened my grip on his neck to bring him closer and kissed him on the cheek.

"I'm genuinely grateful for you, Jae." The young Lieutenant's cheeks flared red, but he smiled softly.

"You have to do your part, Katya. You have to stay safe," he urged, eyes boring intensely into mine.

I touched his cheek with a bittersweet smile. "Only if you promise to protect me."

With a smirk, he echoed Lamar's parting words, "What wouldn't I do for the Balancer?"

33

A Night with Troop Five

Four imposing figures made a beeline for the entrance as we exited the tower.

"I trust everything is well," Demetrius said first, his eyes on Young Jae.

Jae quickly nodded. "Yes, sir. I was just about to escort the Lady into your care."

Demetrius glared at him, but he nodded as well. "You may take your leave, Lieutenant."

Jae saluted the Quad and then turned to me. "Have a pleasant evening, my lady," he said solemnly. He bowed, but his mischievous eyes betrayed him.

I rolled my eyes but followed his lead by returning the bow, "Goodnight, Lieutenant."

Demetrius gently nudged my back, guiding me, while the other three took positions covering my front and sides. The Quad operated like a protective pack, each member playing a role. "Are you really going to let me see what happens there?" I said, grinning widely, eager for a distraction from my dreamwalking nightmares.

Zenobia grinned, stretching and cracking vertebrae in her back. "Sure, just as long as we get you back to your room on time. I don't know about you, but I could use a little fun."

Demetrius didn't look convinced. "If General Nabil ever found out..."

"Pssh, when was Old Man Nabil's last trip to the barracks? Don't worry," Sebastian cut him off. "We're not going to tell. She's certainly not going to tell. And the fellas aren't going to tell."

"The fellas?" I asked.

Addy grinned. "We could explain, but why don't you meet them yourself?"

We weaved through a maze of glass domes shimmering under the twilight. Standing tall and imposing, each dome reflected the pale blue moonlight, casting eerie silhouettes on the cobblestone path beneath our feet. These were the barracks, I realized, each uniquely marked and housing a distinct aura. I snuck a look at the Quad. "So General Nabil isn't a fan of barracks life?"

Addy snorted. "Our Head General is too good to be down there. As if he was never a lower-ranking Kyrios."

"So we're not fans of him?"

They all, including Demetrius, made various noises that I understood as "Meh." *So much for Lamar's guess about Nabil's plans.*

Sebastian smirked, "He's an old man, Katya. He was taught that high-ranking officials must know their place. Old men forget their origins."

"He did say he was over eleven hundred years old," I said. "It makes sense if you think about it. My granddad hated me trying to change the channel whenever he was at our house. Nabil's crankiness is just like an old man who wants to keep the TV on, but not for the sake of watching."

The others laughed at my analogy—even Demetrius, who seemed chagrined at himself at his inability to control his own chuckle.

We had just arrived outside a dome-shaped barrack with five slashes above the doorpost. A look around showed that the other similar domes had different numbers slashed above their door. Addy opened the barrack door and loudly said, "Katya, meet the men of Troop Five!"

The barracks assault my senses—rowdy laughter bouncing off the domed walls, the tang of sweat and leather, scarred tabletops littered with cards and magazines. Several people were seated throughout the covered hangout—about fourteen altogether. All who heard the booming voice turned their attention to the door. The soldiers candidly size me up with fascination. One lanky youth's gaze lingers too long on my chest before dropping away nervously. Sebastian nudged me inside; the Kyrios suddenly looked much beefier close-up. I managed a soft "Hi, everyone."

The soldiers stared at me until a voice from the back said, "Might I remind you, Addy, that there is one less sausage around here?" Stepping from behind a very tall Kyrios came a barely five-foot-tall woman. She was dressed in Kyrios fashion but with a familiar platinum blond haircut that framed silver and steel-gray eyes.

Sebastien sighed loudly. "Yes, we know, sis. You are a woman. Keep your panties on." He scratched the back of his head, taking a nonchalant stance. "One time someone confuses you for a young boy and you just can't let it go," Sebastian smirked.

The petite woman scowled. In a flash, she was directly in front of Sebastian and flat-out kicked him in the jaw. My jaw brushed the floor as Sebastian dropped to his knees. "Damn it, Jaya!" he yelled, clutching his face. "What the Abyss is wrong with you?"

Jaya ignored him and turned to me, grinning widely. "Hello, my lady! I'm Jaya. It's a pleasure to meet you!" She grasped my hand and led me toward the rest of the slack-jawed Kyrios. A glance behind me showed Zenobia, Demetrius, and Addy exasperated but amused. Jaya squeezed my hand, gaining my attention again. "My lady, let me just say this: don't be intimidated by this group. Like my brother just demonstrated, they are a bunch of softies."

"Sure. And call me Katya. I'm not big on titles."

Jaya began to bounce on her toes like a five-year-old. "Really? Come and sit down with us." She led me to the table where the rest of the men were seated and placed me at the head.

I noticed the men were still standing and said, "Guys, please, sit down too. There's no ceremony here, okay? I'm not General Nabil."

The men chuckled, looked at each other, and looked at the Quad, who nodded their consent. There was a sudden mad dash to grab chairs, almost coming to playful blows to get the chairs closest to me. Up close, I notice scars and tattoos on their tanned skin, hints of old battles. But their faces beam with excitement to meet me. It's endearing, these soldiers rendered giddy as schoolboys.

I smiled widely. "This is so great. I've been waiting for my chance to come and meet you all."

"And we as well, my lady," a voice said towards the back. The rest of the men murmured in agreement.

I hadn't been the only one told to stay away. The male who'd won the coveted seat to my left next to me said eagerly, "My lady—

"Guys, please, no more of this 'lady' stuff. Just call me Katya." I said sternly. "And that's an order!"

They all grinned widely and answered in chorus, "Yes, miss!"

The man closest to me cleared his throat and introduced himself as Santiago, his wavy brown hair softly swooped in front of his eyes, giving him a debonair flair. His warm brown eyes put me at ease. "I think I speak for all of us when I say we are pleased you are here. We all have wanted to meet the fabled Balancer."

I rolled my eyes. "I'm nothing special, trust me. I've wanted to interact with you since I started training, but every time I step out, there's no soul outside." I sighed deeply, pouting dramatically. "I guess Nabil is working your tails off."

I noticed that some of the men looked at each other with odd looks, but Santiago pulled my attention away. "There have been several orders, but we all were curious about you. We've never had someone here in Ager that was not a Kyrios."

"How old are you?" someone called out.

"I turned eighteen a couple of months ago."

The Kyrios looked shocked. Quiet murmurs filled the room. "She's just a child."

"Why are they sending someone so young into battle?"

"Do the Generals realize how young she is?"

I eyed one of the men who said loudly, "She's nothing but a

baby!" He was a tall, auburn-haired man who didn't seem much older than twenty-two. Demetrius scowled at the offender, ready to set him straight.

I stood from my chair, my hands finding my hips. "My position has nothing to do with my age." I made a point to bring my power to the surface and glowed blue from head to toe. I was pleased to see some of the men impressed. I was impressed with myself that I could even do it on command. "I can take care of myself." I turned to the yeller. "And you don't seem much older than me anyway, Babyface!"

He smiled as the rest of the Kyrios guffawed at my point. "I'm five hundred and eighty-three years old, Miss Katya."

I paused. "What?"

Auburn-Haired Man laughed. "I'm five hundred and eighty-three years old!" I looked around and realized that the Kyrios were mixed in age. Some looked as young as me. Others looked old enough to be my grandfather.

I looked at one particular gray-templed man. "How old are you?"

"One hundred and fifty-three."

And to a freckled young boy, I asked the same question. "Four hundred and twelve."

I arched an eyebrow. "I assume the wide range of your ages corresponds to when each of you transformed into a Kyrios. Is that how it works?" I turned to the Quad. "What about you guys?"

Zenobia frowned. "I think I'm six hundred and sixty-four, last time I checked."

"Eight hundred and forty-two," Addy answered.

"Six hundred and ten," said Sebastian.

Demetrius proudly grinned, "I'm eight hundred and five years old."

I shook my head. "You guys are ancient!" The men laughed at that.

Santiago spoke up again. "What Kevon meant," he pointed to Auburn-Haired Man, "was that, compared to us, you are like a child. We've all been around for quite some time."

I nodded, but a thought came to mind: *Yes, they were all alive at one point. But what does it take to be a Kyrios?* Not sure I wanted to bring that question to the group at large, I moved on to something else.

"You said it's rare for outsiders to come to Ager?"

"Extremely," Santiago said excitedly. "I can't think of a time that someone has been here without passing on. The other troops will be furious when they find out you've been here. They'll feel your footprint and be instantly jealous."

I looked blankly at him. "My footprint?"

"You leak Vis like a running faucet," Jaya said beside me.

I looked at her, puzzled, but then laughed. "Actually, now that I think about it, when I first met Gregor, he told me that I leak energy so much it was amazing I went on unnoticed."

Jaya nodded in agreement. "He is right. I noticed you the first time you walked through the East Gate. You have so much Vis that it just runs out of you constantly. Your training has helped, but you still have a bit of drip still going. Any strong spiritual entity could find you quite quickly."

I frowned and turned to the Quad. "Why haven't we addressed this yet? Isn't it going to be important to move about undetected?"

Addy said, "I think Gregor's been more focused on getting you to bring out your Vis and communicate better. I'm sure he will add stealth if he finds it appropriate."

Jaya turned to her brother and gave him a dirty look. "When is stealth not appropriate? What are you teaching her in the dome? How to hold her breath?"

Sebastian rolled his eyes. "We don't teach her. We're just there as containment shields. Plus, what would you know about teaching anything to anyone, midget?"

She growled, rolling up her sleeves. "I'll teach you something right now, you son of a bitch!"

"She was your mother too, idiot," he replied.

Jaya gave a loud howl and tackled him to the ground, trading blows. I looked at Zenobia and mouthed, *Are they serious?*

Zenobia looked bored. "They always do this. It'll be over soon." She was right. Jaya had successfully pinned her brother down with him screaming, "Okay! You win! You win!"

The petite blond laughed triumphantly, giving Sebastian a parting kick. She repositioned herself beside me again and said gleefully, "I think this proves that I should be Katya's bodyguard instead."

Kevon shot out of his seat, a prankish glint in his eyes. "Are you kidding me? This comes from the girl who hightailed it out of her first battle, leaving a puddle behind!"

The men guffawed, and I caught myself giggling, giving an apologetic look to Jaya. Kevon threw me a wink.

Jaya jumped up on the table and stomped in front of Kevon. "Last time I checked, someone couldn't stop weeping after *his* first battle!" She patted his head condescendingly. "Poor baby needed his bottle?"

The way Kevon's face matched his hair got me giggling harder and gasping for air. Sebastien frowned, noticing the frenetic energy radiating between the two. "Oh God, you two. Would you both admit that you like each other? This play fighting for over a century is getting old."

They both ignored him. Kevon stood from his chair, now eye to eye with Jaya, his smirk growing. "At least I got on Squad Five by my own merits, not because my brother pulled some strings, you bitch." The men suddenly got eerily quiet. The atmosphere immediately changed. And if the crackling energy around Jaya didn't indicate something wrong, it would've been the men's nervous sideways glances for an exit.

Jaya clutched Kevon's collar, yanking him off balance. "What did you call me?" Her voice was dangerously soft.

Kevon sneered, though excitement flashed across his face, knowing he hit Jaya's button. "Why not show us all that mighty power of yours?"

"Jaya, why don't you calm down?" Sebastian said quickly, looking at me, concerned.

"Shut up!" she yelled, her eyes never leaving Kevon. "Kevon here thinks I'm weak. Why don't I show him now how weak I am?"

Jaya's eyes flashed red and blue, reminiscent of Gregor's that night in the alley. Before I could ask, the Quad shouted at her to stop. Kevon stood firm, ready to brawl. The men backed away nervously, eyes darting toward the exit.

But all of it didn't matter. The door burst open and everyone turned in unison toward the hulking figure filling the doorway, radiating fury.

"Where is she?" Gregor's brogue was heavy with fury. All eyes swiveled to me at the table's head, surrounded by disarray. It probably looked like I had ordered them to fight for my entertainment! Gregor's furious expression flashed briefly with relief at seeing me. But just as quickly, his brows snapped together in frustration.

I hesitated, slowly raising my hand amidst the disarray. "Um, Gregor! You're back! How was your trip?"

He wordlessly quickstepped beside me, had me in his arms, and was out the door. He paused in the doorway and said over his shoulder, "I'll come talk to you lot after I take care of this one." He slammed the door behind us and stalked towards my tower.

Outside, the cold air hit us. I tried to break the heavy silence, "Hey buddy, wanna talk about it?"

"Don't test me, lass," Gregor warned, eyes flinty. I took the hint and shut up. The tense silence continued when we reached my bedroom, and he stood there staring at the floor.

The longer the silence went on, the more horrible I felt. "Will you just say something?" I begged. "Please, it's killing me."

"Killing you?" he asked incredulously. "Killing you? Lass, how do you think I felt when I was supposed to find you protected and guarded in your room but found it completely empty? Not an ounce of energy in the room?"

"We need to talk about that leaking—" He shot me a sharp look. *We can talk about that later.*

Gregor ran a hand through his tousled hair. "And where do I find you? In the middle of the fourth-strongest Kyrios group, a brawl about to break out! Are you thick?"

Thick? As in stupid? My gut twisted with mingled defiance and shame under Gregor's blistering glare. Feeling my own anger rising, I said, "They didn't fight! The Quad had it under control...somewhat." I sighed, realizing he was right. "Gregor, I just... I wanted to understand them, to be one of them."

He sighed, running a hand through his hair. "Katya, there are things I don't think you are ready to face yet."

"Like what? Why is everything a mystery with you?" Frustration bubbled up in me.

He paused, searching for words. "There's a bigger picture involving more than just Kyrios and barracks. You—" he beseeched me for some understanding. Gregor shook his head. "Never mind. Please stay away from the barracks. The men there are a bit too rowdy for my taste. You might get caught up in something."

I contemplated this, sensing layers to his words I hadn't grasped before. "All I'm asking is for some trust. When we arrived here, someone told me he was no better than anyone else and preferred to be with his troop. Maybe I'm just taking his lead." I inched closer to him, gently caressing his cheek. "Let me be part of this world."

He gave me a stern look. "Let me think about it."

He turned for the door, but I called him back. "You aren't going to tell Nabil about the Quad taking me there, are you?"

Gregor's blank stare turned into a smirk. "No, but they don't know that yet." With that, he bid me goodnight and closed the door behind him.

34

Sparring Day

Three weeks had passed in the Live Realm since I'd bid farewell to my mother; in Ager, it had been seven full days. Gregor had been relentless in his training regimen. His grueling sessions reflected his urgency to turn me into a fighter worthy of Ager's standards. But every so often, I'd catch a softness in his eyes—a pride he wouldn't voice, at least not yet.

The Quad took the brunt of his dissatisfaction after our barracks misadventure. They were his constant shadows for the subsequent days, sometimes partnering with me for training sessions. The worst part was they went completely formal on me, refusing to look me in the eye. When I refused to speak to Gregor, he came clean, and they gradually let their guard down.

I had to give Gregor credit. After the first couple of training sessions, I'd gained better control over my Vis, so I could now move about relatively undetected. Gregor also taught me how to increase my speed by sending Vis to my feet and increasing my stamina. I wasn't at full quickstep yet, but I was faster than the fastest human in the Live Realm.

We then moved to hand-to-hand combat. Throwing punches at Gregor while he barked orders at me was cathartic, to say the least. In one hand-to-hand session, I was able to bring up a barrier around me at will, and I got so excited that I lost focus and caused another explosion. *Oops.* After convincing Gregor that I could bring up my barrier without accidental explosions, Gregor told me it was time to pull out my Havadar on our seventh training day.

"It's time?" I asked nervously.

The Scot nodded and had me focus all of my energy into my right hand. "Do you feel pressure behind your hand?" Gregor barked from behind me.

"Yes," I grunted, trying to hold my focus, anchoring my glowing hand with my left.

Gregor moved to stand in front of me. I almost lost my focus with his broad, naked torso now in my view. "I want you to push that pressure to the tips of your fingers."

"What?"

"Come on, you can do it."

I panted, focusing intently on my fingertips. Sweat poured down my face. When an amber glow came from my fingertips, Gregor met my eyes with an unrelenting stare and asked, "Why do you want to fight?"

"To get back at the Want for making my life miserable, for my father's death," I said through gritted teeth, closing my eyes.

I could sense Gregor shaking his head. "That's not good enough. Why do you want to fight?"

"To make the Want pay—"

"No!" he thundered. "Why do you want to fight, Katya? What makes you do this? Why are you in Ager? Why did you take this role?"

My body vibrated painfully from exertion and my desperate focus on the Vis while trying to think simultaneously. *What brought me here? They ruined my home! They attacked my mother! They put my best friend in a spiritual coma. Amie and my other friends from school are in danger. I need—*

"I need to protect my family!" I cried out. "I want to protect my friends. I don't want others to suffer. I don't want to experience pain anymore. I want to protect my world!"

A scorching feeling blanketed my hand, and I felt a weight drop into the palm of my hand. I felt my fingers close around a cold yet soft leather handle with several tassels attached. I opened my eyes to see a beautiful silver sword. The handle was wrapped in silver leather with stray shinning granite leather tassels at the end. The blade was light in weight, thin but long, the length of my arm and then some. Diantha had come forth.

It was awesome.

"Is this what Mika meant? Did I master my heart?" I marveled at how easily I could handle the sword.

Gregor grinned, pride shining through. "Do you understand now? That's the real reason, the heart of your mission. A Havadar couldn't have come out unless it came from a place and purpose to protect. Your anger and revenge towards the Want had only clouded your true warrior heart. Congratulations. You are officially a Vis warrior." He showed me how to return the Havadar back to my body.

He pulled out his own after I showed him I could pull it out several times.

At his battle stance, my eyes widened. "What are you doing?"

Gregor's eyebrow arched up. "Taking a page out of General Raf's book and getting you ready for battle. What do you think?" he said innocently. "Let's see how you do!"

I mimicked his stance with trepidation. "B-b-but I just pulled my sword out. Let's take a break, huh?" I faked a yawn for good measure. "Man, am I tired!"

Girl, don't be such a baby! You have more attitude than that! Cynthia's voice filled my head.

I stared at the sword, incredulous. *No way! Cynthia?*

Who else would it be? And about time, too. I've been waiting for you to get control over your feelings. Finally, I can come out to play.

"Hey!" Gregor called out, getting my attention, grinning widely. "If you don't lift that sword, I will scar your pretty little face."

"Wait!" I shouted as he charged at me. He stopped and gave me an exasperated look. Not having anything else to say, I batted my eyes. "You think I'm pretty?"

He came at me anyway, and I had to lift my Vis sword to protect myself—just in time.

We then focused on battling repeatedly to the point I had difficulty lifting my arms. But with every fight, I knew I was improving significantly. Cynthia, or Diantha rather, coached me as well. At times, fighting moves just came to me as if I had always known them. Hacking, feints, defensive poses, kicks, punches, you name it. Every time I fought, I got a better handle on Diantha.

When I could finally maneuver Gregor into a compromising position, he grinned and said, "That's my girl."

That night, I went to my room with immense pride. I didn't share with Gregor that I could speak to Cynthia at will now without wielding Diantha. While I stared at my best friend's body, still encased in her sphere, I conversed with her and continued to understand more techniques and how to manipulate my Vis into different things better.

Cynthia said, *The Kyrios have their methods for how to get you ready, but we need to get to the next level—you, me, and Mika.*

I'm unsure whether Gregor sensed my energy levels going off that night, but he never said a word.

* * *

The next day, when Jae escorted me to the sphere, he looked odd, Like he had swallowed a lemon.

"What's with the face, Jae?" I swung my arm around his neck. An easy friendship had formed between us over the past week. Jae had become the older brother I never had. Being open with him, complaining about everything, and being myself felt so easy. He allowed himself the same luxury sometimes, but sometimes, he would seem put off or angry. He never explained it, and I chose not to pry.

But the look on his face this morning had prompted the question before I could catch it.

Oddly enough, he answered readily. "I have a mission, Katya, and it's hard to wrap my head around it."

"Are you going to the Live Realm?" I asked worriedly. No one would tell me outright, but I knew the situation in Los Angeles was becoming beyond bothersome. The day's training was to show Nabil that I was ready to head out and begin closing the gates. I looked Jae over and gave him a brave smile. "Whatever it is, I know you can do it. You're one of the best people here. Whatever the mission is, I'm sure you'll do your best."

His smile looked forced. "Of course, Katya. Thank you." He held me back as I was about to step into the sphere. "Katya?"

"Hmm?"

He opened his mouth to speak but then fell silent. I felt an eyebrow arch in response. "Jae?"

Jae's forced smile appeared again. "Good fighting today, okay?"

I rolled my eyes and chuckled. "Of course. It's time to get out of Ager! Let's keep our fingers crossed that Gregor isn't successful in killing me today." I waved goodbye and entered the dome to find several people awaiting my arrival. I approached Gregor first, who was whispering to Generals Nabil, Lamar, Victor, Raf, plus a woman who I wasn't particularly excited to see. *Sophia is here? Why?*

Over the last week, when Gregor and I would return to our tower, Sophia appeared in the oddest places – at the training dome's entrance, behind another adjacent building, or making her way to Ager's gate to the Live Realm. Every encounter, she never spoke to either one of us, but her eyes always glittered with malice. On one occasion, I swore that I saw her eyes flash crimson.

I told Gregor, who answered, "I must have tired you out to start seeing things." His barb didn't hide his uneasiness.

As the Generals discussed our training progress, I couldn't help but notice Sophia. Her eyes flitted between Gregor and me. There was an intensity in her gaze, a spark of something I couldn't quite place.

"Lady Katya, I think we've all been waiting for this day," Nabil said.

I bowed my head in mock reverence. "General, I can't wait to pass this test and get a change of scenery and people."

Raf guffawed. "Seems like my time away has done nothing to my lady's sass."

Nabil's eyes narrowed, but he didn't remark on my tone. "Gregor reported your success with your training. The swelling gate in LA brings a high risk of catastrophic breach between realms. We must seal that rift immediately. So, with today's training, we need you to do and show your best."

My ears perked. "Will you be staying to watch, General Nabil?"

Nabil shook his head. "Unfortunately, no. Raf has returned with intel that the Generals and I must review and apply to your next raid. While we trust Gregor's abilities, we decided the best way to test your abilities is to give you a new sparring partner."

General Lamar interjected before Nabil could continue. "Nabil, perhaps we should—"

"Lamar!" he said sharply. "We've all already decided."

The dark-skinned General's lips became thin with displeasure. Nabil cleared his throat. "As I said, we have decided you should have a different sparring partner." He motioned for Sophia to move forward. "I'm not sure you've met Sophia yet."

Tall, statuesque, and radiating confidence, she had the air of someone well-versed in combat. As she stepped forward, her icy gaze fixated on me. "Lady Katya, we haven't been introduced."

I raised an eyebrow, taking a slight dig at her. "Wait, weren't you the one serving dinner the other night?"

A fleeting shadow crossed her face, and her voice had a sharp edge. "A temporary assignment. Today, however, I'm here in my true capacity."

I gave her a side eye and smiled.

Nabil looked at the both of us, giving me a warning look. "Sophia will assess your skills and provide us with a report. Please abide by her instructions. Gregor, we'll leave you with this." Gregor looked greatly displeased. I wasn't sure who he was angry with—me, Sophia, or the Generals. I gave him a shrug. *I didn't ask Ms. Pinch-Face to join us.*

The Scot entered trainer mode as soon as the General exited the dome. "Get into your stances, ladies."

Drawing my sword, I adopted the stance Gregor had taught me. However, Sophia assumed an unfamiliar stance. "Oh crap," I muttered."

"Begin!"

Sophia charged at me. Hard. Unlike Gregor, whose moves I'd become accustomed to, Sophia was unpredictable. She'd shift between stances I had never seen, catching me off guard. As I swung Diantha, her blade met mine with a loud clang, sending vibrations up my arm. The air was tense, and every move became a dance of wit and skill.

And it felt personal. There were moments when her strikes seemed fueled by something more than just a training exercise. Once or twice, I could've sworn I saw a hint of satisfaction in her eyes when her blade came close.

Cynthia murmured within me, *She is going for blood. Be careful.* My opponent threw her weight behind her attack, but I could hold up. We didn't move, wanting to see who would break first.

"My Gregor's been teaching you, I see," she hissed, the jealousy evident in her tone.

I deflected another blow. "You mean our Gregor?"

Anger contorted her face. "He was mine long before you blundered into our world. We trained side by side, and he's always watched out for me."

She jumped back and charged again, this time slashing at me. The extra sessions with Cynthia were paying off. I could counter every time. She began to speed up, forcing me to dodge. I tapped into Mika for a bit more speed to keep up.

"Hmm, that's funny," I said loud enough as our swords met in a deadlock again. "He never mentioned you once."

She snarled and aimed a kick at my midsection. It connected. I yelped in pain but still managed to block another blow. Sophia's eyes widened as she sent me a flurry of kicks and sword thrusts. Somehow, I withstood it, though I was wearing out faster than she was.

She suddenly flipped back, watching me gasping from exertion. "This is the savior of the Live Realm? I knew she couldn't handle it. Gregor, I thought I told you to get rid of her."

Excuse me, what?

"Enough with the talking, Sophia!" Gregor barked from the far corner, not fully hearing our low conversation. "Focus on the sparring."

I put on my best smile. "Gregor doesn't respond to whining, Sophia. Besides, he is the last person who would ask me to leave."

Sophia's eyes narrowed. "What did you say?"

Knowing I now had buttons to push, I leaned on my sword, studying my nails. "Now, was that before we kissed in my room or after?" I said, murmuring. "Or was it that wonderful time we spent on the roof together?"

Ouch! Good one! Cynthia snickered.

"When did this become tea time?" Gregor yelled from his corner. "I said *spar!*"

"Gregor kissed you?" she whispered, her frame shaking.

I chuckled, lifting my sword and pointing it at her. "Not yours, is he?" I readied my stance again. "You know what? General Nabil was right – this spar was a great idea!"

"He has never... Even when I ...You're a human!" she cried. Her face morphed into a wild look that immediately put me on edge. "You think this is funny? Let's see how you laugh now," she sneered.

Suddenly, Sophia's form began to shift in a disturbing way. Heat radiated from her, making the air itself shimmer. As she locked eyes with me, the humanity faded, replaced with menacing blood-red pupils.

Up your guard, Kat. She's changing!

Changing into what, Mika?

Sophia's face distended into a gaping maw, eyes burning blood-red. Spikes protruded along her spine, skin leathery and charcoal gray. Her energy spiked, and the entire room's temperature rose. This was no Kyrios.

The warped creature unleashed an unearthly screech that struck a chord in me.

My heart hammered. "You're a Wanter!"

"Sophia!" Gregor shouted. "Stop it!"

The energy radiating from her was almost stifling. It took tapping into Mika to not succumb to its heavy weight and remain firm on my feet. With her transformation complete, she stood tall, changing her stance again. "Oh, that feels much better. Balancer," her voice now guttural and disturbing, "let's have some fun."

Sophia moved with uncanny speed, a blur of slashes and blows. I barely deflected them, driven by frenzied desperation. The only thing keeping me from being cut down was Diantha; I threw the sword up as a defense against her as she slashed, banged, and thrashed her sword at me.

Judging from the pain I was feeling, she was winning. I moved to defend myself and slipped on my blood. *Where did that come from?*

Gregor quickstepped in between us, throwing his arms in front of me. "Sophia, stand down now!"

Sophia's anger flared. "Out of my way!" She struck Gregor, sending him crashing into the sphere's wall.

Rushing to his aid, I was halted by Sophia's blade, narrowly dodging her attack. "You're the Balancer everyone's been talking about? A frail human? The Kyrios must've lowered their standards." She darted around, her blade leaving stinging cuts on my skin.

"Can't even fend off one Kyrios. Imagine facing a Wrecker or Stuffer!" She jeered, her laughter cold. With a forceful strike, my Havadar flew across the room. My injured arm rendered me defenseless.

Kneeling, I clutched my bleeding wound. Sophia loomed, raising her sword. "Consider this a mercy."

Desperately, I thought, *Mika, shield!*

A barrier formed just in time to block her blow. She scoffed, "That shield won't last long, especially with you fading."

Weakly, I met her gaze, refusing to back down.

Sophia's voice sank to a chilling whisper, her malevolent smirk unmistakable. "You want revenge on the Want? Tell me, Balancer, how do you plan to face an entire army of Kyrios?"

"What the hell are you playing at, Sophia?

She gave a guttural laugh that sounded more like a rumbling growl. "Kyrios and Wanters are one and the same. Gregor and the others have been deceiving you to defeat the Archs." She laughed.

My mind reeled. *Deceived?* Gregor shouted protests, but his words faded into the clash of steel against my weakening shield.

"This spar's purpose was to see if you could be a threat to us. Since you aren't, we will use you as a battery." She grinned, baring her teeth. "But we won't kill you, sweetheart. You will be alive the entire time. Feeling the excruciating pain of having your energy sucked from you for the rest of your existence."

Rage roared through my veins. *Lies, all of them.* I held onto my faith in Gregor, even as seeds of doubt sprouted. A crack appeared in the barrier, an unfortunate sign of my slipping away. Sophia lifted her hand, smirking, and a red, crackling sphere formed in her palm.

At the confusion splashed across my face, she chuckled, "Something else you don't know, Balancer? This Want ability is called a Seizure Sphere. This little sphere has the force of three earthquakes." She bared her teeth again at the panic in my eyes. "But here is the good news for you," she cooed. "While they might want you, I don't. Trust me, consider this an act of mercy."

Clutching my bleeding arm, I closed my eyes and silently prayed.

A deafening boom echoed as Gregor tackled Sophia, sobs of relief escaping me.

"Enough, Sophia!" he bellowed. She struggled initially, but Gregor quickly pressed two fingers to her neck, sending an electrical charge through her body and knocking her out completely. Her limp form crashed to the ground, and her face returned to normal—whatever that even meant anymore.

I wished I was pleased. I wished I could've jumped up for joy at Gregor's rescue. I wish I could've said something.

I was rendered speechless.

Because the man who I defended, whose attention I hungered for, who I trusted the most in Ager and Live Realm was staring back at me with blood-red eyes, distorted facial features, and white pointy teeth.

35

Revelations Unbound

"No," I whispered, disbelief weighing heavy on my voice. My heart raced, and the horrifying reality set in. "This can't be real," I murmured. I blinked, hoping the nightmare before me would vanish, but the monstrous image of Gregor remained.

His face, moments ago so twisted and terrifying, softened, the familiar blue eyes I'd cherished now clouded with pain. "No!" The word ripped from me, raw and filled with denial.

Gregor rushed towards me urgently. "Katya, please let me explain—"

Pushing off from where I stood, I backed away, shaking my head in horror. "Stay away from me!" My legs faltered, and I found myself sinking to the ground.

He looked around, desperate. "Please, let me help you!"

"Stay away!" My voice cracked with emotion. I held out a trembling hand, summoning my protective shield. My shield sizzled, repelling him.

Gregor recoiled in pain but persisted. "Katya, you're bleeding!"

"Just... stay away." I struggled to catch my breath. My resolve hardened, and fury surged through my veins. *Mika, lend me strength.* Empowered, I pushed myself to my feet, clutching my bleeding arm, and ran from the dome, my shield pulsing with each heartbeat.

Anger consumed my thoughts. *How could I have been so blind? So trusting?* The Quad must have sensed my anguish because they quickly emerged from the barracks.

Addy's eyes widened in shock. "Katya! What happened? We felt—"

A cold glare was all she received in response. Before anyone else could speak, I summoned Vis, propelling me to my tower sanctuary. Once inside, the door slammed shut, sealing me from the rest of the world. My protective shield shattered, its fragments reflecting the pain I felt.

Cynthia's voice echoed softly, *Kat, we need to treat that wound.*

I don't want anyone near me. We'll do it ourselves.

I managed to bind my injury using a torn piece from my satin sheets. The wound throbbed, but my mind was elsewhere, consumed by feelings of betrayal. Every comforting word, every smile from Gregor felt like a cruel jest.

How could I ally myself with monsters I swore to vanquish?

A hesitant knock jolted me from my reverie.

"Katya, please. Can I come in?"

My initial retort died on my lips when Mika said, **You won't get any answers to your questions if you hide yourself away. You won't gain anything unless you let him in.**

I rose, noting the Vis glow and reduced pain around my arm. **Your Vis is helping you heal.**

I wrenched it the door open and stalked away, letting Gregor trail after me. He stood there, a shadow of the confident man I knew, weariness evident in his slouched posture and curls in a disheveled mess.

Silently, I gestured for him to sit.

"You sit there," I pointed to the furthest chair.

He complied. "Katya, I'm sorry. It's not what you think. I did it to protect you."

His words hit hard, but I refused to show it. I scoffed, "Protect? Or deceive?"

His eyes pleaded. "Every tale you shared about the Wanters was filled with pain. I wanted to spare you that, to earn your trust."

I wheeled on him. "Don't spew that bullshit. You hid the truth because you needed my allegiance against the Archs! I bared my soul to you! And you repaid me with lies."

My cold chuckle held no mirth. "Was this a setup from the beginning? Am I really closing Abyss gates? Am I really protecting people? Do you really send souls to the Room of Apofasi? Or maybe you devour them and their Vis as the other Wanters do!"

Gregor blanched. "No!" He shot up, desperation evident. "I am not them! Yes, I have the blood of a Wanter, but I chose to be Kyrios."

"Chose? What do you mean?"

He sighed, settling back agitated and visibly exhausted. "To truly understand, I need to share my past, a past I've tried to forget for six centuries."

Gregor took a deep breath, his Scottish burr becoming more pronounced, and his voice wobbled as he began his tale. "You must understand, Katya, Scotland in the 1700s was not the most welcoming place for people who looked like me."

I tilted my head. "But...how? Why were you there?"

He looked into the distance as if picturing a long-lost memory. "My mother was African. She hailed from a proud lineage, and her journey to Scotland was remarkable and challenging. For several centuries, many Africans had made their way to Scotland, primarily due to trading, exploration, and the complexities of colonial politics. Some were brought as servants or slaves, while others came of their own volition, driven by ambition or curiosity."

Seeing my deep interest, he continued, "My mother was among the latter. She was intelligent, charismatic, and had an uncanny ability to navigate the intricacies of Scottish court life. Her wisdom and charm didn't go unnoticed, and she quickly became a respected figure in the court. In time, she met my father, a proud member of the Clan MacGregor. Despite the social prejudices of the era, they fell deeply in love."

Gregor's eyes lit up with fondness and wistfulness as he remembered. "Their union was more than just a marriage of two souls; it was a strategic alliance that would bring prosperity to both worlds. As a gesture of goodwill and appreciation for her services to the court, the king granted my parents a sizable portion of land. This increased the holdings of the Clan MacGregor and solidified their influence and power."

I blinked in amazement. "That sounds...progressive for the time."

Gregor nodded. "It was. But it also sowed the seeds of envy and animosity among certain rival clans. Particularly, the MacCollins."

He paused, the weight of old memories pressing down on him. "Fast forward a few years, and my parents had me. Growing up biracial in such times was...challenging. But my parents raised me with love, teaching me the values of both my heritages.

"When I was but 21, a young husband and father, tragedy struck. Fueled by jealousy and a growing power, the MacCollins clan saw an opportunity. They spun tales of deceit, convincing the then-English king that the MacGregors, under the future leadership of a biracial man as laird, were a threat."

Tears glistened in Gregor's eyes. He shifted uncomfortably as if the memory burned inside of him. "My Dah was captured by the English army, given a sham of a trial, and beheaded as a traitor. They captured me and tortured me for almost two years. Their hatred for my heritage and my parents' love story was evident in every blow they landed. They brought forth my wife and son when they realized they couldn't break me."

My heart ached as I watched the pain play out on his face.

"They paraded my remaining clansmen in front of me and killed them one by one. They made me watch as they took away the two most precious people in my life, screaming for me," he murmured, his voice filled with agony. "I was the last. And when I transitioned to the afterlife, the fury, the injustice, and the sheer pain of it all... consumed me. It turned me into a Wanter."

I felt nauseous as Gregor's words sank in. His fierce gaze bored into me. "Remember how I told you the Wanters are formed? Either they stay behind, bitter and enraged, or their rage at death transforms them. When I died, I wanted revenge on everyone and everything for what happened to me, my family, my clan. I became a Wrecker, bent on making the entire world suffer.

"My soul tore apart as the change overtook me. Within hours, I had decimated the MacCollins. But it wasn't enough – I hated everything and wanted everything destroyed. Yet part of me longed for the grief to end. That shard of humanity allowed me to meet Nabil and Demetrius. They said I had a choice: perpetuate my pain and rage or let it go and be part of the solution. I had only hours before the change became permanent.

Gregor's voice lowered, "They showed me a mirror to my soul, a horrifying reflection of what I had become. The sight of it... it terrified me. I didn't want that body, that future. With their help, I began reverting to my former self. But my old life was gone – I was now Kyrios, caught between life and death.

He continued, "Nabil explained that I had evolved into a Kyrios—a fusion of Wanter and human essence. While I'm no longer tethered to the world of the living, I'm not entirely consumed by death either. I stand as a guardian at the threshold.

"When we need strength, we take on the wrathful half-formed state. It's the essence of our internal conflict—drawing upon the dormant fury within us to shield the sacred balance we've sworn to protect. So, in a way, it's like armor."

Gregor's eyes implored me to understand. "All Kyrios went through an ordeal like this but chose not to be agents of destruction, as our killers were. I've wrestled with that anger ever since."

I hesitated for a moment, gathering the courage to ask, "What about your wife and son?"

A mixture of sadness and peace graced his features. "They crossed over. I heard they're in Paradiso now."

The weight of Gregor's story hung heavily between us, and I instinctively glanced at Cynthia's encased body. Her earlier question echoed in my mind – "Do you trust them?"

"So," I began hesitantly, "was it just a coincidence that you all chose to keep your true nature from me?"

His brow furrowed. "What are you talking about?"

Exasperation overcame me, and I threw a pillow at him. "Don't play dumb! Sophia's not the only one who told me about Nabil's plans to outdo the Archs because the fabled Balancer chose the Kyrios. There was no intention to strengthen me, just keep me weak and reliant on you! Is that why you didn't want me fighting?"

Tears blurred my vision. "I'm furious, not just at you or the Generals, but at myself for being so naïve."

Gregor's face crumpled. "Look, tensions between Nabil and the Archs are common knowledge. But I swear I have never heard of any scheme like this. My fear has always been about your well-being."

He stepped closer, but I recoiled instinctively.

His expression hardened, and he took several steps back. "Understand this—every moment I spend near you is a tug-of-war between my humanity and Wanter nature. I resist the Wanter side so I can be with you to protect you. So I can feel more of my humanity again. If you can't accept the dark parts of me after all this, I will do as you wish. Whatever it may be."

I sighed, weariness seeping in. "I need time, Gregor. To think, to process."

Gregor paused at the door, a last glance revealing the depths of his turmoil. "I'll update the Generals that you're not seriously hurt, nothing more." And he left.

Grief overwhelmed me, and at some point, exhaustion pulled me into a restless slumber. Awakening, I sought comfort beside Cynthia's resting form.

I felt hollow like a shell scraped empty of all feeling. Gregor's words swirled in my mind, apologies and explanations I could barely comprehend. Part of me longed to understand, to make sense of it all. But the hurt and anger still simmered below the surface, threatening to boil over again.

Cyn, you were warning me, weren't you?

Kat, I wasn't sure of anything at that time. It's just that I knew that something was off about their energy. I didn't know exactly what it was.

Mika began nudging at me. I tried to ignore her, but she was insistent. *Mika, I don't even want to talk to you right now. You probably knew about this the entire time!*

She ignored my attempts to fight with her. **There is something for you on your bed.**

A note had been laid on the corner of my bedspread. No one here had ever written to me, so I was a bit surprised to see the small, neat writing that belonged to Gregor:

Katya,

I know you need time, but I just needed to say one more thing. Being with you, I feel like my twenty-three-year-old self. You make me laugh. You tick me off, but I want to kiss your tears away anytime I see them. I admire your fire, lass, but I want to keep you safe, too. I feel alive again because of you.

Misconceptions are swirling around you, I know. But I don't want to lose you over this. We need to talk. Come when you're ready.

Gregor

What am I supposed to do? Now calmer, I understood Gregor better. But I couldn't dismiss what Sophia said either, as she was right in some ways. *Could I trust them?* I sighed, the weight of uncertainty heavy on my shoulders. *Could I move past this betrayal? Did I even want to try?* A knock at the door jarred me from my thoughts.

"I'm not in the mood for talks, Gregor," I began.

"It's Jae, Katya." Hearing Jae's voice was the last thing I expected. "We need to speak. Urgently."

I paused, recalling his earlier warning. Tentatively, I opened the door just a sliver. "What's going on, Young Jae?"

Jae looked around anxiously before whispering, "General Lamar sent me. He's offering an escape for you and your friend."

I yanked him inside. "What are you talking about?"

He hesitated, eyes scanning my face with palpable concern. "Are you alright, Katya?"

The genuine concern in his voice nearly crumbled my composure. "All of this... it's too much. You tried to tell me earlier, but I wouldn't hear it."

Jae embraced me, murmuring comfort as I clung to him. "Don't cry, Katya. I wanted to tell you everything, but they forbade it. We were under gag orders."

I managed a weak smile, grateful for his attempted warnings. His face mirrored a mosaic of emotions – fury, sorrow, regret, and a flicker of hope.

With a sudden intensity, he clasped my hands to his chest. "Come away with me, Katya."

I stared, bewildered. "Jae?"

He tightened his grip, imploringly looking into my eyes. "I know of a route out, a way to vanish undetected. We can vanish into the Live Realm. We can start anew," he breathed, wiping away my tears. "All this chaos, Sophia, Gregor—it doesn't have to be your life. Tell me, and I'll prioritize you above all else. Give me the word, just one word, and you will become my entire world. One word, and I will give you everything I have and more."

Stunned, I stared as Jae leaned in to kiss me softly, and I froze. His lips met mine, gentle at first. A small voice told me to pull away, but the warmth of his skin drowned it out. This was comfort, an escape from the chaos around me.

When I didn't immediately pull away, he deepened the kiss. Jae's fingers tangled in my hair, drawing me closer. For a moment, I let go, melting into his embrace. My mind went blissfully blank as his mouth moved with mine. Emotions swirled inside both of us, melded, intensified. His affections for me, once subtle, were obvious now. And for a split second, the allure of freedom and escape was intoxicating.

I started to pull him closer when I felt the letter crunch underfoot. *Gregor.* The name was like cold water, shocking me back to reality. *What was I doing?* I cared for them both, but this would only complicate matters.

The trance was broken.

Slowly, I drew away, tapping his chest. "I can't. I'm sorry. We shouldn't have."

Jae recoiled as if burned. His arms fell limply, and his once warm demeanor transformed. "They'll keep lying, you know. He will keep lying to you." Desperation tinged his voice.

I cringed, knowing who he meant by "he." *Apparently, we weren't as discrete as we thought.* Guilt gnawed at my resolve. "I've got to give it a chance. I'm in too deep."

Jae's heartbreak was palpable as he went rigid cold. In that instant, he couldn't stand the sight of me. Alright then," he said with an icy detachment. He turned away, reaching for the door. He stopped and threw over his shoulder, "Follow me to the General's tower. He's waiting."

With a swift turn, he left, and I found myself trailing behind, my heart heavy with choices and what-ifs. He didn't glance back. Not even once.

36

His True Nature

We converged silently at Lamar's tower base. Without warning, Jae gripped me and soared to the tower's summit, entering the security chamber. To my surprise, the room was enshrouded in darkness, not a single monitor aglow. Almost abruptly, Jae released me, and I landed hard on my healing bicep.

"Hey!" I protested. He retreated without a word, positioning himself in a distant corner.

A familiar voice broke the quiet. "Are you all right?"

Blinking, I tried adjusting to the dimness. "General? Is that you?" A single monitor flickered to life, casting a pale glow that revealed Lamar in his chair, staring at me. Still, the pervasive shadows made me uneasy.

"A few more monitors would be appreciated, General."

Lamar illuminated additional screens with a nonchalant shrug, providing a dim luminescence. He then crouched before me, eyes filled with concern. "I trust you're not gravely injured?"

Rubbing my sore bicep, I replied, "It's healing faster now, though not fully healed. I should be fine."

His face brightened. "Splendid. Let's proceed then." Suddenly, with a theatrical snap of his fingers, a chair materialized beneath me, binding me with metallic restraints.

Startled, I demanded, "General, what's happening?"

Lamar grinned, inhaling deeply. "The surge of your energy... It's delightful." He seemed tempted to touch me but hesitated.

"We mustn't touch what isn't ours," he whispered, reminding himself.

Struggling, I called out, "Jae! Why? What's happening?"

The General's voice oozed with condescension. "My dear, he never really was your friend. He was following orders from me from the moment he met you."

I strained to see Lamar's face, eyes widening, "You? I don't understand. Why are you doing this to me?"

His fingers toyed with a small device. "Before our guest arrives, let me enlighten you."

"Guest? Who?"

The General snapped his fingers again, and a small chair emerged from the floor. He sat with such flourish that I imagined he was enjoying himself very much. "Patience is not your strong suit.

Now, if you allow me, I'll start immediately. How do humans start a story again? Oh yes," he delivered with chilling glee.

"Once upon a time, there was a sweet Kyrios major named Sherene. She was gifted, powerful, and could've been a general. But she declined, and I, madly in love with her, was content as her deputy. We were inseparable. Sherene had an uncanny ability to prevent souls from turning into Wanters. But one fateful assignment changed everything."

My heart raced as he continued, "Sherene went on a mission alone, against my wishes. She encountered a particularly ferocious turning and didn't survive. The remaining parts of my soul died alongside with her."

Listening intently, I realized the depth of his pain. "That's tragic, but why betray everyone?"

His eyes sparkled with a combination of madness and clarity. "Her death gave me all the answers I needed about this system. There is no point. Day in. and day out, our protection accomplishes nothing. Humans have become increasingly weak, constantly susceptible to the prodding of the Want. One mere suggestion, and they are ready to hate, harm others, and burn everything in sight to the ground. But no one was ready to hear the truth."

Lamar's eyes sparkled malevolently. "I rose in the ranks to reveal the truth behind this facade called Ager."

Bitterness laced my voice. "So, you've been sabotaging the Kyrios?"

He grinned. "Precisely. Sabotaging, manipulation, whatever it took. And what better way to do that than as the head of security? It did, unfortunately, require the death of the previous general, but overall, I think it was a good plan. Most importantly, you will be my master-piece. Your arrival, training, and hatred for the Want could not have gone better."

Lamar pulled out the silver bracelet he had given me from his pocket and snapped it back onto my wrist. It gave me such a horrible jolt that I screamed. "What the – it was you! You messed with my energy in the Live Realm."

Lamar sniffed the air with relish. "I will never get enough of that. Your training has done wonders on your reserves." He tapped the bracelet, sending more painful shocks that had tears streaming down my face. "Your friend's energy, the enigma it was, also had a delicious flare. It's unfortunate she was such an unknown liability that I had to put her in a coma."

"God, you are fucking sick! You are actually enjoying this!" I shouted after catching my breath.

He sat back in his chair, despondent. "Yes, and since you are at the end of your training, my fun and manipulation have come to an end. Nabil wants you out in the Live Realm closing gates. And we can't have that, so Sophia made such a show for you today to burst your bubble effectively. So you can see the ugly truth about us. Jae has been instrumental in setting this up, hasn't he?"

Lamar gave Jae a look of pride. "Jae has also been hurt by the de-cisions of this pseudo-soul-saving group. He lost his twin brother. They died together, you know, but they are now separated forever. Because of this blasted system. Such a shame."

He shook his head. "Anyway, His Lordship thought it best to make it look like you had cut your ties with the Kyrios after discovering that we are part Wanters. You know, to make your disappearance look purposeful rather than sinister."

I shuddered, feeling the weight of his gaze. Every instinct screamed at me to break free, fight back, or do something. "You won't get away with this," I hissed, starting to pull against the cuffs, realizing my true danger.

Interrupted by a knock, Lamar announced with mock cheerfulness, "Ah, our guest is here. He's been eager to reunite with you."

Reunite?

The door opened to reveal Sophia, the devious Kyrios major, with her signature smirk. She gave me a wink and stood by the door next to Jae.

But my attention was on the strange man who had walked in beside her. He sauntered gracefully in a full gray suit, focusing solely on me. He wore a black bowler hat that concealed his slicked-back blond hair. He grinned as my eyebrows disappeared into my hair.

"Detective Sloan?"

He sauntered towards me, still grinning. "Katya, you certainly have grown in the few weeks you've been away. Ager has been good to you."

My heart raced, every past interaction with him rushing back, painting a clearer, more sinister picture. "How are you here?"

He wagged his finger dismissively. "I couldn't stand to be away from you. I first sensed your unique Vis on a bus before our official intro-duction. Since then, your Vis has been my siren call. Lamar had hinted at someone special, but meeting you confirmed it. In the presence of the fabled Balancer – a divine gift during humanity's troubled times. Hilarious, really." He circled me like a predator. "I wanted to confront you earlier, but that Kyrios major was always by your side. Thankfully, Lamar organized this reunion."

Jae's story about the fall of Archs and Phims immediately came to mind. *"The more powerful Archs-turned-Wanters kept a humanoid form and sowed dissension and chaos among the humans."*

"You're a Want General?" I asked slowly.

The man in the bowler hat chuckled, mockingly bowing to me. "My name is General Krenlin of Want Fleet Five, and you are about to send me into history." He smirked and turned to Lamar. "Is she ready?"

General Lamar nodded eagerly. "Yes. Her Vis reserves have grown exponentially since she started her training. Just smell the air, sir."

"Hey, assholes! Stop talking about me like I am not here!" I yelled.

Krenlin flashed before me, slamming his hands on the back of my chair. The force reverberated like a sudden clash of lightning had just exploded within the small confines of our room. Hovering over me, his dark blue eyes gleamed angrily. "You are in a precarious situation, little one. I orchestrated your mother's anguish, deployed my soldier to infiltrate her, and ordered attacks on everyone dear to you. Everything you lost, I orchestrated. You will respect me."

Krenlin smiled smugly, sniffing the air, sensing my anguish. "Here's a fact you may not know. As a Wanter, the more powerful you are, the more readily able you are to assume the image of the souls you absorb. This next form is my absolute favorite."

His form began to shimmer and melt into a mousy-looking girl with large glasses and flat brown hair. Her large brown eyes, which usually shined with ready tears, had a distinct coldness.

Amie stood over me and smiled deviously.

Cynthia's internal sobs turned into my own. "Amie," I whispered brokenly. "You...you..."

"Amie fought to stay alive valiantly, likely trying to find you amidst the chaos that was your home. She was trapped beneath the debris, desperately calling out for rescue — for her mother, you, Cynthia, and even the peers who tormented her at school. Hours passed; her cries grew faint until they ceased. By the time help arrived, she was gone."

He resumed his original form, locking eyes with me. "She died because of her loyalty to you. And in her death, she offered me her potent Vis. A gift I attribute to you, Balancer.

Pain. Anguish. But rage turned my body impossibly hot as my power flared violently. "I will destroy you!" I bellowed. Every nerve in my body was on fire and wanted to explode to directly hit the smug bastard. But the cuffs stopped me cold, absorbing the massive power flare.

Krenlin took a deep breath of the air, sniffing the frail remnant of my power like fine wine. "Oh, yes, you were right, Lamar. She is ready for absorption. Pure Vis rolls off her body." I struggled against the cuff, hoping that they would melt from the heat I was giving off. Krenlin shook his head, chuckling at my feeble attempts. "Oh, don't worry, sweetie. You'll join your friend soon enough. There's no happy ending, no reunion in Paradiso for you. Simply darkness."

I turned to Jae, betrayal sharp in my eyes. "You promised my mother. How could you betray us?"

My last shout moved him from the door to the front of my chair. He bent over until he was at eye level and said softly, "I gave you a chance. I guess you're really 'in too deep' now." Never had I seen his eyes so cold and expressionless.

Angry and guilty tears burned the corners of my eyes. "I'm sorry, Young Jae," I whispered brokenly. He didn't say a word. He turned around and returned to the door, standing guard.

Krenlin smiled, amused at my despondency. "Now that all that is out of the way, can we get started?"

Lamar, with a devious smile, lifted his hand over my chest. "This might hurt a bit."

A purple sphere emerged from his hand and was thrust into my core. The room echoed with my agonizing screams. I felt an icy coldness clawing its way into my chest, trying to wrench my soul and Vis from their core. It was nothing like any pain I'd experienced before— not the Vis bind, not the feeling of fighting with Sophia. Every fiber of my body ignited in resistance against the extraction. The agony was unbearable.

The room was now filled with an odd beeping that caught everyone's attention. "What is that, Lamar?" Krenlin demanded.

"The shield outside the tower is being attacked. Someone knows where we are," Lamar answered tersely.

"What—argh!" Krenlin was suddenly thrown to the wall by a red blast of energy. Lamar and Sophia met the same fate, sending them into the wall and knocking them out. I looked around to find Jae dropping his hands, still glowing red.

"Why did you...?"

Jae rushed for me. "We don't have time. Krenlin and Lamar are too strong to be stunned for long." He quickly pried open the cuffs, and I finally freed myself from the chair. My knees buckled as my body attempted to cool down. He caught me and took hold of my arm. "Come on, we need to get you out of here."

The urgency in his eyes said more than words could. "No, Jae, wait –"

He gave me a small smile. "I'm making my peace with you. I made a promise to you and your mother. Now come on, we've got—"

He paused. I stilled as well, too afraid as to why he'd stopped.

"Jae?"

The Lieutenant's eyes flared with blue Vis energy, and he gently touched my face. "I love you, Katya." I stood in shock as his eyes turned violently bright, and he grabbed me by my jumpsuit and threw me out the nearby window.

Time seemed to stretch infinitely. As glass shards sparkled around me, I locked eyes with Jae. The familiar warmth had returned to his gaze, a calm amidst the storm. But any light in his eyes soon disappeared, and his slight smile slipped away as a hand, crackling with red energy, protruded from the middle of his chest.

37

Steeling Resolve

Jae's body crumpled beyond the windowsill and out of sight as I plummeted. I could only stare at the cloudy sky as it rapidly pulled away. As I hurled to the ground, I could only think: *Jae's dead.* I barely noticed the two arms slipping underneath me in midair, cradling me close to a broad chest.

A familiar brogue frantically cried, "Katya! Are you all right?" As we descended slowly to the ground, my eyes sought out my favorite blue-grey eyes, and everything from the betrayal and hurt melted away.

"Gregor," I said brokenly. "He's dead."

Gregor looked at me strangely. "Who are you—" BOOM! An explosion sent us careening to the ground. Gregor took the brunt of the force and slammed into the concrete. Shouts surrounded us as the troops emerged from their barracks, responding to the noises. The ceiling and roof of the security tower had been blasted clear off, leaving only the top floor. Standing among the debris and acrid dust floating through the air were Krenlin, Lamar, and Sophia with bored expressions.

"Well," Krenlin said in a loud voice, catching every Kyrios' attention, "looks like the Balancer is in the arms of her beloved protector. Poor Young Jae." He picked up Jae's lifeless body by the head. "Looks like he loved in vain. Poor sod." Krenlin threw the body to the ground below but it never made it; his lifeless limbs glowed eerily until it evaporated. Green particles danced with the wind, leaving Jae's clothes to flutter to the bottom.

"Lamar, you bastard!" Nabil cried furiously, making his entrance. "What is the meaning of this?"

Lamar laughed heartily. "As if you didn't have some inkling! I've made some new friends and shifted around some priorities." I could hear murmuring from the Kyrios troops. Every face mirrored the same confusion and anger.

"Lamar, think about what you are doing. You made a choice many years ago! Don't throw everything away," Nabil tried.

"And where has that decision led me? Led us? Endless battles! More of us die in vain with the humans unappreciative of our sacrifices. More souls are turning Want every day. If they are going to change and continue to change at this rate, what is the point of all this?"

"Because it's an outcome worth fighting for. We save the souls the Want would prey on!" Michiko shouted back. She and Victor appeared behind Nabil, looking just as furious.

Lamar snorted. "Maybe for you. But I think it's time I take a new direction." He removed his black coat and threw his General medallion to the ground. He gestured to Krenlin. "Lord Krenlin has a wonderful crusade I couldn't help but join." He then clasped hands with Krenlin and began to change.

Spikes made of bone emerged at his elbows and shoulders. His plain black pants and shirt changed into the same three-piece suit Krenlin wore. Lastly, the former General's brown eyes went completely red. Sophia underwent a similar transformation, with spikes protruding out of her chin and her navel. Her clothes shifted into a red, fitted gown with long slits along her sides.

Gregor tightened his hold on me. "Krenlin is here in Ager? How?" he hissed. I felt angry power spikes from the rest of the Kyrios around me. Everyone knew precisely who Krenlin was.

The smug bastard came forward and bowed with a smirk. "Long

time, no see Nabil! I don't think we've ever met outside of the Live Realm."

Nabil's power surge shook the ground underneath us. A blue sphere, humming with electric currents, grew to the size of a beach ball in his hands. "Do not call me 'friend.'" Several other Kyrios reacted as well, and soon, the courtyard glowed blue with numerous powerful spheres.

Krenlin shook his head in mirth. "Sophia and Lamar, I think we've overstayed our welcome. It's time to go. I believe we are needed in the Abyss."

"Do not let them escape!" Nabil shouted. "I want those traitors in custody now!" Several Kyrios leaped into the air as he commanded, only to be met by a large barrier protecting the three traitors now floating above.

Sophia laughed loudly at their crashing into the barrier. "I'm afraid I'm never coming back, Generals. But I'll surely see you all again in the Live Realm." Her eyes bore into mine, taking in Gregor clutching me to his chest. "Especially you, Balancer," she said bitingly.

"Sophie!" Krenlin chided. "Hands off now." He waved to me. "Katya is my one and only. No one can touch her but me." I couldn't help the shiver that traveled down my spine. Gregor felt it and impossibly tightened his grip further.

"Well," Krenlin said, bored. "Plan A didn't work. Now on to Plan B!" A black hole emerged over their head with a snap of his fingers. All three leaped in, and it closed right after them. No one made a sound —everyone was shocked that a well-liked General had suddenly gone AWOL, with a high-ranking Wanter at that.

Nabil snapped out of it first. "Troops, our security has been compromised. If your loyalty is true in the security unit, I want you to reconfigure and reinforce the wards and barriers as best as you can. I want all exits sealed now.

"Victor, take a unit to block the main entrance. Michiko, send a message to all units in the Live Realm about the closure. Everyone else, remain in your quadrants and stand guard. They may launch an attack on Ager at any time. Go!"

Bodies flew, Kyrios running everywhere. Gregor had just put me down when Nabil turned to us. "I want you two to follow me to Central Command." We arrived there silently and entered a small room to the side, where Michiko and several others were furiously working the controls, sending messages out. Nabil closed the door behind us and gestured for me to sit down.

"All right, Lady Katya. Tell me what happened."

I robotically relayed the details, including what had happened in my room and Jae's sacrifice. I could see Gregor's jaw tightening as I described the kiss. But I didn't have the chance to react to the flash of jealousy. I just felt horrible. Amie and Jae were gone forever, and I couldn't help them. Moments of Jae's face came to mind. His sacrifice and his love all felt like a heavy burden. But this wasn't the time for tears.

At the end of my explanation, both men looked down pensively. I couldn't help but whisper, "I'm sorry."

"No," Nabil said tiredly, "I'm sorry. I have failed you, my lady."

"What do you mean?"

Nabil suddenly aged before my eyes, looking like a man of more than five thousand years old rather than his typical appearance of a thirty-five-year-old. "I have suspected Lamar for some time now. I just wasn't able to prove it. When word of you came, he immediately took an interest. Lingered in places you once were. Now we know he was taking in your residual Vis energy.

"When you came back, nearly soul-crushed, he said that your power had fought the soul bind. I suspected he might have been behind it. And I am sorry I couldn't spare you from this."

He attempted to massage the fatigue away from his temples. "There is something you need to know that very few do. Gregor, I expect your utmost confidence in this. It must stay in this room."

We both nodded. "Lamar was correct about one thing. Yes, I did want you and your allegiance with us. I will not make excuses for that. I thoroughly believe your role is to close the gates. But my desire for your allegiance was not about flexing our newly attained Balancer in front of the Archs. It was to keep them from finding out about your awakening."

"I don't understand."

Nabil sighed. "In the same records that General Michiko found, it said that once the Archs find out that you've awakened, they are to take to the sky and descend upon the Live Realm with you as their leader. If you were to team with the Archs, it would mean it was time for the world to end."

I felt faint. "So you are saying I'm not the savior, but that I end everyone's life? End the entire world?"

Nabil shook his head. "The records are vague at best, but that's how the Archs will take it. And with your training, they might take it as gospel. That you were preparing for them. We are lucky—because they are so high above everything, they haven't found out about the Want's current onslaught or kept track of who you are. I swore Michiko to secrecy so that this news would not travel. The rumor you heard probably came from Michiko, who must have used it to explain my actions to someone less conscientious than they should have been."

A sharp knock at the door interrupted us. Michiko stuck her head in. "Nabil, Gregor, you need to see this." Her face was grim.

We returned to the Central Command console to see a screen with Raf featured in the center. In a word, Raf looked rough. The General's white hair was now peppered with black dirt and grime. Scratches and cuts plagued his upper body. A bleeding gash over his left eye forced him to squint and periodically wipe the blood away from his vision.

"Raf, what news?" Nabil asked.

"The situation is at a critical stage. More small Wanters have attempted to overrun the Los Angeles Abyss gate. The ensuing accidents caused by the Cravers and Posers have reached an all-time high. The gate over Los Angeles has grown exponentially in the last twelve hours. The Wanters are overly excited, chanting that their own Balancer is awakening."

"Huh?" I asked. But a withering look from Gregor shut me up quickly.

Not missing a beat, Raf continued. "There also has been a huge surge of negative Vis energy from the LA gate. And the Want has become particularly concentrated there. Five large tremors have occurred in the last two days."

I could only imagine the panic down in California.

"Nabil, the situation cannot wait any longer. We need the Balancer to close the rift here to clear the Want."

Everyone at Central Command froze and turned to stare at me. My stomach dropped to my toes. Nabil again rubbed his temples in fatigue. "Raf, stand by for further instruction." The screen went blank. Nabil eyed me, gauging my reaction. "What do you think, Balancer?" he asked softly.

I wanted to scream, *No! It's chaotic out there! Gregor was right. I'm in way over my head, and I quit.* Just as I was about to open my mouth, I remembered Amie and how I hadn't been there to help. So many others were like her in the Live Realm, and while I didn't know what was going on with the Archs and what my work in the Live Realm might mean to them, I couldn't abandon everyone in the Live Realm either. Even if I wanted to run and hide. My mom used to say to me, "Women can be emotional and broken people, but never in the face of what needs to be done."

"I can do this," I said, surprising everyone. "We must do this." As I took in their faces, a new sense of determination also fell over me. I was still scared, but I felt Mika spread through my body and strengthen me. Nabil scrutinized me from head to toe, and whatever he found, he was satisfied. He turned to a technician at the control. "Get General Raf back on. Tell him to expect a squad with the Balancer within two Live Realm hours."

I exhaled the breath I held as I watched the scurry of movement in response to the order. The Kyrios moved with more purpose, with more fervor than before. And with the furtive glances I received, I was sure I was the cause.

Nabil looked at Gregor and me. "Prepare to leave from the East Gate in two Live Realm hours. Gregor, set her up with some battle armor.

Lady Katya," he said quietly, "we are putting all our faith in the idea of the Balancer. Let us hope our faith is not misplaced." I nodded and followed Gregor out the door.

Our trip to our tower was quiet, save for the urgent marching and shouts outside. As we entered my bedroom and the door clicked shut, the weight of everything pressed in. Gregor's gaze met mine, a mix of fear, longing, and determination. His voice, thick with emotion, whispered, "Do you realize this might be the last quiet moment we have together?"

Without answering, I stepped into his embrace. My body was flattened against the wall as Gregor covered me completely, his lips devouring me with desperation. His hands were everywhere, as if memorizing every curve, every inch of me. My hands were in his hair, over the flat planes of his chest, and stroking his hard-lined jaw. It wasn't just passion. It was a promise, a plea, a moment of solace amidst chaos. Our world might be crumbling, but this connection was unbreakable despite the lies and omissions.

After several moments, Gregor pulled away, resting his forehead against mine.

"I desperately don't want you to go."

"Gregor—" I started.

"But at the same time, I know you have to do this. After our talk with Nabil, it's even more important now."

I gnawed on my bottom lip. "What if I really bring the end of the world?"

He shook his head. "One battle at a time, Kat. Let's deal with the immediate crisis first. Before anything else happens, I want you to know I am proud of you."

My insides turned to mush. "Really?"

He cradled my face and searched my eyes, seeking something. He said, "There is one thing I want you to promise me. Stay alive. Stay by my side. I don't want you to join me on this side yet."

I gave him a small smile. "I'll promise to do that if you do one thing for me. Well, two."

"What is it?"

I inched as close as possible and gave him a soft kiss, filled with everything I felt but couldn't voice. I think he understood because his eyes softened with a smile as we separated.

"Hold on to that kiss for me. I'll want it back later."

A grin lit up his face. "Well, what if I don't want to return it?"

"There is a 'must return' policy on that kiss. Think of it as a loan."

Gregor chuckled. "Okay, fine. What's the second thing?"

My smile dimmed slightly. "Could you hold me until I have to leave?" I asked in a small voice.

Gregor pulled me into his arms and kissed me on my forehead. "I'm not leaving your side." We laid on my bed, his chest to my back. Being held close stopped the jitters and the shock of Nabil's news from overtaking me. *Could I bring the end of the world? If the Archs found me, would they try to convince me of their vision? What if this all turned into something I didn't want? Could I be my own version of the Balancer?*

I'm unsure how long we rested there, enjoying the contact, but it felt like it was over too soon. Gregor said, "It is time to get ready."

Gregor left and then returned with two boxes. Each box contained several pieces of armor of various sizes – one for me and the other for him. He began unzipping his bodysuit, revealing his taut torso. With sudden dryness in my mouth, I asked incredulously, "Um, what are you doing?"

He smirked, stretching his arms over his head, elongating his taut torso. "What do you think I'm doing? I'm not leaving your side. I meant that." He looked at me, daring me to ask him to leave to change.

I returned his smirk, "That's right. You did say that."

Our eyes never strayed from the other. I let my eyes drink in the rugged ridges of his chest, the smooth bronze skin over taut muscle. I slowly released the front zipper of my bodysuit, with him watching hungrily at me. Gregor's eyes roamed over me, studying and memorizing every curve.

Finally, he dropped his own, leaving himself completely bare. To say this man was magnificent would be an understatement. Piece by piece,

I shed my clothes until nothing remained between us. Gregor's eyes blazed as they roamed my bare skin, his chest heaving with exertion. Every nerve in me longed to close the gap, to run my hands over the angles and valleys of his body.

This was the reminder we needed – this moment of tension, of promises unfulfilled, awaited us on the other side.

But time was against us, and duty called. Gregor took a deep breath and expelled any lingering hard-charged desire. He turned to his box of armor and gestured to my own. We dressed silently, donning our new jumpsuits and each piece of armor – chest and back, shoulder guards, arm and wrist guards, and leg guards. Each piece was sleek and futuristic, with a glossy black finish with the blue and gold thread undertones. Each piece fit perfectly, as though custom-made for me. As I adjusted the jumpsuit and armor, I could feel its fibers amplifying my Vis energy; I felt more flexible and more mobile. I quickly released my twists, fluffing my hair and releasing my curls to cascade wildly over my shoulders. If anything, I was going in with my curls ablaze.

Gregor adjusted the last piece of my armor, his fingers lingering a moment too long on my neck. Our eyes met, reflections of longing and fear swimming in them. We shared one final, desperate kiss before duty tore us apart. I wanted nothing more than to melt into Gregor's embrace, to feel the comfort of his arms around me, but time was against us.

This was it. Without another word, we marched out for the East Gate to meet our battalion.

I glanced back again at the tower that had been a haven, now fading in the distance. The hollow pit in my stomach grew with each step. *What horrors awaited us beyond the gate? Would I make it back?* My eyes briefly clouded over, settling on the spot where I last saw Jae. Grief attempted to claw its way out, but just as quickly, I shook my head and pulled myself back to the present.

Gregor, sensing my distraction, gently cupped my face. "You're thinking of him."

I looked away, nodding slightly. "It's hard not to, but I need to focus on now—it's what he would've wanted."

Gregor squeezed my hand, a silent promise to stick together no matter what. Side by side, we went forth into the unknown.

38

Now or Never

By the time we reached the East Gate, General Nabil, the Quad, Jaya, Kevon, and Santiago were waiting for us.

"I've taken the liberty to increase your number of guards, my lady. I'm told you have already met these individuals," he motioned to Jaya, Kevon, and Santiago. "I hope that despite everything, you all can work together." He gave me a meaningful look.

I cleared my throat. "While I don't appreciate the secrets that have been kept from me, in some ways, I can understand. Many people back home don't know about my past because of my fear of rejection." I looked at all of them in the eye, including Gregor. "I am willing to put all of that aside. We have work to do. Together."

The relief and grins on their faces were clear, and they answered, "Yes, miss!"

A ghost of a smile flitted across Nabil's face. "Your mission is clear, Kyrios. Get the Balancer to the rift and give her the necessary cover to get the job done by any means necessary."

They all nodded. I guess that meant they were going to transform into their Want counterparts. I began to coach myself. *Don't freak out. Don't freak. Do. Not. Freak.*

General Nabil took another look at us, looking grim but determined. "We wait for your return. Depart."

The Kyrios saluted him, and we moved quickly out of the gate. The Kyrios formed a small circle around me, with Gregor on my left and Demetrius to my right. We headed far outside the gates so Zenobia could open a portal large enough for all of us to walk through at once.

On the other side, we arrived in what looked like the middle of downtown LA. Night had just fallen, and the area was relatively deserted, save a few cars that looked like they had been abandoned. I guess they hadn't been kidding about the increasing number of accidents. As much as I wanted to marvel at finally making it to California, the presence of the otherworldly guard dampened my thrill.

The group ushered me to a nearby alley where we found a disheveled General Raf with several injured Kyrios resting against the buildings' walls.

"General Raf—" Demetrius started.

"Shh," Raf said.

All of us fell silent. A loud screech could be heard about a mile away, quickly fading. When Raf felt it was safe, he said, "We've been reduced to hiding out here until you all arrived. As you can see," he said bitingly, "we've gotten a couple of scratches." Some Kyrios looked about to keel over from exhaustion and injuries.

"General Raf," Gregor interjected. "What's the plan to get to the gate?"

The General grimaced. "The Wanters have drastically increased their numbers in the past few hours." He held out his hand and manipulated a ball of energy until it looked like a city map. "The gate is about one and a half miles east, towards the Arts District. We are here." He pointed to a large building directly in front of the gate. "Between us and the gate, we are looking at more than a hundred Wanters, ranking from the lowest to level-three Stuffers and Wreckers. We have two other Kyrios groups in a building to the east and west, ready to strike with us." He pointed to a smaller building standing directly to the rift's right.

"And the humans?" Demetrius asked.

Raf shook his head. "Humans have evacuated the area for the last few days." He pointed to the middle ground between us and the gate. "This is all a mess due to our fighting. Much of it is just debris from the clipped buildings or craters formed in the street. Before the hard fighting occurred, the skirmishes alone were freaking the humans out, and the place was evacuated. Now rumors have been flying that this place is either the epicenter of the tremors or just plain cursed. Either way, those in charge of the Live Realm figured out a way to explain away what they can't understand as usual. It's just us and the Wanters here."

"What's your plan to move us, General?" Gregor asked.

He sighed. "We'll move forward and engage the Want from the west and the east, pressing them into the middle. Gregor, Demetrius, and Jaya, you will take Lady Katya around the fighting from the west and get to the gate. We'll close the Want in a circle long enough to close the rift." He turned to me. "How long do you need?"

Everyone looked at me. I inwardly turned to Mika. *Well?*

A pause. **Seven minutes.**

"Seven minutes," I repeated.

Raf nodded. "Then we'll do our best to give you that. Gregor, Demetrius, and Jaya, you three stay with Lady Katya. The rest of you come with me. We'll alert the others of the plan. Move out in fifteen." Zenobia, Addy, and Sebastian turned to me and bowed deeply, their right hand over their hearts. "It has been a pleasure to serve you, my lady." Santiago and Kevon joined them on their knees.

I desperately held back the tears that wanted to fall. "I expect to see all of you when I get back. There are more gates to close." They each smiled at me and left, following after General Raf.

I took a deep breath, stealing a glance at Demetrius and Jaya. Their expressions were passive, but both of their bodies looked rigid. I guessed they were getting themselves ready. Gregor's body also looked rigid, but he focused on me, looking very grim.

I was about to ask what was wrong when I felt Mika prodding me. I moved to a corner, sat on the floor, and closed my eyes. I hoped it looked like I was meditating and that no one would bother me.

Mika? I asked.

Katya, Mika's voice was a gentle whisper. **There are things you're not ready for that are beyond your comprehension. But for now, we must focus.**

Yeah, we do. How are we going to do this?

The power needed to close the rift is too vast for you to wield in your current state.

What? If I can't do this, why did you let me say we could?

We can do it together. But you need to do exactly what I tell you. Diantha, you will need to listen well. This concerns you, too.

What is it I have to do? Cynthia asked.

There was a long pause. Each second felt like an eternity. Then, Mika's gentle yet firm voice echoed within me:

Katya, you need to die.

A cold shiver ran down my spine. *Die?* The word echoed in the hollows of my mind, turning louder and more insistent. Was this some cruel joke? A desperate anger bubbled within, but a rising tide of fear and sorrow threatened to drown me beneath it. I had fought, struggled, and survived for so long. *Was it all for this?*

I screamed in my head, *Are you crazy?* Cynthia just sputtered in the background, not believing her orders.

Quite sane, thank you.

This is no time for jokes, Mika! I can't do that. Not willingly! All the battles, the close calls, the friendships, and betrayals – was it all leading to this one heart-wrenching moment? The thought of never seeing Gregor again, of leaving him and the others behind, gripped my heart with an unbearable pain.

Katya, listen, Mika's voice carried an urgency I had never felt before. **There are paths and decisions that even you cannot fathom. I wish we had more time, but you must trust me now. This gate will not yield to an unfinished power. For this battle, you must let me guide us. If you cannot access the power, I must do it for all our sakes. The current path requires a sacrifice, one I wish we didn't have to make. You must let**

go, and we shall close the gate as one. The universe and its equilibrium hang in the balance. This is our duty.

My mind involuntarily flashed back to a moment with my mother, her warm eyes looking into mine, telling me always to be brave, no matter what. Would she consider this bravery or foolishness?

I couldn't answer Mika. I didn't have to. She felt my acceptance.

Cynthia was still sputtering. *This is going to be the hardest thing I have ever done. To just let Katya die?*

Mika's calm voice answered. **You can, Diantha, and you will. Katya, I will tell you when it is time.**

"Katya, we need to move out."

I opened my eyes to find Gregor, Demetrius, and Jaya with their Havadars out. I pulled Diantha out as well. Knowing it was my best friend, it oddly felt comforting in my hands. We all left through our designated entrance to find Raf's team moving toward the west. Raf grinned at me. "We'll meet again, my lady."

I nodded. With that, he was gone. Gregor led us a bit further down the middle to a deserted street. We waited in silence for the General's signal. It was several moments before we saw blue sparks glowing in the sky.

"Move!" Gregor shouted. We ran down the street, looping around pieces of debris and cars to return to the middle. We heard clangs of fighting in the background as we sprinted to the gate. The massive gate loomed before us, casting an oppressive shadow stretching into downtown LA's moonlit streets. Unlike the distant views from Central Command, up close, it seemed almost alive, a pulsing behemoth that dwarfed the surrounding buildings. It stood a daunting one hundred feet tall and at least twice as wide. The ground near it felt different, cooler, and more brittle, as though the earth itself was being affected by its presence. Abandoned cars lay strewn about, silent witnesses to the unfolded chaos.

It sent chills up and down my spine, raising the hair on my neck. It was the same turbulent energy I'd felt in my mother's dream – this is what Raf meant by negative Vis. But the worst part was, deep inside the tear itself, a loud, deep breathing could be heard.

"What is that?" Jaya asked.

"No idea and I'd rather not find out. Lady Katya?" Demetrius said.

I gulped. "Right." I tried to summon my own energy, but it felt like nothing would come up. Being next to the dark rift had blocked the Vis reserves I had. "Something is off. I can't bring up my power!" I panicked.

"Lady Katya, you are just delaying the inevitable." Lamar, Sophia, and two other men I didn't recognize were hovering over our heads. At least they looked like men. At a closer look at their claws, their jagged teeth, their horns protruding from their backs, and their red eyes, I realized they were Wanters.

"Oh great," Jaya muttered. "The Thirsty. Level three, too."

Lamar grinned down at us. "The power you feel from the gate is the future. This realm's new awakening. Even after all that training, I think this is too much for our precious Balancer to handle," he sneered.

Gregor stepped forward in front of me. "Think about what you are doing, Lamar! Sophia!"

"We didn't come here to talk," Sophia laughed. "We came to end this—and her."

"Over my dead body," Gregor growled, his eyes glowing blue.

"That can be arranged!" Lamar shouted. The traitors charged at us. Our swords clashed against our opponents. My combatant was Sophia.

"Look like we get to pick up where we left off, Balancer!" Sophia charged; a feral grin stretched across her face. Her strikes came swiftly as a viper, each blow intended to maim. I darted left and right, using the debris scattered around us to my advantage. A fallen concrete slab became my springboard to leap over Sophia's head and flank her.

She anticipated the move, whipping around with her Havadar, slicing through the space I'd just occupied. The blade whistled past my ear as I contorted my body out of its path. We clashed again, the screech of metal on metal piercing the air.

"Getting tired yet, little girl?" Sophia taunted.

I tuned my senses to the environment - the waft of smoke in the air, the crunch of rubble under my feet, the faint trembling still emanating from the looming gate. This was my terrain now.

In answer, I feinted left before diving right, driving Sophia back towards a crater's edge. She stumbled on the unstable footing, and in that split-second vulnerability, I disarmed her. Her Havadar spun into the debris.

But Sophia was far from finished. As I struck forward, she vanished into thin air. I whirled, struggling to spot any ripple or displacement. Too late, I sensed the disturbance at my back. She kicked hard, sending me crashing twenty feet away. I landed hard on the ground with my free hand, trying to break my fall. I instantly knew I'd broken my wrist. Sophia must have heard it snap because she grinned widely. "Already? I told Krenlin I wouldn't need to do much to send you into pieces."

I managed to muster some energy to jump back some feet to get breathing space. I gingerly touched my wrist, holding it close to my body.

Cyn, can you help out here? I sensed her grin.

Let's try out some of that extra training!

I smirked at Sophia. "You caught me off guard once, Sophia. Not again." With a flash, Diantha reformed into two new, short blades while the hilt was wrapped with a cloth that shimmied up my wrist to my elbow. The new weapon reinforced my broken wrist, and I could tap into some previously blocked Vis. I quickly used some of that energy to mend my break. It was a short-term solution that Cynthia had taught me, but the moment I relaxed, it would be rendered useless again. "Besides, I thought Krenlin wanted me for himself."

Sophia didn't look impressed. Shrugging, she said, "I don't care what he wants. I want you dead now." She attacked again, but the two blades gave me some advantage. Our Havadars sang and clanged, blow by blow. I could only imagine how we looked, fighting and quickstepping as fast as we were.

Frustrated, Sophia leaped back. "Let's see how you do with this, little girl." Her eyes flashed maliciously as she lifted her free hand and formed a small black hole the size of a bowling ball. The black hole began to suck in all the air around us, taking in everything nearby—trees, dirt, even a car or two. After sliding towards her about fifty feet, I slammed my blades into the ground and held on for dear life. The sucking suddenly stopped, but Sophia's gleeful eyes glittered dangerously. She crashed the sphere into the ground, causing all the wind and debris sucked in to explode into a mighty gale storm solely aimed at me.

"Mika!" An enormous shield formed around my body, blocking the heavy metal debris from hitting me. I could hear someone calling my name, but I couldn't lose focus now. By the time the gale force winds stopped, I was exhausted. Mika had used most of my available energy to protect me. Diantha returned to her original form. My wrist hurt like hell. My shield cracked and shattered into pieces. I barely had the strength to stand up.

Sophia was right. Mika was right. *I'm not ready for this.*

I watched Sophia approach me leisurely, sensing I had nothing else up my sleeve.

Katya, Diantha, Mika's voice was a soft echo. **There's a crossing we must make. A merging of souls and powers. Trust me. It's time.**

"Okay," I whispered. I leaned on my Havadar and tried to look bored. "Nice trick, Sophia. Got any more?" I yawned. "You're kinda boring me here."

She stopped dead in her tracks, baffled. "What?"

I rolled my eyes. "I mean, if you were trying to rough me up, take a page out of Gregor's book," I said with a smirk. "Gregor has shown me better tricks than that, and we've been together..." I counted my fingers, "a handful of times now. And let me tell you, the man does not disappoint. He is such an animal!" I winked at her.

Her expression was pure rage, her eyes bleeding red. With her sword raised, she quickly charged at me with murderous intent. And I did nothing as her Havadar ran through my stomach.

39

Rebirth in Battle

The experience of dying was nothing like I imagined. Honestly, it sucked.

Forget the pain licking at your body like fire. Forget the "my-life-flashed-before-my-eyes" montage. What surprised me was the slow motion. I never imagined my final moments stretching out like one of those overdone "slo-mo" scenes in movies, where every second feels like an eternity.

It took an eternity for my body to crash to the ground.

I remembered being very aware of everything around me. Clashes of power, screams of rage, and cries for mercy. The wonderful cacophony of a battle winding up to its pinnacle. The players' faces were unclear, but each sound was heard distinctly. It's incredible how your ears seem to hit their peak as life leaks out, like a light bulb getting brighter and brighter before it explodes.

I remembered someone calling my name and saw how his quick movements sent him zipping to my side. His cries echoed through me, making me wish I had enough strength to lift my hand and brush against his cheek. I wished I could say his name one more time. To remind him one last time of all the times he annoyed me. To confess the many moments he left me flustered and breathless. To say how in the short time we'd known each other, he'd become my most important person.

To say that I was sorry.

His cries became more incessant, urging me to hold on. But there was nothing else I could hold on to. I had to let go. The sounds became mumbles, buzzing in the background. My eyelids became heavier.

The moment is here, Katya. Are you ready?

If I could have nodded, my head would have bobbed up and down. But she understood. She knew my agony, my pain.

As my eyes closed on the scene before it, on the most beautiful set of blue eyes I had ever seen, I felt the light within me dim, as if it too was dying out.

My heart completely stopped. And then the light erupted.

In an instant, a shift occurred. Mika and I exchanged places, leaving me a spectator in my own body. I could see right through my eyes but no longer had the controls. Seeing my body rise on its own and Gregor's tear-stricken face respond with confusion was bizarre. But it was incredible seeing Sophia's shocked and angered face. She tried to charge at me, but Mika lifted our hand and sent our own gale wind, careening the traitor into a nearby building.

"Katya," Gregor whispered.

I felt myself smile. "Everything will be fine now, Gregor," Mika said. I think Gregor instantly knew it wasn't me talking but someone else. Mika didn't wait for a response and began to walk towards the rift. As Mika and I approached the rift, I felt that familiar pooling of energy, like the surge of water behind a dam. It wasn't just from within but from all around, the essence of the Live Realm rallying to our cause. We drew from the very fabric of the realm: every flicker of light and shadow, every whisper of wind, every heartbeat echoing in unison with our purpose. Nearby, I could feel everyone's individual energy. Demetrius's fierce aura. Jaya's prideful energy. Gregor's apprehension. Even the Wanters that fought against us. It was overwhelming but remarkable at the same time.

Our body rose in the air until we hovered before the gate. She clapped our hands and closed our eyes to focus, siphoning an enormous amount of Vis through our body and channeling it into our hands.

"I wish I had absorbed you when I had the chance."

We opened our eyes to find Krenlin floating fifty feet away, looking fascinated and ticked off. "I'm afraid I can't let you do this. The gate must remain open. The new Master insists on it."

As if on cue, the horrible dark energy surged. We could see a massive pair of eyes staring at us from deep within. We didn't hear a word, but a distinct roar could be heard from the dark energy.

Krenlin smirked. "He says hello."

Mika hadn't moved an inch since Krenlin's arrival. We said, "What must be done will be done."

The Want General sighed. "I'm not even talking to Lady Katya now, am I?" He shook his head. "It's truly a pity. You and I could have been together forever. Now, I have to destroy you."

He removed his bowler hat and revealed a long, skeletal spike at the top of his head. With a loud grunt, he pulled the spike out of his head, wielding his own long sword. As he readied himself to attack, a red sphere shot Krenlin in the face, sending him careening to the ground. We found Gregor in his own battle stance, his Havadar pointing at the Wanter General, who was struggling to get up. Gregor had already transformed into his half-Want form.

"Your battle is with me, Krenlin," he said in an unearthly tone.

Krenlin stood from the ground, touching his bruised face. "Do you know how many souls I had to devour and absorb to get this face?" he screeched.

Gregor grinned ferociously. "Wait till you see what I'm going to do." The two met head-on, and the force of their power clashed and sent tremors into the earth. Mika returned to gathering positive Vis energy into our body. The "new Master" watched from inside the rift and sent enough ripples through it that we couldn't help but shudder from the dark energy that moved around us.

What is that? I asked Mika.

A synthetic malevolence, Katya. One that should never have been created.

Mika finally moved. **We have enough energy.** Speaking in a loud voice, speaking in another language I couldn't understand, Mika directed the power in our hands toward the top of the rift. The seam between the realms began to slowly close—like a vast zipper pulling together two pieces of fabric. Our body became increasingly hot from the Vis energy from the Live Realm, but we stuck to our task. One inch at a time, working to return this part of the world back to normal.

Our dark voyeur from inside the rift fought against the closing with each inch. It became a battle of wills. Dark versus light. When we couldn't move it any further, with the zipper stuck halfway down, Mika told me, **Katya, remember what I said. We need to do this together.**

What do you want me to do?

Think about this world. The world you love. Consider love and peace, and remember all the emotions and sentiments the Want despises.

Who do I love? My mother, the parent who gave up everything for me, patiently awaited my return. I wanted to see my mom's proud smile as I got my college degree.

My best friend, my Havadar, waiting to be freed from her coma prison. Waiting to return to her body.

And Gregor. I loved him. He was my protector, my friend. And I didn't want to leave his side ever.

The touch of my mother's hand, the mischievous glint in my best friend's eyes, and the warmth in Gregor's gaze.

That's it, Katya. Think about everyone you love. Your mate, Gregor.

Millions of images flitted through my mind centered on my beloved Kyrios. Thought of the first time I had seen him at Amie's party. Gregor in the alley. Gregor telling me what he was. Our adventures with my friends. Our falling out after I learned who I was. Faking at husband and wife. Training together. Gregor holding me before the battle, telling me how he cared.

The rift closed with every thought I had about my family, my friends, and Gregor. We could feel the "new Master's" frustration when he only had five feet left.

We sank to the ground to close the remaining space when a humanoid hand shot out of the rift and closed around our neck. A low, rumbling voice said, "Do not think you won here. Your Vis will be mine."

Our body began to convulse from the lack of air, and I could tell Mika was beginning to lose control. The hand tightened its grip and started to siphon off our power. With everything within us, taking whatever energy we had left, I pushed from inside and yelled, *You are not getting her!*

An explosion of raw energy erupted from within us, the intensity so fierce that the encroaching hand recoiled, releasing its grasp, and the rift sealed shut. As I chanted, *You're not getting her*, our body continued to burn like fire. *No one is getting you.* The ground shook as we became a pure beacon of light, releasing all the Vis energy we had gathered into the earth and air.

At the last second, I felt something significant depart from my body before the controls were returned to me, and my limp body fell to the ground.

As encroaching darkness threatened to consume me, the last thing I heard was Mika's voice, growing fainter, murmuring, **It is done**, before everything went silent.

40

Promises Kept

And now for the top story worldwide. The entire planet breathed a sigh of relief. For over seventy-two hours, no tremors have been reported. Experts warn that this may be the eye of the storm, but they are hopeful that we might still find an answer to the source of these quakes. After declaring a state of emergency for the entire nation, the President of the United States directed supplies and medical help to shelters and hospitals as needed.

The President reminds us that now is not the time to panic but to remain calm and vigilant...

* * *

I felt a hand caress my cheek, pausing to trace a small scar that had formed on the corner of my eye when I was eight years old. Only one person in the world would know that scar. I cracked open my eyes to find my mother gently caressing my face with tears in her eyes. "My Kitty Kat."

"Mom," I said hoarsely. "Where am I?"

"Argentina, sweetie. You're at my safe house."

A look around confirmed her words. The room was modest, with white plastered walls that hinted at age. A window stood open, the gentle breeze carrying the scent of blooming jacaranda flowers. From the street below, the soft murmur of Spanish mingled with the distant sounds of a guitar, creating a comforting lullaby for the city. Outside, I glimpsed palm trees, tropical plants swaying gently, and a colorful toucan resting on a branch, its beak a vivid orange contrast to the deep greens.

Before I could ask another question, a pair of footsteps thundered down the hallway until they came to a stop at my door. Cynthia, in her redheaded glory, grinned widely as our eyes met.

"Kat!"

"Cynthia," I said tearfully. She looked like she wanted to give me a bear hug but opted to sit down at the foot of my bed instead. "You're back to normal—" I darted a look at my mother. "How are you feeling?"

My mother smirked at me. "You don't have to watch your words around me, silly. I remembered the dream, and Cynthia gave me a refresher. You can ask Cynthia how she got back into her body."

With a huge grin, I asked, "How did you get back into your body, Cyn?"

She waved her hand flippantly. "Eh, it was nothing. Once the Kyrios figured out that Lamar had placed a soul bind on me, they removed it, and I got the ol' strength back." She grinned. "But don't be confused. Just because some of our energy has returned to this body, it doesn't mean you don't have the other bits of me still inside you. Besides, we need more training. Sophia got to you way too easy!"

I cringed, remembering. "Hmm, maybe I'll want a different trainer."

"Sorry, honey. There are certain things Gregor can't teach you about me. Anyway, this is a girls' club. No boy Kyrios allowed!"

My smile died at the mention of the dark-haired Kyrios's name. "Where is he? Is he alright?"

"I'm right here." Gregor's voice, usually so steady and sure, was tinged with an unfamiliar rawness. He leaned against the door, his blue-grey eyes locked onto mine, intense and emotion-filled. Out of the corner of my eye, I caught Mom and Cynthia exchanging knowing glances.

"Hi," I said breathlessly.

"Hi, yourself." He sauntered into the room with an easy smile.

Mom cleared her throat gently. ""Perhaps it's time for Cynthia and me to give you two some privacy." With one last squeeze of my hand, she left, taking Cynthia.

Gregor sat at my bedside, his eyes roaming over my face. "How do you feel?"

I blinked slowly, trying to gather my thoughts amidst the haze of fatigue. "Just exhausted." After a brief pause, memories flashed, and I looked up at him with concern. "What happened?"

He sighed. "When you closed the rift, a huge shaking stopped us from fighting. When the Want realized that the rift was closed, they immediately retreated. Krenlin's parting words were, 'This is only the beginning.'"

My eyes dropped to my fidgeting hands. "How many gates are there?" I said quietly.

Gregor lifted my chin up. "At last count, about nine. Yes, this is the beginning, but we will make it to the end."

"What about what Nabil said?" I said uneasily. "If I continue doing what I do, what if the Archs find me?"

"We deal with it when the time comes. We need to just focus on the gates. As soon as you get better, we'll close the rest of the open gates and try to move as quietly as possible." He smiled. "Fancy taking that trip around the world?"

The corners of my mouth quirked up. "I've always wanted to see the world. But wait, did anyone else get hurt?"

His eyes saddened a bit. "We did lose a few men in the fight."

I held my breath. "Anyone I know?"

Gregor shook his head. "No. Your guards suffered some injuries, but they'll recover."

I sighed happily. "Thank God."

The curly-haired Kyrios took a deep breath and folded his arms over his chest, as though steadying himself. "Katya," he began, his voice strained, "when you... when I felt you slip away, a part of me broke. The world went dark. Every moment that your heart wasn't beating was an eternity for me. I felt helpless, lost..."

"I'm not dead," I smiled sheepishly. I waved my arms and hands, noting my left wrist was healed. "See, I'm fine."

He shook his head, "I distinctly felt you die. You broke your promise." He ran a hand through his dark hair to find the right words. "Seeing you here now, alive and talking, it's like the sun breaking through the darkest storm. I can't... I can't even begin to describe the weight lifted and my gratitude. I'd been holding onto a thread of hope, praying you'd come back to us, to me."

His eyes, typically so fierce and confident, glistened with unshed tears. "Every time I close my eyes, I see that moment. I felt your absence like a physical pain. And now, feeling your presence, hearing your voice... It's a gift, Katya. One I won't ever take for granted."

I took his hand in mine, kissing him softly across his knuckles. "I'm sorry you had to see that, but I had to. Mika said—" I stopped short, sensing something was off.

Gregor looked at me, puzzled. "What did Mika say?"

I ignored him and searched deeper and deeper. Found nothing. "Mika's gone," I whispered.

"What?"

"Mika's gone, Gregor! Where is she?" I panicked. I was about to get out of bed when Gregor held me down.

"Katya, calm down. She may have gone dormant again. You released all of your Vis in that blast. She may be within your soulscape again."

I relaxed a bit, but I wasn't completely convinced. "Are you sure?"

He nodded, trying to be reassuring, but I could feel the void where Mika once resided. I closed my eyes, trying to reach out to her, to feel that familiar, comforting presence, but there was only silence. A chill ran down my spine, the emptiness echoing within me, threatening to swallow me whole. Tears prickled my eyes.

He gently wiped the corners of my eyes. "Peace, lass. I still sense a lot of Vis energy in you. She has to be there somewhere. Where else could she be?"

I nodded, hoping he was right.

Gregor took my hand into his again. "I don't know whether to be cross with you or to kiss you," his brogue thickened with emotion. "Even though you broke your promise for a moment, I'm very glad you kept it in the end." He tucked a loose strand of hair behind my ear.

I remembered my last thought before I died. "Gregor." I looked down at our joined hands. "Sometimes you annoy the bejesus out of me."

He chuckled. "Okay?"

"Hold on, let me get this all out." I took a deep breath. "You can tick me off within seconds, but make me want to cover you with kisses in the same amount of time. As my heart stopped, I realized I had never told you how much your smile means to me or how much I enjoy feeling your arms around me. How much I enjoy our banter and how I can be myself around you. Or how you have my favorite pair of eyes. And I know I'm human, and you're not," I took a deep breath. "I told myself before I died that, if I ever got the chance, I would tell you that I love—"

My lips became preoccupied. The same passion and urgency I'd felt expressing myself to him was returned as Gregor encased me in his arms, driving me insane with the movement of his lips and tongue. My hands gripped his shoulders, moving to massage his scalp, earning a groan.

He pulled away, leaving a trail of kisses on my face. "Silly girl. I think I fell in love with you the moment I saw you. The way this beautiful lass stared me down sent shivers through me, reminding me I even had a body."

A soft smile rested on my face. "You know, Mika has referred to you several times as my mate. What do you think that's about?"

He nuzzled my nose with his own, "She's an all-knowing entity. She probably always knew we would gravitate to each other. Especially given how cute and ferocious you can be. Who else could handle such a woman?"

I laughed and rested my head on his shoulders. "So, we love each other. Now what?"

"We'll break the rules together. Not sure how Nabil will take this, but right now, I don't care."

I smirked at him. "Hey, that's your beloved mentor there. Be careful, Kyrios." I eased back into my pillow, letting my hand linger in his. "When will I see the others?"

He grinned, his shoulders relaxed as he kissed my fingers, "Funny you should mention the others. Because of your upcoming work, General Nabil decided you should have a full guard during this world tour. The Quad, Jaya, Santiago, and Kevon have been designated as your personal guards and will be stationed here."

"This road trip will be memorable, that's for sure. Let's pray that Jaya and Kevon keep the play fighting to a minimum."

As the sun streamed into my room, Gregor paused to take another look at me, painting me with a serene look that warmed me to the core. He arched an eyebrow as if waiting for something.

I rolled my eyes but could not keep the smile off my face. "What is it?"

"Aren't you going to ask?"

"Ask what?"

Both his eyebrows rose. "If you're not going to ask, I'll just keep it." He made to leave, but I pulled him back down.

"What are you talking about?"

His eyes warmed over, and he tweaked my nose. "I kept *my* promises."

Giggling, I threw my arms around his neck. I asked sweetly, "Can I have my kiss back, please?"

"Gladly."

As our lips met for a sweet and soft kiss, I let go of my worries about Mika and what the Want was planning next. For now, I decided to let go of the imminent threat of the Archs finding out about me. For a moment, I even let go of my worries about closing the gates for the next few months.

For now, I decided to take Gregor's advice. *Enjoy the sweet moments while you can, for you're never promised another.*

ABOUT THE AUTHOR
K. T. CONTE

K.T. Conte, a devotee of the written word and all things wild and fascinating, first discovered her passion for books at the tender age of two.. An African-American author with a flair for breathing life into stories, K.T. holds a B.A. in English from Boston College and a law degree from Suffolk University Law School. While she is a licensed and practicing attorney, K.T.'s first love has always remained books. The enchanting dance of words across a page and the powerful narratives they weave continue to captivate and inspire her daily. Over the years, she has shared her Massachusetts home with a delightful blend of characters - the enchanting specters in the closet, her loving husband Everett, mischievous building fairies, and her beloved daughter, Ella.

Afterword

Dear Reader,

Thank you for embarking on this extraordinary journey through the pages of "Awoke." Your engagement with the story and the characters is deeply meaningful to me, and I hope this book has touched your heart in a special way.

The creation of "Awoke" has been a labor of love, and your reaching the end of this book signifies that you've experienced every emotion and twist alongside the characters. I would be immensely grateful if you chose to share your thoughts and experiences with others. Your reviews and word-of-mouth recommendations are instrumental in bringing this story to a wider audience.

Special Invitation: I invite you to stay connected and be the first to receive updates about the "Unseen War" series, including the eagerly anticipated next installment, "Rise," slated for 2025. By visiting my website and subscribing to my newsletter, you'll gain access to the latest news, exclusive content, digital assets, behind-the-scenes materials, a Book of Monsters to explore and dive into the world behind "Awoke.", and other special offers. Join the community at www.ktconte.com/awoke.

As we look forward to the continued journey of the "Unseen War" series, your enthusiasm and support are invaluable. If "Awoke" has captured your imagination, I hope you'll consider spreading the word to friends, family, and fellow book enthusiasts.

Your support is the foundation that allows these stories to soar. Thank you for being an integral part of this adventure.

With heartfelt appreciation,

K. T.

THE UNSEEN WAR SERIES

EXPECTED 2025

Milton Keynes UK
Ingram Content Group UK Ltd.
UKHW012255090224
437600UK00012B/184/J